Fletcher and the Constitution

FLETCHER
AND THE
CONSTITUTION

JOHN DRAKE

LUME BOOKS
A JOFFE BOOKS COMPANY

Lume Books, London

A Joffe Books Company

www.lumebooks.co.uk

This paperback edition first published in Great Britain 2024

We love to hear from our readers!

Please email any feedback you have to: feedback@joffebooks.com

Cover design by Imogen Buchanan

Cover images © iStock by Getty Images

ISBN: 978-1-83901-590-8

INTRODUCTION

The mighty and all-powerful USA very nearly did not happen. It very nearly did not happen because as the nineteenth century began, vast chunks of North America were owned by others. Thus the British owned Canada, the French owned Louisiana, and the Spanish owned the near unbelievable list of California, Mexico, New Mexico, Arizona, Colorado, Oklahoma, Kansas and Wyoming — and if that's not enough, the Russians owned the entire and colossal bulk of Alaska.

Furthermore, none of these colonial powers had any intention of going home, having implanted their colonists and culture, their rival versions of Christianity, and their forts and soldiers to defend them. At the same time, the Americans on the east coast were divided into thirteen separate states, each cherishing its independence from the rest, and the supposedly *United* States was nipped in between the British to the north and the French to the south: the two most powerful seagoing nations in the world.

So this was the America known to Admiral Sir Jacob Fletcher (1775–1875) in this eighth volume of his memoirs covering the years 1805–1808. If this is the first you have heard of him, then note that he was a huge man of enormous strength, and a magnificent seaman and gunner. He was greatly attractive to women, while the men who served under him would have followed him down the cannon's mouth. He was instantly recognisable not only for his bulk, but by a thin streak of white in his dark hair, and was both rogue and hero to the popular press of Britain and America in the nineteenth century. Finally, and remarkably, he was unique among seafaring heroes in declaring that he never wanted to go to sea at all, but having been press-ganged into service his true desire was to go ashore for a career in trade.

Thus these memoirs contain Fletcher's own account of his life, as dictated in the 1870s to his clerk/secretary the Reverend Dr Samuel Pettit, who transcribed them into bound volumes. In 2012 I bought the entire set at auction, together with a trunk containing papers, memorabilia and letters. So the Fletcher books are mainly Fletcher's voice bellowing at the reader, together with a few chastising inserts added by the Reverend Doctor, who was shocked by some of the text he was compelled to set down. These inserts I represent *in this different font.* S.P.

Meanwhile, in addition to offering Fletcher's own words, and since the original trunkful of papers has vastly grown via research and generous donations, I have included entire letters or articles where these speak for themselves. Also I have used letters to construct third-person chapters between Fletcher's narrative, to give a wider perspective. Please note that these third-person chapters are only my inventions, but they are as accurate as I can make them and each one is preceded by an extract from the letter — or letters — which guided my hand in writing it.

Thus I draw attention to my created chapter two of this volume, which features Lady Sarah Coignwood, the beautiful witch-queen who hated Fletcher throughout his life. She was his stepmother, having married Fletcher's father, Sir Henry Coignwood, the billionaire industrialist who was long since dead by the time of this volume. Note that Fletcher was illegitimately born and raised as an orphan, never knowing his father, nor even his sister Mary, for many years.

Finally I would like to thank my respected friend, Dr Nikola Tanyavichova of The Alexander Nevsky Free University of Moscow, for her patient translation of documents from the Russian, and for sending me Mr David Nash's letter to his wife, which was lost to Western scholarship for over 200 years. See chapter thirty-two for the colossal historic importance of this letter.

John Drake,
Cheshire, England,
November 2023.

CHAPTER 1

Now listen to me, because your Uncle Jacob has something to tell you about pistols, because pistols can either be toys or fighting weapons. By "toys" I mean the pieces of ironware that a man uses to impress the world by hitting a playing-card's ace of spades at twenty paces in a shooting gallery. Either that or — even more stupid — he uses it to blow holes in some other stupid idiot in a duel at twenty paces. In that case yes, a rifled barrel is useful and the very best of luck to you.

But if you're hand-to-hand in a boarding action, and the enemy is bearing down with a cutlass, then you've no time to take aim at twenty paces because he's coming on so fast. Furthermore, even if you did try to take aim at long range, being in dreadful fear of your life, and your heart thumping like a mad drum, any advantage of a rifled barrel is doomed and damned, because you can't even think let alone aim, and you can't stop your hand from shaking. Believe me, my jolly boys, that's what it's like and I know because I've been there.

So never mind a rifled barrel. What you want before all else is certainty of fire such that when you pull the trigger the weapon goes *bang*! If it misfires you'll never live to worry about it, because the enemy will kill you. So you want the best that money can buy in a sure-fire pistol lock. Added to that, you want a pistol with a heavy bore so that when you hit your man you knock out of his head any idea of doing you harm. You want that, not shooting-gallery accuracy, because you'll give fire just beyond arm's length, and you'll do it instinctively.

In that case, my own choice for years was a pair of sixteen-bores by

Mr Henry Nock of Ludgate Street, London, built to take the sea service cartridge, with belt hooks so a man can take them into action, and with locks as crisp as a Swiss watch.

So that's what saved me close by Bannerman's Bay, Alaska, in 1805 when a creature from hell came at me in the woods, all screaming and howling with many others the same astern of it, and the whole horde of them, jumping and leaping and gibbering and as far from being human as was possible to imagine. Their heads alone were fit to shrivel your withers: monstrous, hideous-coloured and grotesque. By George I'd seen things afloat that landmen never dream off, and it was a thing uncanny that put the white streak in my hair, but I'd never seen real live demons before. Nonetheless I aimed my musket on the first of them, and its damned lock sputtered useless, it being a nasty Russian trade gun that didn't even have a bayonet. So I dropped it and hauled out one of my Nock barkers and fired, even though I feared that lead alone might not serve, and wished I'd loaded silver.

But the Nock went off with a crack and a flash, and down went the demon, stumbling so close that its hands dropped a stone-head war club right on my foot, as I slung the empty pistol full at the head of the next demon. But the pistol bounced off such that he kept coming and he'd have had me for sure, if he hadn't tripped over the first one and messed up his thrust of a spear with a wickedly sharp head. That gave me time to draw, cock and fire my second pistol, which flashed and roared with the muzzle jammed hard into his collar bone, such that he fell on me, in the stink of him, all scorched and burning from the powder, and the ball deep inside of him.

So I shoved him clear, and winced as there came a volley from the Russian-Alaskans behind me, and then another volley as they managed to load without firing away their ramrods or stuffing ball down the barrel before power. I say this with contempt, my jolly boys, because the Rusky-Alaskies are very hard to like, and I never tried very hard. But there were sixty of them with muskets, they filled the woods with powder smoke. I heard the thud of balls going home into some of the demons, and several of them dropped their clubs and fell to their knees

4

clutching their wounded bellies, even as the rest of the pack turned and ran.

But that wasn't enough for one of the Rusky-Alaskies — Father Nikolai, a priest — who ran forward from the rest, spitting fury into his whiskers, and swung his musket by the barrel with the full force of his arms, smashing the butt with a fearful *clap* into one of the demon-heads. The gun was rubbish and broke at the wrist of the stock, but the demon's head came right off and, instead, there was a brown-skinned oriental-looking man with long black hair in a top-knot, who gaped with open mouth as the good Father beat out his brains with the musket barrel and lock.

Duly encouraged by this victory, the other Rusky-Alaskies pounded forwards, bellowing and blowing, and got themselves busy with musket-butts smashing and mashing the heads of the other three fallen demons, dead or alive alike, such that all I could see was arms going up and down, and all I could hear was grunting as the deed was done. Then Father Nikolai was coming up and shoving something at me and gabbling in his own language and so close I could smell the drink on his breath. By Jove he was excited. His eyes were round and he had the cheek to grab my arm with one hand, while thrusting something at me with the other. It was a wolf's head, with huge white teeth and ferocious eyes.

"English, you swab!" says I. "None of your damned Russian!" I knew the blighter could speak English and speak it well, after his fashion, though he spoke with a Yankee nasal twang, which was odd.

"*Da*," says he. "You English! You see how they fight? These are Tlingit. Tlingit warriors. Dangerous!" He had a point. He did indeed, because the demon-heads wore helmets made from hard wood. They fitted all the way down to wooden collars to take the weight and they had eye-slits for the wearer to see out. They were cunningly made and were carved and painted to scare the daylights out of an enemy. "And see!" says Father Nikolai, throwing away the helmet, and falling to his knees to poke at the one he'd personally battered, and whose head was once again unrecognisable as human. "See, Captain?" says he. "Armour of the body!" He was right, the dead man had a coat of thick hide, and over that he had a sort of breast-and-back of horn and hardwood plates, all neatly drilled and beautifully sewn together, then painted with grotesque faces. It wouldn't do against muskets or pistols, but it showed how dedicated these people were to warfare on their own terms, with knives, clubs and spears.

"But no guns," says I, "at least I can't see any."

"Some have guns, some not," says he. "Different clans, different arms. This time we lucky. But more may come. And with guns. So we must be quick."

"Come on then," says I, and pointing at the men who were still busily beating the remains of the fallen, "call off them swabs from what they're doing."

"Yes, yes," says he, and he threw away his broken musket and was yelling in Russian and going among the men, calling them off, and twisting their noses and tugging their beards such that they actually laughed. There's Russians for you, since Father Nikolai had influence as a priest. Also, the Father was slightly less of a drunkard than the rest of them, which — I would point out — still left him plenty of sea room for alcohol because while I thought that British tars liked their drink, I'd seen nothing 'til I met Russians.

I have here removed a prolonged rant by Fletcher regarding catastrophic drunkenness among the Russian colonists of Alaska. I have likewise removed his comments on the Russian language except to note that — much to his own amazement — he had finally found a language that he disliked more than French. S.P.

"Now quick, Captain," says Father Nikolai, "before others come with guns." He turned to the rest and I suppose he said the same in Russian.

"Da! Da! Da!" says they, which is Russian for yes, and they were about to follow Father Nikolai further into the woods, when I grabbed hold of Nikolai and stopped him.

"For God almighty's sake," says I, "get the sods to reload first!" And I snatched up the pistol that had bounced off the demon — or whatever he was — then took out a cartridge and made a pantomime business before them all, out of biting it then priming the lock and ramming home. Then I loaded the other, which I'd stuck in my belt, and picked up my nasty trade gun and primed the lock so it should fire next time. I did that and waved it at them.

"Ahhhh," says they. "Da! Da! Da!" So they did the same, and the ramrods went up and down, and Father Nikolai pinched a loaded musket off one of them, who scowled and muttered something rude, and got clouted for it by one of his mates for disrespect to a priest.

"Now Captain," says Father Nikolai, "we go?"

"Now!" says I. "And as quick as you please."

So off we went, with a scout in front who knew the way, and all of us looking every way for demons with guns, and Father Nikolai gabbling loudly, to urge everyone on. The trouble was, you see, they'd been at the vodka to summon up courage before we started, since I'd never have got them on the march without Dutch courage.

Fortunately, very soon the scout was yelling and we came on our destination, a fur-trapping station in the form of a very large log house with a planked roof — much decayed and badly mended, with dense layers of thin branches woven into a thatch. By George it looked miserable, but there was smoke from the stone chimney and when Father Nikolai called out, the door opened and a dozen or more people poured out, including the British lieutenant and the midshipmen we'd come to rescue. They ran out full of joy, straight towards me.

"Cap'n Fletcher!" they said.

"Sir!"

"Thank God you're here!"

"I knew you'd come, sir! We all knew it, sir!"

It was the lieutenant who said that — Lieutenant Dawson — and despite his words I could see that every one of them had been in dread that I would *not* come. Not in time, anyway. But my people had the decency to salute like Englishmen. So later I made sure that each of them had a musket, powder and shot, and told them to keep by me. But meanwhile, the Rusky-Alaskies from the log house ran towards us with arms stretched out and faces full of joy. They were mainly women, and mainly Creoles of half-Russian, half-native blood.

"Gabble-gabble-gabble!" says every one of them, near hysterical with relief at being rescued, and the Rusky-Alasky musketeers yelled back at them, and there was a universal embracing and kissing, which extended even to me. I didn't mind at all when the kisses came from a lovely little girlie with plaits curled on top of her head. She leaped into my arms and kissed me square on the mouth, so not everything Russian was bad. I could have eaten that one alive. She was tall and slim but tasty. But a man who looked 100 years old did exactly the same, and he tasted of bad breath and garlic. Then Father Nikolai was grabbing my arm again.

"Captain!" says he, with a bright gleam in his eyes. "We save the furs?"

"No," says I, "we've come to save people, not bloody furs. So let's get 'em safe back in the fort, before the Tlingit come on again."

"No," says he, "they don't come back. Not now. They've been beaten."

"Really?" says I. "Are you sure?" And he said nothing because he wasn't sure, the swab. I could see it in his face. So I'd have said, damn the furs, but I was too late. All the Rusky-Alaskies were running to the log house, hauling open the doors, dashing inside and heaving bundles of furs into a line of big-wheeled hand carts standing by.

"Avast!" says I, in a masthead bellow that made them look. "Belay that! All hands back to the fort!" My lieutenant and mids tried to stop the fur-loading, but the Rusky-Alaskies didn't or wouldn't understand, and just got on with their loading. At least they were quick about it. They heaved mightily and the bundles of fur flew into the carts, because the furs were very precious and they wanted their profit on them.

Now! You youngsters will know that there's nothing your Uncle Jacob likes more than a profit, and such profit comes from Alaskan furs as you'd barely believe. But sometimes there are greater considerations, such as not waiting to be butchered, since the entire Tlingit nation lived close nearby and if their warriors came in a horde we'd be outnumbered beyond hope. So by God and all his little angels I wanted to be gone and safe behind a stockade where the carriage-guns were loaded with grape.

"Father," says I, "can you get them moving? We've got to be gone before any more of the savages turn up."

"Yes, yes, yes!" says he. "Da, da, da!" And he darted off, yelling out words, such that the whole party of musket-men and log-house people got into something like good order, and off we set at a good quick march, with eager hands hauling the carts, and those not hauling walking outside the carts, with muskets cocked and eyes sharp.

Then Father Nikolai got them singing. Well done to him for doing that! It was something they all knew and could join in with, to get their feet moving. It was a song with challenges and responses. The men would sing one line in deep voices, and the women would respond in wonderful harmony and wonderful melody. So even I, who cannot abide the Alaskan Russians, have to say that they sang it well, and it shivered my spine to hear it, there in a twilight forest, because while it never got fully dark in Alaska, there was a sort of twilight in the small hours, and it wasn't even twilight as we know it in England. It was the magical, fairy twilight of the Northern Lights. We were marching under the aurora borealis: a whole sky of blue and green, like an enormous curtain that shimmers and moves and folds, and strikes you with wonder the first time you see it, but then you get used to it. Well, normally you do, but not when you're waiting for unknown numbers of enemies to come howling down on you.

So we all sang, with Lieutenant Dawson, the mids and me picking up the tune, if not the words. So we cheered up. I grinned at Father Nikolai, who grinned back, and jabbered about furs, and would have kissed me if I hadn't fended him off. He laughed at that.

"You English!" says he. "No blood inside. No passion."

So, weren't we all merry and bright? Weren't we happy to be nearly home and clear, with the fort just round the bend, on the rising ground that looked out over Bannerman's Bay? That's Bannerman's Bay where the Russian America Company's ships came in to anchor. What a fine bay it was too, so nicely sheltered, but with a sandy beach where boats could land to bring in supplies and take off the tight, fat bundles of sea otter furs that sold for such magnificent prices in China.

So we all cheered up something wonderful until, just before we came in sight of the fort, marching through a dense curve of forest — pine, spruce and cedar — there came the most appalling howling and shrieking, of countless wild voices, and a straggling *boom ... boom-boom ... boom* of artillery.

Oh Jesus, that was a bad moment. The Russians all froze, Father Nikolai grabbed hold of me like a child in fear of the bogey-man, and the women began to moan.

"None of that!" says I, shaking off the Father. "Dawson! Get 'em off the path! Get 'em in the woods!"

"Aye-aye, sir," says he, and set to with the mids, to push the Rusky-Alaskies into hiding.

"And do it quiet!" says I. "No shouting!"

"Aye-aye, sir!"

So, with myself and Father Nikolai helping, we got everyone off the road and under cover, and the cart-loads of furs with them.

"Right!" says I when that was done. "Mr Dawson, you're in command here!"

"Aye-aye, sir!"

"You stay here, keep everyone together and quiet, and no letting off firelocks unless the savages are actually bearing down on you! Have you got that?"

"Sir!"

"And Father Nikolai," says I, "you tell the rest of them to sit down, stay here and be quiet." So he gabbled and they nodded and sat down.

"Now, you're coming with me," says I to Father Nikolai, "to see what's going forward." He didn't like that, didn't Father Nikolai — and his face went white, around the black beard. But I took hold of him and dragged him a step or two until he got the idea. "Shhh," says I, finger to lips.

"Da," says he — and note well that all the while we'd been talking and getting under cover, the noise from round the bend was getting worse as a major battle took place, with muskets crackling and guns booming. So while it might have been wise for us to hide and be quiet, I doubt anyone would have heard if we'd all blown trumpets. Then off we set, Father Nikolai and myself, stopping to peer round the trees before moving on, and just before we came into full sight of the fort, there was a renewed howling and screaming from the savages, and the red light of fire glowing over the treetops. We saw that, and heard a crackle and roar of flames, and more musketry, and shouting in Russian, but no more booming of guns.

Then we saw it.

"Jesus!" says I, and Father Nikolai groaned.

There must have been thousands of Tlingit warriors, all in their demon masks, and many of them with muskets. They were dancing in glee, and shooting at anyone who raised his head over the ramparts of Fort Alexander: a big, square, earth-and-timber fortification enclosed within a palisade of pine-trunks, with bastions at the corners and guns mounted in the bastions. But the damned thing was too near the forest, and the Tlingit had obviously rushed it with sheer weight of numbers — and while I could see the dead bodies of those who'd been caught in the first fire of the guns, they were now swarming all over the gun ports, and blazing away at the gunners inside. They'd even brought ladders to get to the ports.

Worse than that, the Tlingit had brought up bundles of sticks, all trimmed and neat-bound, and in great numbers. My guess would be that every man of their attack had carried one, then piled them in a heap against the palisade wall in a chosen spot, then the bundles were set alight, and from the quick blazing up of them, they'd doubtless soaked the bundles in some sort of oil. So, seeing the systematic manner of their attack, and the obvious planning of it, then from that moment on I stopped thinking of the Tlingit as savages. Not when the Duke of Wellington himself couldn't have done it better.

After that, Father Nikolai and I had the best seats in the house, to witness the palisade breached by fire, the Tlingit breaking in, and the complete rout, massacre and burning of the fort where a few hours ago, we'd thought ourselves totally safe — before we sallied out to rescue the outlying trappers.

Some of what we saw was not very nice, my jolly boys, so I'll spare you the details of what the Tlingit did to the Russians they caught, but it was enough to convince Father Nikolai and myself that there would be nothing left whole or alive in Fort Alexander when the Tlingit were done with it.

So let this be a lesson to you youngsters, of the punishment that a man gets for being greedy, because I never should have been in Bannerman's Bay, Alaska; not when I'd been safe ashore and in trade. But I was forever seeking further opportunity and was led astray by the fur trade, especially the trade in the fur of the sea otter.

So it served me right to be where I was in that moment, and very deeply unsure as to how — in all imagination — I might get myself and the others safe away without falling into the hands of the Tlingit, who most certainly did not take prisoners.

CHAPTER 2

I did not say the word. Even as the Lord liveth and I hope for redemption, I did not say it.

(Extract of a letter from Samuel Franklin Bache to his mother in Philadelphia.)

Lady Sarah Coignwood — reigning queen of London society — was amused to see that here in America's London embassy, the republicans aped the style of the aristocracy. Thus the dinner was lavish, candles twinkled, wine was without limit, and a dozen of elect society sat round the table, while liveried servants grovelled in attendance.

She whispered this to Mr Charles James Fox, the formidable Whig politician who was her beau for the evening. He was bulging fat, with jowls so dark that no razor could shave them, but he was a famous wit and admired by Americans for his radical opinions. He shuddered at the exquisite sensation of her lips brushing his ear, then raised his voice.

"Mr Monroe?" he cried.

"Sir?" said James Monroe, American ambassador to England.

"Here's Lady Sarah," said Fox, "who says that you keep the table of a duke!"

"Only an American duke, sir!" said Monroe, and everybody laughed, and Lady Sarah smiled at Monroe, who goggled at her from one end of the table while his wife Elizabeth gnashed teeth at the other, because until meeting Lady Sarah, she had thought herself a beauty.

But Lady Sarah hardly gave Monroe another glance because he was

13

plain, with a long nose and narrow eyes. Thus she concentrated her fire upon the man directly opposite: Mr Samuel Franklin Bache, a God-fearing young man who was a great-grandson of Benjamin Franklin, whom Lady Sarah understood to be one of those responsible for the Declaration of Independence, the American rebellion, etc, etc, etc, and therefore of no interest to herself whatever.

But great-grandson Samuel *was* interesting. He was exceedingly lovely, broad-shouldered, well dressed and very young: seventeen, eighteen or thereabouts, and these days — for reasons she chose not to examine — Lady Sarah preferred young men. So Samuel was appealing in that respect, and also for his naivety. So she led him on, giving a look of soulful adulation.

"Tell me more of your great ancestor," she said, and Samuel blushed at her close attention, and all the ladies affected disdain at another seduction under way, and all the gentlemen envied young Samuel.

But Sam had not understood what was on offer, and instead of smiling into Lady Sarah's eyes, he gave a lecture on the colossal achievement of Benjamin Franklin, in founding and creating the United States of America.

"Labour of years, ma'am!" he said, and much more: "… Bill of Rights … ten amendments … Mount Vernon Conference … constitutional convention … Rhode Island ratification …" By now she was bored, but Fox beat the table in emphasis to every word and bellowed approval.

"A constitution most glorious!" he cried. "Bringing forth a shining republic in the midst of tyranny! God bless and save the Founding Fathers!"

"God bless you too, sir!" said young Sam, and among those around there was much applause and satisfaction.

So it was not until the ladies withdrew, leaving the gentlemen to their port, that the bomb burst. Thus, as Lady Sarah left the room beside a sour-faced Elizabeth Monroe, she passed by Sam Franklin, and whispered to him. The result was a flinching from the innocent Sam, who was still a true virgin.

"Too bold, ma'am," he muttered. "You're too bold for me."

That's what he said, but that's not what everyone heard, or afterwards *said* they had heard, because Fox laughed aloud, poked Sam in the chest and declared, "Too old? She's been thirty-eight for years, so she can't be too old!"

Lady Sarah's heart stopped. Her breath froze. Her jaw clenched.

Old? *Old?* Too old? *Too old!*

Horror of horrors!

Bolts and shackles!

Thunder and lightning!

Fox was never forgiven.

He was vilified and execrated.

He was forbidden Lady Sarah's company.

Forever.

Nonetheless, every salon in London had the tale next day because the tongues of gossip moved fast … but not as fast as Lady Sarah, who was waiting in the early hours in her town carriage with a driver and footmen, outside the offices of Smart Robinson and Partridge, solicitors of Hanover Crescent. She was there when Mr Smart arrived to open up for the day's work, with clerks and minions waiting, hats in hand, at the door. He blinked at the glossy chaise, and bowed to Lady Sarah — who glared at him, as her servants let down the step for her.

"My husband's private papers," she said. "At once!"

Mr Smart bowed again, and blinked. He was elderly, frail and terrified of her. "Papers, my lady?" he said. "What of them?"

Her response was a hysterical abuse heard the length of Hanover Crescent by all early risers, not to mention the entirety of Mr Smart's staff. He gaped and gulped.

"Yes, yes," he said, "the late Sir Henry's private papers. At once, m'lady."

Thus Mr Smart — knowing what was good for him — himself personally took his keys, opened many doors, and lit lanterns all the way downstairs to the stone-vaulted cellar of the Great Archive. Then he stood by Lady Sarah, gazing at the rows of iron-bound trunks in the dim light. Each trunk had a number painted on the side.

"Which one?" she said. "I want the American papers."

"American papers?" said Mr Smart. "That would be number fifteen."

"Open it, then go away!" she said. "Now! Instantly!"

Soon after, irrespective of dust and expensive clothes, she was on her knees hurling papers out of the trunk, then digging for more. Something was on the edge of memory, from the days when she and her husband still talked. It was something from his long stay in Pennsylvania before the rebellion of the colonists, when he was attempting to establish a pottery-works. He'd met everyone in those days: Washington, Jefferson, Adams and Benjamin Franklin, too.

Franklin? Sam Franklin? That name caused a howl of pain, clenched teeth, clenched fists and uttermost purest hatred. There had to be some very special, very personal and very appropriate revenge. Something to hit Franklin and everything that his ancestors revered. So she threw more papers aside until — even in a cellar — the sun came out in his glory, because she found the document her husband had showed her long ago. It was a few pages in an oilskin package, and he'd laughed, and she'd sneered, then it was put away for years.

But now she realised that it was the most enormous gunpowder mine, just waiting for someone to light the fuse. The only problem was, who should do the lighting? It would have to be someone seriously political because this was a matter between nations. But which nation should receive the gift? Britain? Prussia? Russia? Even France, despite the war?

She made a swift decision, thinking of the gorgeous Count Pavel Pavelovich — dear, dear Pavel — the Russian ambassador, who was gorgeously handsome in uniform and gorgeously wonderful in bed. So Pavel must have the papers. But she frowned. Would he understand the power of them? Would he believe them?

CHAPTER 3

I assume that since I am here dictating this, and that you — in later years — are there reading it, then you will have calculated that your Uncle Jacob did not get butchered by the Tlingit on Bannerman's Island. In case of doubt, be assured that I was not thus butchered. I was not, nor were the trappers and log-cabin folk. Most especially the lovely little blondie with the plaits was not: she who kissed me and was so tasty. She was saved, and was very grateful for the saving. She was very grateful indeed and later on she acted accordingly towards myself. But more of that in due course because first I must explain what the damned hell I was doing on Bannerman's Island.

It began over nine months earlier when I was living with my sister Mary and her husband Josiah Hyde, at Hyde House in Kent, and for once in my life I was entirely content — or at least, I thought I was. I had finally come ashore, having parted with the Royal Navy — and I should add that I'd parted badly. This was because the navy, egged on by the blasted politicians, God damn them, had repeatedly betrayed me, by sending me on such expeditions of espionage and underhand work as would shame a common burglar. So I blame the politicians before all others.

I have here deleted another of Fletcher's rants, since his opinions regarding politicians were expressed by him in terms of such profanity and blasphemy as I would spare the reader. S.P.

Consequently, I was out of the navy in that year of 1805 when French invasion was most feared. But I was confident the navy could

17

do without me, and I was proven right when Nelson thrashed them at Trafalgar and serve the rascals right!

So, I was then ashore with a knighthood and a fortune, and I was content with my sister Mary and her husband Josiah at their house in Kent, where we were building a fine business of ever-expanding enterprises. I was particularly happy because Mary and I had been separated years ago, and I'd only recently found her. But she was as mad for business as me, with a steam-powered calculating engine for a brain. She and Josiah had built up the finest carriage-building business in England and were even selling into America. But we — or rather I— was always looking for further opportunities: steam engines, coal mining, wool and cotton manufactories. Indeed Mary had the sharp wit to apprise me of the reason for this, just days before I received some visitors.

She and I were walking in the gardens after the day's work, and by rare chance we were alone. My brother-in-law Josiah was also Member of Parliament for Bishopsbourne East — one decent soul among the dishonourable members — and was in London, while the nieces and nephews — seven of them, by then — were in the charge of servants. So Mary and I had a nice walk in the sunshine, then sat on a rustic bench in an arbour surrounded by roses, in the gardens designed by Mary herself. So we sat and talked for a while, and I went over my latest plan, which was for a steam-engine shed with a fresh team of young engineers. But she interrupted me.

"Jacky," says she, "you're babbling."

I looked at her. She was a woman in her early forties with a fine figure, a pretty face and the same dark curly hair as mine. Being so rich as we were, she always dressed well: neat and smart, and never flash. Not Paris fashion or even London. But what anyone noticed first about my sister was her intelligence, even aside from her brain for business. She looked straight at you and looked inside, and made judgement. She especially did that to me, because she was thirteen years older than me and could never forget that she'd held me in the crook of her arm as an infant. So she called me Jacky and never ceased to think she was responsible for me.

"Jacky, you're babbling," says she again. "It's all about the sea, isn't it?"

"What?" says I, for I'd not seen that coming. But it stabbed me.

"You're never easy," says she, "you never stop looking beyond."

"Beyond what?" says I.

"Beyond all this," says she, waving a hand at the house and the sheds. That stabbed me again. I didn't know what to say. I didn't ... but she did.

"You've got our father's gift for trade," says she, "it's in our blood and can't be denied. But the sea's in your blood as well, and there's a part of you that wants to be doing ..." — she paused for words — "doing halliards and capstans and whatever else you do on a ship."

"*In* a ship," says I, correcting her.

"See!" says she, pointing at me.

"Oh," says I.

"And another thing," says she. "When we go to church or round the town, every woman that sees you, gives you the likely look."

"What's that?" says I.

"Don't pretend you don't know," says she, "they give it to you because you're a rogue."

"No, I'm not!"

"They think you are! And some women are mad enough to love a handsome rogue. They think he's romantic and they love him more than a decent man like my Josiah — because he certainly doesn't get the likely look."

"Does it matter?" says I, and she smiled.

"Yes," says she, "because, while you've been good so far, sooner or later you will take what's on offer and bring scandal on our heads." She stopped smiling. "Sir Roger Coltrain's wife was goggling at you in church last Sunday and you were smiling back, and Sir Roger is Worshipful Mayor of Canterbury."

I said nothing. I had indeed noticed the lady, who was tall and slender with a hungry look which had nothing to do with food, but rather the fact that her husband was old and ugly. I had indeed noticed her and had been wondering how I might arrange a meeting.

"There!" says she, guessing my thoughts. "So what I'm saying, Jacky,

19

is that while we all love you, and while you are a huge asset to our business, if any opportunity presents — a seafaring opportunity — then it's best that you should take it."

Again I said nothing because such powerful emotions were stirred up within me. But my sister had a fortune-teller's gift, as well as her other talents, because even greater emotions were aroused within me a few days later, when a post-chaise rolled up in the drive of Hyde House, all smart in its yellow paint, with two most superior gentlemen inside and a postboy on the lead horse, who jumped down, came knocking at the door and asked for me.

Within ten minutes they were sitting down with my sister and me, in the counting house of the main carriage shed: a good plain office with bright windows, a clean-swept floor and high stools and benches for our staff. But the staff were all sent out, madeira and cakes were summoned, and Mary and I sat on one side of a big table, facing the two gentlemen on the other. They had brought some leather satchels and they were expensively dressed: cravats, tailored coats, tight breeches and top boots; they both had sashes and stars of knightly orders under their coats, and while they were obviously foreigners of some species, they looked like serious men. They were tired from a ten-hour journey from London, with nine changes of horses, but they were mustard-keen to meet me and came with a letter of introduction.

But they didn't show that straight away. First, one of them spoke. He bowed his head to my sister, gave a diplomat's smile, and looked at me.

"Sir Jacob," says he to me in excellent English, "we have grave matters to discuss. Will not this most charming lady wish to withdraw?"

"No, sir," says I, "the lady is my sister. She is my confidante in all matters and I keep no secrets from her."

He sniffed and frowned and the two of them looked at each other and shrugged the way Frenchmen do — though they weren't French, but Russian.

"So be it," says he, took the letter from his satchel, and gave it to me with another little bow so nice and polite, and another little smile. So I represent the letter here.

Commanded by the Commissioners for executing the Office of
Lord High Admiral of Great Britain and Ireland & of all His
Majesty's Plantations and colonies, this despatch is directed to:
Jacob Fletcher, Knight of the Bath, Lately Commodore in
His Majesty's Sea Service, now resident at Hyde House, near
Canterbury in the County of Kent,

Sir Jacob,
This shall inform you, with all due approval of Their
Lordships of the Admiralty, that the bearers are true and
esteemed servants of His Imperial Majesty, Alexander I of the
House Romanov, Tsar of all the Russias: viz

Count Stepan Mikaelovich Doyetov,
Deputy Ambassador to the Court of St James.
Vice Admiral Alekesy Adamovich Adadurov,
Flag Officer in His Imperial Majesty's Sea Service.

Given the vital importance of securing the continuation of His
Imperial Majesty Tsar Alexander's alliance with Great Britain
in persecution of the war against France, you are requested and
beseeched to render unto these aforesaid gentlemen every assis-
tance within your powers in bringing success to the enterprise
that they shall expound. Note well that a ship with all seafaring
stores, officers and men will be provided you in this purpose.

Given this day Thursday August 1st 1805,
At the Admiralty in Whitehall.
Charles James Florint,
Admiral of the White, Principal Officer of Foreign Affairs to
Their Lordships.

This letter, on top-quality note paper, was elaborately sealed and signed,
and was drafted in the flourishing pen-hand of the Admiralty's senior clerks.

I read it and passed it to Mary, noting that Mikaelovich and Adamovich frowned as I did so, then switched back to smiles. Incidentally, note that I shall use just the middle of their three names, as Russians themselves mostly do, since the full three is only for formal matters. But I was amused by their frowns and smiles, and I thought, Like it or lump it, my lads, 'cos I can see from your dear little faces that you want something from me and you want me sweet.

When Mary had read it through, she looked at me with raised eyebrows. She was signalling, Is this genuine? I just nodded, and she nodded back. I'd seen too many Admiralty letters not to know the real thing. I knew Charley Florint, too. He was exceedingly dull and had got his promotions by family influence, but he was a diligent pen-pusher, and I recognised his signature.

"So, gentlemen," says I, "here's the two of you, just come all the way from London, and I'm told that you wish to make a proposal. So please begin!"

"It begins with this, Sir Jacob," says Count Mikaelovich. He drew a piece of fur from one of his bags and passed it to us. It was a couple of feet square, dark brown and most wonderfully soft and lustrous. Mary and I could not help but stroke it. "This is the fur of the sea otter," says Mikaelovich, "it is the finest in the world, and worth a fortune if sold in China, where it can be exchanged for porcelain, tea and silk. And then, when those items are sold on in Europe, the profit on the original investment in getting that fur ..." — he paused for effect — "is between one thousand and two thousand percent."

Mary and I both laughed at that. We couldn't help that, either. But the two Russians stayed straight-faced and even then I had the odd feeling that they weren't talking nonsense. They weren't sharps or villains, and had just had their backsides hammered in a ten-hour journey, with another ten hours to get them back to London. So why do that, just to spout nonsense?

"Those are fine figures, gentlemen," says my sister, "but can you explain them?"

"With pleasure, ma'am," says Mikaelovich, and he and Adamovich got out a series of maps which they spread on the table. "See here, ma'am and sir," says he, pointing to a map of the North American continent, "here is Alaska, which is sovereign territory of the Russian Empire."

"Is it?" says Mary.

"Yes," says I and the Russians together.

"Huh!" says she. "Go on, gentlemen."

"See here," says Mikaelovich, "where Alaska reaches out, via the Aleutian Islands towards Russia. And north of that, at the closest point ..."

"The Straits of Baring," says I, and he bowed in respect.

"The Straits of Baring indeed," he says. "At this point Mother Russia is less than sixty miles from Alaska, and for many years our fur-trappers have moved towards Alaska, and made it Russian." He paused again and looked at me. "And all this in pursuit of the sea otters, present there in vast numbers, which they catch and skin." I nodded, for he'd caught my attention, then he pointed to another map, his finger moving across the North Pacific. "And we carry the furs by ship, to Okhotsk, on the far western coast of Russia in Siberia." He nodded to Adamovich, who laid out another map. This one showed how Siberia butted up against China. "Then, by land," says Mikaelovich, "the furs go to the ancient trading town of Kyachta, on the border with China, where the furs are sold, and exchanged for silks and tea and porcelain."

"Very nice," says I. "But what's this to do with me?"

"Next map, please," says Mikaelovich, and Adamovich spread it out. It showed the vast continent that is Russia, and it showed a zig-zagging route, drawn in red, from Siberia to Moscow. "Look," says Mikaelovich, "see how the furs move now. They move by roads, rivers and canals, and through every climate from snow to drought."

"And so?" says I.

"Last map, please," says he, and Adamovich obliged. This one was a projection of the whole world. "Now," says Mikaelovich, "it is not just Russians that hunt the sea otter. The Americans are there, too. And even some British. But they do not use a land route to take home the benefits of trade. They deal with Chinese merchants in Canton — a seaport — and they take home the tea and porcelain and silks entirely by sea. The Americans go south and east, round Cape Horn and up the coast of South America, to New York and Boston. The British go south and west, past India, Cape of Good Hope, and north up the coast of Africa to Britain, yes?"

"Very likely," says I, "and enormous voyages those are too! They're precious near sailing the whole world around. Those are voyages of half a year or more. Far more, probably." And I smiled, because by now I could guess what was coming. "But once again, what's this to do with me?"

"Admiral," says he, "would you please explain?"

"Yes, Your Honour," says Adamovich, and he laboured a bit because his English was nowhere near as good as Mikaelovich's. "The Company cannot do these voyages," says he, and shrugged. "We — the Tsar's ships — we could make voyage. But not ships of the Company."

"What company?" says Mary.

"Russian American Company," says Adamovich. "Company has, has ..." He looked at Mikaelovich for a word.

"A monopoly," says Mikaelovich, "granted by the Tsars. The Russian American Company is entirely responsible for the fur trade: for the fur trade and for the colony of Alaska."

"Yes, yes," says Adamovich. "So! Company has ships. But not so good ships. Not so good crew. Not so good officer."

"Ahhhh," says I, leaning back in my chair. "So you want somebody to put that right. Somebody to take your furs to Canton, then a shipload of porcelain, and tea and silk, out of Canton and all round the world, past the Cape of Good Hope, to the Baltic and Moscow. Is that it?"

"Da!" says Adamovich.

"Yes!" says Mikaelovich. "We need that, and more than that. We need a man who can teach our mariners to do the same for themselves."

"Well, gentlemen," says I, "it might be that I know someone who could do that."

"Da?" says Adamovich, pleased as a boy on his birthday; but Mikaelovich had the bargaining sense to keep quiet.

"I might know somebody who could do that ..." I paused. "For an appropriate share of the profits — and it'd be a good, fat share, believe me!"

"Da!" says Adamovich eagerly, and Mikaelovich sighed, irritated with Adamovich's transparent enthusiasm.

"But something puzzles me," says I.

"What?" says Adamovich, and would have said more, but Mikaelovich motioned him to be silent.

"Well," says I, "just looking at that map and making calculations in my mind, then the voyage from Canton to Moscow — even leaving aside storms, pirates and other perils — is the matter of six months' to a year's sailing, with the need for going into friendly harbours from time to time on the way, for fresh water, supplies, repairs and other matters. So you should best assume a year at sea."

"Da!" says Adamovich, nodding.

"So," says I, "how can a voyage of a whole year be better than taking the goods nice and dry overland from China to Moscow, with no perils of seafaring whatsoever?"

"Sir Jacob," says Mikaelovich, "you do not appreciate the size of Russia. The journey from China to Moscow is long and troubled. The cargoes are carried variously along the route by pack-mules, camels, wagons, barges and sleighs: whatever suits the land and the climate. The roads vary in quality from bad to appalling. The cargo passes through many hands, constantly loaded and unloaded, and the route straggles this way and that, and is six thousand miles long — six thousand miles!" He looked me in the eye for emphasis. "So the journey takes a year to complete and the whole way is plagued by theft, accidents, bandits and corruption. So, Sir Jacob! So, Captain Fletcher the celebrated mariner! Consider this: even if the journey by sea took longer than a year, then once the cargo was secured aboard ship in Canton, at least it would all arrive in Moscow."

Well, my jolly boys, never mind the Russians trapping fur, because they trapped your Uncle Jacob then and there, and it was all my own greedy fault. In all truth, Mikaelovich and whoever was behind him

25

were naïve in thinking that all the goods taken aboard ships will arrive at their destination — because they won't, not all of them. Not when the sea turns nasty and naughty sailor men have hooked fingers for pilfering cargoes. But I was trapped by the idea of it, and the romance of it. That, and the thought of 2,000 percent profit.

So we talked some more, shook hands, made Mikaelovich, Adamovich and their post boy welcome for the night, and they were off and gone satisfied next morning. Within a month, I was outbound aboard ship from Portsmouth, destined for Cape Horn and Alaska. The agreement I made with the Russian embassy was drawn up and secured under British law, the Admiralty itself provided a ship, and my share of the profits was very great indeed. So even my sister thought I was right to go; or at least, she understood why I couldn't refuse.

But what a crying shame it was that we couldn't see round the next corner.

CHAPTER 4

The conjunction of opportunities was by chance. We had planned to bring silk, porcelain and tea to Moscow by ship, but then a vengeful woman gave me such a document!

(Extract of a letter from Pavel Pavelovich Stroganov, in London, to his father Pavel Sergeyevich Stroganov, in St Petersburg. Translated from Russian.)

Tsar Alexander looked down on the grand salon of his embassy in London: a large and noble house on three floors and a basement, and finished in white-plastered stucco, so as to appear as if it were carved from a single, massive block of stone. It was without doubt the finest of all the fine buildings in St James's Square. It glistened and gleamed in the bright sunshine that threw such excellent light through the tall, round-topped windows of the grand salon, with its lush carpets, ormolu vases and gilded furniture. Better still, the sunshine illuminated His Imperial Majesty in his ornate frame, for the three gentlemen who gazed up at him in discussion, and for the servants and guards in their various uniforms. But these lower beings stood rigidly stiff, staring straight ahead and taking no part in the conversation. They dared not even think of such impertinence.

"It's a copy, of course," said Count Pavel, the ambassador, a tall and handsome man of thirty-three, immaculate in expensive civilian clothes. Thus the two other gentlemen — Mikaelovich the deputy ambassador, and Vice Admiral Adamovich — nodded respectfully, since Count Pavel came of a powerful family, yet had won high position by intelligence and diplomatic skills.

"A copy but extremely well done, Your Excellency," said Mikaelovich.

"Who did you say painted it, Your Excellency?" asked Vice Admiral Adamovich.

"The Englishman, George Dawe," said Count Pavel. "He's young, but very good. He took the likeness of His Imperial Majesty during a visit to St Petersburg, last year. He painted the main image for His Imperial Majesty, then copies for others, including ourselves." He smiled. "Well, his studio did the copies. Not the great man himself."

"These artists!" said Mikaelovich, and the three shook their heads.

"So, gentlemen," said Count Pavel, "it's new, and has just arrived, so I thought you might like to see it."

"We are grateful, Your Excellency," said Adamovich, "and His Imperial Majesty looks magnificent in his uniform!"

"Yes," said Count Pavel, "but it shows his bald head, doesn't it?" Mikaelovich laughed with Count Pavel, but Adamovich thought it better not to laugh, not in front of the guards and servants. "Now," said Count Pavel, "having given respect to His Imperial Majesty, let's get to business! Mikaelovich and Adamovich, you have done very well with Captain Fletcher, whom I am advised is a most tremendous seaman and navigator. So, if he can show the way — by sea — to bring home the Chinese wares that we get from the fur trade, then the entire Alaska colony will thrive and grow, to the glory of the Motherland. Meanwhile, I have ..." He paused. "I have *the document*" — he spoke with emphasis — "in my private study, and have summoned advisors."

Count Pavel led the way. Mikaelovich and Adamovich followed. Doors whisked open before them and closed silently after. A brief walk into a smaller room: oak-panelled, lined with books, a large Orthodox icon on its own stand, and the walls hung with watercolour paintings of the aristocracy and royalty. There was even a picture of King George of England, the celebrated lunatic.

As they entered, two persons — who had been sitting in wait — leaped to attention and bowed. They were the embassy's lawyers. They wore grey wigs, black coats and white stocks. One wore small gold-rimmed spectacles. He was the elder and senior and he clutched an oilskin package to his very bosom. He held it as a priest would hold a holy relic.

"Wine!" said Count Pavel as he entered, nodding at the two lawyers, and he sat behind a huge mahogany desk, displaying colza oil lamps and beautiful silver figures of mounted cavalrymen. Wine and glasses instantly appeared, as Mikaelovich and Adamovich sat where Count Pavel indicated — to either side of the desk. Wine was poured and sipped. Count Pavel waved a hand towards the lawyers. "Have you read it?" he asked, and the senior lawyer clutched the oilskin even closer.

"Yes, Honoured and Noble Sir," he said.

"And is it as good as we were told? As powerful?" The two lawyers looked at one another then swept eyes to heaven in wonderment.

"With all respect, Honoured and Noble Sir," said the elder, "my colleague and I are practised scholars of the legal forms of international treaties and accords, and also of constitutional forms, and therefore ..."

"Yes, yes, yes!" said Count Pavel. "I know that. So answer my question. How powerful is this document?"

The elder lawyer drew breath. He delivered careful words.

"It is immensely powerful, Honoured and Noble Sir," he said. "It concerns the Founding Fathers who framed the Constitution of the United States of America." He stepped forward, bowed, and laid the document on Count Pavel's desk.

Much further discussion followed, then Count Pavel sat back in his chair and took more wine. "So," he said, "it is not only the *west* coast of the American continent that is ours to seize!" He looked to Mikaelovich and Adamovich, who nodded. "I must take this news to Moscow," said Count Pavel. "I must go at once, because we shall need a movement of armies and ships."

CHAPTER 5

They gave me one of my old ships for the Russian enterprise, did the Admiralty. Charley Florint was as good as his word, and I was given command of *Enable*, that had taken me to Africa and back some years before — as I've told in earlier volumes of these memoirs.

I'd last seen her in Portsmouth in March of 1803, when she was tired from hard usage and in need of a re-fit, which by Jove they'd given her since then, and she was clean, fresh-rigged and smart from main truck to keelson, and from bowsprit to taffrail. Also, Charley had ordered her magazines stuffed with extra powder and shot, knowing my taste for live-firing drills. He'd even given me a range of shot from round shot to grape and chain-shot. Well done that man! She was fresh-coppered too, which makes a world of difference, as every mariner knows who's tried to get good sailing out of a bottom that's thick with weed and drilled with the sea-worm.

So she was smart as paint but she wasn't beautiful, and she wasn't beautiful because she wasn't meant to be. She wasn't one of your modern, fast-flying clippers that takes your breath away for loveliness. She was a three-masted Newcastle ship, taken into the King's service. She was a collier, built for the east-coast trade bringing coals down to London; and a hard school for ships and men it is too, for it means following the coast, ever fearful of rocks and shoals. So colliers are built hardy and strong, and are bluff-bowed to rise to the seas and not get swamped.

In fact she was the twin of HMS *Endeavour*, chosen by the famous

Captain Cook for the voyages in which he mapped Australia, and various islands including How-why-ee.

Hawaii is the accepted form but Fletcher would tolerate no correction of his spelling of foreign words, but would lapse into his usual denunciation and detestation of the very existence of any language other than English. S.P.

Cook — a man whom I greatly admired — always declared that no finer ship than a Newcastle collier could ever be devised for a voyage of exploration, since a collier is tremendously seaworthy, will survive going aground, and is so deep and broad in hold that provisions can be stored for a vast great number of months. That was Cook's judgement and it's likewise that of your Uncle Jacob, so if ever you youngsters get command of a voyage around the world, then you should sail in a Newcastle collier.

Aside from that, *Enable* was ninety-five feet long, thirty feet broad, and 400 tons in burden, and she now mounted fourteen nine-pounder long guns and four twenty-four-pounder carronades. This was a purposeful increase on her armament from my last commission in her, and the extra gun ports were fresh cut by the dockyard people, because I'd made clear that since we were at war, the ship must be able to defend herself, and because it was my plan — among other things — to instruct her crew in gunnery. The Russian crew that is, and more of them later, because *Enable* came under my command with a core of British officers whom I list as follows:

Mr James Bentley, first lieutenant
Mr Frederic Dawson, second lieutenant
Mr David Arkwright, boatswain
Mr Peter Holding, gunner
Mr Steven Longfield, carpenter

The boatswain, gunner and carpenter were veterans in their forties, as was commonplace aboard ship, since it takes years to breed up men to such heavy responsibilities. But the two lieutenants were quite young. Dawson was barely twenty and Bentley a few years older, and Bentley always sticks in my mind as a great rarity among seamen, being a convinced Bible-basher. He was a short, round fellow with an earnest face, and always begging me to hold divine service on Sundays, even though the Russians have some other religion entirely — whatever that might be, for such matters are beyond my interest. But I advise you youngsters never to interfere in the superstitions of foreigners, since they will turn nasty beyond belief in the denying of them. Nonetheless, once we were at sea I let Bentley get on with it, preaching to the half-dozen grinning Russians who turned up just for the fun of it, and strictly voluntarily besides, at my insistence. God knows if they understood him, since he tried to preach in Russian. It was a caution to see him at it, and I tried not to laugh.

Incidentally, I hope you'll notice that I named Bentley and Dawson as lieutenants even though *Enable* was not one of His Majesty's ships, and she wasn't even one of the Russian Tsar's. Thus *Enable* was a merchantman and Bentley and Dawson were strictly first and second mates. But any ship under my command runs Royal Navy fashion, and there's an end of it.

There were four midshipmen too, the eldest sixteen, the youngest just twelve:

Mr Joseph Blacker
Mr Patrick Conner
Mr Paul Galliware
Mr Evan Cardiff

Fortunately all of the aforesaid — from lieutenants to mids — were fine seamen, plucked out of the King's service under orders from Charley Florint. So thank you yet again Charley my lad, because the Russian crew was something else entirely.

I met them when I went aboard with my trunks and traps, wearing full dress of a British sea service captain, despite the fact that the flag flying over *Enable* was that of the Russian American Company. It was horizontal stripes of white, over blue, over red, with a black double-headed eagle in the middle, and if that precious company ever had a uniform, then I never found out, because they certainly never gave me one.

I went aboard with Vice Admiral Adamovich, him that had come to see me in Kent with Mikaelovich, the deputy ambassador. Adamovich was about fifty years old and wore a beard, but had a seaman's face. I was in the same hotel as him the previous night — the Royal George, Portsmouth — where we'd dined together, and I'd been amazed at the drink he swilled down. But he was the one decent Russian I ever met. He was merry and laughed, and tried to tell Russian jokes in English. So you have to imagine him red-faced, sweating, leaning across the table, spilling wine from his glass and knocking things over, and him shouting so loud that all the other diners are looking on from other tables, some laughing, some frowning. Here's a flavour of it:

"Peasant woman's daughter: not married, but pregnant. What woman say?"

"Don't know," says I.

"Who's the mother? How you get peasants out of bath house?"

"Don't know."

"Throw in some soap! What difference between unicorn and clever peasant?"

"Don't know."

"Nothing! They both fairy tales."

The jokes weren't funny, but the man was. He laughed, he made me laugh, and when he'd taken a bottle or two, he pinched the bums of the servant girls, and got slapped for it, and he laughed even more. So I liked him too, which is more than I can say for some of the other Russians I met afloat, and who should have been heaved over the side with a sack of shot tied to their feet. But Adamovich was his honest self, and he did have a proper uniform — which was much like ours, but with different buttons and lace.

He grinned as our boat pulled out from Portsmouth Point the next day, with ourselves sat in the stern thwart of a sea service launch — six tars pulling and a coxswain in charge — courtesy of Charley Florint. I turned and looked back at the beach from which countless bold sailor

33

men have set forth, saying goodbye to tearful women. There was a small crowd waving us off. Some of them even called out to me, since my name was known to the public by then.

Indeed it was. In my company Fletcher could not walk down a street without the vulgar and the curious pointing him out, which considering the great bulk of him, was not surprising. Women in particular gazed upon him with an admiration which was both immodest and embarrassing to myself. S.P.

But Adamovich was looking ahead.

"See, Fletcher," says he, pointing to *Enable*, among all the herds and hosts of shipping anchored, and the busy boats pulling to and fro. "Your ship! She is old friend, yes?"

"Old friend and good friend," says I, smiling back at the memory of past times.

"You know is Russian crew? You know that?" says he.

"But with British officers," says I, "that's all been agreed."

"Da! Yes! But with …" — he struggled for words — "with *ghost* crew, to learn, yes?"

"Yes," says I. "Just so long as they don't run foul of my cables."

"Ooof!" says he, and wagged his head from side to side. "We know you," says he. "We know you, Fletcher. We ask all people, and we know." He raised fists as if he were a pugilist. "We know how you come aboard. I will see this, yes?"

"Most likely," says I, and put my mind to seeing how *Enable* was trimmed in the water, and already thinking that cargo would need to be shifted. She was too much down by the bow for my liking. But then we were bumping alongside where a stairway had been rigged, and I was out of the boat and going up and over the side, and boatswain's calls were sounding salute with all hands paraded at attention. *Enable* didn't have a quarterdeck as such, just a long poop deck that ran for'ard to just before the mainmast. Since it sloped downwards, the place of honour was the stern, from where all else could be looked down upon.

So there I stood, with Adamovich beside me, and I looked at everything. The ship was in good order: decks white, rigging neat, boats on skids at the waist, guns under tarpaulins and boarding pikes secured round the mainmast. Then there were the ship's people. There were two clumps of officers: one to larboard, one to starboard of the main body of sixty-five hands, the hands being entirely Russian. Mind you, the hands looked much the same as any other nation's matelots: tarred hats, slop britches and short blue jackets. In fact, most looked entirely English, as some Russians do, though others had a high-cheekboned, sloping-eyed look.

But then there were the officers, standing apart in their two groups — five British and six Russian — and I could see the distrust of each for the other. I'd have spotted British from Russian officers at a glance, since some of the Russians had beards, which are never seen in our service, and they had odds and ends of faded gold lace on their coats, as if reaching out for uniform but never finding it. But in any case, Bentley the first lieutenant greeted me as I came aboard, and made the introductions.

I have to say that aside from being an angel-maker, Bentley was one of those few in the service who admired myself, and Dawson the second lieutenant was another.

Note that officers of the Royal Navy were forever divided concerning Fletcher. He was greatly admired by some, but never forgiven by others for his sinking of HMS Calipheme *in Boston Harbour on October 4 1795, by the use of a submarine boat towing an explosive mine.* S.P.

"Honour to serve under you, Sir Jacob," says Bentley on first meeting, and with all the Russians looking on and listening.

"Honour and pleasure, sir," says Dawson, and the two rascals damn near bowed. Which is all very nice, my jolly boys, but beware of such sentiments in those you command, for it may lead to familiarity, which I can easily squash, but which you may find embarrassing.

But now there were matters of ceremony to address.

"Admiral," says I to Adamovich, "would you be so kind as to read the paper that you brought with you?" And I turned to Bentley and the other Englishmen. "This is the *reading-in*, gentlemen. It can't be the King's commission, so I shall receive this command by order of the Russian American Company."

"Ah!" says they, and nodded, because the first duty of any captain taking command of one of His Majesty's ships is to read out the commission that gives him the right to do so.

"Admiral?" says I.

"Da!" says he, and read aloud a great bucket of heathen gibberish, written in devil's writing on an elaborate scroll, stamped and embossed and hung with seals. God knows what it meant, but the Russians all nodded, and mumbled "*da, da, da*" which I took to be approval. When he was done, he touched his hat to me in salute.

"*Kapitan!*" says he. "The ship is yours!"

"Hurrah!" says Bentley and the other Englishmen. Then Bentley turned to the ship's people: the Russians.

"Three cheers for Captain Fletcher!" says he in a roar, and they got the message as he continued. "Hip-hip-hip ..."

"Hooooo-*rah*," says they, with little enthusiasm.

"Hip-hip-hip ..."

"Hooo-rah."

"Hip-hip-hip ..."

"Mumble, mumble, mumble."

Right, you swabs, thinks I to myself, and I took off my cocked hat and dress coat and dropped them on the deck, to puzzlement from every Russian face — but not the English, because they'd heard of me and knew what was coming. They grinned and nudged one another. So I pulled off my waistcoat and shirt, and dropped them on the deck with my stockings and shoes following straight after. The Russians were all gabbling by then, with round eyes and shuffling feet.

You see, my jolly boys, these poor innocent Russians did not know— as the entire British Fleet now knew — the manner whereby your Uncle Jacob comes aboard a fresh command, to impress the crew with the extreme need to behave and to follow your Uncle Jacob's orders. Just you believe me. Just you ask any man who has ever served under my command, and a kindly and gentle way it is too, since having established my authority, in my own way, I never had need for cruel and savage punishment. And so:

36

"*Alllll hands*!" says I in the biggest voice that I could deliver, such that the wavers-off on Portsmouth Point probably heard me. "*Alllll hands*!" And I stepped forward, barefoot and bare-chested, to let them get a good look at me. Then I turned to Adamovich.

"Admiral?" says I.

"Kapitan?" says he — the only one among all the Russians who was grinning.

"Would you kindly ask the ship's people," says I, "to bring forward the best man among them? The one who's cock of the walk and bully-boy? Will you ask them that, on my behalf?" He laughed, turned to the crew, and yelled at them in Russian, then touched his hat to me again.

"I'm obliged, Admiral," says I; and I took a good look at the crew, because they were moving about, chattering and arguing. Then there was a bit of a cheer among them as they pushed forward a squat, slimy-haired creature with a broken nose, and ears all deformed by battering. I smiled. There's always one among any ship's crew, and this one would do very nicely.

"Admiral?" says I.

"Kapitan?"

"Tell this good man to fight back hard, or God help him!"

"I tell him," says Adamovich. "I tell him to fight for his mother and for Holy Russia!" Which I suppose is what he said, and there was a mixture of cheers and puzzled silence from the crew. But the squat ugly one got the message all right, and he threw off his jacket and shirt and stepped forward, stretching out his arms to grapple, at which he got the most enormous cheer from his mates, while Bentley and the rest yelled out my lower-deck name.

"Jacky Flash! Jacky Flash! Jacky Flash!"

And so we set to, myself and Shuska Veleslav, which was his name. His style was grab, bite, then jerk up the knee to mash my precious assets. But when you've fought the jiu-jitsu men of Japan, as I have, that isn't going to win him the bout, even if I did come away aching from his knee-jabs, for he caught me once or twice. But my style was hammering right and left with the fists, just as hard and fast as I can, and since I've the strength to turn over a mail coach single-handed on its roof — which I can and have done — then believe me, the blows come hard. But it took me a few minutes to put him down, what with the way he hung on, and while we fought, the ship shivered from end to end with the cheers, howls and curses, with all present jumping up and down with excitement and bellowing with every atom of breath.

But in the end, there he was, flat on the deck was Shuska Veleslav, and you'll think I'm boasting who reads these words. But look at the size of me. As I've said a thousand times before, I can knock down other men as easily as you would a child.

So I knocked down Veleslav, then did another thing that I always do on these occasions. I hauled him to his feet, presented him to them all, and gave *hip-hip-hip* so that all should cheer him for being man enough to take me on — and all his mates cheered.

"Double grog for this fine man and his messmates!" says I. Adamovich translated that and I got a full-hearted cheer from the crew. Then Bentley and the other Englishmen were coming forward with my clothes and shoes.

"Well done, sir!" says Bentley.

"Well done, sir," says the boatswain, "that's shown them swabs!"

"Good! Good! Good!" says Adamovich. "We Russians like the strong leader *silny lider! Silny lider*, yes? You understand? *Silny* is strong, and you are strong!"

"Thank you, gentlemen," says I, "but there's more to do."

Bentley nodded his head at that, because he certainly did know my ways. "Shall we clear and run out, sir? I believe that is your usual practice?"

"It is indeed, Mr Bentley; I'd be obliged if you'd beat to quarters and do it by the clock!"

"Aye-aye, sir!" says he, and up came a boy drummer, to sound general quarters. And then I had that ship turned inside out with drills. Yes, I had them clear for action and run out the guns, with all things proper other than loading powder and shot, because you can't load and fire in port. Then, since they did it far too slow, I had them put the ship all to rights: powder magazine locked and keys given back to the first lieutenant, and guns secured away. And then I made them do it all over again.

After that, eight bells of the forenoon watch sounded and it was dinner time, which I advise you youngsters never, ever to neglect unless the enemy is bearing down or a hurricane blowing, for the loss of dinner unsettles the men. So we stopped for that, and I looked kindly on Veleslav and his mates being near unconscious after double grog, since I'd ordered it myself, and I had them hauled down to the cable tier to sleep it off.

But then it was all hands to launch and man a boat, and myself rowed round the ship, and the cargo shifted to my commands to get *Enable* trimmed to my liking: a fearful job of work, since massive fresh water casks on the ballast down below must be shifted, as well as other stores above, and even shot taken from the fore locker to the aft. Then I had the upper yards sent down, then sent up again, and we had a fire drill, and a man overboard drill. By Jove but they slept well, did the ship's people, over the next days, and got the best of vittles that could be contrived, since being in port I had the boats come alongside — which are always plentiful at Portsmouth — selling fresh bread, fresh greens, chickens, eggs and other tasties. Once again, I exhort you youngsters never, ever to compromise on the men's food, since food is the fuel that powers a seaman just as surely as it's coal that powers a steam engine.

Aside from shaking up the hands with these exercises, and letting them know what to expect of me before even we went to sea, I had the chance to go among them as they worked, and see how Bentley and the rest managed a ship where the hands spoke no English, not with Vice Admiral Adamovich long since gone. It also gave me the opportunity to reinforce my earlier lesson as given to Veleslav, when one or two of the hands attempted a surly look, and had to be knocked down for it. I should add that I was doing only what was common practice in those days, and not just in the King's ships but merchantmen, too. So don't think that officers aboard merchant ships kept command with

39

a kind word and a friendly smile. Not them, my jolly boys, because it was a punch on the nose and a kick up the arse. So I was doing nothing unusual — but on this occasion it was close to being the end of me.

It was on my first day aboard, the second time I had them run out the guns, and I was on the gun deck with Mr Dawson, our second lieutenant, and a Russian who I took to be his shadow, which word — shadow — is what the British officers called their Russian equivalents who were supposed to be learning from them. But in fact, this shadow was *not* Dawson's shadow. The Russian's name was Gregorovich; he was a skinny man with a completely bald head and a beard all over his chest. Now: the way of working for Bentley, Dawson and the other Englishmen was to give commands in English, to be translated by the Russian shadows, who did have a bit of seaman's English.

On that occasion, Gregorovich wasn't giving close attention to Dawson, but was knelt down spinning the elevating screw on one of the stern-mounted carronades: to show the gun crew how to do it, since carronades were new to them. But Gregorovich kept fumbling. He was worse at it than the gun captain, and Dawson spoke to him.

"Never mind," says he, polite as could be, "just let him do it," and he pointed at the gun captain. But Gregorovich stood up, gave Dawson an insolent look, then turned to me and said something in Russian that made the gun crew laugh at me; them and others, too, who heard it. So *smack*! Down he went, my jolly boys: *smack*. I didn't even use full force, just enough to put him in his place.

But I'd made a mistake, because even though I'd already met Gregorovich when Bentley made the introductions, I couldn't follow the Russian names, and when Bentley introduced him the fellow was wearing his laced coat. But later, for working the guns, he had just a shirt and britches and he wasn't wearing the hat which had covered his bald head. So I hadn't recognised him as Pitr Gregorovich Vinogradov, senior Russian aboard, who was highly regarded by the Russian American Company, and the man I was supposed to train up as captain in his own right.

Oh dear. Oh dear. Oh very dear. And this despite all my best intentions. Thus Gregorovich never forgave me and much worse was to follow — very much worse — and all this after Charley Florint, bless his heart, had placed me so snug and secure that it seemed too good to be true. Thus it was, indeed, too good to be true.

CHAPTER 6

Sir! If you think your anger was too great — that anger expressed in your letter on Fletcher's being sent to Alaska — then apologise not, sir, since my own anger is excessively, vastly bigger!!!

(Extract of a letter from Earl Wilshaw, First Lord of the Admiralty, and addressed to William Pitt the Prime Minister, at Downing Street, London.)

"Good God Almighty, Florint! What damn well possessed you to do it? Don't you know the bloody man? Don't you know his bloody reputation?"

The First Lord thumped the long table with his fist, while sitting beside him, the Second, Third, Fourth, Fifth and Sixth Lords growled agreement. So did the senior clerks and other bureaucrats, even the least of whom was a powerful man in his own right. But none were as powerful as John James Wilshaw, Knight of the Garter, ninth Earl of Wilshaw and First Sea Lord, because Wilshaw sat in the government's cabinet as one of the men who ruled over Britannia herself.

So he thumped the table again.

"God Almighty!" he said.

He — Wilshaw — was an oddity: nobly born into vast estates, but away with the gypsy poachers as a boy and living with them in the wild for years. He joined the sea service late at twenty-five years old, then pursued an illustrious career, rising entirely on merit and serving in dozens of hot actions. He was renowned for his foul temper and worse language, and was still formidable at seventy-nine years old. He ran fingers through his mane of white hair, then rubbed a handkerchief across his face, gathered himself, attempted to control his rage, and stared at Admiral Charles Florint, who was cringing on the other side of the table.

Florint groaned, and couldn't meet Wilshaw's eyes. So he looked round the Admiralty boardroom for inspiration — not that any came. The weather was unseasonable and the room was gloomy despite the large windows looking out on Horse Guards Parade, where dismal persons scuttled forward, bent against the rain and clutching their hats.

Then, as is often the case for persons under stress, the details of Florint's surroundings forced themselves into his mind: the elaborately decorated ceiling, one wall hung with rolls of maps, a great globe of the world at the end of the room, and above that a wind-indicator like a giant clock face, giving the wind direction to men commanding ships that moved only by sail. But he dwelt too long in his thoughts.

"Florint, damn you!" cried Wilshaw. "I'm damn well speaking to you! Why in God's name did you send Jacob Fletcher to Alaska?"

"Ah, ah," said Florint, avoiding the question. "M'lord, I have sent a fast ship to recall him. I sent … ah, ah, a revenue cutter." He fumbled with a sheaf of notes. "Ah, ah, in fact I sent three of them, m'lord. Three! They are fast ships and very nimble in stays."

"Nimble in stays?" cried Wilshaw. "Might as well be your bloody grandmother's stays for all the chance they'll have of catching him!"

"With utmost respect, m'lord," said Florint, "his course is known, m'lord, and the cutters will follow it such that …"

"Follow it be damned!" said Wilshaw. "'Cos even if they *do* catch him, those cutters are cockleshells armed with pop-guns, while *Enable* has man-o'-war timbers and a man-o'-war broadside!"

"But m'lord," said Florint, "Fletcher would never fire on the British flag."

"Would he not?" said Wilshaw. "Would he not? If you think *not*, then you don't know bloody Fletcher!" Then Wilshaw tried again to calm down. "Why did you send Fletcher?" he said.

"To assist the Russians, m'lord," said Florint. "Were we not exhorted to assist the Russians? To ensure their continuance in the war against France? Indeed I did my very best with a fine ship well-equipped, and in any case they asked specifically for Fletcher."

"God bloody save us all!" said Wilshaw. "Do you not meet with your equals? Do you not talk? Do you not understand the politics? Our intention — well known to every other person in this room — was to give the Russians every *sign* of assistance, every *pretence* of assistance, in this Alaskan-Chinese business, but to take bloody good care that they don't expand out of Alaska. It's bloody tragic enough that *we* lost America, let alone helping the bloody Russians to grab it!"

"But they asked for Fletcher," said Florint. "They asked for him by name."

"Of course they bloody well did," said Wilshaw. "The man's a bloody prodigy. He gets things done. He walks on water. He wriggles out of scrapes. He's famous for it, and we've used him ourselves when things turned ugly. But the bugger can't be controlled once he's set in motion. He always gets what he's going after, and in this case that's dangerous, 'cos he'll help the bloody Russians too bloody much. You should've passed off some damned old fogey on the Russians, and never given them Fletcher! Him and a ship provisioned for circum-bloody-navigation! He could go anywhere in that ship!"

"But I thought, m'lord ..." said Florint. "I thought ..."

"You thought, did you?" said Wilshaw, completely losing his temper. "You thought! You thought? D'you know what Thought did? Well, do you?"

"No, m'lord."

"'Thought he farted and shit himself! And so have you!'"

CHAPTER 7

Of course, I had to apologise to Gregorovich. I didn't need to be a genius to work that out. I had him aft to the taffrail, once gun drill was finished, and spoke to him before all hands, gasping and panting as they were in the sweat from the drill. I spoke before all hands since there's no hiding such matters aboard ship, where word goes round like a cat with its tail on fire. So I wanted the people to hear me direct, not second-hand, and I had Gregorovich aft with the ship's officers mustered and shook his hand, speaking English for want of anything better.

"Mr Gregorovich," says I, "it was a bad mistake on my part, for which I apologise." I paused to see his reaction and was surprised when Mr Bentley the first lieutenant stepped in.

"Mossoo Gregorovich," says he in French. "Mossoo le capitain ill sekskyuse."

Properly: 'Monsieur Gregorovich, Monsieur Le Capitain il s'excuse.' But in French of all languages, Fletcher would never accept correction and insisted — with fearful anger — on his phonetic rendering. S.P.

"Ah!" says Gregorovich, and he looked at me, looked around at his mates, shrugged and nodded and chattered some French at Bentley, since the pair of them both spoke it: a fact that proved invaluable later on, because how else was I to instruct the blighters in their duties?

"Cap'n, sir!" says Bentley when they were done. "Mr Gregorovich accepts your apology, sir!" And he touched his hat in salute. In fact, looking at Gregorovich's nasty face, I could see that he still cherished a grievance. But damn the swab, I wasn't apologising any more, and that

45

had to be the end of it for that moment. In any case, there was much work to do to get the ship fit for sea. She was already well provisioned with ship's stores: biscuits, salt beef, split peas, pickles and the rest. Every hold and locker in the ship was full, and there was enough drink on board to float the ship. But there was nothing fresh, and it was near three days' work to get the livestock aboard.

If you don't know what this means, then I'll remind you that when a ship of those times set sail for a long voyage, she upped anchor with an entire menagerie of beasts on board. She had chickens, ducks, sheep … even cattle on the big ships: as many of them as could be crammed into coops and pens, rigged by the carpenter and his mates, for how else were we to have fresh meat? So when sails were set and the noble vessel spread her wings and set forth on the azure ocean, she clucked and mooed, and baahed and the shite ran out of the scuppers in brown streams, driven by the wash-deck pumps. Which is something they don't tell you in the romantic novels of the sea. She stank pretty foul too, but you didn't mind that when you sat down to a fine dinner of chicken or tucked into a boiled egg.

There was something else besides, which I insisted upon before setting sail — in addition to my constant drills — and that was making the officers mess together and not apart. Thus I would not allow what I found when I came aboard, which was the British officers messing separate from the Russian. So I had that out with them, there and then.

"See here, Mr Bentley," says I, "you'll oblige me by putting my words into French for Mr Gregorovich to turn into Russian for all hands to hear."

"Aye-aye, sir!" says he.

"All hands pay heed now!" says I, and glared at the pack of them.

"Gabble-gabble-gabble!" says Bentley in French.

"Gabble-gabble-gabble!" says Gregorovich in Russian, and so it continued, but I won't mention the gabbling again, since I'm sure you've understood the way of it.

"All hands take heed," says I, "that from this moment, we shall not be Englishmen and Russians, but shipmates! We shall be united in the enterprise of this voyage, and in facing the sea in our ship!" I let them think about that, and some of them nodded and some did not. "And to that end," says I, "the lieutenants — those who were once Russian and English — shall now mess together, and the ship's craftsmen shall do the same, with no divisions between them!" Some were frowning now, so I delivered a piece of theatre. "Where's Mr Veleslav?" says I. "Where are you? Step forward!"

The hands were gaping wide-open-mouthed now, but Veleslav came forward, greasy and ugly, and looked at me, and he touched his hat in salute.

"Kapitan!" says he. That was useful. Very much so.

"So!" says I. "Any man that won't mess with a shipmate — whether he be Russian or English — can take his choice, to face either myself or Mr Veleslav. So, do I have any takers of that offer?" Silence followed. Then Veleslav laughed at the looks on all their faces, and as he laughed they all laughed, and the tension was broke and the bargain was made. And so:

"Mr Boatswain!" says I.

"Aye-aye, sir!" says the boatswain.

"Up spirits and a tot for all hands to salute the ship!"

I got my second full-hearted cheer for that, and the united messes worked well for gunners, boatswains and carpenters, since these trade professionals quickly united with their fellows. Later, and to my great satisfaction, I was even asked by the men themselves to make these friendly arrangements official, by rating the equivalent Russians as first mates to the British gunner, boatswain and carpenter, leaving each pair to choose among the crew for second mates, as needed. So that was good, but it didn't turn out so well for the lieutenants, since Bentley and Dawson rightly considered themselves gentlemen, while some of their Russian equivalents were not. Most definitely they were not, since they weren't particularly clean and they regularly got drunk.

So I kept all hands busy, and later on when we'd set sail, and cleared Portsmouth and were well out to sea, I had the drummer boy beat to quarters, for yet another gun drill. But this time I had powder and shot loaded for thundering detonations and billows of smoke. By Jove it brought back memories, it did indeed! Just the smell of it and the grit of the smoke in my teeth.

I ordered live firing firstly to keep the men sharp, but also — and any ship's officer will tell you this — because the men love to hear the cannon speak. It's like fireworks. Every man loves the flash and the roar, and they chuckle most mightily as the guns discharge. I've seen it a thousand times, and it never fails. So I had a good few broadsides fired away, leaving Mr Bentley to give the orders as first lieutenant, while I went up and down the gun deck to see how the men behaved. And by Jove they were slack, and nowhere near British standard. They were slack and slow, but at least they heaved with a will, and I noticed something else too.

As is usual aboard ship, the midshipmen had charge of the guns in action: each mid commanding one or two pairs — larboard and starboard — under orders of the first lieutenant. So the mids were yelling at the gunners in the most amazing mixture of English and Russian, and bits of French too, with a Russian lad shadowing each mid, to learn his trade.

"*Vite! Vite!* Quick!" says one of the mids, and something in Russian too.

"Da!" says the gun crew, ramming home a shot.

"Da!" says the mid.

"Da! Quick-quick!" says the Russian shadow-lad. It was all very strange to me, since I could never understand a foreign word, but this was the way of things aboard *Enable*, where the ship's people soon had a bizarre language peculiar to themselves, especially among the mids and their shadows. Then, when broadside drill was finished, I had a cask heaved over the side, bearing a spar with bits of red cloth as a flag, then brought the ship about, for her guns to bear on the cask from a cable's length off.

"Now then, Mr Bentley and Mr Gregorovich," says I, "I'll have steady, aimed fire — five rounds each gun — and the gun crew that gets closest gets sippers of every other crew's grog!" Another huge cheer followed, then the first lieutenant was going to each gun, to give the time, and the mids were yelling at the gun crews as they heaved their pieces left and right to aim.

"Left-*gauche-levo*!" says one mid.

"*Pravo*-right-*droit*!" says another.

It was a caution to hear: French, Russian and English all mixed together in some of the few foreign words that I ever learned.

In the event, one of the carronade crews won the sippers, which was pure chance, since carronades, with their short barrels, wide bore and cunning swivel-carriages, are excellent for close work; indeed that's what they were designed for. But they haven't the range of long guns and nobody would choose one for distant firing. So the carronade crew threw up their arms and cheered and danced up and down when I gave judgement.

"Number two gun, larboard!" says I, pointing them out, since their shot was by far the best, drenching cask and flag with the huge water-spout that went up when a twenty-four-pound shot hit the sea with a fat *chop*!

"Hooooo-rah! Hooooo-rah!" says they, while Bentley turned to Dawson the second lieutenant, as they stood by me among other officers at the stern.

"Lucky devils," says he, "they never even hit it."

"Indeed, Mr Bentley," says I, "but that's not the point of the drill. The point is to make sure that the men take care with their firing, because one day we may actually be obliged to fight at long range, and even at close range a slack crew can manage to miss if they're stupid enough."

"Aye-aye, sir!" says Bentley.

"Of course, sir!" says Dawson.

"Da!" says Gregorovich, who caught the drift if not the words, and he looked at me pensive and thinking inside of him, because all the crew were cheering now. They were giving the Russian hooooo-rah! They were cheering because they were happy not just with the gunfire, but because all the tars of all the nations are like the Russians in that they want a strong leader. They want a captain who's master of his ship. So I suppose they thought that I was one.

False modesty. Fletcher had the gift to inspire tremendous loyalty in the

49

men who served under him. He knew this very well indeed and was most vainly proud of it. S.P.

But as regards Mr Pitr Gregorovich Vinogradov, I think the blighter might have forgiven me for knocking him down, but I don't think he ever forgave me for being a better man than him in the eyes of the crew. Not for that, nor for the troubles I had in getting Gregorovich to find longitude by chronometer, of which he was profoundly ignorant, him and the rest of the supposed navigating officers that came with him. More of that later, because something more acutely difficult really did foul my cable in the very earliest days of the voyage.

Thus a week out from Portsmouth we were to the west of the Bay of Biscay, working south to pick up the trade winds for the Atlantic crossing, when our mainmast lookout spotted an oncoming vessel, and yelled down in Russian.

"Sail on the larboard quarter, sir!" says Bentley, who'd picked up a deal of Russian by now.

"Sail. Yes!" says Gregorovich, and I raised my best Dolland telescope to look. I saw nothing at first on an empty grey-blue ocean with a stiff wind and big swell. Then the lookout yelled again, and even I guessed what *Britansky* meant, in the midst of his words, and I was right.

"British colours, sir!" said Bentley.

"Da! Britansky!" says Gregorovich, and all the other Russians nodded.

"Fast ship, sir, " says Bentley. "Fore and aft rig. Bearing down upon us."

Soon, anyone with a glass could see what was coming, and there must have been a dozen of us looking, including the mids and some of the Russian lads who were their equivalent of mids. The stranger was a most lovely little ship, perhaps 100 tons burthen, with two masts, a bit of topsail on the foremast, a huge mainsail stretched fore and aft on a spanker and boom to the mainmast, and great bulging staysails to the forestays. She was heeled hard over, and thrashing along at a tremendous rate. She had three times our speed at least, and she looked so nimble as to come about on a pocket handkerchief. All this, and a white ensign flying from the peak of the mainmast.

Then ... *puff!* A silent ball of white smoke burst from her bow, and was blown to atoms by the wind. Then … *thud!* We heard the sound. Soon after another puff of smoke, followed by another thud, all flat-sounding across the ocean. Then a hoist of colours went up, and everyone aboard who was British swiftly recognised the signal. The mids all muttered and Bentley looked at me.

"Yes, Mr Bentley," says I, "I can see: it's *heave-to!*"

"Yes, sir," says he. "What do we do, sir?"

Then there was the most furious argument. Gregorovich, who had a glass of his own, was studying the oncoming ship, which looked to me like a revenue cutter, and he saw the signal even if he couldn't read it. But he'd heard what Bentley said, and shouted into my face.

"*Nyet*, Kapitan!" says he. "Not stop. Not heave-to. *Nyet, nyet, nyet!*"

I must confess, my jolly boys, that Mr Gregorovich very nearly got another fist in the face for telling me what to do aboard my ship. But, but, but … a little memory tickled my ear. Back in Portsmouth, when Adamovich was yelling jokes at the entire company in the dining room of the Royal George Hotel, a seafaring gentleman among the company had yelled back. He'd yelled at *me*, not Adamovich. He was merchant service, not King George's, so I'd paid him no heed.

"Fletcher!" says he. "Put a stopper in that Rusky's scuttle, before their lordships realise what they've done and call you back!" In later years I wondered what that gentleman knew, and how he knew it. Sea gossip, I suppose. But at the time, aboard *Enable,* with the white ensign bearing down at high speed, that feeling came back of it being too good to be true. The feeling came back that they were going to snatch it all away from me. Meanwhile, Gregorovich and the other Russians were yelling at me, and pointing to the mainmast, where the Russian America Company's flag was flying.

"We Ruskiy ship!" says Gregorovich. "Not heave-to!"

"Nyet! Nyet! Nyet!" says the rest. Thinking of the fur trade, no doubt, just as I was. Then Gregorovich was pointing at the oncoming ship, and then stamping a foot on the deck, and went off in Russian, all passionate and angry. Then he chattered French at Bentley, who frowned, and looked at me.

51

"He says we should fight, sir," says he. "We're the bigger ship with better guns and more men. He says we're under a Russian flag, and if the other fires on us, then it's war. But damn the swab," says Bentley, fiercely, "we shan't do that, sir, shall we? Not fire on a King's ship!" Before I could reply, Gregorovich was off in French again, pointing back to the Russian hands now clustered together and looking on.

"Sir! Sir!" says Bentley. "He says he'll call on the hands, sir. Call on them in the name of the Motherland. He says they'll fight, even if you won't."

"Da! Da! Da!" says Gregorovich, and all the Russian officers were with him, though I'm not so sure about the hands, because they stared at him, then me, then back again. But if it came to it, I couldn't be entirely sure that they'd ignore Gregorovich and obey me. They were Russian, after all. It was a very nasty moment. Very nasty indeed. So, taking time to think, I raised my Dolland glass and looked at the approaching ship. If she was indeed a revenue cutter then she'd be light-built for speed, with a token armament of four-pounders. I hadn't the slightest doubt that if it came to close action, then *Enable* would smash her and sink her in short order.

But then the skies opened and the heavenly choir sang.

"Mr Bentley! Mr Dawson!" says I. "Beat to quarters, load with shot."

"Ah!" says Gregorovich, and he grinned. He might not have understood entirely, but he could see the looks on Bentley and Dawson's faces. He nudged his Russian mates and they grinned too. But Bentley and Dawson were horrified.

"Beat, sir? Beat to quarters, sir?" says Bentley, in fearful dismay.

"Load shot?" says Dawson, equally horrified.

"But we can't, sir," says Bentley. "Not fire on the flag, sir. It'd be treason!"

"Treason, sir," says Dawson. "We can't do that!"

"Gentlemen," says I, "if you don't do as I say, then it will be treason indeed." So I explained, and as the drum rolled, the hands ran to their station, cast off the sea-lashings from the guns as shot was brought up from the lockers below, then rammed home over powder and wads, and by Jove you could almost taste the excitement on the hands. They knew what was coming, you see, and such is the manner of human nature that firing into an enemy that can't hit back touches off the devil's glee inside of a man. It ain't a pretty thing, my jolly boys, but it's a fact. So they heaved with a will, did those Russians, with grins all over their faces. Then, finally:

"Both batteries stood ready for action, sir," says Bentley, touching his hat. "Larboard and starboard, whichever side might need to engage, according to your orders, sir."

"Well done, Mr Bentley," says I. "But it'll have to be faster next time."

He smiled. "Aye-aye, sir," says he, and I raised my glass towards the speeding cutter just in time to see another blank round fired from her bow ... *thud* ... to emphasise her order that we must heave-to. She was close enough now that I could see the hands aboard her running to their duties, as she came about to sweep around us with the white water boiling under her bow: a very fine sight indeed, and a very smart little ship.

"Mr Bentley," says I.

"Sir?"

"Shorten sail and back the main topsail. Heave-to!"

"Aye-aye, sir!"

Then there was a deal of yelling from the boatswain and his mates, since *Enable* was not yet a smart ship, which happy state takes a month or two at sea to achieve. But soon enough our courses were furled, the ship was brought into the wind, and the main topsail yard swung to leave its sail blown flat against the mast and opposing the forward pressure of the fore topsail; the standard means whereby a ship at sea is brought to a wallowing stop. And *Enable* wallowed heavy, being so flat-bottomed as she was, without much depth of keel.

Meanwhile, the cutter came round us like a swallow. She came round, backed sails so nice and neat as to deserve applause, and laid alongside us so close that I could see faces, uniforms, curled lines, polished brass and a young officer at the stern, about to raise a speaking trumpet to hail. He was close enough that he recognised me.

"Ahoy, Cap'n Fletcher!" says he. *Captain* Fletcher, indeed. That was nice. What a nice young lad he was, in command of such a nice little ship. "Ahoy, Fletcher," says he. "You are required by Their Lordships of the Admiralty to come about ..." He said more, but I wasn't listening.

"Port lids, Mr Bentley," says I, "and wait for my orders!"

"Aye-aye, sir!" says he, and the hands cheered.

"Hoooo-rah!"

Then up came the lids of the larboard gun ports, since the cutter had chosen to come aboard us on that side. Up came the lids that had hidden our guns from the cutter. I even saw the amazement on the faces of the cutter's crew, while our men cheered.

"Hooooo-rah! Hoooo-rah! Hoooo-rah!" they cried as they hauled on the tackles and the guns ran out, with gun captains taking up the lanyards of the guns' firelocks.

"Wait for it ... wait for it!" says I, with all the force of my lungs. "And ... *Fire!*"

Thunder and smoke, flashing flame, and a broadside of chain-shot — the rigging smasher — poured from our guns, and into the masts of the cutter, splintering spars, shredding sails, parting lines and blowing the foremast into a stump. The cutter was swamped with wreckage, draped in ruined sail-cloth, and totally helpless.

But I place the greatest possible emphasis on the fact that I'd taken care to fire on the upward roll — and good deep roll it was in that ship — such that none of our shot went into the cutter's hull or swept her decks. Our broadside went entirely into her rigging, to disable not sink, to hamper not kill. Yes, there would have been some sore heads from falling wreckage, but that's a hazard of the seas, and a good crew will always make shift to heave the mess overside, and press on with jury-rigged sails. No crew would ever go to sea that couldn't do that, but nonetheless I held back from getting *Enable* under way, until I could see that the cutter wasn't sinking and the hands were busy making good.

Her name was *Firefly* and she was under Lieutenant Charles Trentham, who bawled across at the top of his voice, once he'd got the ruined mainsail off of him.

"Fletcher!" says he in a wild scream. "You bloody-handed-bastard-traitor, I'll see you swing for this! I'll see you broken, I'll see you hoist to the yardarm …" And so on and so on, blah, blah, blah. Ungrateful swab! I saved his life by not aiming into *Firefly*'s hull as Gregorovich would have done. So it was only thanks to me that Trentham eventually dropped anchor in Falmouth, and went on to damn me before the Admiralty, the world and the newspapers. Which indeed he did. He did it for years. He never forgave me.

However, note the perversity that Lieutenant — later Admiral — Trentham's sustained campaign against Fletcher succeeded only in enhancing rather than diminishing Fletcher's reputation as a charming rogue, in the eyes of the foolish public. See Proverbs 10:23, "It is sport to a fool to do mischief." S.P.

But Gregorovich was satisfied with what we'd done, even though I saw the nastiness in him: he who'd have done worse. But the other Russian officers threw arms around me and tried to kiss me as Russians will. So who can understand foreigners? I shoved them off, and pointed to the hands who were stood grinning beside their guns.

"Get those idle sods to work, Mr Bentley," says I, "and make sail!"

"Aye-aye, sir!" says he, and got the ship under way, leaving *Firefly* to her repairs.

"So was that treason or not?" says I to him, privately, later on.

"It was not, sir."

"Indeed not, 'cos the Russians would have sunk that cutter and drowned her people."

"Aye-aye, sir."

"So we'll need to be watchful of some of those aboard this ship."

"Really, sir?"

"Yes," says I, and I was right.

CHAPTER 8

I entered the church in such a state of fear as previously I had experienced only when facing the bayonets of the enemy. Believe me, Little Kitten, I did not — I absolutely did not — know whom I could trust.

(Extract of a letter from Pavel Pavelovich Stroganov to his mistress, the dancer Lydia Markovitz, later 'La Markova of Petersburg', described by Sergei Diaghilev — supreme impresario of ballet — as 'the muse whose life was my inspiration'. Translated from Russian.)

Count Pavel kissed his wife. It was a formal kiss, French style: left-right-left. Thus Russia might be at war with France — for the moment — but the Russian aristocracy lived in a French world and Countess Irena wore the latest in French fashion: a gown in white muslin, caught under the bust with a blue ribbon, and a white ostrich feather in her hair. She had been a great beauty once, but she was older than her husband, and now the low cut of the gown merely emphasised her wrinkles.

"Monsieur Le Comte!" she said.

"Madame La Comtesse!" he said, since they *spoke* French as well as lived it, and the foyer of their grand house in Moscow's elite Stoleshnikov Lane was entirely in French style — as were the liveries of the servants in attendance, one standing just behind Count Pavel with his master's dress sword, busby and pelisse.

The count and countess spoke on in French, which for once was practical since the servants could not understand.

"Are you sure?" said the count.

"I am sure," said the countess, and they looked at each other, these two who were bound together by family and politics and who could almost trust one another because there was a degree of trust still left, despite several dozen lovers taken by one or another of them over the years. What were lovers, in any case? A man might change from one horse to another, so why not a lover? At least, that is what the count hoped. So he pressed on.

"Are you sure that the Patriarch will approve?" he said.

"Yes," she said. "My father the duke and my brother the archbishop have prepared him, and so have I. We have been working on him for months."

"And the Tsar?" he said.

"You look ill," she said, stepping back.

"What do you expect?" he said. "Three weeks on that ship from London and seasick every day. I shall never go to sea again."

"Not even if you must?" she said.

"You're avoiding the question," he said. "What about the Tsar?"

She took a breath. "If the Patriarch approves, the Tsar will approve," she said.

"What about the generals?"

"They will follow the Tsar, and so will the admirals."

"But are you sure?"

Countess Irena chose not to answer that particular question. Instead: "You look ill," she said, "but you must go and be brave."

Since those two statements were undeniably true, and since Count Pavel was not a coward, he nodded, and stood straight as he left the house. His carriage was waiting. It was an open landau set to a pair of splendid black horses, with a uniformed driver to the front saluting with his whip, two footmen raising hats to the rear, and Count Pavel's three equerries stood bowing beside the carriage, all in the uniform of his regiment, as he was himself: the uniform of the elite Kutzak Hussars, flamboyant in gold-laced pelisse and fur busby with white plume.

He climbed in, the young officers climbed in beside him, and a stage-managed crowd of Muscovites waved and cheered as he set off. They waved thin branches, sharpened at one end, but with green leaves at the other. Everyone in Moscow waved such branches on this saint's day, and the city was decorated with them in memory of St Konstantine, put to death by the Vikings in the tenth century when the cruel pagans — laughing at what they had done to him — proclaimed that they had given him a tail of green feathers.

The carriage drove off, crossed the Moskva river by the Holy Trinity bridge, and soon came up against a line of carriages. There, a company of great dignitaries was alighting, to be cheered by a host of merry people, all waving branches, outside the centuries-old and deeply revered Church of the Martyred Konstantine: an edifice of ancient brick and pointed domes, where the bones of the saint resided in a crystal casket and were known to effect miraculous cures of afflictions of the bowel.

There was much greeting and saluting among the great men present, as Count Pavel and his equerries made their way through a crowd held back by guardsmen with muskets, and into the church, which glittered with uniforms and resounded with the chanting of a choir of young priests and high-born boys. But — by tradition — no ladies were present on St Konstantine's day, since the saint had always disdained women as pathways to sin, and had never defiled himself among them.

The church's interior was gloriously Russian, with ancient arches and faded icons, and gold leaf, and relics, and vessels swung by priests to emit clouds of incense. But Count Pavel's stomach turned at the stench of incense, he cursed the seasickness yet again, and struggled into the place reserved for him, pushing past epaulettes, uniform lace and plumed hats held under one arm. Uniforms were everywhere, because St Konstantine had dearly loved soldiers. And sailors.

Sick as he was, Count Pavel did his best to catch the eye of as many generals as he could, in the attempt to guess their thoughts. But each one merely nodded, in stone-faced impartiality such that Count Pavel feared that his project might be dying, and that the risks he had taken were now lethal. Thus his entrails began to churn so painfully that he wondered if touching the crystal casket might help. But there was no chance of that, because the chanting rose to a crescendo as a procession entered the church, and all present bowed heads in respect of the venerable Konstantine — Patriarch of Moscow and all the Russians — as he passed down the aisle, with a trail of acolytes, towards the high altar. He had respectfully taken the name of his favourite saint, and was supreme head of the Orthodox faith, subject only to the will of the Tsar, who marched just one footfall ahead of the Patriarch.

Tsar Alexander I marched ahead because — as all Russia knew — he had been divinely appointed and was supreme in all matters, whether civil or military, legal or commercial, imperial or regional, sacred or profane. Thus whosoever insulted the Tsar, insulted Almighty God.

The Tsar wore the uniform of Supreme Marshal of All the Armies, beneath a cape of cloth-of-gold, and since he wore no hat, it was obvious that his rumoured baldness must have been a malicious falsehood, since he seemed to have a fine head of hair. Meanwhile, Patriarch Konstantine advanced with noble and splendid bearing. He was blessed with a huge white beard, and wore the sacred kouklion headdress: a great dome surmounted by a golden cross, with lappets descending to his breast. Each lappet bore the image of St Konstantine, naked from the waist down with his protruding tail of green leaves picked out in emeralds, and an uncertain look on his face.

To Count Pavel, the service was tedious beyond bearing. It was agony and every last second — every last sniff of nauseating incense — was the torture of the damned in hell. But all things pass, and eventually all persons other than the most senior generals and admirals were removed from the church. Thus the priests and high-born boys were removed, the deacons and servants were removed, and — to Count Pavel's inexpressible relief — the incense swingers went with them, and the great doors of the church boomed shut.

Then everyone looked at Count Pavel, whose face was the colour of soap, and who was wondering if his wife had truly acted on his behalf, or had she betrayed him? But now he was invited by the most senior general to step forward with his proposal. And so, since Count Pavel cared deeply for Mother Russia, and believed deeply in his Campaign of the Americas, he stepped forward towards the altar, crossed himself, and bowed to His Imperial Majesty the Tsar, and to His Holiness the Patriarch.

"Pavel Pavelovich Stroganov," said the Tsar, "we take advantage of this fortunate conjunction of the leaders of our forces of land and sea." He waved a hand at the stars and sashes, the swords and the uniforms.

"God bless Your Imperial Majesty!" said the generals and admirals, and their voices rumbled, echoing around the church.

"Since all are present," said the Tsar, "then, Pavel Pavelovich Stroganov, you have our permission to present your case."

"Imperial Majesty," said Count Pavel. "It is with honour and respect that I offer you a great pincer movement. I offer a military and political attack on the colonial American powers of Spain and Britain." He paused. "And most particularly on the thirteen colonies of the eastern coast: the so-called United States of America! It is my honour to present to you the means whereby — according to its manifest destiny — Your Imperial Majesty's empire can be enormously expanded, and our holy faith—" Pavel bowed to the Patriarch — "equally according to manifest destiny, may likewise be spread across a vast continent."

Count Pavel did his best not to show the dread of doubt that filled him up. He tried not to show his doubt in the matter of his wife's loyalty. Had she — and the duke and the archbishop — whispered *for* him or *against* him, into the ear of the Patriarch? How could he know? He tried to control the ghastly doubt, and he tried to be a good advocate. But when he was done, the fear within him was so great that he could barely stand. So he bowed and looked to the Tsar for judgement, since he could do no more.

The Tsar looked at Count Pavel. He looked around the church at a congregation of veteran military politicians who never, never, *ever* gave an opinion until they knew that the Tsar would approve. Then he turned to Patriarch Konstantine.

"What is your opinion, Holy Father?" he said. "Do you support Count Pavel's proposal?"

60

There followed a long instant which was so paralysed in silence that even the dust twinkling in the window-light dared not descend to the marble floor.

"Holy and Reverend Father," said the Tsar again. "Do you support the proposal? And do you believe in the power of the document which was given to Count Pavel by the English woman?"

Patriarch Konstantine looked at the Tsar and made his judgement.

He pondered for a time that was agony.

Then, slowly, he nodded.

It was enough.

CHAPTER 9

Having left the Bay of Biscay behind us we made a good crossing with the trades, and took on extra supplies and fresh water at Bermuda, all of which was good for the ship and good for her people, because with myself and Mr Bentley driving them, the crew settled down, settled in and were approaching something like smartness — though I must admit that I found it hard going with the Russians, and drunkenness was a constant problem.

I should explain here that the charge of drunk aboard ship didn't mean just slurred speech and a dizzy head — not with the daily rum ration of those times — it meant so blind-sozzled that a man couldn't get up to his duties when the boatswain kicked him. But the trouble was that the Russians thought nothing of being blind drunk. They thought it was funny and manly, and the hands contrived every imaginable way to get hold of drink, especially spirits. They'd sneak into the hold, drill holes in casks and draw off the fluid into pig-bladders for hiding, then plug the holes so craftily you'd never know they'd been, and that adds theft to the charge, since it's stealing of ship's stores.

Now the usual punishment for drunkenness was flogging, but I despise the very idea of a man being triced up with bound hands, and unable even to face, let alone defend himself, from a beating on his back. So I hope you youngsters will forgive your Uncle Jacob for being soft-hearted, but there was no flogging aboard any ship of mine. And so, you may ask, what was I to do? Although I always established discipline aboard ship by knocking a man down, I couldn't constantly be doing that for fear they should become accustomed to it. So I was obliged to employ other means.

The first time this problem arose, I had the entire crew mustered, at two bells of the forenoon watch, and the ship going a comfortable five knots under a steady blow. The weather was fine, the sky blue, and there were even some porpoises following along in our wake, all leaping and shining.

"All hands pay heed!" says I, with a bit of translation by Bentley and Gregorovich, though by now there was less need of it, since the officers and men were learning bits of each other's languages. "Pay heed," says I, "and look at these fellows." I pointed to five foremast hands in the clutches of the boatswain and his mates, and which hands had trouble in standing. They already nursed headaches and had been roused only by the cutting of their hammock lashings such that they fell to the deck. "These men were too drunk for duty when the last watch turned," says I.

I saw some of the Russians chuckle at that. Gregorovich and his officers included.

"So pay heed, all of you," says I. "And because I will not have such behaviour aboard ship, then these men ..." I pointed to them, and paused for effect, before delivering the most cruel and sadistic punishment afloat, the one that fills sailor men with dread. "These men," says I, "are on *stopped* grog for a *week*!"

By Jesus, God and all his angels, you'd think that I'd sentenced them to being skinned alive and salt rubbed in. The entire crew gave such a gasp as made the porpoises ask each other what was going on. The condemned men wept, and one by one they fell to their knees and raised hands in supplication. They groaned and groaned. The crew looked on in horror and it's a shame that the Frenchman Chopin didn't write his miserable "Death March" until later years, because it would have suited the moment.

Nonetheless, I'm afraid that even by such means I never quite clapped a hitch on that crew's taste for drink. It's in their blood, I suppose: something that softens the pain of their country's winter with more dark than light and snow ten feet deep. God knows how they stand it because I certainly could not. Meanwhile, I soon wished that drunkenness was my only problem because it was not. That was Gregorovich and his blasted officers, and my attempts to teach them proper navigation.

It began early on in the voyage, when first we took our noon observation, to determine our position on the sea. I'll spare you the full details of how this is done because years of experience have convinced me that no landman will ever understand it. So I might have had some sympathy for Gregorovich and the rest if they hadn't been seamen. But they were indeed seamen — or what passed as such within the service of the Russian American Company. So here's a concoction of my attempts to teach, putting together bits and pieces of the many times that I attempted to educate Mr Pitr Gregorovich. Once again, I leave out Bentley's assistance in French in order that I might converse with Gregorovich. But believe me that Bentley was there, and sweating with the effort.

So it was noon, the ship rolling along, the hands sent to dinner, and myself, Bentley and Dawson, with our sextants, likewise Gregorovich and two others, and our mids as well, though the Russian mids had less idea of navigation than Boris the ship's dog, a nasty great beast that dropped its dung in dark corners for men to tread on, which the Russians thought was funny.

"So, Mr Gregorovich," says I, "have you taken your sighting?"

"Yes," says he, "I took the altitude of the sun, for latitude."

"Good," says I. "So shall we go below now, to the chronometer, to get our longitude?"

He said nothing, but shrugged and looked at the other Russians, who did the same.

"Mr Gregorovich," says I, "are we going below?"

He shrugged again. "No," says he, "that's Imperial Navy. We don't do that."

"*Nyet!*" says the other Russians.

"Imperial Navy?" says I. "What does that mean?"

"The Tsar's navy does those things," says he, "with the clock and figures. But we don't need that. We find latitude, then run it down."

"Da!" says the others, looking superior, and not just superior but affronted. They looked as if I'd given them turd pie for dinner. You see, they were generations behind, using the same style of navigation as Francis Drake. That meant sailing roughly in the right direction then north or south to find the latitude of the destination, then east or west along that line of latitude in the hope of finding it. Yes, Drake and the rest made it work in the old days when nobody knew better, but it meant a slow zig-zag across the ocean and was highly inaccurate: a ship might make landfall 100, even 200, miles from its true destination, or it might run onto unknown rocks.

"Mr Gregorovich," says I, "we'll go below this instant minute, and that's an order!" I stepped forward and stared him in the eye. He blinked, sniffed and shrugged.

"Da. We go below," he said, and so we did. We all crowded into the small stern cabin, astern of the gun deck. We had two chronometers there, thanks to Charley Florint, since they were enormously expensive. "See here," says I, "ship's time is noon, while London time — given by the chronometer — is …" But most of them weren't listening. The Russians were looking at one another, scratching their beards and picking their noses, and in that moment I realised what a task lay before me if I was to show men like these how to sail from Alaska to St Petersburg. They weren't only ignorant, but arrogant besides.

"So how the hell do you manage in Alaska?" says I. "You sail between Alaska and Siberia, don't you?" They all smiled at that, just as you would smile at an idiot, who didn't know two plus two equals four. Then Gregorovich and some of the others were off into deep Russian, and occasional bits of French, and staring at me. I looked to Bentley. He was struggling to keep up and constantly shaking his head.

"As best I can make out, sir," says he finally, "for the fur trade, heading east from Siberia, they work along the Aleutian island chain, finding their way with a sounding lead and local knowledge, and for open-sea work, they run their latitude, as they've said. With them, it's lead-log-and-latitude, sir. They're not deep-sea men at all. Not blue water. Not really."

"In that case," says I, "God help us every one, when we try to get round Cape Horn, westbound."

The only thing I will say is that not all the Russians refused to learn. Gregorovich had a second in command called Turganev. He was by far the youngest of them, and while he was as thirsty for drink as the rest, he was different. He wanted to learn, and was fascinated by the chronometers. I caught him once gazing at them, down in the stern cabin where he shouldn't have been without my permission.

"Oh! Oh!" says Turganev, touching his forelock like a tar caught with his hand in the pickle jar. "Oh, oh, Kapitan," and he gabbled off in Russian for want of English. But I saw a little spark there. A spark in the dark. There had to be one of the blighters who wasn't useless.

"So," says I, "you want to have a look, do you?"

"Da!" says he. "Da, Kapitan." So I showed him how the instruments were mounted on their gimbals, and how they were wound up with a key, and I spoke a bit about finding longitude. He smiled and nodded, keen as could be, and it was the best few minutes' work I did that voyage, as you youngsters shall see later.

Meanwhile, Cape Horn! Mark well the name of it, because you've no idea what it meant in those days to round Cape Horn westbound: Cape Horn at the southern end of Chile, which was the cause of troubles even before we reached it. The troubles began in the stern cabin with myself attempting to explain the course that I proposed to set. I had our charts spread out: the best that Charley Florint could provide. They were Dutch, by Van Oosterhout of Amsterdam, the Dutch being as good seamen as any that ever sailed.

"See here," says I, pointing to the tip of South America, with the ship's officers clustered round, "we shall coast downward south-east, around Tierra del Fuego, then westbound south of the Horn Islands, then north-west, clearing these hundreds of islands that—" But I was interrupted.

"Nyet!" says Gregorovich, then he gabbled in Russian, and among all that tripe and offal I recognised the word "Magellan". That or something like it.

"Beg pardon, sir," says Bentley, "but he's saying ..."

"Straits of Magellan?" says I.

"Yes, sir."

"Da! Da!" says Gregorovich, and gabbled some more tripe with some — but not all — of the Russians gabbling with him, and pointing at the chart and nodding.

"Mr Bentley?" says I. "You will do your best to translate."

"Aye-aye, sir!" And I suppose he did his best as I read them the rule book. I did so with one finger moving across the map, while struggling to keep my temper.

"See here," says I. "Yes, the Straits of Magellan offer a route from Atlantic to Pacific."

"Da!" says Gregorovich, with a truly insolent scowl.

"Yes," says I, wanting to punch his head, "and we'll need to run onward past the Straits, for three days' sail to get down to the Horn."

"Da! Da! Da!" from all of them.

"And," says I, "we'll face seas like mountains, and sleet and ice, and fierce winds in our faces, going westbound round the Horn."

"Da! Da! Da! Da!"

"But!" says I, "the Straits of Magellan is a land-locked seaway that's thirty miles wide at best, down to one mile at worst, and there's miles and miles of that, with rocks and shoals and lee shores and fog. So it's—"

Gregorovich interrupted again. "Gabble-gabble-gabble!"

I turned to Bentley.

"He says that's what they're used to, sir," says he, "fog and coast-hugging. They're used to that in the Aleutian Islands: with the sounding lead, and finding their way." He looked at me. "I'm sorry, sir, but now he's saying that no man can sail the deep seas and find his way. Not with a stupid clock he can't find his way." Bentley sighed. "That's what he says, sir."

"Thank you, Mr Bentley," says I, and looked at Gregorovich. "Can't find the way says you? You? You couldn't find your own dick in the dark — don't translate that, Mr Bentley."

"Aye-aye, sir!"

"Just tell these Russian gentlemen that we're going round the Horn.

I'm captain of this ship, appointed by their own damned Russian American Company, and it's damn well going to be run my way."

So we did, and the further south we got, with Spanish America on the larboard beam, we ran down what later became Argentina, then Chile, and the sea turned ugly.

I was on deck myself when the first big waves came aboard. All hands were in oilskins and whatever beneath that kept in some warmth, and there were hand lines rigged for us to take hold of, and I had chafing rigged around every line that might rub against a sail (that's strips of canvas and old rope, wrapped round and round the lines such that neither they, nor the sails, might be worn through by the rubbing, and which I exhort you youngsters never to neglect when rounding the Horn).

Gregorovich was beside me, as was Turganev, and of course Bentley. *Enable* was heeled over something steep, and rising magnificently to the swell, under topsails and spritsails, and running a grand seven knots, which was splendid sailing for such a ship in such weather. Then the waves really got up under a gusting blow, that came with sleet that stung the face, and blinded the eye, and now, my jolly boys, you have to believe your Uncle Jacob in the exhilaration of such a moment. It's like nothing else in the world: with a taut ship riding waves so big that you can't believe them. That's riding them and beating them. It's a wonderful time to be alive. It's why men go to sea.

All those who doubt Fletcher's hypocrisy in claiming that he despised the seafaring life, should read the above once again. S.P.

We'd seen some rollers in the Atlantic, but nothing like those that rise up round the tail end of the Americas. They come white-capped, heaving and charging. They come forty, fifty, sixty feet high, and even more: much, much more, and an endless line of others coming up behind. So one instant the ship is raised up to see wide horizons, and the next plunged in to a grey-green slippery valley that shuts out all the world.

So ponder on that my lads, and forget all your invulnerable iron steam-ships and think of a wooden ship under sail, and the seams of her leaking apart under the strain, and nothing below decks ever dry, and soggy-wet hammocks to sleep in. All that and cold food — because you can't stand the risk of the oven being overthrown and setting the ship afire — and all of which was normal and usual for a ship in those waters, and all those who can't abide it should stay safe ashore.

Which meant that since I was aboard to instruct Gregorovich and the rest, then I had to give Gregorovich his chance to make his mistakes and be corrected, for that's how any seaman learns, and I'd done the same with him and the other Russian officers earlier, under easier weather. To give them their due, I suppose, they weren't completely hopeless. They could hold a compass course, change sail as need be, and keep lookout for squalls, though none of them — officers and men together — were ever going to come near Royal Navy standards, nor Yankee nor Dutch either. And so:

"Mr Gregorovich," says I, "are you happy with the sail we're wearing?" I didn't even need Bentley to translate. Not for that.

"Reef!" says Gregorovich, pointing to the main topsail, and remember my jolly boys that this was all shouted into one another's ears, since the wind in the rigging made such a howling scream, as sounded like beasts in torment.

"Your ship, mister!" says I, because he was right. So I touched my hat in signal that he should take over. So he did, and he bellowed in Russian, and the boatswain's calls sounded, and the topmen went aloft, and they did manage to shorten sail, leaning over the yard with their feet on the foot ropes, and they didn't make a bad job of it. After all, the blighters had sailed before, up in the north off Alaska. But there was one thing I didn't like at all. Boris the ship's dog was always a part of Gregorovich's orders. The dog was Gregorovich's great favourite. He loved it and fed it tasty scraps and encouraged it, to encourage the men to their duties — so he said.

Boris was some sort of sled-pulling breed from Siberia. He was thick-furred, long-nosed and had the most amazing blue eyes. But he was vicious, a nasty creature, which may be why Gregorovich liked him: because whenever Gregorovich gave an order, such as sending the topmen aloft, Boris would bark, and chase them, nipping the legs of the last man. Gregorovich thought that no end of a joke, and he would point to the dog, and nudge me, as if challenging me to approve, though in all truth the swab was really challenging my authority as such, being confident that I'd not dare hit him again.

But this time, Boris turned really nasty. He caught the topmen as they came down the shrouds to the deck. He seized the last man by the leg. He bit fierce and hard, and actually pulled the man off his feet, and did so just as a huge wave broke over the deck and we clung to the safety lines, for fear of being swept away. But the damned dog hung on such that there was blood in the white water as he and the topman were washed up the deck right to where we officers were standing, and by the grace of God I managed to grab a good hold of the seaman, who for sure would otherwise have gone over the rail.

So the man was saved, but the dog wouldn't let go of him. I could see the brute's teeth sunk into the man's ankle, where the nasty creature had got his nose up under oilskins and britches to find white flesh.

"Get off, you sod!" says I, clinging to the man with one hand and a safety line with the other, and stamping Boris with the heel of my boot a good half-dozen times, such that the animal turned its blue eyes on me, let go of the seaman and went for me with teeth and fury. I lost my hold on the line, the ship heaved, and the dog, and myself and the seaman — who I clung on to — slid across the deck as the wave drained through the scuppers. Then by George I had to let go of the man, because the dog was pushing and nuzzling with the stink of his breath in my nose, and mad energy, trying to reach my throat and kill me!

But two can play that game, and I got my hands on his throat first, though it took all my strength, such that he'd have done for most men in one bite. Then it was him or me, and it wasn't going to be me, and it ended with blue-eyed Boris going over the side as an offering to King Neptune, courtesy of myself throwing him with all my might.

Then I grabbed a line, Bentley came to help me and I saw the Russian seaman was held by two of his mates, since he couldn't properly stand and was bleeding bad.

"Are you all right, sir?" says Bentley, with concern all over his pale, round face. He looked as if his grandpa had fallen down stairs. I think he actually liked me, as well as false-idolising me. But Gregorovich tried to push past him, and Bentley shoved back.

"Haul off, you no-seaman swab!" says Bentley. "Didn't you see what the captain just did, you swab? And your bloody dog going for him!"

"Thank you, Mr Bentley," says I, "but stand clear, and leave him to me." I said that because Gregorovich was screaming at me in Russian, and pointing where I'd thrown his blasted dog, and totally lost in anger. He pushed right up to me. "Shut up, mister!" says I, and pushed him back. But the swab stepped forward and I couldn't believe what he did next, because he spat at me! He actually spat in my face! What sort of a seaman would do that? I was disgusted with him, disgusted to the marrow of my bones, contemptible brute that he was. So there was only one thing to do.

Smack! Down he went.

Which is when the mutiny began.

CHAPTER 10

> You'd not believe what these Russians are contriving, nor
> how stubborn Uncle James is become, nor what shore-talk is
> reporting of Count Pavel and the Tsar.
>
> (Extract of a letter from Duncan Argyll, Argyll House
> Kronstadt, to his friend Ian Cameron, of 13 Carrick St,
> Edinburgh.)

The sun shone in his glory. He shone so well that, just for once, the
waters of the Gulf of Finland were as blue as those of classical Greece: a
respectful nod, perhaps, to the huge and wonderful piece of history —
a war galley — that was pulling steadily towards the Kronstadt Naval
Base on its island in the Gulf of Finland, having left St Petersburg just
three hours ago.

The galley was far bigger than any vessel of Greek antiquity, bearing
three masts rigged for lateen sails. But these sails were furled and the
galley was under way thanks to the combined muscle-power of 200
men sat five to a bench pulling forty great oars: five men to each oar,
twenty oars to each side. They pulled to the beat of a solemn drum, and
their own deep-voiced singing. They were the pick of the Tsar's fleet
and wore splendid uniforms of scarlet and gold, just as the galley itself
was painted and gilded, and hung with banners, because His Imperial
Majesty Tsar Alexander stood on the command deck at the stern, with
his suite of nobles and the officers of the galley.

"It's a grand sight, I'll grant you that," said Duncan Argyll.

"Of course it is," said his uncle, James Argyll. "What did you expect?"

"Not something from the past," said Duncan.

"It's not from the past," said James, "oared ships are common in the Baltic. Sweden and other powers have fleets of them, just like the Russians. Oars are useful in narrow waters with shifting winds."

"Still sounds old-fashioned to me," said Duncan. "Like the Russians themselves."

"Hush your mouth," said James.

"What for?" said Duncan. "Who'd know?"

They stood on the quarterdeck of *Pietr Velikiy* — Peter the Great — flagship of the Americas fleet, a vessel of seventy-four guns, embarking 600 men, with their officers — in their gorgeous uniforms — standing elbow-to-elbow beside the Argylls. But these officers spoke only Russian or French. They couldn't follow even plain English, let alone broad Scots.

Thus Duncan Argyll came of a group — almost a clan — of Scots shipwrights and navigators, who'd been in Kronstadt for generations — since Russia had once welcomed foreign knowledge where shipbuilding was concerned. So at sixty years old, James Argyll was born a Russian citizen and had a Russian wife, sons and grandchildren. But he'd grown up in Scots tradition as well as Russian, while young Duncan — just twenty-three years old — had come out to follow opportunity at his uncle's invitation, having studied the shipwright trade in Aberdeen, Newcastle and Portsmouth.

"Will you look at that, now!" said Duncan. "Even our fathers' fathers never saw such a thing!"

Indeed, the galley was magnificent as it approached the seventy-four and backed oars as neat as a six-oared launch, then it lost way, and raised the great sweeps to vertical by sheer seamanly strength, such that the galley could come hard alongside, and the Tsar and his suite could mount the white-roped, gleaming-brass-railed steps rigged for His Imperial Majesty's convenience.

"One, two!" cried the bandmaster, and the ship's musicians and choir delivered a spine-tingling harmony of sombre music as the Tsar ascended the quarterdeck, to be greeted by Grand Admiral Fyodor Orlov, who stepped forward, bowed low and kissed the Tsar's hand.

"Uncle?" said Duncan Argyll, whispering. "Isn't that 'God Save the King', that the English sing?"

"No," said James, "it's 'Prayer of the Russian Folk' in honour of the Tsar. They've got their own words to it. Now hush and give a good low bow to His Majesty!"

So Duncan hushed as the Tsar and his nobles moved among the ship's officers, and favoured ones were presented. Duncan bowed as the Tsar and suite paused and actually stopped in front of Uncle James! Then the Tsar offered his hand for Uncle James to kiss, and Duncan listened as the Tsar spoke incomprehensible Russian, to which Uncle James repeatedly replied, "*Da, Imperatorskoye Velichestvo*." (Yes, Imperial Majesty.) Duncan was amazed at the respect his uncle was given, and the smiles of those in company with the Tsar, and he noticed the Tsar's elaborate uniform, his multiple stars of knightly orders, his pale face and his small, pursed lips. More than that, since Duncan was tall, he noticed that His Imperial Majesty's side-hair was cunningly slicked over with Macassar oil dressing to cover His Imperial head, so bald as it was in the centre.

Then the Tsar moved on, as Grand Admiral Orlov led him and the nobles on a tour of the ship, and finally to a splendid lunch in the stern cabin. Then all those of *Pietr Velikiy*'s officers not invited to table could relax, look round the harbour and chat, while the band played merry airs, the choir sang, and the foremast hands went to their duties.

"What did he say to you?" asked Duncan.

"His Majesty was gracious enough to thank me for my help in making ready these fine ships," said James. "Look there!" And among all the pleasure craft, out to see the Tsar and his galley, James pointed towards two of the line anchored with a number of merchant ships clustered around them, just a cable's length from *Pietr Velikiy*. But Duncan frowned.

"They're none of them ready for sea," he said, "no more than this

74

ship. And they're only seventy-four-gun ships. The English and French always have a three-decker or two in their fleets, and they bear one hundred guns."

"Our ships don't need to be ready for sea," said James, "not yet, and seventy-fours are adequate for this purpose. They're perfectly good for the Americas."

"Huh!" said Duncan. "And I grant you there's a fine frigate over there, beyond them, and she's got yards crossed, and looks fully manned."

"That's *Svatoy Eudoxia,*" said James, "*Saint Eudoxia* in English. She's ready for sea, according to plan. Your trouble, my lad, is that you don't know Russian ways!"

Duncan laughed. "Such as the fact that half their ships are bad-timbered and leaky?"

"Duncan, you're new to Russia. You've barely arrived."

"Yes, Uncle, but you've never been *out* of Russia. You haven't seen what's a-building in the English and American yards. Every ship's copper-bottomed and heavy-gunned."

"Yes! Yes! You've said that. You say it all the time."

"It's more than that. I don't like the English any more than you, but you should see them at gun drill: three broadsides in five minutes!"

"Duncan!" said James Argyll, slipping into anger. "Now you listen to me!" And since James was more Russian than Scots, and since Duncan was already regretting having left Portsmouth, the discussion became an argument.

But down in the great cabin, among a press of land service and sea service officers, and before lunch was served, the Tsar and a favoured few stood out on the stern gallery in the fine fresh air, with a view of Kronstadt's massive fortifications, the harbour, the pleasure craft, and most particularly the warships brought together for this special purpose. Thus Count Pavel Pavelovich Stroganov explained the Expedition of the Americas to the Tsar, Grand Admiral Orlov and the rest.

"*Pietr Velikiy* shall be the flagship, Imperial Majesty," said Count Pavel, "in command of the east-coast squadron, which shall comprise the flagship, two other seventy-fours, and merchantmen with two thousand infantrymen." The Tsar nodded. "While the seventy-four-gun *Aleksy Senyavin*—" Count Pavel pointed to the ship — "shall lead the west-coast squadron, with two seventy-fours and merchantmen with two thousand infantrymen. But, of course, the west-coast squadron shall sail only after the east-coast squadron has achieved its aims."

"Good," said the Tsar, "and what artillery shall be embarked?"

"One field gun per half-battalion," said Count Pavel, "and siege guns shall be contrived from the batteries of the fleet, with extemporised carriages, should need arise, Imperial Majesty."

"And cavalry?" questioned the Tsar.

"More difficult, Majesty," said Count Pavel, "considering the need to keep horses healthy — even alive — within a ship, on a voyage of such duration. So we shall take just one hundred horses: fifty for each squadron."

"And I believe that you shall go in advance," said the Tsar.

"Indeed, Majesty," said Count Pavel, "I shall go aboard the frigate *Svatoy Eudoxia,* in advance of the two squadrons. That is our plan."

"*Your* plan, Count Pavel," said the Tsar, smiling. "*Yours* is the credit."

"God bless Your Imperial Majesty," said Count Pavel, bowing. "Your Imperial Majesty is most gracious." So everyone smiled, including Count Pavel, even though he knew that the man who took credit for a plan was punished if it failed, and the greater the plan, the greater the punishment. But Count Pavel knew no other way. He was bred up to that. He was Russian.

Later, Count Pavel was indeed aboard *Svatoy Eudoxia* when she upped anchor. She was cheered by the two squadrons with bands playing and banners waving, while — in order to seek God's blessing — a priest sprinkled holy water over the ship's figurehead: a life-sized and lifelike depiction of a lovely nun with eyes half-closed and mouth agape in a shuddering ecstasy which surely was *religious* ecstasy, since what other kind might be visited upon a nun?

But Pavel Pavelovich Stroganov was seasick even before the ship left the Gulf of Finland and entered the Baltic. Despite all his considerable talents he was one of those unfortunates who suffer greatly from a ship's motion. So he didn't care what was going on around him. He just wanted to die. He didn't care that his plan was going forward: his plan whereby Russia would seize the entire North American continent.

CHAPTER 11

I took Gregorovich below. I did it myself. I shoved him semi-conscious through a hatchway. I relished the *bumpity-bumpity-bump* of him making his way down the companionway ladder, and if he'd broken his neck I shouldn't have cared. Then I turned to Mr Bentley, standing by the helmsmen at the ship's wheel; four of them given the state of the sea, and the ship heaving and groaning, and the scream of the wind in the rigging, and every man of them staring at me.

"All yours, Mr Bentley!" says I. "Keep course, and mind she don't get took aback by squalls." He probably never heard me, what with the wind, and thundering seas. But he knew his work and I knew him, so he'd have done what I said regardless.

Then I was below decks, and the hatch was slammed over me to stop the seas coming in, and I was in the sloping, rolling berthing deck, where the men sling their hammocks, and them gaping at Gregorovich and myself. They especially gaped when he woke up and looked up at me with his broken nose and blood-stained mouth, and I delivered him the boot, good and hard.

"Get up, you swab!" says I, and he cringed and pulled himself up by the ladder and hung on. And now you have to imagine what it was like, my lads, below decks in such weather. It was dim-lit by swinging candle-lanterns and damp, stinking, slippery, and the whole wooden world following the ship's movement. There was never a steady deck beneath a man's feet, and all the bulkheads swayed, and tried to throw you over.

So I looked at the faces in the gloom, and braced against the motion. A dozen hands of the off-duty starboard watch were staring at me and Gregorovich, and I didn't like the looks on their faces: not when they'd seen me throw Gregorovich down a hatchway then kick him. Him that was Pitr Gregorovich Vinogradov who was beloved of the Russian American Company and who was their captain before I came aboard, and supposed to be captain when I left. In that moment I dearly wished I had marines behind me as I would have done aboard a King's ship, but I had to make do with what I'd got.

"Where's the boatswain's mate?" says I. The boatswain himself was on deck, but his Russian mate was not. I just hoped he'd follow ship's discipline. "Boatswain's mate?" says I, hoping they'd recognise the title.

"Kapitan?" says a voice, and one of the Russians came forward. He was the boatswain's mate, but he wasn't the sort who kept order with his fists. He was a good seaman but a small man. Worse still, he was scowling at me and showing no respect. So there was angry muttering among the hands in support of Gregorovich, and some of them were reaching for their seaman's knives.

But then I got support I'd not expected. Someone came forward from aft where the officers berthed. He gabbled some Russian, I looked round, and there was Turganev, the admirer of chronometers. He was with some officers and mids who'd come to see what was happening. Second Lieutenant Dawson was among them. Then Veleslav, the ship's bully-boy, came out of the gloom, and he too stared at Gregorovich. But Turganev gabbled some more Russian and pointed at me.

"Da," says Veleslav, then, "Kapitan!" says he to me, touching his brow, stamping a foot and coming to attention just like our own tars did. So with him on my side, there was no more fingering of knives, and I seized the moment.

"This man is to be clapped in irons!" says I, seizing Gregorovich by the arm and giving the words in a masthead bellow. "You can ask your larboard watch mates what he did, because they all saw him do it." The hands looked blank, so I turned to Turganev. "Do you understand?" says I, and he shook his head. "He ... spat ... in ... my ... face!" says

I, pointing at Gregorovich, and then myself, and doing some mime to illustrate. That did it. Turganev gasped at such atrocity, and I grabbed hold of Gregorovich and shook him. "You did that, didn't you, you piss-house swab?" says I, and Gregorovich said nothing.

So the crisis was gone for the moment. Gregorovich was taken down to the hold, and leg irons put on to keep him there. They were hammered on by the carpenter, there being no blacksmith aboard. Neither did we have a surgeon, so the poor devil with the dog bite — Kolosha, his name was — got treated by Turganev, who fancied himself a bit of a doctor. Later when the weather calmed down a little, I made a point of going to see Kolosha in his hammock, taking Bentley with me as translator, and Turganev to show off his doctoring. He took the blanket off Kolosha's hammock, showed me the bandaging, and explained via Bentley's French.

"Shirt linen for bandages," says Bentley, with Turganev nodding, "and the wound washed with vodka, to purify it." It worked too. Kolosha was on his feet within days.

Kolosha himself was embarrassing. He took my hand and kissed it, even as his hammock swayed, and he crossed himself with two fingers and thumb as Russians do, while chattering at me. I looked to Turganev and Bentley who between them told me what I'd have guessed anyway. Kolosha was very grateful indeed.

"He says he's your man after only ..." Bentley turned to Turganev, obviously puzzled, then Turganev gabbled some French, and Bentley said something in French in great surprise.

"Da," says Turganev.

Then Bentley shook his head and spoke to me. "Kolosha says that he's your man, Captain, after only his master."

"Da," says Turganev, smiling.

Bentley shook his head again. "Captain," says Bentley, "Mr Turganev says he *owns* Kolosha. He owns Kolosha and Veleslav and some others. They are bond-servants, slaves: *serfs*, I think we'd say. His family owns them — or rather his father does — and his father sent them with him when he went to sea. They're property, like horses and sheep. That's what Turganev says. That's how the Russians go on, sir."

"Well, I'm damned," says I.

"Oh never say that, sir," says Bentley, anxiety all over his round face. "There is always redemption after repentance."

Bless his heart, he meant it too. Though I doubt that God takes interest in me because my sister was absolutely right: I go to church to see the ladies. Mind you, in later years I have become profoundly moved by the hymn "Eternal Father Strong to Save", and such religion as I have is found entirely within it.

In emphasis of Fletcher's words I record that with his family I once accompanied him to Canterbury Cathedral for the dedication of a shot-torn battle-ensign, from a ship he had commanded. The bishop preached on Ch. 27, Acts of the Apostles, concerning the shipwreck of St Paul, and the next hymn was "Eternal Father". Whereupon Fletcher began to sing in his powerful bass voice, but as the organ thundered in resounding melody and accompanied by the choir, he could not continue, and all present remarked on the spectacle of this huge and powerful man, so moved by the emotion of the music as to be shaken by sobs, and the tears streaming down his face. S.P.

So that was the worst of rounding the Horn, which we did via Drake's Passage. It was the worst part in many ways of that voyage, though not all of the worst, my jolly boys. After all, it's not often aboard ship that a wolf-dog goes for the captain's throat, and the captain gets spat upon. After that it was pure perils of the sea that we faced, and perhaps the Eternal Father did save us, since we steered our course westward, despite all the efforts of the sea to throw us back.

I'll not give details day by day, because although each day was furious and full of adventure, the adventures sound much the same when written down. Thus we had sails ripped and shredded, and the topmen aloft to replace them, with masts and yards whirling, such that even monkeys couldn't have hung on. But seamen can do it, even Russian seamen. It's in the nature of the breed. We had a topmast sprung, lines parted, leaks opening and all hands to the pumps, including myself, all taking turns to heave the cranks up and down in the worst and most spine-cracking labour that exists aboard ship. We had to take observation and calculate position when the sun and stars were barely visible, and we had to be always aware of the lee shore waiting, ever ready on our starboard beam, with Davy Jones and all his minions grinning and beckoning.

Worst of all, we suffered two men lost overboard, with no possibility even to think of coming about to save them. They were washed away when the sea came aboard, still green and hardly broken, and swept the deck from stem to stern, and so strong that we lost a nine-pounder, as well, despite the heavy ring-bolts to which its lashings were secured, which bolts were screwed deep into the ship's timbers. But the sea drew them out like corks from a bottle.

All we could do was hold a service in remembrance of our lost shipmates. Turganev did that before all the hands who could be spared. He did it Russian Orthodox style, and did it below decks, since more men would have been lost had he done it anywhere else. I had to be on watch — the sea demanded it — so Bentley represented me, and said he found the service interesting. But then, he would.

Finally, there came a day when the sky was blue, and the sea wasn't quite entirely trying to kill us, and we were northbound up the coast of what later became Chile. Incidentally, my jolly boys, if you like a wild story then look at how the Spanish — like the British — lost an enormous empire in America, which empire became a clutch of separate nations first fighting Spain, and then one another, for their existence. There were more battles, broken treaties, great men and lovely women than stars in the sky. I was there for some of it, but that comes later on than this particular adventure.

So, we were on safe course, facing no more than usual sea hazards, the ship was sound, repairs made good, leaks plugged, and the oven afire so we could enjoy hot food again. So it should have been all plain sailing, my lads, but it was not, because while ship's people are bound close together by storms and perils, it's not like that in gentle seas. Thus there's never a mutiny during a tempest, nor when the enemy bears down. But in sunny weather, the people may become divided if there is a grievance unsettled. With British tars the grievance is usually one of the following: no pay, no shore-leave or too many floggings.

But aboard *Enable*, it was bloody Gregorovich, shackled down in the hold, but talking to the hands who took him his vittles and emptied his chamber pot.

I knew there was something going on, since there was a surliness among some of the foremast hands: some, but not all. But with not understanding Russian, it was only when I was warned of it that I learned what was brewing. I got the warning during the middle watch in calm seas off Isla Carrenas, one of the thousands of islands off the south-western coast of Chile. It was a clear night with fair winds and five bells striking — that's half past two of the morning — and I was in my hammock asleep. Note that in a small ship like *Enable*, the great cabin spans the ship at the very stern, and I slung my hammock there. But just for'ard of the great cabin there's what passes for a wardroom: a narrow passageway with a table and chairs in the middle and cramped little cabins for the officers, contrived out of lath and canvas, on either side of the passageway.

In a King's ship, there would always have been a marine with his musket to guard the captain's quarters, but there were no marines aboard *Enable*, so I awoke to find the Russian Turganev, with First Lieutenant Bentley and Second Lieutenant Dawson, standing beside me in the moonlight coming from the cabin windows. Bentley was shaking my arm and I was awake on the instant. The sea teaches that, especially the dangerous sea. You sleep fully dressed apart from shoes, and you don't waste time waking up, 'cos wasting time might kill you.

"What's this?" says I, noting that all three had pistols in their belts.

"Shhh, sir! Begging your pardon, sir!" says Bentley, whispering. "Quiet, sir! It's Gregorovich: he's raised the hands in mutiny against us."

"What?" says I. "Damn the bastard! How could he do that?"

Turganev nodded then gabbled in French.

"Yes, yes!" says Bentley, listening. Then he turned to me. "Gregorovich is very powerful among the Russians of Alaska, sir. He has shares in the Company, and owns ships, and has followers, and he's threatened the hands with the knout if they don't obey him."

"What's that?" says I. "The knout?"

"Knout!" says Turganev. "Da!"

"It's a horrible great whip, sir," says Bentley, "a giant whip with metal ends."

"Da! Da! Knout!" says Turganev, and gabbled some more, and Bentley translated, with Dawson and me listening.

"He's frightened them with the knout, sir," says Bentley, "and he's promised huge rewards — paid in otter fur — to every man that follows him." Bentley licked his lips then looked me in the eye. "And that means following him against you, sir! And he says all the British officers are to go over the side, except you, sir, 'cos he's saving you for the knout in Alaska. He says he'll have you flogged to death."

"Oh will he, by Jove?" says I. "Not when we've got the arms chest and he hasn't!"

"But they do have arms, sir!" says Bentley. "Mr Turganev says they've got arms down in the hold: trade guns, that they sell to the natives for furs. They've got guns and powder and shot."

"Oh, Jesus," says I. "How many has he turned? How many of the hands are against us?"

Bentley and Turganev chattered in French, then Bentley spoke. "About fifty, sir," he says, "but Veleslav is loyal. It was him that told Mr Turganev what's going forward. Him and a few others and Kolosha, of course, him with the bitten leg. They're Mr Turganev's serfs, sir."

"So," says I, "fifty of the bastards, probably with firelocks. Who have *we* got?"

"Us three, sir, and the mids, and Mr Turganev's folk, and the boat-swain, gunner and carpenter of course. But not their mates. They've all been turned."

"What about Gregorovich?" says I. "Is he still in irons?"

"No, sir," says Bentley, "they've released him and he's down in the fore-hold with the mutinous hands. He's giving out guns."

That made me think, believe me, and it took a moment before my mind cleared. But then I thought of other times and other threats, and of deception and surprise. And so, my lovely lads, in case you should think that what happened next was a trifle harsh, then ponder on the fact that mutiny — especially with violence against officers — is a vile crime under any law that ever ruled a ship.

"Right!" says I. "Here's what we'll do. First I'll unlock the arms chest, then you gentlemen must rouse out the loyal hands — quiet as you can — then I want two parties: one to follow me, one to follow you, Mr Dawson and one of the mids, on special duties."

"Aye-aye, sir!" says Bentley and Dawson.

"Da, Kapitan!" says Turganev.

Minutes later I was creeping for'ard with no boots and on tiptoes, with my Nock pistols primed and loaded, and a midshipman's dirk in my belt, it being handier than sword or cutlass below decks. I was followed, likewise on tiptoes, by Bentley, then the carpenter, the gunner and the boatswain, all with as many sea service barkers in their belts as they could cram in. We went along the berthing deck — empty of life as it was, with mutiny afoot below — and heard the murmur of voices in Russian from the forehold even as a great noise sounded.

It was the ship's bell, rung like a mad thing, as one of the mids hurled the rope and clapper to and fro. That was the alarm summoning all hands to face the worst peril that can afflict a ship: fire at sea! It's in the marrow of a seaman's bones to attend to that alarm, dropping all else to muster at the bell. There was a yelling and shouting from the forehold, and I heard Gregorovich loudest of all.

"Nyet! Nyet! Nyet!" says he, which is their word for no. But that did no good. The hands poured up the companionway ladders, running to the sound of the bell, some with trade guns clutched, and others dropping them as they went.

"Wait! Wait!" says I to my party, and us not even noticed where we hid in the dark. Then, when most of the hands were up on deck and a small clump of them jammed on a ladder — with Gregorovich one of them — "Now!" says I. "Fire!" And it was flame and smoke and a galloping volley of sixteen-bore shot as a dozen or so pistols fired.

Screams and yells followed and bodies falling into the hold, even if Gregorovich — the filthy swine — managed to get off a shot from his gun, which whistled past me and did me no harm other than the flash dazzling my eyes and the powder grit stinging my mouth. Then more noise came from above as another volley roared out into the hands that had reached the deck, straight into the musket fire of Mr Dawson, three mids and Turganev's men.

So much for the mutiny. It ended there and then in a cloud of smoke with eight of the mutineers killed outright and five wounded. But first of all, I was down into the forehold after Gregorovich, who'd ducked back, dropping his empty gun. I jumped more than climbed down, and saw the blighter stumbling over a whole clutter of trade guns, hauled out of a chest, and then trying to hide his precious self among the casks and bales and barrels, where I had the pleasure of grabbing a leg, dragging him out, and so to business with the dirk. Have me flogged to death, would he? Not when I'd done with him! So he made a lot of noise. He squealed like a pig in a slaughterhouse. God knows what he was saying, but if he was begging for mercy then he didn't get any. And heave my officers over the side, would he? He got heaved over the side himself, soon enough: him and the rest of the dead 'uns. They went over the side like rubbish.

So much for them. But I am most sorry to report that the mutineers weren't the only ones to die. The shot that missed me, hit someone else. When I came out of the hold, having finished with Gregorovich, I found poor Bentley propped against a bulkhead with Turganev and Veleslav holding him. Bentley's hands were clutched about his chest with blood seeping through his fingers.

"Oh no," says I, which is what a man says, my jolly boys, to deny the reality of what he sees. "Oh no." I knelt down beside him. "How are you, Mr Bentley?" says I.

He was nearly gone, but he looked at me and managed a few words before his eyes closed. "I know you aren't a great believer, sir," says he, "but you will say some words over me, won't you, sir? From the Bible?"

How could I not? So I did. But other duties came first. We cleared the ship of the aforesaid rubbish, and later on Turganev doctored the wounded: five of them, of which two died and three lived. More important, since I needed a crew to sail the ship, I had all hands mustered on deck, even in the dark of the night, and some still bleeding and broken, and every one of us shaken as men are after a fight. The night was blessed clear, the ship running smooth, and the surviving mutineers were under guard of the loyal hands with loaded firelocks. But I went among them all, and stared every man in the eye and I read them the book of rules, with Turganev translating via one of the mids who spoke French.

"*All* hands!" says I. "Listen well, for this is how it shall be! We're heading for Russian Alaska, where mutiny is punishable by death!" That was only my guess, but it proved true, and the Russians knew it, since there was groaning and hanging of heads. I let them ponder on that before going on. "And so," says I, "this is how it shall be from this moment. There was indeed a mutiny aboard this ship, and it was led by Gregorovich, who was mad with drink. But his mutiny was put down, and now he's gone. He's gone and his threats of the knout gone with him. He's gone because his mutiny was put down, by all present here." I paused for effect. "And that's you, my lads, you who are loyal hands and true!" Again, I let them think, since this lie was their path to salvation, and they needed to understand it as such. "So this is the tale we shall tell," says I. "This tale and none other!" I had to repeat it a few times to get it into thick skulls, but finally they looked up, cheered up, and nodded, and Turganev called for three cheers for myself.

"Hoooooo-rah! Hoooooo-rah! Hoooooo-rah!"

As for Mr Bentley, we gave him the best honours that the ship could contrive. He was sewn into his hammock with a round shot at his feet and a Union Flag over him, as we laid him on a plank, and the plank on the ship's rail with all hands mustered in best clothes. Then I read the twenty-third Psalm, which I represent here in case it's been forgotten, given the strange times in which we now live.

The Lord is my shepherd, I shall not want.
He maketh me to lie down in green pastures: he leadeth me beside
*   the still waters:*
He restoreth my soul: he leadeth me in the paths of righteousness
*   for his name's sake.*

Yea though I walk through the valley of the shadow of death, I will
fear no evil: for thou art with me; thy rod and thy staff they
comfort me.
Thou preparest a table before me in the presence of mine enemies:
thou anointeth my head with oil; my cup overflows.
Surely goodness and mercy shall follow me all the days of my life:
and I will dwell in the house of the Lord forever.

Then the boatswain's pipe gave a long call and Mr Bentley was committed to the deep: a fine shipmate, a good man, and much missed.

After that, aboard *Enable*, even if we weren't a band of jolly companions united, we were at least a working ship's company. In addition I was worried that the tale of Gregorovich's mutiny — as amended by your Uncle Jacob — might not be entirely believed in Russian Alaska.

But first there was Aunty Mary: *Tia Maria*, as the Spanish say.

CHAPTER 12

I rejoice, Little Kitten, that the ghastly seasickness has now passed, and I was able to prepare myself for the great task ahead, taking advice and help from the ship's people.

(Extract of a letter from Count Pavel, in mid-Atlantic aboard His Imperial Russian Majesty's frigate Svatoy Eudoxia, to his mistress.)

As a direct appointee of the Tsar, Count Pavel was treated with nervous respect when finally he appeared on the quarterdeck, having been dressed, combed and made ready by his valet. He wore his regimental uniform, and gaped with landman's eyes at the arcane sea-world all around him: enormously tall masts, cross-grids of black-tarred lines, bulging sails, and the decks cluttered with an incomprehensible confusion of tackles and gear which seemed designed to trip a man and throw him headlong. Yet hordes of common mariners ran barefoot between them, with never a glance or a stumble. Though of course they grovelled whenever Count Pavel glanced at them.

The worst part was the constant movement of the vessel, which was never still, and which even at best, was inclined at a tilt such that Count Pavel had to hang on to something — anything — merely to stand upright. On the other hand the air was fresh and cold, and merely to be on deck was preferable to the suffocating confinement of his cabin below, which stank horribly of vomit. At least his staff could now make good and make clean.

"Your Excellency!" said the foremost of a group of officers who approached him, raising hats in salute.

"Honoured, sir!" they said.

"Your Honour!"

"Excellency!"

Count Pavel recognised Kapitan Komandor Vorishilov, most senior of the ship's officers: a veteran seaman in his sixties, who nonetheless bowed to Count Pavel, since Count Pavel was so very seriously political.

"I rejoice to see you recovered, Your Excellency!" said Vorishilov, and his officers concurred.

"All hands rejoice, Your Excellency."

"A happy day, Your Excellency!"

"Happy day!"

"Indeed, indeed!"

"Thank you, Kapitan Komandor," said Count Pavel, raising his busby, "I thank all of you gentlemen," he paused and smiled, "and I hope you'll forgive me for being a gut-heaving, land-lubber on your fine ship!" A weak joke, which brought a strong laugh, because Count Pavel was indeed political. He had a politician's talent to be charming, and — as he had intended — he won the goodwill of the ship's officer corps from that moment.

"If Your Excellency is indeed recovered," said Vorishilov, "perhaps you would like to see the ship?"

"I *am* indeed recovered, and I *should* indeed like to see the ship!" said Count Pavel, to more smiles. Vorishilov bowed again. Then:

"Kapitan Lieutenant!" said Vorishilov, to one of his officers. "Take the watch! I must attend His Excellency."

"Kapitan Komandor!" said the officer, saluting, and the tour began.

"*Svatoy Eudoxia* is built on French lines, Excellency," said Vorishilov, "after the Republican ship *Indomptable*." Vorishilov pointed towards the guns lashed in their sea-mountings. "She mounts twenty-six main-deck eighteen-pounders, and unlike British frigates, she does not have cant frames at the bow ..."

Count Pavel was happy to indulge Vorishilov, who was hugely proud of his ship, and overjoyed with a mission to take her out of the Baltic and into the greater maritime world. Also, Count Pavel was not truly, entirely freed from affliction, and anything that kept his mind from *that* was welcome. So he was shown everything from riding bitts to capstan, and from bowsprit to taffrail. He was even taken down to the magazine's light room, to peer through a window at the ominous casks and the racks of made-up cartridges: fat tubes of flannel cloth filled with gunpowder, each one a single charge for a single main-deck gun.

"Your Excellency will forgive me if we do not enter the magazine proper," said Vorishilov, "since the magazine is illuminated only through the window by light-room lanterns, and the gunner and his mates must wear special clothes and felt boots on entering the magazine, to avoid any possibility of a spark, since even one single spark — here in this most dangerous place — would cause such an explosion as would blow our ship, and all aboard of us, into fragments, and in the blink of an eye." Count Pavel frowned at that, and looked around as if searching for sparks. "But never fear, Excellency," said Vorishilov, "we take the most absolute of precautions."

The tour continued, and ended just as eight bells of the morning watch sounded, when ship's routine sent the foremast hands to their dinner, and the ship's navigating officers to their noon observation. Afterwards, with the hands on the lower deck shovelling down their food with knife and spoon, a formal dinner was given in the great cabin at the stern, swiftly extemporised by Vorishilov's personal cook, and delivered by white-gloved ship's servants.

Count Pavel was guest of honour, and sat facing Vorishilov, with the ship's officers in order of precedence round the dining table. In addition there were three civilian gentlemen, who were introduced to the count. Each stood as he was named, and gave a neat bow to Count Pavel, who smiled at them while noting something of sourness in their middle-aged, bearded faces. They were trying to hide the sourness but it was there. Count Pavel was adept at reading such expressions.

"Professor Fitzhummer, Dr Barkovskiy and Dr Menchikov," said Vorishilov, "who have generously volunteered to take leave of their posts in the University of St Petersburg." Vorishilov gave them a small bow. "They are the university's foremost experts in the history of the thirteen English-speaking colonies, especially as regards the building of their Constitution."

"Thank you, learned sirs," said Count Pavel to the three academics, "I applaud your patriotism in being here on the ocean, rather than safe in St Petersburg." Three heads nodded. Three faces smiled weakly, while inside himself Count Pavel laughed, knowing that all the *volunteering* they'd done was gather their books in haste, when the St Petersburg Polizeimeister arrived at the university with a dozen troopers and told them that they were conscripted, that their families would be informed, and that everything they'd need would be provided other than books. They were told what sort of books to bring using their own judgement and expertise.

But the three relaxed during dinner, which was accompanied generously with wine, and with vodka to follow, toasting the Tsar, the Tsarina, the Imperial Family, Our Lady the Holy Virgin, and much else. Also Count Pavel exerted his charm to enliven the company, giving hilarious stories of the mad English King's behaviour, having made great study of this while in London. Thus he made the cabin rock with laughter.

But later, since Count Pavel had drunk far less than was supposed, he had the cabin cleared.

"My dear Kapitan Komandor Vorishilov," he said, and waved a hand at him. "I have matters to discuss with these learned scholars which would be boring to others."

"Of course, Excellency," said Vorishilov, reading the dismissal code. "We shall leave you to your discussion immediately."

"How kind," said Count Pavel, "and perhaps a guard at the door?"

"Of course," said Vorishilov, and stood, beckoning his officers. When the door closed behind them, the cabin was suddenly quiet. No more laughter, no more clatter of plates, no slapping of backs; just sea noises: the creak of timbers and ever-present sound of the ocean.

"Gentlemen," said Count Pavel to Fitzhummer, Barkovskiy and Menchikov. "I hope that after such fine food and wine, you are not drowsy?" He stared at each one in turn, and since Count Pavel's talents included the ability to set a mood — and set it formidably hard — each one realised that this would be a very bad time to be drowsy. The realisation cleared their heads most wonderfully.

"Not at all, Excellency," said Fitzhummer.

"Not at all," said Barkovskiy and Menchikov.

"Good," said Count Pavel. "Now pay attention."

"Yes, Excellency," they said.

"Later on I shall give each of you a copy of a document." He paused. "The document is in English." He smiled. "Can I assume that you gentlemen read English?"

"Huh!" said Fitzhummer, in a supremacy of self-satisfied conceit. Then he looked at his colleagues, who likewise smiled.

"Ah," said Count Pavel, "I see that I was asking if a fish can swim."

"Your Excellency is too kind," said Fitzhummer.

"So," said Count Pavel, "you will study this document carefully, then discuss it with me."

"Yes, Excellency."

"The document concerns the drafting of the Constitution of the United States, and in the weeks ahead, as we sail to America, I want you to tell me everything you know of the men who signed the Constitution, and the discussions between them which led to the Constitution. In particular, I wish to know of any problems or disputes in the matter."

Instantly Fitzhummer looked at Menchikov and Barkovskiy. They became alert, alive and focussed, and Count Pavel smiled to himself, recognising the delight that falls upon a lonely expert when — at last — someone takes interest in his field of study.

"Excellency," said Fitzhummer, "we can answer one of your questions immediately."

"Of course," said Menchikov.

"Indeed," said Barkovskiy.

"Thus the present American Constitution," said Fitzhummer, "replaced an earlier version of 1781, which failed."

"That one was called the Articles of Confederation," said Menchikov.

"Yes," said Barkovskiy.

"So," said Fitzhummer, "a better version — which became the final version — was proposed among the Americans at a constitutional convention in 1787. But not all the thirteen states wanted it."

"Indeed not," said Menchikov.

"The states are jealous of each other," said Barkovskiy.

"And proud of their individual identities," said Menchikov.

"Quite so, gentlemen," said Fitzhummer, "thus some of the colonies distrust the Union and the Constitution was saved only by the Connecticut Compromise, which—"

"Ah!" said Count Pavel, raising a hand. "Forgive me if I stop you, Professor, because the document that I shall show you, concerns this," he paused, "this *Connecticut Compromise*."

"Oh?" said Fitzhummer, Menchikov and Barkovskiy, totally fascinated.

"So," said Count Pavel, "what if the Connecticut Compromise were overthrown and broken? How would that affect the American Constitution?"

Fitzhummer, Menchikov and Barkovskiy looked at one another in sorrow, given their deep immersion in the study of the American Constitution, and the fact that any keeper of a beast — even a foreign beast — comes to love it.

"If the Connecticut Compromise is overthrown," said Fitzhummer, "then the Constitution is overthrown."

"And broken," said Menchikov.

"Shattered," said Barkovskiy.

"And the Union with it!" said Menchikov. All three were aghast. But Fitzhummer offered some reprieve.

"All this overthrow and destruction," he said, "depends on the document being genuine, and not some fake put together with malicious intent."

"Ah!" said Menchikov and Barkovskiy, eagerly.

But Count Pavel then dashed hopes. "Don't worry, Professors," he said, "it is entirely genuine, and our duty in America is to present the document itself — and the hundreds of copies that I have had printed

94

— to present the document to some person or persons having the ability to *certify* the document as genuine, and the influence to place it before the ruling elite of the thirteen colonies." Count Pavel paused to let the three academics ponder on that.

Then he spoke again. "And so, gentlemen, who shall it be? Who is this person or persons?"

Fitzhummer, Menchikov and Barkovskiy looked to each other and began a busy conversation, throwing out one name after another, then arguing against each, until Count Pavel frowned.

"Gentlemen," he said, "it is indispensably vital that the Americans believe in our document. So can you answer my question or not? If you cannot give me a name, then this entire project fails."

CHAPTER 13

Tia Maria? There's a Spanish American legend that in the early 1700s, during the reign of their King Philip V, a young Spanish girl had to run from persecution and ended up in Jamaica, accompanied by an old servant woman who had a recipe for a drink made of alcohol and coffee beans. Being fond of the servant — whose name was Mary — the girl called her *Aunty* Mary: that's *Tia Maria* in Spanish. Hence the name of a sickly-sweet, revolting concoction fit only for those who won't drink decent wine, beer or rum, and much good may it do them.

But to your Uncle Jacob, Tia Maria means something entirely different. It means a lady who gave him a likely look with extreme seriousness, and went into action wielding a riding crop while wearing nothing more than a pair of high-heeled, laced-up boots. Not one for the faint-hearted, my jolly boys! Strictly for connoisseurs — and more of her later.

Meanwhile, as we sailed north up the coast of the Americas, for the sole and only time in my career afloat I never had a happy ship under me aboard poor old *Enable*. It wasn't the ship's fault: of course not, not one plank or stitch of her. It was those damned Rusky-Alaskies on the lower deck. They didn't dare mutiny again, but they were surly and you can't keep punishing men for that 'cos it just makes them worse. Or at least, it does if they know your time in command is coming to a close, and new rules will soon apply, and with some of the rascals planning to tell a different tale about Gregorovich than the one I wanted told.

One of the mids gave warning: Joe Blacker his name was, born of a

Bristol family and with an education behind him. He had a talent for languages, and spoke French fluently and was working at Russian. He was a nice lad, sixteen years old and bright and tall, and red-haired. He came to me just on the turn of the forenoon watch, with the ship off lower California, when I had all hands mustered for striking the whole suit of sails — courses, topsails, t'gallants, staysails and all — which now were bleached clean by the sun, such that some fresh ones could be brought up and bent to the masts.

You youngsters take note that this is a fine and seamanly practice which you must never neglect, especially in a ship that's been battered going round the Horn, with seams opened and nothing fully dry below decks, but always so damp as to foster mildew in the sail lockers. More than that, it was one of many heavy tasks that I insisted upon: setting up the standing rigging, greasing the blocks, shifting the trim, worming and parcelling of cables and hawsers, manning the pumps and daily holy-stoning of the decks. There should never be an end to such work in a ship under sail, since it leads to a busy ship, which is an efficient ship and a happy ship. But it didn't quite work that way with Rusky-Alaskies. So:

"Cap'n, sir?" says Blacker, with the ship steady and all hands at work. He chose a moment when I was far aft by the taffrail, talking to Lieutenant Dawson. Nobody else was close enough to hear.

"Mr Blacker?" says I. "What is it? You don't look happy."

"It's the hands, sir," says he. "I've picked up quite a bit of their speech, and I think some of them are still loyal to Gregorovich, him that started the mutiny."

I'll spare you youngsters what I said about that, for you shouldn't hear such language. But fortunately, things weren't quite that bad.

"It's not all of them, sir," says Blacker. "Just some of them. They shut up when Veleslav's about, and Mr Turganev too, though they don't know that I can understand them. But it's why they're unhappy, sir, 'cos of Gregorovich. They're divided among themselves." He paused a moment. "Or at least I *think* that's the reason, sir."

"Oh?" says I, and I was about to question him on that when Turganev himself came on deck with yet another problem. I must admit that he was another Russian that I liked, perhaps because he was modelling himself on me. He'd smartened up considerably, was trying his utmost with celestial navigation, and he wore his blue uniform coat and cocked hat on deck. So he saluted me Royal Navy fashion as he approached, raising his hat.

"Kapitan!" says he, "Mr Dawson! Mr Blacker!" Then he chattered at Blacker in French, occasionally nodding at me. It was a good, long chatter, and I saw Blacker frown and shake his head a few times. Then Turganev saluted me, and Blacker spoke.

"It's scurvy, sir," says he, "we've got scurvy aboard, among the hands."

"Da!" says Turganev. "*Scurrr-vy.*"

"How can that be," says I, "with lime juice in their grog?"

"Ah, but that's the problem, sir," says Blacker, "the hands don't like it, it's never used in the Russian American Company's ships, and the cook's mates have been dumping it in the bilge rather than mix it in the grog. Mr Turganev has only just found out that they've been doing that."

Again, I will control my temper, which rises even now at such abysmal, wicked stupidity. I will only point out that before the British sea service put lime juice in the grog, then scurvy was the worst and most dreadful affliction to curse a seaman's life. It saps the strength, it makes the gums bleed, it opens up wounds long-healed, and it lays a dreadful lethargy upon a man such that he cannot discharge his duties. In past times, scurvy caused more deaths among seamen than all of England's enemies combined: more even than the sea itself. It was a dreadful horror.

Fletcher does not exaggerate. Consider the case of Admiral Lord Anson's circumnavigation of 1740–1744, which is celebrated for the colossal treasure he took from the Spanish. But in dreadful contrast to this success, it must be remembered that while Anson left England with eight ships and 1,935 men, he returned with only one ship and 145 men, because over 1,300 had died of scurvy. S.P.

Then Turganev was gabbling French again, and Blacker nodding, then turning to me.

"Mr Turganev says the hands have been keeping quiet," says Blacker, "'cos they know you'd be angry …"

"By God I am too!" says I.

"Aye-aye, sir!" says Blacker, "but some of them have lost teeth and can't chew their vittles and came to Mr Turganev as ship's doctor."

"Da!" says Turganev. "Dok-tor!" And he bared his own teeth — and a fine row of gnashers they were, since he had indeed taken his lime juice — then he jabbed a finger at them and chattered some more.

"He says it's an early sign," says Blacker. "Puffed-up gums and loose teeth. Early sign of the scurvy, sir."

"Right!" says I. "Damnation on the lot of 'em! Stopped grog for all those as won't take it with lime juice, which is a sovereign remedy for scurvy." Turganev must have understood, because he shook his head and chattered some more.

"Ah," says Blacker, "the dirty swabs! Sir," he said, "it's even worse! The blighters have been draining the lime juice casks. There's hardly any left in the ship."

Well, my jolly boys, that was a broadside between wind and water. What in the Lord's name was I to do? Go round and knock them all down? Flog 'em? Hang 'em from the yardarm? Bring on another mutiny and kill half the hands in the fighting? No. None of that. Not when the ship wouldn't sail herself, and we were only just passing California with a month's sail or more before Alaska, even assuming fair winds and a kind sea. So I needed a fit and willing crew, not one dropping down with sickness, and there was only one answer.

"Mr Blacker," says I, "tell the boatswain that he has the watch, and tell the helmsman to keep course on one point west of north."

"Aye-aye, sir!"

"Then will all three of you gentlemen please follow me to the great cabin."

"Aye-aye, sir!"

"Aye-aye, sir!"

"Da, Kapitan!"

I had charts laid out on the table. We sat round them. Two oil lamps swung unlit from the deckhead above, while pistols and cutlasses gleamed in the racks, and two chronometer boxes looked down on their student

Turganev. The charts were the best that the Admiralty could provide, and gave the location of every known settlement, harbour or seaport on the west coast of the Americas.

"See here, gentlemen," says I, "we must have a run ashore on fresh greens and shore-food, to get rid of the scurvy among the hands." I looked at Turganev. "I suppose they won't mind that?"

Blacker translated to and fro, then smiled at me. "Mr Turganev says they won't mind a bit, sir. Not if there's women ashore."

So we looked at the maps.

"Here," says I, pointing, "Yerba Buena! It's only a day's sail to the north." I addressed Turganev, via Blacker. "What do you know of Yerba Buena, Mr Turganev?"

He shrugged a bit, then chattered, and Blacker explained. "He says it's the furthest north of the Spanish settlements. There's a fort with soldiers, and a lot of Spanish-Mexicano peasants." Blacker grinned. "He called them *serfs*, sir."

"Never mind that," says I, "have they got fresh food? Greens and fruit especially."

"Oh yes, sir," say Blacker. "They have crops in the fields, and trees and cattle and vineyards," Turganev chattered a bit more. "Chickens too, sir," says Blacker. "But he says they have guns trained on the harbour, so it might be dangerous to attempt a landing since we're at war with Spain."

So we were, my jolly boys, but now you must forget two things. First you must forget this modern world of morse keys, electricity and instant messages across oceans, because there was none of that in 1805! So I could smile.

"Gentlemen," says I, "half of Europe's been fighting the other half, since the French chopped off King Louis' head in '93, and only England has stood firm against the French. By contrast, everyone else has shifted alliances, year by year, and Yerba Buena is so far from Spain that they probably don't know who's on their side and who isn't at the present moment, especially if we go in under Russian colours, not British, 'cos we've been fighting the Dons since Francis Drake's time but the Russians have not."

So that's what we did.

Just before the first dog watch next day, having run down a long line of sandy beaches with forest and rising ground behind, we came about and headed eastward past a rocky headland, then onward through a narrow channel, where the high forest-lands rose up on either side and nipped inwards leaving a channel less than a mile wide. Beyond that, we found one enormous bay to the north, and another to the south, and both so big that they stretched beyond the horizon. Thus we were sailing into the most grand and magnificent anchorage that God ever made. It could have welcomed all the fleets of all the world with room for twice that left over. A magnificent sight indeed, and with hardly a sign of human habitation.

Hardly any, but not none at all, because the settlement of Yerba Buena was soon visible on our starboard beam as we shortened sail and made ready to anchor. There was a line of miserable-looking buildings high up on the crest of the land, with wispy smoke rising over them, and two earthwork-and-timber forts looking out over the settlement's landing ground. There was no proper harbour, since the beach ran straight for miles. Instead there were two timber piers reaching out into the bay, some small boats secured to the piers, others bottom-up on the sand, a few log huts, some people shading their eyes to look at our ship, and Spain's banners of scarlet and gold — which in fact meant weather-faded red and yellow — flew over it all. But aside from these scraps of civilisation, we were in a limitless wilderness owned by the birds of the air, the fish of the deep and the beasts that roared and leaped and chased each other with hungry intent.

And now my jolly boys, pay attention — since the sharpest of you will have noticed that your Uncle Jacob told you to forget *two* things. The first was electric messaging across the globe, but now here comes the second, which is the mighty metropolis of San Francisco! You must forget San Francisco as it is today, having boomed enormously from the gold rush of 1848 and filled with Chinese thousands who came to build the railroads. You must forget the dense forest of masts in the purpose-built harbour, the streets full of brash men, proud women and fabulous business opportunity. You must forget all that, because in 1805 San Francisco *wasn't* San Francisco: not then, not yet. Eventually it became San Francisco, named after St Francis of Assisi, but when I first dropped anchor there it was Yerba Buena, which means something in Spanish which I disdain to investigate, since the Lord God intended all decent men to speak English.

Here, I delete another prolonged Fletcher rant, abusing all foreign languages, especially French, even though French was irrelevant to the matter in hand. Instead I record that Yerba Buena *means fine herb, or good herb, which is the name of a mint-like plant which once grew thickly in the lands which became San Francisco.* S.P.

So, having forgotten the present, now grasp the past and know that — as I discovered later — Yerba Buena was just a small settlement of Spaniards and Mexicanos, with a shifting population of the native Ohlone Indian people, while the two forts that defended the landing mounted just two eighteen-pounders, six twelves and a few old nines. But we gave honours nonetheless.

"Mr Dawson," says I.

"Sir?"

"Salute the batteries!"

"Aye-aye, sir!"

So the order was given, the guns run out, and an un-shotted charge fired from each gun, nice and slowly as we came about to show that we were not aiming at the forts. At the same time, we dipped the Russian American Company's banners and I was much relieved to see the forts dip their colours in response, because you never know, my lads, and I wanted *Enable* to be received with fresh greens rather than hot shot.

But after that, all was well and there followed one of the jolliest runs ashore a ship's people ever had, especially myself. Nonetheless, as the anchor went down and our launch was lowered, I had a final word with the landing party, while the Russian crew crowded round, grinning their faces off and looking ashore in expectation.

"Mr Blacker," says I, "you will translate for Mr Turganev and he will translate for the people."

"Aye-aye, sir!" says Blacker.

"Da, Kapitan!" says Turganev, who was catching on fast these days.

"The tale shall be," says I, "as close to truth as possible, that this ship is under Russian American Company command, with some hired-in officers from the British merchant service. Is that understood?"

"Aye-aye, sir!" says everyone British.

"Da, Kapitan!" says all the rest.

"Good!" says I, looking at Turganev, who was turned out in his best uniform, and Blacker, who like myself was in a plain blue coat and round hat with nothing Navy about us, because if you're acting a role, you act it thorough.

"And above all," says I, "Russia is at peace with Spain. Is that understood?"

"Aye-aye, sir!"

"Da, Kapitan!"

"At peace!" says I, for emphasis, then looked round and caught them in my eye. "At peace, 'cos without that … you'll not be rolling in the hay with the local trollops!" That got the biggest cheer I ever had from that load of no-seaman Alaskies, while Turganev — being Russian — kissed me on both cheeks. I never will understand foreigners. Not if I live to be a thousand.

Then we were down into the launch and the oars going *clunk*, *clunk*, *clunk*.

"Look, sir!" says Blacker. "They're getting ready for us, and there's horses too!"

So they were. On the beach, a couple of hundred yards off, a line of soldiers came out from one of the log houses, just half a dozen of them, clapping on their hats and clasping muskets, and an officer shouting, while a whole clump of horsemen was galloping down a winding track from the settlement, raising dust as they came. Meanwhile, the coxswain pulled for the beach, avoiding the piers which looked rickety and unsafe, and in any case the beach sloped gently, and soon I was out, with Turganev and Blacker, and we hardly wet our shoes.

"Gabble-gabble!" yells the Spanish officer, and his men presented arms, as the horsemen swirled their mounts to a stop and leaped from the saddles something neat to behold, and some dark-skinned Indians — damn near naked they were — came forward from somewhere to hold the horses. Then it was face-to-face, explaining and greeting and looking one another over; the Spanish and ourselves, though I stress that most of the time they were gazing at the ship, in a manner which told me that they didn't get many visitors and that our arrival was an occasion.

There were three men in fancy uniforms which looked as if they'd come out of store and been rapidly hauled on. There were some civilians too, a couple of them being priests, clad all in black with wide-brimmed hats, and wooden crosses round their necks. They stood just behind the uniformed men. But front and centre, before even the uniforms, there was a woman, and quite a woman. She was about forty but exceedingly tasty. She wore men's clothes with britches and boots, a white shirt belted at the waist, and a straw hat to keep the sun off her complexion. She had the words *Little Madam* about her, as plain as could be. She was about five foot two, olive-skinned, dark eyes, dark hair and the trimmest figure that a woman ever had. It was the classic hourglass shape, and — though it is to her discredit — she put me in mind of my bloody damned witch of a stepmother, Lady Sarah Coignwood.

But then the uniforms came forward, one clearly being the superior — a man in his thirties — who was so deferential towards the woman that I took her for being his wife. He too chattered at me, most politely, and we doffed hats in mutual respect.

After that, since we had no Spanish and they had no English, a problem presented itself, which was solved in the oddest of ways. Thus Blacker tried French, which the lady and the uniforms didn't understand. Then Turganev had a go in Russian and some other heathen languages, and that failed too. But we all smiled, and introduced ourselves anyway, speaking slow and loud to be understood, as always you do with foreigners even though it never works. But then one of the priests was introduced and he said something, raised two fingers in blessing, and Blacker cried out.

"Latin?" says he.

"Latin!" says the priest and smiled, and they were off — Blacker and him — and all the crucial matters of negotiation between us and Yerba Buena were then and later carried out in that dead language which came suddenly to life. So what a bright little chap Blacker really was, with his education.

Better still, while Blacker was chattering away like Caesar's ghost, and the Spanish uniforms concentrating on the priest's translations, Little Madam came close and looked me over again, fixed me with her eye, quite solemn and serious, and said something quite softly, which I did not understand but which gave the impression of a signal being hoist. As I've said before, there is no such signal in the code book as "permission to lay alongside". It's just a seaman's joke. Nonetheless, she hoisted something closely similar, and did so within mere yards of her husband! Also she had the most lovely teeth and lips and a waft of most lovely perfume.

I guessed then and there that Yerba Buena would offer benefits beyond the banishment of scurvy and I was absolutely right. By Jove I was, indeed.

CHAPTER 14

Good cheer today, dear Chris, with a parcel of worthy farmers come to gape at the Constitution, and may fortune bless their respectful bearing compared to men of politics who demand instant service, as if we were their Library of Congress.

(Extract of a letter from Mr David Nash, Principal of the Library Company of Philadelphia, to his wife Mrs Christine Nash, then visiting her sister on Stone St, Manhattan.)

The honourable members of the Tun Tavern Masonic lodge gaped at the splendid building on Fifth Street, Philadelphia. They gaped at a Palladian pediment with white pilasters on fine red brick. They gaped at the two fine staircases curving up to the main entrance, above which stood a noble white statue of Benjamin Franklin, draped in a Roman toga. Like most Americans they were yeoman farmers living on the land, and they rarely came into civilisation except for monthly visits to the lodge. They were entirely unused to brick buildings, glazed windows, city clothes and bright linen.

Yet the wonders increased. Facing them in the entrance hall was a gloriously bright painting of the goddess Liberty offering learning to the world. But then they were greeted by Mr Nash himself, who shook hands most cordially with each of the six men as individuals. Then he welcomed them one after another.

"Welcome, sir!" he said. "Welcome, sir! Welcome, sir!" And finally: "Gentlemen! Philadelphians all! Be proud in your city. The Congress may have moved to Washington, but Washington is new-invented, festering hot and alive with mosquitos, while Philadelphia remains the metropolis of the Union, and the centre of its politics!"

"Yes, yes," they said, though they were nervous of him at first, since he was famous as a polymath — a renaissance man — who had been an engineer, then a teacher and was now a renowned scholar — master of Latin and Greek, and famous for his prodigious and detailed memory of historical events. But he was a most friendly man, some fifty years old, well dressed, stout of build, balding and with a cheerful, smiling face. He put the farmers entirely at ease and they all smiled. They smiled even more when refreshment was offered, and later when Mr Nash took them personally to tour the library and its magnificent collection of books. But the holy of holies, the splendour of splendours, was displayed in a cool basement away from bright light, dampness and infestations of insects. Mr Nash led them proudly to see it, late in the afternoon. It lay in a glass-topped case, and was magnificent. The farmers gazed upon it and without a word said, each man took off his hat in respect.

"Our Constitution, gentlemen," said Mr Nash, "the original first draft executed in 1787, in a fine round hand upon vellum, by the scribe Mr Jacob Shallus, who was paid thirty dollars for the work." He leaned forward and beckoned the farmers to come close. "Look carefully, gentlemen," he said, "and you will see how the calligraphy was guided by pencil lines ruled from side to side, between needle-pricks at measured intervals down the edges of the vellum sheet."

"Ahhhhh ..." they breathed. Then they nodded. They were so solemn that Mr Nash could not help himself when another side of his character was aroused: one that was not solemn at all.

"The needlework reminds me of a sad story of my own experience," he said.

"What is that, sir?" said the farmers' leader.

"I hardly wish to tell," said Nash, shaking his head.

"Oh do, sir," said the leader.

"Aye," said the rest.

"Well since you ask," said Nash, "some years ago I was waiting to be shaved by the local barber, and a neighbour was beside me who was shaved first. But a sudden storm arose with a huge clap of thunder, causing the barber to jump and to take off my neighbour's ear at a single stroke." The farmers gasped. Mr Nash paused, then resumed. "But, gentlemen, I recalled that a seamstress shop was next door, I hurried out, and returned with needle and thread with which I swiftly sewed back the ear, such that it took, and flourished."

"Ah!" said the farmers.

"And yet," said Mr Nash, "my neighbour never forgave me."

"Why?" said the farmers.

"Because I sewed on the ear back-to-front."

A brief and sad silence followed until the farmers' leader saw the look on Mr Nash's face.

"You rogue, sir!" he said, and laughed.

"Indeed I am, sir!" said Mr Nash, and everybody laughed. They laughed very loudly. After that, the tour of archives continued in lighter mood, with great merriment and further refreshment to follow. Nonetheless, the farmers went home knowing that the Library Company of Philadelphia housed a tremendous and complete collection — a collection unrivalled in all the world — of all the documents concerning the negotiations that led to the Constitution of the United States of America.

Yet Mr Nash was constantly searching for any further documents. He was searching for anything that might have been missed: anything at all. He was constantly searching because in all the thirteen states, Mr Nash was the most renowned and respected expert on the history of the Constitution.

Indeed, his word was law in such matters.

CHAPTER 15

I'm pleased to say that we were very well received at Yerba Buena, where they believed our pretence that Russia and England were at peace with Spain. Either that, or they thought it better to forget such trivial matters and to welcome the trade that we offered, since I wanted all sorts of supplies from them to keep the ship free of scurvy once we'd got rid of it.

What's more, they merrily accepted our money, since we paid in the big, silver, Spanish dollars which in those days served as the world's currency, and of which coins *Enable* had a full strongbox by courtesy of the Admiralty. Thus once again you youngsters should note that not all things in the past were the same as today, when the world worships the pound sterling and the US dollar.

So *Enable*'s foremast hands got their holiday ashore on fresh greens, and I could forget all fears of them running off as tars might in a friendly port, since there was only wilderness to run into, and in any case the Rusky-Alaskies all had shares in the Alaska fur trade. Better still there was strong drink in the cantinas, together with women — both Mexicano and Ohlone Indian — and even the music of Spanish guitars. Most nights they were up all hours singing their Russian songs, since the cantinas never closed. Believe me, they didn't! Not while there was money being spent.

Meanwhile I received an education in just how light a hold the Spanish had on this particular scrap of America. I learned that because we were most courteously received by the comandante of the settlement, José Raymundo Domingo Carillo, better known as Don José. Perhaps it was the Spanish dollars that made him happy, but I think he was actually proud of his command, such as it was, because — judging from the look of him — he wasn't the brightest spark ever struck by flint, and probably knew he'd never get anything better. So the day after we anchored, he took us on a grand tour, providing horses and saddles, and himself and his officers dressed in their fancy uniforms again. We gathered inside the main fort up on the high ground, and mounted outside the stables, with myself begging the assistance of a stool as a ladder, to climb on.

Just a word about horses: I don't greatly like riding them, and horses don't like me at all. I'm too heavy for the poor beasts, especially such small horses as they had in Spanish California. So I never ride easy on horseback. The only thing that kept me on a saddle at all, was the advice — given years before — by my old sea-daddy Sammy Bone, who despite never having been on a horse, once said, "It's the reins as does it, lad. Haul larboard for larboard, haul starboard for starboard, and haul both to throw all aback."

So I bumped and rolled something heavy, and I saw Little Madam smiling in amusement at my discomfort, since she came too, all turned out in a man's clothing as before. She came along, and so did one of the priests who spoke Latin. It was quite a party, a dozen of us at least, since I had Turganev with me, who we pretended was in command of *Enable*, and Mr Blacker as translator, since all conversation went through him and the priest. Young Blacker was soon sweating like a pig with the strain of it, since he had to deliver Latin then English, then since Blacker wasn't perfect in Russian, he had to give some French for Turganev who had scraps of English but was far from perfect. I've seen slaughterhouse floors that were less of a mess. So for shortness, I'll represent these conversations as if we spoke to one another direct.

"See here, Capitán," says Don José to Turganev, as we rode out through the gates, "the fort is a great square, with adobe walls for musketry, and a ditch in front of the walls, and bastions at the corners for artillery." Turganev nodded, we all looked and saw a slightly decrepit fort, sitting under the hot sun, all dusty and dry about 100 yards square, with walls too long for the small garrison to man, since they had only some seventy soldiers, every one of them as dusty and worn as the fort. As for adobe — that's mud bricks stiffened with straw and dried in the sun. It wouldn't be my choice to stop a musket ball or a round shot, and it turns right back into mud if the rain comes on hard. Also, there were bastions at the fort corners all right, but I didn't see any guns.

"Don José, sir," says I, "what guns are mounted in the bastions?"

He thought a bit, then answered. "We are waiting," says he, "waiting for guns to come up from Mexico. They will come soon."

"Thank you, sir," says I, guessing that he'd have a long wait. After that, and in succession, we saw a couple of churches, also adobe, and all painted neat, bright white; then some rather jolly little houses, with gardens and trees, and the people coming out, hats in hand to give respect; and then we saw a school, with the teachers and children in rows. We also saw lots of fields and fruit trees and some vineyards. But mainly we saw a vast emptiness rolling away to the eastern horizon, because there were very few people in Yerba Buena — just a few hundred — and a colossal continent beyond; all savage, unknown and unconquered.

In addition, while there was the fort — under-manned and with no guns — and while there were the two batteries covering the landing place, very much of Yerba Buena was unprotected. Thus most of the folk lived in tiny villages, each with its church and cantina, or in isolated houses with a bit of garden and some chickens. I never saw a frontier settlement so open to any hostile force that wanted to grab it.

So much for the lesson of geography, but what was more interesting at the time was an education concerning Don José's family. I got that when at last we were back inside the fort, a quadrangle lined with adobe buildings: barracks, guard houses, magazines, a chapel and some civilian living quarters. Then the horses were taken away and a meal was served on the shady side of the quadrangle, where servants had laid out a table with food and drink. We all sat down, the priest gave a blessing, and Little Madam contrived to sit next to me, and looked me up and down with a bold stare, while Turganev was given the place of honour at one end of the table facing Don José at the other. Blacker and the

111

priest were close enough that, with some raised voices and translation, I managed a conversation with the lady, as follows:

"So," says she, looking me in the eye, "what thoughts do you have of Yerba Buena?"

"Madam," says I, "before all else we appreciate your husband's hospitality."

"Husband?" says she. "You mean Don José?"

"Yes."

"He is my brother," says she. "I am Maria Martina Domingo Carillo." She looked across to where a row of servants was standing. They wore plain clothes and white aprons, but to one side, just apart, there was a young woman and a girl in elaborate embroidered costume, who stood just looking on. "My brother's wife is over there, with her daughter," says Little Madam, and waved a hand as if dismissing a fly, "but they do not go into society." I saw the woman bob a curtsey as I looked at her. She made her daughter do the same. They were very much Mexicano, and they didn't get their knees under the table, not in Yerba Buena. I instantly understood what was going on, having seen the like in Bombay where the East India Company's staff marry native girls chosen for beauty, but who are never seen on formal occasions.

A couple of days after that, most of *Enable*'s people were found accommodation ashore — we paid for it in dollars — since part of the cure for scurvy is to be ashore, not confined in a ship. I kept anchor watch aboard, and drew up a rota for ship duties to keep all in trim, but mostly I wanted the hands ashore to wander around and get well. So the ship's officers — including myself — had to be ashore to keep an eye on the men, bless their hearts, to kick them up the breech if they misbehaved.

Thus one evening near bedtime, Blacker explained about Little Madam. We were in the rooms in the fort that we shared with Turganev, who was bare-chested, pouring water from a big jug into the washstand basin. Since I have no truck with foreign speech, I looked to Blacker and Turganev to keep me informed of what was going on in Yerba Buena, and the talk turned to Don José's sister.

112

"Her name's Maria, sir," says Blacker, "and Don José's wife is also called Maria, and so is his daughter. So she's *Aunt* Maria: *Tia Maria.*" He lowered his voice. "And I think they're all frightened of her, sir. Don José certainly is. That's what the priest said. She's got a temper, sir, and does much what she likes."

"Does she, by George?" says I.

Then Turganev laughed, since he could follow a bit of English. He laughed and said something in Russian.

"Mr Turganev says she likes you, sir," says Blacker, "he's seen her looking at you, sir, and he wishes he was you." Blacker looked puzzled. He was good at languages, but still quite young. Blacker was puzzled, but Turganev was not. He laughed again, put down the jug and started singing a song in Russian, stamping a foot in time, and making lewd gestures with his hands.

So I laughed, because earlier that day Tia Maria had managed to pass me a handwritten invitation on a scrap of paper, which incidentally proved that she wasn't as innocent of English as she pretended. Thus an hour or two later, I was recovering from exertions in a large bed with curtains and carving, and gazing at Tia Maria, who had the most amazing pair of bouncers. She wasn't sixteen any more, and the charms of some women head south with age, but not Tia Maria's, and she knew it, and knew what she'd got and was proud of them. They jutted like figureheads, swayed when she walked, and pointed the way when she entered a room, and all entirely without support. Even aside from that, she had lovely round limbs, a most gorgeous colour of skin, and a pear-shaped stern that makes a man's mouth water, for wanting to bite it. Also, and just as we'd finished the latest encounter, she got out of bed with never a thought for a shift or dressing gown, laced on her boots stark naked as she was, and stepped forward pretending a need to peer out into the dark night through the shutters. But really, she was parading for my benefit — or more likely her own — because right by the window she had a couple of big mirrors on stands, with candles for light, so that she could keep an eye on herself at the same time.

With her, in all truth, it was sham and theatricals delivered by a lady full of her own pride. But who should blame her? Not me, for sure. She was a fine sight, and I roused out, darted forward to grab her and throw her back to bed. By George it was fun. But she was expecting that.

"No! No! No, In-gless!" That's what she called me: *In-gless*. Then she turned round, jumped clear, and snatched up her blasted riding crop from atop of a chest of drawers. "Ohhhhhh-lay!" says she, and caught me a whack across the shoulders, as she stepped aside of my charge. It left a stripe and it bloody well hurt. I never did understand why some men like that kind of treatment, and I offer as evidence the fact that in all the history of navy flogging no man ever said, "By Jove that was nice, could I please have some more?".

"Damn that!" says I, and there was a brief chase till I caught her in a corner, swept her up, grabbed the whip, threw it, and heaved her on to the sheets, boots and all. Then she was shouting out orders, and pushing and shoving at me with a frown on her face as she took command. It was hilarious really, considering the size of her and the size of me, and she never gave a smile. She just gave commands: serious commands, which ain't quite my choice of behaviour on such occasions. But it was exciting since she didn't actually shout — for fear of waking the house — but delivered an urgent whispering right into my ears, that was prickling delightful for the sound and feel of it, and I did like that.

"Whoosh-wish-whoosh!" says she. "Whish-whish-whish!"

I couldn't understand a word, but I knew what she wanted and once again, I don't blame her. I am so big that all my life the ladies have preferred that I lie back and let them come aboard as best suits their comfort and convenience. So why should I object? Who would? I love women and always have. I am a sailor, after all.

So all in all, we *Enables* had a jolly fine time in Yerba Buena. I certainly did, and so did Turganev, who took a great fancy to the Ohlone girls, until he gave some sort of offence. Indeed he did and I saw the result.

I was standing at the fort gates with Blacker, bargaining with some Mexicano peasants over a wagon-load of wine casks, while a couple of sentries leaned on their muskets and looked on in boredom. Then everyone turned round as a screeching came from a cantina some few hundred yards from the fort, and there was Turganev running hell for leather towards us, with a crowd of women after him, led by an old hag — something wonderful nimble for her years — who was doing the screeching and waving an axe. He'd clearly taken a drop or two, and was only just keeping ahead, but he made it to the gates, pushed past myself and the rest, and threw himself down, gasping and groaning, and laughing like an idiot.

After that he was safe, because the women didn't dare enter the fort. They just stood yelling at the rest of us, and the Mexicano farmers and the sentries laughed and yelled in return, until the women gave up and went back to the cantina. When Turganev got his breath back I had Blacker ask him what was going on. Turganev chuckled and gabbled, until Blacker blushed pink. It took me some time to get out of him what precisely Turganev had done, but eventually Blacker found the words and I must confess that I laughed aloud. I laughed till my hat fell off. But I regret, my jolly boys, that I cannot tell you what Turganev did in the cantina, since your mothers would never forgive me if I did.

On the other hand, I can certainly report Turganev's warning that my exercises with Tia Maria couldn't last. He was up to all the Yerba Buena gossip, was Turganev, that was until he got banned from the cantinas. He gave warning that Tia Maria had no husband and could never keep a lover because she was too keen on that blasted riding crop. Mind you, I'd already guessed as much. That's why I bit her arse: that, and for the pleasure of doing it.

Best of all, the scurvy was washed away, the Rusky-Alaskies were as merry as ever they were, and eventually with all hands aboard and stores replenished, we upped anchor for the voyage northward. We went out on the morning tide, with all Yerba Buena waving other than Tia Maria, and with the sounding lead going, for fear of rocks. Thus we found sixty fathoms under the ship, in the narrows at the mouth of the great bay, whereas the bay itself — San Francisco Bay, we'd call it now — was remarkably shallow: not more than three or four fathoms in general.

Then we came about, and set course for our final destination, since we were heading for Fort Arkhangelsk, which was the Russian America

115

Company's main port and settlement, located on Baranov Island in the Alexander Archipelago. That meant a voyage of 1,300 sea miles, running north up the western coast of the American continent, which was entirely wilderness and free of any man's flag, save that of the primordial native peoples if only they'd had one. So it was over three weeks' sailing to reach Fort Arkhangelsk, and even then the main mass of Russian forts, settlements and shipyards was 700 miles further north of that! They were up in the Gulf of Alaska, where the 1,000-mile chain of the Aleutian Islands reaches eastward towards Russia, in the deep of the Bering Sea.

That's how big the world was in those day. It was so big, and so wonderful besides, since the Aleutian Islands are incredibly varied with gorges, peaks and gullies. They are misty and mysterious. They are riven with vicious currents. They are home to dozens of snow-capped smoking volcanoes. They have hot springs that burst steaming out of the ground, and the native Aleut people say that some of these islands are so new-born, and thrust up by the gods, that they are too hot to walk upon.

The only trouble was that while the Aleutians might have been wonderful, Fort Arkhangelsk was not, at least not to your Uncle Jacob. The Rusky-Alaskies liked it and the blighters got more cheery the closer we got. I suppose they were looking forward to the vodka and the tarts, as well as their shares in the fur trade. So up the coast we went, keeping well clear of the land for fear of being embayed by the westerly winds that would have run us ashore if we'd let them.

Then finally we had the Alexander Archipelago on our starboard beam. That's hundreds and hundreds of islands, and some of them very large. They clustered just off the north-west coast of what's since become Canada. But they were Russian then, and some have Russian names to this very day. They have Russian misery, too, for the miserable damp and misty lot they are, since we'd long since lost the Californian sunshine. In the Alexanders it was neither very hot nor very cold: just damp, wet and raining.

But all voyages end, and we came in sight of Fort Arkhangelsk with all hands on deck, or in the shrouds for a better view, and the Alaskies grinning and chattering, and myself standing back to let Turganev take

116

the con. It was plain sense to give him command, since he knew the ground and knew its hazards. He was a good seaman and didn't need a translator now since his English was just about good enough.

"Steady!" says he to the helmsman. Then he yelled at the topmen, "Easy sail! Tops'ls alone!" Then: "'Ware of rocks to larboard!" to the helmsman. When he was satisfied, he turned to me and waved a hand at all around us. "Here is Angelsk Sound, Kapitan!" says he. "Angelsk Sound and Baranov Island." He nodded. "Baranov Island is hundred miles long. Has many bays. Has many inlets. But Angelsk Sound is best for anchorage."

He went on, and I listened and looked around with my telescope just as all others were doing that had one. The anchorage was a good 'un, with rocky hills all around, and a thick growth of pines on them, and I saw Fort Angelsk with the Russian America Company's flag flying over it. It was a great big timber fortification, on a steep hill at the end of a peninsula, with the sea all round. It was the real thing. It was what poor Yerba Buena's fort was trying to be. It was well placed and well built, within a massive palisade of tree trunks, and with the pitched roofs of large buildings rising over the palisade. What's more, there were proper piers and quays at the foot of the hill, for the convenience of shipping. Beyond that, there was a surprising number of buildings on the mainland beyond the palisade.

"Kapitan?" says Turganev. "We give honours?"

"Give honours," says I, and he bellowed something in Russian, and our gunners gave blank charges with rolling cloud banks of white powder smoke, and we dipped our ensigns in salute. The hands cheered as the guns spoke.

Boom! Boom! Boom!

"Hooooo-rah! Hooooo-rah! Hoooo-rah!"

So we arrived in swaggering, full-blooded, seamanly style and the fort dipped flag and fired in return because, by Jove, there were guns in this fort all right! Plenty of them, and heavy guns. Then we let go the anchor close by the fort and the hands cheered again. Which cheered me up something wonderful. For all the troubles of the voyage, we'd come safe to anchor at last, and perhaps not all the Rusky-Alaskies were bad — look at Turganev — and above all, and which was the whole purpose of the entire enterprise, I was on course for colossal profits in a new and wonderful line of business: the Alaskan trade in the furs of the sea otter. The sun had come out at last. Or so I thought, my lads, so I thought.

CHAPTER 16

Not all of the town's youth are gone to the dogs. Today's class behaved most splendidly. Then, when I told the tale of the bear, you would have loved their little faces. Eyes as round as pennies.

(Extract of a letter from Mr David Nash, Principal of the Library Company of Philadelphia, to his wife in Manhattan.)

The schoolroom of the library was on an upper floor, lit with bright sunshine from the long windows. It had rows of desks and benches, the walls were hung with maps of the Union's thirteen states, and a large, printed facsimile of the Constitution itself was prominent above all else. Likewise there were portraits of the Union's presidents — three so far — Washington, Adams and Jefferson.

Mr Nash loved the room, because he loved to bring in children from Philadelphia's schools to give them a grasp of his beloved Constitution and his beloved United States. He even loved the fake documents that he displayed on these occasions. He loved them for the fun he enjoyed in finding them out! So now he gazed happily upon the twenty-five youngsters who were enwrapped in fascination with his charisma as a teacher, just as he was enwrapped with them for their enthusiasm, since they came of the finest school in Philadelphia: the Public Grammar, founded by William Penn in 1689.

Being a deeply Quaker school, the Grammar was remarkable — even to a free-thinker like Nash — in that all children *without exception* were

119

admitted. Thus today's twenty-five included not just boys, but girls, and also children of African hue.

"This is a fake!" said Nash, holding up a paper from the pile on his big desk at the front. "Can anyone tell me why we know it to be false?"

"It's on paper, not vellum like the Constitution, sir," said one child.

"Well spotted!" said Nash. "But that alone is not enough. Plenty of authentic documents are written on paper."

"The handwriting, sir?" said another child.

"Well done, young ma'am!" said Nash. "Yes, this pretends to be a letter from George Washington to the mayor of Graniteville, concerning the billeting of troops into the houses of citizens. But it's not Washington's writing, nor his signature. I was given this forgery because everyone knows that I am forever expanding the archive of Constitutional papers, and they come to me with offerings: some generous and true, some greedy and false." He waved the letter again. "This came from a bookseller who himself had been deceived, and was sorry when I told him the truth, because he'd paid good money for it." He put down the letter and held up a printed pamphlet. "What's wrong with *this* little demon?" he asked, and the children made their guesses.

The process went on for some time, enabling Nash to point out the many ways that untruth could be revealed: wrong typeface, wrong size or weight of paper, incorrect watermarks, forged signatures, inconsistency of content, false dates, attempts to change the wording, and much else. Mr Nash concluded, with a modest smile, "I've been at this work so long, that truth and falsehood proclaim themselves at a glance." He clapped hands to make the children jump. "And now, just before I send you to your cakes and lemonade—" the class stirred in happy anticipation — "I shall ask a few questions, to examine you on the degree to which you have learned what was taught here today!"

The class stirred again, and the teacher within Nash was delighted to see that they edged forwards in eagerness, not backwards in sloth. They were a credit to their school — which presumably was why they had been chosen and sent in the first place.

"Now," said Nash, then raised his voice and barked out a question. "When was the Constitution signed, and who signed it?"

"Sir! Sir! Mr Nash!" they cried, with hands up and waving for attention.

"You, boy!" said Nash.

"Seventeenth September 1787, sir," said the boy. "Signed by George Washington, Benjamin Franklin, Roger Sherman ... er ... er ..."

"Me, sir! Me, sir!" cried a girl.

"Proceed, madam!" said Nash.

"There were thirty-nine men signed," said the girl, "John Rutledge, James Madison ... er ... er ..."

"Come on now!" cried Nash with a smile, and sweeping hands up in encouragement. "Do it between you, ladies and gentlemen!" He was so merry that the youngsters laughed, bounced higher and poured out the names higgledy-piggledy and on top of each other, as Nash roared out the count. "That's twenty, twenty-one, twenty-two ..." and so to the final name, which happened to be Thomas Fitzsimons, a delegate from Pennsylvania.

"And *where* was the Constitution signed?" he said. "And you can say it all together!"

"The Independence Hall!" they cried. "The Independence Hall, Philadelphia!"

"Yes!" cried Nash. "Our own Independence Hall not five minutes from here! And a noble and splendid work it was too. So God bless our Union! God bless our Constitution!" But now he waved hands for quiet, he waved both hands palms down, and the boys and girls fell silent and waited for more.

"Now," said Nash, "you surely know that the Constitution nearly failed?"

"Yes," they said in hushed voices.

"It nearly failed over the contentious issue of the manner in which each state was to be represented." He paused. "Represented where?" he asked.

"In Congress!" said the quickest.

"In the Senate and House of Representatives!" yelled the rest.

"Indeed," said Nash, "and how was this issue resolved, and the Constitution saved and our Union saved with it?"

"By the Connecticut Compromise!" they cried.

"Indeed!" said Nash. "The Constitution was saved by a form of rules called the 'Connecticut Compromise'. Without that, the Constitution and the Union would have failed." He let them contemplate this appalling truth, then smiled. "And now," he said, "since you have been so good, then before your cakes and lemonade" — they stirred again and grinned — "I shall tell you of the time that my little brother and I were hunting deer in Lancaster County."

"Ahhh," they said, and settled down to listen.

"We'd just shot a fine buck with our long rifles," said Nash, "those instruments of deadly precision, whereby our ancestors deprived the British of their officers in the revolution. Thus we had just shot a buck and were a-skinning of it, when a bear emerged from the bushes and charged. Foolishly, we'd not re-loaded, and even if we had, our rifles were of thirty-two-bore, taking half-ounce balls which — while suitable for British officers — would never stop a bear! But I thought quickly, and pushing my brother behind me, I threw aside my gun, knife and jacket, and ..."

The tale continued to conclusion, leaving the class sunk in awestruck respect for Mr Nash's skills as a wrestler. This continued until the first child burst out laughing, nearly falling off his bench in the vigour of it.

But later, they all remembered the Connecticut Compromise.

CHAPTER 17

The first thing any seaman notices on coming into port is the other vessels in harbour around him, and there was plenty to see in Fort Arkhangelsk. First of all *Enable* wasn't the only real, seagoing vessel in the anchorage. There were two brigs flying American colours, and moored close together. We got most serious attention from those two, and their people were gaping and pointing, just as ours were gaping and pointing at them. One was *Nancy Biggins*, by the name on her stern, and the other was *Old Man Summers*, both out of Boston, and they showed it in the weather-beaten wear and tear about them, since they must have come round the Horn as we had. So I don't doubt *Enable* looked the same to them.

Both had a few ports for guns, but they were merchantmen first and foremost and had nothing like *Enable*'s fourteen nines and four twenty-fours. They didn't have *Enable*'s collier-trade timbers neither, so we could have battered them mast-less in a few broadsides if it came to a fight. For that matter, in all the time I was in Alaska I saw no ship more powerful than mine, nor any man-o'-war at all, since while the Russians had a navy of sorts, it didn't venture that far away from its home in St Petersburg: not then, anyway, but that's another story.

Aside from the two brigs, there was a shoal of most horrible, slovenly Russian craft that went by the name of *shitik*. Yes, you read that aright: *shitik*. You read it true and the name speaks true, because they stank. You wouldn't want to be downwind of them, though I suppose that was the fault of the crews, not the ships, since none of the Rusky-Alaskies smelt sweet. There was about a dozen of them, clumped together. They were large boats more than small ships, some thirty to fifty feet long, with a single square sail, and various awnings and plankings to cover the cargo, and no keel at all since they'd been invented as shallow-water river craft in Siberia, which is where they came from. So God only knows how they'd come out along the Aleutian chain. They didn't even have nails to fasten the planks, which were actually *sewn* together with tree-root bindings. Nonetheless, these were the seagoing cargo vessels of the Russian American Company.

So they weren't a pretty sight, and nor were they the most numerous craft in the anchorage because the entire area beneath the fort was full of great swarms of the most neat little canoes of the Aleut people. The Aleuts themselves — stout, plump little chaps, black-eyed and swarthy-faced, in furs and skins — were ashore in tents and log houses. There were whole families round their cooking fires who stood up and gazed at us as our anchor cable roared out.

Then it was the usual business of coming ashore at any port. All hands were in best shore-clothes, the RAC officers put on such uniforms as they had, and since there was no need to pretend otherwise, I turned out in full dress and my own officers did the same. So the mood was merry, but there were always formalities on such occasions, so I had a boat lowered and was pulled ashore, taking Turganev and Blacker with me.

Then, by Jove what a reception we were given! It damn near cured my dislike of Rusky-Alaskies. They didn't turn out the garrison because they didn't have one. They didn't have a band, either, not a proper one, but there were some bearded men hammering the hell out of triangular Russian guitars, and two women of advanced age blowing hard down flutes shaped like blunderbusses. But — and it is a great big considerable *but* — everyone in a crowd of at least fifty people was clapping hands and singing along to the tune and I have to admit that Russians sing beautifully. They sing from the heart and soul, and the melody of it grabs hold of you. More than that, some of the men — and they weren't all young — began some mad, crazy dancing whereby they crouch down on their haunches, bounce up and down and kick out their feet. They

124

did it this way and that, they joined hands, they clapped to the music and they sang along. Any theatre in London would have loved them. I'd never seen such dancing before.

But the main event was the leading men of the settlement coming forward through the press to greet me, and I had to keep dignity while every one of the blighters threw arms around me, yelled into my face, and kissed me on both cheeks. They kissed Turganev and Blacker too, so Turganev kissed right back and, to my surprise, so did Blacker. He was a bright lad, and learning Russian ways. Then there was another bugger's muddle of languages, with translations flying, and which I'll represent as I did before to save your precious selves from boredom.

"Kapitan!" says a small chap with a bald head and the remains of fair hair around it. He looked about sixty, with a pointed chin and small lips. He was very smartly dressed — by Rusky-Alasky standards — and he was one of those small men who seem big, since he barely came up to my chin, but he bellowed and waved hands, and all present gave him attention. "Kapitan!" says he, "I am Alexander Andreyevich Baranov." He looked around. "I am Governor of Alaska and Champion of the Manifest Destiny of the Russian Host in the Americas!" They all laughed at that, since — as I learned later — his real title was chief manager and he was a tradesman-bureaucrat, not a nobleman. Also I had no idea what manifest destiny might mean, but I learned more later. Meanwhile Baranov went further. "Because of these duties," says he, "I respond directly to His Imperial Majesty the Tsar!" And more cheers and laughter followed. "And yourself, sir?" says he. "Yourself, who comes in command of the first Russian ship that has come here in …" He turned to the mob. "The first Russian ship in …"

"Two years!" they cried. "Two years!" Which explained an awful lot about Russian Alaska. Then Baranov let something slip.

"Two years," says he, "and such trouble with the Tlingit!"

"Da!" says everyone around him, in a groan.

"But now resolved," says he.

"Hmmm," says everyone around him. I should have pressed him on that, but he cut in quick.

"And you, sir," says he. "Who do I have the pleasure of addressing?"

"I am Captain Jacob Fletcher, sir," says I, "late of King George's Sea Service but now acting for the Russian American Company, and here is the commission giving me command of my ship." I turned to Blacker, who had the document in a waterproof satchel. He handed it to me and I passed it to Baranov.

"Oooof!" said Baranov, gazing at it; then he looked up at me and I saw the politician within him, making his calculations. "You have command of a ship?" he said. "Nothing more?" I could see what he feared, and having no wish for trouble if he really was in charge of this place — and especially of the fur trade — I gave a careful answer.

"Nothing more, sir," says I, and I paused. "Nothing more than my ship, *Mr Governor*."

"Ahhhhh!" says he, and then everything was plain sailing, except that I was surprised at Baranov's next question.

"What food do you have aboard ship?" says he. "What do you have that is fresh?" There were cheers and kisses all round when I told him *Enable*'s holds were still stuffed with the vittles we'd loaded in Yerba Buena.

"There will be a feast!" says Baranov in delight. "A feast tonight. Can you give us something fresh?"

"Of course, Mr Governor," says I. "Mr Blacker, can you arrange that?"

"Aye-aye, sir," says he.

So there was a huge celebration, that very night in the fort's main hall, which was timber-built, long and high, with rafters above and tables below, set out for my ship's officers, Russian and British, together with our boatswain, gunner and carpenter. They were mixed in with Arkhangelsk's best folk, such as they were. I was guest of honour on a high table next to Baranov, with a Russian priest on my other side who spoke English. His name was Father Nikolai, and it was odd to hear him speak because he'd learned English from Yankee seamen, and had their nasal voices. In fact, Arkhangelsk was crawling with priests since, aside from the fur trade, the Russians dreamed of civilising the natives and saving their souls. I suppose you can't blame them — the

126

Spanish priests down south were doing the same, and our own English missionaries too, though in lackadaisical Anglican fashion.

On the other hand, Arkhangelsk was different from Yerba Buena or Bombay since Baranov's wife sat beside him, and she was pure Aleut, middle-aged like him, and not some doxie picked for looks. So it was a true marriage, and there she sat with long black hair in plaits, and wearing her best Russian dress. She beamed and smiled and even toasted my health in carefully learned English.

"Captain Fletcher," says she, raising a glass.

"Ma'am!" says I, smiling. She gave me the likely look too, but I thought it best to ignore that, all things considered. Anyway, she could have been my grandmother.

But she was a full part of society, which in Arkhangelsk meant that she threw down the drink like everyone else, and the hall was full of red faces and loud singing to the triangular guitars and flutes. I thought I had a strong head, but not by Baranov's standards, because he led the way where drink was concerned. His speciality was scalding hot rum punch, brought to table in a bubbling bowl, even as we were still tucking into some sort of meat stew — who knows what meat, because I didn't ask — with vegetables from *Enable*'s store. Everyone had to drink the punch and it was devil's brew. It would have burned the throat even if cold, let alone boiling hot, and Baranov was out of his chair, going up and down the table, slapping backs, kissing heads, and damn near forcing drink down throats.

Meanwhile Baranov blathered on repeatedly about manifest destiny, which seemed to mean that the Russians wanted not just Alaska, but the whole of North America, which struck me as ludicrous and I'd have assumed he was drunk, except that there were a lot of Rusky-Alasky heads nodding when he blathered.

This went on for hours and when at last it was done, they gave my crew another and separate hall to sleep off the drink, since none of them could have got back to the ship. Some of them, and all the mids, had to be carried from the tables where they were unconscious asleep. So they all slept on bare boards, while I got my own room — and

Baranov personally showed me the way, with a couple of servants holding lanterns.

He was bleary-eyed, singing half the time, and hanging on to me to keep upright. When we got to the door, he took hold of my face by the cheeks, and gabbled something at me with raised eyebrows. I shook my head, so he laughed, let go, minced around like a woman and threw out his arms in question, then he pointed along a corridor and mimed beckoning someone.

"Ohhhh," says I, "thank you, but no." I was in no state for that. So he laughed again, pinched my nose and staggered off. As for the room, it was at least private and had a bed. So I took off shoes and coat, fell in, slept sound and woke up knowing that bare boards would have been better, since I was now speckled with the works of the bed bug. I slept aboard ship after that, and had my clothes baked in the ship's oven.

Then, over the next few days, I was mainly in Baranov's counting house, where Arkhangelsk's business was done, and records kept for the whole of Russian Alaska. I do like a counting house with clerks and ledgers, pen and ink, and a quiet mutter of work going forward. So I was happy to sit down with Baranov and his clerks, around a table in a corner raised up and kept private by a low wooden railing. Father Nikolai was with us too, as translator, but I'll continue with direct speech in this summary of what was agreed between myself and Baranov over several days.

"Before all else," says Baranov, looking round at all present, "we regret the tragedy of the mutiny inspired by Pitr Gregorovich Vinogradov." His people muttered and whispered at this, but none of them spoke up. "Thus, all blame resides in Gregorovich!" says Baranov, slapping the tabletop in time with the words. "So the matter is best forgotten, and as far as Moscow is concerned ..." — he paused — "we shall report that Gregorovich was lost at sea." The mutterers and whisperers considered that, then nodded in agreement.

"Da," says they. "Da!" They were a shifty lot, and I don't doubt that local politics was at work. Obviously they wanted the mutiny kept quiet, and for all I know they had their eyes on Gregorovich's shares in the fur trade. But that was the end of the matter, much to my relief, and Baranov pressed on to happier things.

"And so, Captain Fletcher," says he, "you have sailed from England to Alaska!"

"I have, sir," says I, "coming round the Horn by Drake's Passage."

"And you have shown Russian officers how to do this themselves?"

"I have, sir! Mr Turganev in particular is a fine navigator."

"Good. Excellent!" says he with a great smile.

"And the ship *Enable*," says I, "is gifted to the Russian American Company, courtesy of King George."

"Ahhhh!" says every Russian round the table, and they looked at each other in such joy as surprised me.

"Isn't that what was agreed?" says I. "Didn't I explain my negotiations with the Russian embassy in London?"

"Yes, yes, yes," says Baranov, "but promises are like fish, they go bad very fast."

"Not when the British promise!" says I, sitting upright in my chair, and God bless their innocence for believing me.

"Of course," says Baranov, "so now we may bring in our stores of furs from the deep country — which will take some weeks — then load them aboard your ship. And then—" he sighed, and shook his head in amazement so great that it was near disbelief — "you will take the furs and sail, with them—" he drew breath — "you will sail to Canton, exchange furs for tea and porcelain and silk, and then *sail directly to St Petersburg?*"

"Yes, sir," says I, and all the Russians gasped except Father Nikolai, who crossed himself Orthodox style, with a thumb and two fingers of the right hand. "But I ask something else," says I, and all the smiles disappeared.

"You ask what?" says Baranov.

"I ask to see something of the fur trade," says I, "while we are awaiting our cargo of furs. I would like to see how the trapping is done and the furs prepared." The smiles came back. Baranov spread arms and positively beamed in relief.

"Of course," says he. "Father Nikolai will be your guide. While you are here, you can go anywhere you please, and see anything you wish."

So I did, and Father Nikolai went with me. I didn't like him much because he sweated a lot in his long black robes, and he drank a lot, too. He drank Russian-style. Also he too blathered on about manifest destiny, but to him it meant spreading the Russian Orthodox version of Christianity, and ridding the Americas of all rival versions. He said the Patriarch in St Petersburg — whoever he might have been — demanded this and I often had to tell Father Nikolai to shut up, especially when the blighter had the cheek to ask what faith I followed, while he stared me in the eye ready to give correction to a sinner. So:

"Mind your own bloody business!" says I. "One more word and I'll knock you down!" I would have, too, but he had the sense to say nothing.

On the other hand he certainly did his best to show me the colony. Nonetheless, I learned far more than he showed me in a single chance conversation I had with the captains of the two Yankee brigs in harbour. I was in the fort's *stolovya*, which is their word for a canteen. It was midday, I was tired and hungry from walking and Father Nikolai needed his glass — bottle, really — of vodka to keep going.

The *stolovya* was plain wood on all sides: plank floor, plank walls, tables and chairs, and a counter at one end, with grim-faced, dirty-aproned staff to serve and a constant smell of cheap boiled meat from the kitchens next door. Father Nikolai was in the privy relieving himself when two men — seamen by their manner, wearing the long coats of officers — got up to leave and passed me on the way out. They stopped at my table, tipped their hats and one of them spoke.

"Good day, Cap'n," says he, "I'm Cornwich, master of *Nancy Biggins*, and this here's Kirkwell, master of *Old Man Summers*."

"We saw you come to anchor, Cap'n," says Kirkwell.

"Did you now?" says I, wondering what they wanted.

"So would you be Fletcher?" says Cornwich. "Fletcher that blew up British frigate *Calipheme* in Boston Harbour in '95?" They both smiled, and I saw that I was among friends.

"Yes," says I, "I'm Fletcher." And I wasn't surprised that they knew me, since I'm easy to spot and have been in the newspapers for years, on both sides of the Atlantic. Anyway, Arkhangelsk was talking about nothing else than me and my ship.

"We've heard of you, Cap'n," says Cornwich.

"Yeah," says Kirkwell.

"And we like what we hear," says Cornwich, "we like it a lot."

"We hear you've got American papers an' all," says Kirkwell.

"Indeed I have," says I. I'd had American citizenship since 1794.

"So why'd you stay loyal to the British?" asks Cornwich.

"Yeah," says Kirkwell, "them British don't like you, Cap'n" — and he grinned — "but we do! There's lots of us Bostonians as would make you welcome."

That made me think, it really did, since I'd been wondering how the Admiralty would respond to my firing on that revenue cutter and blowing her masts overside. You must never forget, my jolly boys, that a good half of the sea service never forgave your Uncle Jacob for his sinking of HMS *Calipheme*. Thus some of Their Lordships of the Admiralty were only waiting for the chance to do me down. Conversely, I had friends in Boston from past times, I had money in the bank there, and even if my American citizenship papers were left in my cabin aboard *Enable*, the papers had been issued in Boston, where records would be kept. And so, and so … but Cornwich and Kirkwell looked past me to where Father Nikolai was on his way back.

"Word in the ear, Cap'n," says Cornwich, leaning forward and dropping his voice. "Grab your furs quick and get out, 'cos this colony can't last."

"Why not?" says I.

"These Russians think they can have everything," says he, "all the Americas, coast to coast. But this colony is hopeless. Without us coasting ships, they'd starve. We trade food for furs, see? They ain't supposed to trade their furs, but they do because they have to, since they can't grow crops here."

"And they can't get the men, neither," says Kirkwell, "so everything's done by the natives. It's the Aleuts that hunt for furs, while the Russians sit on their asses. So the Aleuts don't *like* the Russians and the Tlingit *hate* them, hate them for taking their land."

"Tlingit?" says I, tripping over the strange sound. "Baranov mentioned them when I first met him. Who are they?"

"The local warrior tribe," says Cornwich, "they've been fighting the Russians since forever. They got beat last time, but they're still out there, just awaiting their time."

"Baranov didn't say that," says I.

"He wouldn't!" says Cornwich. "So watch your back, Cap'n." Then they tipped hats again and were gone, leaving me wondering if I'd been told a fabrication of lies and sent on a fool's errand.

CHAPTER 18

I had expected to sneer at this town which calls itself, 'The Athens of America' but I was favourably surprised. It is their premier seat of learning, politics and culture.

(Extract of a letter from Count Pavel, at Mrs James's House, 25 Chestnut St, Philadelphia, to his mistress.)

"The American pilot asked if the Alaskan colony is doomed," said Count Pavel, "and of course it is!" The others nodded. They were his usual entourage aboard ship: the scholars Barkovskiy, Fitzhummer and Menchikov; the lieutenant who was adviser in seafaring matters; the midshipman who took notes and the midshipman who ran errands; those six and a servant who trailed behind in case there were menial duties to be performed.

They all paced the quarterdeck as *Svatoy Eudoxia* sailed up the Delaware River, passing busy shipping on a bright morning, with the vast American continent fading into the distant horizon beyond.

"The pilot had been talking to American shipmasters, Excellency," said Barkovskiy.

"Yes," said Count Pavel, "it seems to be common knowledge among them that the colony cannot feed itself." The entourage nodded.

"And there is acute shortage of labour," said Barkovskiy, "since free Russians won't go there, and we can't send our serfs because they are bound to the land."

"Not if their owners won't let them go," said Count Pavel, "since

133

they're almost as valuable as horses!" Everybody laughed. It was a joke, but it was true. "But we have the perfect solution to those problems," said Count Pavel. "Once we have dealt with the thirteen colonies of the east coast, our squadron of the west coast will sail from St Petersburg, and will easily take Yerba Buena and other Spanish American colonies, providing food for Alaska, and plentiful numbers of native labour, and Mexicano labour. It will be the work of some years, but it is our manifest destiny." He smiled. "Meanwhile there is this *pilot*. Still talking." Count Pavel and his entourage looked as the American pilot stood with the ship's officers at the wheel, chattering, chattering — always chattering. "Lieutenant," said Count Pavel, "why do we need this man?"

"To con the ship, Excellency," said the lieutenant. "As you saw, pilots come out in fast boats to offer their services to con the ship in."

"Con? What does this mean?"

"It means to steer a safe course, Excellency. Ships need a pilot when coming into an unfamiliar harbour: a local man who knows the shoals and hazards and currents." Then they saw the pilot touch hat to the ship's captain, and orders were shouted.

"Ah!" said the lieutenant. "See, Excellency, we're going about, where the river curves round to larboard."

Count Pavel and the rest watched as the pilot pointed. Then feet rumbled, men chanted as they hauled lines, sails were trimmed high overhead, and the big frigate heeled over and headed northward. But Count Pavel went back to the greater matter.

"The entire Alaskan enterprise is doomed," he said. "Or rather, it *was* doomed. But the enterprise which we have in hand will put that right: *our* enterprise."

"*Your* enterprise, Excellency," said Barkovskiy, who knew very well what was good for him and what was not. "Your creative genius, Excellency," he said, and he bowed. All the entourage bowed. Count Pavel merely nodded, accepting such praise as no more than his due. Then the ship trembled as all hands not on duties moved to the larboard rail to look at the city they were approaching. It was a remarkably bright day and Philadelphia was clearly visible.

"Ah," said Count Pavel, "I had expected log cabins, and turf on the roofs. But it does seem to be something of a city. I see spires and domes, and chimney smoke."

"Oh yes, Excellency," said Barkovskiy.

"Oh yes," said Fitzhummer and Menchikov.

"See there, Excellency," said Barkovskiy, "the whole river front is lined with fine buildings in brick and stone, and there are piers and wharves, and the entire city is laid out on a grid of squares, like those of Ancient Rome."

"Libraries and theatres too," said Fitzhummer, prompting, "and churches."

"Indeed," said Barkovskiy. "The whole of European culture has been brought to this new world. There is everything in Philadelphia from coffee houses to the salons of ladies."

"But nobility is absent," said Count Pavel, "there is no ruling class."

"Not yet, Excellency," said Barkovskiy, and everyone laughed. Another joke, another truth.

Later, with *Svatoy Eudoxia* anchored just off the Custom House Pier, there was a great coming and going of boats between the shore and the ship. There were the usual tradespeople, coming out to sell everything that an incoming ship needed: fresh bread, fresh meat, strong drink, cheap trinkets and whores both cheap and expensive. So there were lively negotiations between the boats alongside and the Russian seamen leaning out of the gunports: everyone bellowing and waving hands. It was a merry time, as is always the case when a big ship comes into the harbour of a big city.

Also there were boat-loads of officials: those who had business with any incoming ship, let alone a man-o'-war flying the colours of a foreign power. Count Pavel left matters of customs and harbour to the ship's officers, but received all political persons himself, in the great cabin. He received them with diplomatic skills and immaculate English, telling them everything that he wanted them to know: that and no more.

"A voyage of friendship, gentlemen!" he said to representatives of

Congress Hall and the County Court. "A voyage of learning and exploration for the sea service of His Imperial Majesty."

"Ah!" said the various gentlemen in their wigs and best clothes.

"And what of the European war, sir?" said one gentleman.

"Russia is allied — reluctantly — with the British, at present, sir," said Count Pavel. "But His Imperial Majesty constantly seeks wider alliances with more—" he smiled — "more *congenial* allies." Everyone was charmed by Count Pavel, and over the next few days social occasions were held in his honour, including a ball. He excelled in dancing, and was adored by the ladies.

"God bless me, sir," said the very lovely wife of a congressman, when he took her in his arms for the waltz, a dance previously unknown to the Americas, "are you sure this is entirely proper?"

"Indeed, dear lady," he said, "look round the room." Which the lady did, for it was the finest in Philadelphia, and attended by the best and finest people. She looked round and saw several dozen couples in bright-coloured evening clothes, jewels twinkling under the chandelier-light, some blushing, some smiling, all moving into fumbling embraces for the dance, brought from Vienna by Count Pavel. They smiled and blushed, but some of the older ladies sat frowning in their chairs, and all the servants frowned with them, since no man is more conservative than a servant.

"One ... *two!*" said the leader of the orchestra, the orchestra played and the couples made the best way they could round the room except for Count Pavel and the congressman's wife, who flew upon wings, with Count Pavel whispering seduction into the lady's ear.

All of which fixed the Philadelphian mind firmly to the proposition that Count Pavel, his ship and his officers were friendly, harmless folk from a friendly, harmless nation. This was a serious objective, and Count Pavel was seriously pleased to have secured it. But he was nowhere near as pleased as he was with a visitor who called on him in his excellent lodgings at 25 Chestnut Street. The visitor had called when Count Pavel was out, but on returning to his lodgings, explanation was given by Count Pavel's butler, a lifetime, trusted servant brought out from St Petersburg.

"Mr John Howard Ducaine awaits Your Excellency in the breakfast room upstairs," said the butler. "He is a most serious person, even though of low birth and in trade."

Count Pavel smiled at that. "As are all the leading men in this place," he said, "it is a truth which we must accept."

"You are most gracious, Excellency," said the butler, "since that was my own judgement."

"So what does he want?"

"He would not say, Excellency, except that he comes to discuss a matter of ..." He paused. "Of *nationhood*."

Count Pavel's eyebrows raised, and soon he was in the breakfast room, where Mr Ducaine stood as he entered.

Count Pavel saw a middle-aged man, shrivelled by a life in the sun: wiry and thin, but with a prominent nose, all dimpled and bulbous and red. He was well dressed, obviously wealthy, and like all these American tradesmen, he had not a scrap of deference about him. He looked Count Pavel in the eye, clearly regarding himself as fully equal to an aristocrat who could trace his ancestors back 500 years. So he stepped forward and held out his hand.

"I'm Ducaine," he said, "Ducaine of Ducaine Forks. That's twelve thousand acres of cotton, rice and tobacco." Count Pavel took the hand and smiled diplomatically. Ducaine spoke on. "I'm also a senator of the General Assembly of the Colony of South Carolina and I represent an interest group, with certain ideas."

"Perhaps you would explain them, Mr Ducaine?" said Count Pavel. "Meanwhile shall we sit; and will you take tea, coffee or wine?"

"Wine, Mr Count, if you please," said Ducaine.

So they sat and talked, and wine was served although Count Pavel took none of it. The conversation was too gripping for that.

"I'll begin with a question," said Ducaine.

"Ask it," said Count Pavel.

"Am I right that you Russians have slaves?" said Ducaine, which Count Pavel thought odd. But he was a diplomat and answered promptly.

"You might call them slaves," he said, "but they are serfs."

Ducaine nodded. "Whatever you call them, they are property, am I right?"

"Yes. They are property."

"And I have five hundred slaves that are property! So, what d'you think of that?"

Count Pavel shrugged. "No doubt you also have horses, cattle and sheep," he said, and Ducaine laughed.

"Well, Count Pavel," he said, "some of the northern colonies don't like slavery, and for that — and other good reasons — there are some in South Carolina who don't approve of the Union, and want out of it! So how d'you like that, Count?"

"Mr Ducaine," said Count Pavel, "I am a guest in a foreign land, and must avoid political matters … unless there is clear benefit to His Imperial Majesty's empire."

"Then here it comes, Count," said Ducaine. "This continent's colossal. There could be Russian colonies on the east as well as the one in Alaska. Meanwhile if we South Carolinians are to break away then we'll need the help of a friendly power, to keep the Union, the British, and the Spanish and French off our backs."

"Mr Ducaine," said Count Pavel, "if South Carolina wishes to leave the Union — to *secede* — then why not do so? And why should any other power be involved?"

"Because we were forced into the Union," said Ducaine, "and later ratified the Constitution. So if we just leave the Union, then the other colonies — especially the northern colonies — will say we're rebels and traitors, and the British and others will believe them, and we'll be at war with the northern colonies."

"But how were you forced into the Union?" said Count Pavel, and his heart began to thump because he already knew the answer and could not believe that, all uninvited and undreamed of, Ducaine — entirely for his own reasons — had come to Count Pavel as a true and wonderful gift of God.

"We were forced into the Union," said Ducaine, "by an agreement that we had to accept even though we didn't like it, and now we cannot get round it — not legally, anyway. It's something you'll never have heard of. It's called the Connecticut Compromise."

139

CHAPTER 19

I thought hard about Alaska. I thought very hard indeed, and in the end I took the advice of the Yankee captains: grab the furs and go! Because a shipload of sea otter fur was immensely precious and I was determined to get *Enable* fit for sea, get her holds stuffed with furs, then take them to Canton for the tea, silk and porcelain which was even more precious, and I'd relish the joy of the trading and bargaining involved, since such has always been a joy of my life, and my love of commerce and trade is beyond measure. So I'd make such a deal as would leave the Chinese merchants gasping. Wouldn't I just! I relished the thought.

After that, my plan would be to take my new — and vastly profitable — cargo where best opportunity might present, which was certainly not St Petersburg: not when a fine welcome might be awaiting me in Boston. So it was in my mind to take tea, silk and porcelain back round the Horn to America, except that I'd have a crew of Rusky-Alaskies who'd never agree to it. But life is never simple, my jolly boys, and I'd just have to think about that one, and see if a way might be found.

Note well that Fletcher is here contemplating outright theft of furs, and betrayal of his contract with the Russian American Company, and he is doing so without the least moral compunction. He was indeed a rogue and pirate at heart. S.P.

Meanwhile there had to be jolly smiles to Mr Governor Baranov, and my mouth shut concerning the future of his colony, since I needed him to gather in his furs. I likewise needed Fort Arkhangelsk's shipyard to re-fit *Enable* for the onward voyage, which would take a while. So, within a day of our arrival, I had Turganev and the other RAC officers, with my gunner, carpenter and boatswain, in the shipyard assisting in *Enable's* fitting out. Then, since I really did want to understand the fur trade, I sent Lieutenant Dawson, with Blacker and the other mids, to report on Fort Alexander in Bannerman's Bay: the RAC's biggest up-country depot, where vast quantities of raw furs were processed and stored.

As for myself, later on, I wanted to see how the animals — the sea otters — were actually caught, and again Father Nikolai was most helpful.

"You come-along-a-me," says he in his Yankee voice, and he led me down from Fort Arkhangelsk, down to the huge, misty damp harbour, under a grey sky with the hills around, and the sea beckoning from beyond the anchorage. "See, Captain," says he. "Aleuts. Hundreds of Aleuts. We do not catch otters, *they* do! And today is good, 'cos they go out today. So you go with them, and you see how they find the otters. They know where to go, these Aleuts. You watch and you learn."

He was right. The harbour was busy with dozens and dozens of Aleuts bidding farewell to their women and children, and dozens and dozens of their wonderful neat little canoes. They were called *bidarkas* and they were like the kayaks of the Eskimo: about fifteen to twenty feet long, slim amidships, sharp fore and aft, with a light timber frame covered with sealskin and completely decked over. They were so light that a child could lift one, and they had hatches lined with sealskin, so that a paddler could lash the linings tight about his middle to be watertight.

Then Father Nikolai was gabbling at the Aleuts, and them clustering round gawping at me, till I was quite surrounded. Small chaps they were, with little kiddies peering round their legs, and their women pointing at me and giggling. I didn't understand what was going on until two of the women brought me the most amazing garment. It was a great tube of some shiny material, with sleeves and a hood, and you put it on over your head. The Aleut women laughed as they hauled it onto me. Indeed everyone laughed, especially the children. When it was properly on it came down well below my knees, and Father Nikolai explained.

"Is *kamleika*, Captain," says he. "Intestine of otter. Is cut open, flattened out and sewn in rows. Very light, very waterproof." Then he pointed: "Look! Look!" says he, and everyone looked at an Aleut, afloat in his canoe, wearing a *kamleika* and with the canoe's sealskin linings lashed about his middle. He shouted something then deliberately rolled the canoe over then rolled it back up again, to howls of approval on all sides. "You next," says Father Nikolai.

"Bugger that!" says I, but he just laughed. Then there was much merry chatter and the Aleut men stood back, while the women dragged me to a double-seater canoe, with a grinning Aleut already aboard with his paddle. He was brown-faced and wrinkled as old leather, and his fingernails were black as ink. Father Nikolai made the introductions.

"This Captain Fletcher," says he.

"Cap'n!" says the Aleut, touching his brow like a tar.

"And this Tookarni."

"Tookarni!" says I. He grinned at me as the women got me to crouch down in my long robe and get into the canoe. They were all merry, and some of the women were pretty enough, and this was obviously some sort of test. So I was a good boy, and sat myself down in the canoe with my legs forward while they shoved food and water into the canoe, then lashed me into the sealskin linings, and Tookarni got the canoe under way with a few strokes, then brought it swirling to a stop in deep water, where we paused and he chattered at me saying I know not what.

Then everyone ashore — the Aleuts, Father Nikolai and a few Ruskies — all began clapping hands and giving out some sort of Aleut chant, which got faster and faster, then suddenly stopped. And then, oh God help me, Tookarni rolled us over! I swallowed half the bay, inhaled the rest, and knew for sure I was drowning. But then I wasn't, 'cos he rolled us right back over, and I was hacking my lungs up and spouting like a whale. It was not a thing I ever want to repeat, but I was amazed how little water got inside the kamleika garment: a little at the hood, less at the sleeves, but I was mainly dry. So yes, my lads, we're clever folk in Britain with our steam power and precision machinery, but don't ever think the native peoples aren't just as clever, since that garment was better at its work than any oilskins a seaman ever wore.

After that, I very nearly did see how the sea otters were caught, because the whole fleet of bidarka canoes pulled out from the shore and headed for the open sea, and once again I was impressed. To begin with they were very fast, with remarkably little effort needed on the double-ended paddles that propelled them. They were fast and nimble, and mostly single-manned, but some were two seaters, which seemed to be command boats, since the for'ard man aboard would shout orders that the rest obeyed. Tookarni was one of these commanders, and seemed to be senior among them from the respect he got when he spoke.

So out we went in a shoal, hugging the coast, searching out bays and inlets, and the Aleuts finding their way by the signs of the sea coast: the shape of the cliffs; changes in the water's colour and current; growth of weed; the behaviour of the birds and fishes; and even the way the wind shifts. That's how folk made their way before maps, and I've seen it done by the fisherfolk of Devon and Cornwall, so I suppose it's the same everywhere.

After some hours, things got exciting, and even I could see furry beasts diving and surfacing ahead as we entered one particular bay. At this the Aleuts prepared for the hunt, bringing out harpoon spears which were laid handy on the canoes while the paddlers inched us forward, preserving the most disciplined silence, with all commands given by hand signals. But then it all went bad. We ceased to be the hunters and became the hunted, and all praise to the Aleuts who'd taken care that we were not caught entirely by surprise.

A shout went up from behind the shoal of canoes, and we all looked round to three canoes, spread out over the entrance to the bay as look-outs. The shout was a warning, and the Aleuts acted fast. The spears went away. The paddles dipped in hard. The canoes turned in their own length, and the whole fleet of us ran for the open sea, just as hard as muscle and skill could drive us.

We were running because another fleet had crept up on us, or tried to, as some twenty or more huge dug-out canoes bore down on us with evil intent. They were utterly different from the little Aleut bidarkas: not light and cunning but massive things hacked out of tree trunks. They were forty feet long, painted in bright, bizarre colours with huge, sharp prows rising out of the water all carved in the likeness of monster beasts. They were crammed with men, paddles going furiously on either side, and one man standing just behind each prow-figurehead, dressed as an eagle, with flapping wings and hook-beak mask. They were fearsome enough even to look at, but the sound they made was worse: howling and screaming and blowing horns.

"Tlingit! Tlingit!" says Tookarni, and damn near bust himself driving our canoe onward at lightning speed. The whole shoal of us did the same, and we damn near made it clear of the bay since our canoes were so much faster than the dugouts. But some of ours got caught fair and square. They got rammed and run down and men stood up in the dugouts jabbing down with spears, to kill the helpless Aleuts in the water. It was as ugly a fight as I've ever seen, and we must have lost a dozen or more canoes in the first instance.

But that wasn't the end of it. The dugouts that had entered the bay were just their vanguard. There were more of the buggers out at sea waiting to pounce, and these had nets between them on lines, to catch the Aleuts, which they did in some numbers with utter butchery, and stabbing spears, and no quarter given. The Aleuts fought back with their harpoons, but the dugouts had height advantage and the fight was one-sided.

As for me, I felt the most absolute fool for coming out with not so much as a penknife to fight with. Mind you, my sword and pistols wouldn't have been much use — not just two rounds of ball, and myself trying to chop heads while sitting down. So the only thing that saved me was Tookarni's seamanship, since he darted us in and out of the fight, with canoes crunching, men screaming and blood in the water. There was jammed confusion all round, until he saw a gap between two of the dugouts — or rather, two that had come so close together that the netting between them sank enough for us to slide over the top of it.

"Hi! Hi! Hi!" says Tookarni, and shot us through the gap with a long, strong pull and the fight falling astern of us. When we were clear, he heaved-to, swung us round for a look and a judgement of what to do. He chattered at me, while pointing up the coast *away* from Arkhangelsk.

"No!" says I. "Take us back!"

"Chatter-chatter-chatter!" says he, shaking his head, and pointing to other Aleut canoes that had escaped just as we had, and he headed for them and we closed up alongside of each other: some fifty little vessels bobbing on the waves, a whole raft of us, with the Aleuts yelling at each other in discussion, until Tookarni raised his voice, gave a long speech, and everyone nodded. Then he led and they followed, and he did try to tell me what we were doing, but I didn't understand a word.

After that we were three days at sea, during which time I drank some of the water we'd taken aboard, but ate none of the food. The Lord God Alone knows what it was, and the Aleuts gobbled it down, but it stank like a leper's toenails. So the food was bad but Tookarni's judgement was good. We couldn't go back the way we'd come, for fear of the Tlingit war-fleet, so Tookarni led us away from the coast, out to sea in a great loop then back to Arkhangelsk.

But he did something else: something that took courage, and his judgement that the entire Tlingit fleet was at sea. Thus he took us up-coast right past the main Tlingit coastal settlement! We went close by it. Since he knew the hazards of the coast and I did not, I can only assume that this made better sense than turning straight out to sea. In whatever case it gave me the opportunity to see what a formidable people the Tlingit were, since while I hadn't brought blade and barkers, I never go on any expedition without a pocket telescope: a neat little brass two-draw by Dolland.

So, as our canoes put on speed in case any of the war canoes were still in port, I took a good look at Tlingit-town-on-sea, and was duly amazed, and I warn you youngsters once again, that it is seriously wrong to assume that native peoples are not as clever as us. It is seriously wrong and it is dangerous besides, because it can get you killed. Thus I was amazed at the strength and solidity of Tlingit building. There were heavy log houses of timbers shaped and squared, all painted in bright colours. There were proper piers, with piles driven into the shoreline and planking on top, and above all there were huge posts, unbelievably tall, formed of tree trunks smoothed of limbs, and carved in grotesque and monstrous shapes, all neatly merging one into another with a spread of eagle wings at the top. Today we call them totem poles, but by any name they were impressive, and they still are.

When finally we got back to Arkhangelsk, the fort was on war-footing, everyone had been brought inside its walls, and the outlying settlements evacuated, though the two Yankee ships were still there. When we landed, there was a great weeping and crying from the Aleut women over the men killed by the Tlingit, and I was hauling myself out of the canoe, and stretching my legs for the first time in days. It was painful to move at first: very painful. I'd not have got up at all without Tookarni's help, since he was out and up before me, being used to such confinement. Then, my jolly boys, since he'd undoubtedly saved my life, I threw my arms around him and hugged him. Perhaps it was seeing all the surviving Aleuts hugging their women.

"Cap'n, Cap'n," says he.

"Shipmate," says I, "Shipmate." At least I didn't kiss him. I let his wife do that. Then there came Baranov, running down from the fort with Father Nikolai in tow, and a large number of men with muskets, who looked in every direction at once, in considerable fear.

"Captain Fletcher," says Baranov.

"Captain!" says Father Nikolai.

"Gentlemen," says I. "We were attacked by the Tlingit. Attacked by their fleet. What the hell is going on?"

"Ah, yes, yes," says Father Nikolai, "they have risen again. Risen against us in war."

"I thought you'd settled all that," says I to Baranov, who pretended not to understand, even when Father Nikolai translated. Instead, he gabbled at me.

"Governor Baranov says we must get back inside the fort," says Father Nikolai.

"Gabble-gabble," says Baranov.

"Quickly," says Father Nikolai.

"Da!" says all the men with muskets, and by Jove they meant it.

So that's what we did, with me throwing off my waterproof, then stamping my feet to make them work, then insisting that before all else we went straight to the stolovya canteen, because I was famished. So my briefing on latest events took place with me sat down wolfing some Russian meat stew with dumplings. I ate it out of a chipped bowl with a dirty spoon and it was one of the finest meals of my life. They even had a drop of rum to go with it. Baranov and Father Nikolai sat with me, and drank vodka — plenty of it, and it wasn't the first they'd taken that day, so I record a summary of what they said, since it came in a jumble, what with them being so nervous as well and Nikolai having to translate.

"The Tlingit are risen in force," says Baranov.

"Out in thousands," says Nikolai, "joined by allied tribes of the interior."

"They have driven in many of our settlements," says Baranov.

"And Fort Alexander is threatened," says Nikolai.

I put down my spoon at that. "Fort Alexander?" says I. "That's where my lieutenants and mids have gone! Are they safe?"

The two of them looked at one another and spoke Russian with many shrugged shoulders. I didn't like that, and I got angry.

"Well you can damn well put together a relief column," says I. "Every man who can be spared, to march to Fort Alexander and take the people to safety!" They looked away and muttered in Russian again, and that feeling came back in a wave that in this whole Alaska furs business, I'd been taken for a fool. So I lost my temper good and hard. I stood up and shouted.

"Now see here you shifty bastards!" says I. "You never told me about no damn tribal wars, and here's my shipmates stuck in a fort that might fall at any minute. So pay good heed because it comes to this. If you don't send a relief column — which I shall command — you can shove the fur voyage to St Petersburg straight up your beam ends, and your whole damn colony with it, and sod the lot of you to bloody buggery!"

In fact I wasn't as polite as that, but you don't want to hear what I really said. So there was a deal of yelling on all sides and thumping of tables, until finally the Ruskies shrugged and did something which reveals everything about why the Alaska project was going down the plughole.

Thus for once they used their lazy brains. They made proper use of an opportunity that was there for them to grasp if only they weren't so block-headed soaked in drink. So in the end — since they knew what I did not — *their* idea was better than *my* idea of a marching relief column.

CHAPTER 20

All three of us were out-manoeuvred by Ducaine. He is clever
and Count Pavel values him greatly.

(Extract of a letter from Professor Fitzhummer, lodging
at Ingleby's Hotel, Philadelphia to his eldest son Igor in St
Petersburg. Translated from Russian.)

"Mr Ducaine for you, gentlemen," said Ingleby. It was Ingleby himself,
owner of the hotel, since the three Russian gentlemen were most superior
guests who paid in gold roubles at a time when Pennsylvania was struggling to establish a proper currency. Thus anybody's gold was welcome.
Indeed it was more than welcome: it was received with rapture. "Mr
Ducaine comes with a letter of recommendation," said Ingleby, "a letter
of recommendation from …" He paused before pronouncing the words,
"The Count Pavel!" Then Ingleby bowed, having being bred up as a
servant in England, and retaining — even in wealthy middle age — a
servant's respect for rank.

"Thank you, Mr Ingleby," said Professor Fitzhummer in English so
perfect that there was only a trace of accent about it. "Please bring Mr
Ducaine to us," he said.

"Gentlemen," said Ingleby, and stood back to allow Ducaine to enter,
who stood in the doorway and instantly took command of the room,
since it was occupied only by men of book learning. It was a comfortable day-room, on the ground floor, well furnished in yellow maple,
with a run of windows giving a view of a cobbled market square busy

with trade and people. But most of all Ducaine saw the three scholarly, academical gentlemen he'd been sent to meet: Professor Fitzhummer, Dr Barkovskiy and Dr Menchikov, all of St Petersburg University, who were seated round a table, with a wine flask and glasses, enjoying the tobacco pipes they'd been forbidden aboard ship for fear of fire. Thus each man had hold of a long-stemmed, china-clay pipe and was busily filling the room with smoke.

"Thank you, Mr Ingleby," said Professor Fitzhummer, "that will be all." Ingleby bowed once more to the men who paid in gold, and went out, closing the door behind him, at which Ducaine tossed his letter of introduction on the table, gave a steady smile and spoke.

"Gentlemen," he said, "I'm here on the orders of your Count Pavel, and I'm here to make things happen."

"Good!" said Fitzhummer, attempting to take charge. "But you needn't have bothered with the letter of introduction."

"We knew you were coming," said Menchikov.

"Count Pavel told us," said Borkovskiy.

"Sit here," said Fitzhummer. "Will you take a glass and a pipe?"

"Glass please, but not a pipe," said Ducaine. "I don't smoke." He sat. A glass was poured. He drained it, and in the confidence of his dominance he took the decanter himself, re-filled his glass, and took another gulp. Then he looked at the other three, staring them out of countenance and grinning. But Fitzhummer gathered himself, sat up straight and spoke.

"What do you know?" he demanded.

"Yes!" said the other two.

"I know about …" He paused. "The *document*!" He said the two words with heavy emphasis, and once again he was pierced with wonderment that such power could exist, handwritten on a piece of vellum. But then the American Constitution itself was only words on vellum. "I know about that," said Ducaine, "and I know that it is a matter of finding the right man to receive the document, and vouch for its truth."

"And have you found the man?" asked Fitzhummer.

"Yes," said Ducaine, "I think that I have found him."

Fitzhummer instantly pounced on that. "You *think?*" he said. "You only *think?* We'll need better than that if we're all to come safe out of this!"

"Huh!" said Ducaine, spotting the attempt to shift blame in case of trouble. But he dealt with that easily. "I know Philadelphia," he said, "I know Philadelphia's society, and I know the same for Washington and New York." He leaned forward in emphasis. "I know much else, but choosing the right man is a heavy matter, and we may get only one chance!" He looked at each of the other three. "So you gentlemen—" he grinned — "you, with your expert knowledge of American Constitutional law, must be part of the final decision." He nodded firmly. "Count Pavel says as much, so it's already decided that you must go to see him."

Fitzhummer and the others frowned, but Ducaine had got them in a corner. He was right. They'd been brought all these thousands of miles precisely because they were Russia's experts in the American Constitution.

Fitzhummer sighed and spoke.

"Who is this man?"

CHAPTER 21

Captain Cornwich chewed tobacco, which I have always thought to be a nasty habit because it makes a man spit. It makes him spit a jet of dirty-brown fluid when, by mastication of his quid, he has too much liquid in his mouth, and it's a liquid which nobody wants to swallow. That's bad enough on shore where there are spittoons on public house floors to test the accuracy of the spitters. But aboard ship it's really nasty, since it stains the nice white decks that the hands have holy-stoned to make clean. Or at least it does unless the chewer regularly takes himself to the rail to spit into the sea, which in a man-o'-war he damn well had to, it being a flogging offence in any man's navy to spit tobacco juice on the decks. So, since Cornwich ran his ship to man-o'-war standards:

"'Scuse me, Cap'n," says he, to me, as he went to the rail to spit. I looked at him, and so did Father Nikolai. So did the fifty Rusky-Alaskies sat on their haunches in the waist, with muskets over their knees, trying to keep out of the way of the Yankee seaman as Cornwich worked the ship up the estuary. Thus we were the relief column, but we were going to Fort Alexander by sea rather than on foot. We were under way with an easy wind, the ship hardly heeling, and the canyon-like high ground sliding past, thickly wooded and seemingly empty of life.

Then Cornwich came back, taking his place by the wheel which was just aft of the mainmast aboard the brig *Nancy Biggins*.

"You see, Cap'n," says he, "we're safe aboard ship."

"Baranov said that," says I, "and I took it on trust, since it's only hours by ship, which would have been three days' march through the

152

woods, with the chance of being ambushed all the way. So I want to hear it from you. Why are we safe aboard ship?"

"'Cos them Tlingit ain't stupid," says Cornwich, "they've tried attacking ships and found out what these can do—" he pointed to the line of swivel-guns along the rail on either hand — "two-pounders, Cap'n, each one primed and ready, with a good few handfuls of pistol balls loaded. Any one of them can clear a Tlingit war canoe from end to end, and there ain't nothing they can do, 'cos we rig boarding nettings, so they can't get into the ship, and we stick 'em with pikes if they try. And we got these, too." He pointed to wicker baskets lashed by the rail. "Grenades," he said. "If they do get alongside, we light the fuses and drop these on their heads." He grinned. "*Boom*!" says he.

"What about bows and arrows?" says I. "Or muskets? Have they got guns?"

"They have some guns, but we keep mid-channel out of range of the shore, and if they're shooting from dugouts, they're lower than us and shooting upwards with the ship's rail in the way."

"What about at night?" says I. "Can't they creep up on you, and board on the sly?"

"Nope!" says he. "You don't hardly get no night, this time o' year. Not with the Northern Lights an' all. And we don't come here in the winter: you bet your sweet ass we don't! So I'm telling you, Cap'n, you're safe aboard ship." He smiled. "'Cos I wouldn't be here otherwise, however much Baranov is paying me."

Nonetheless, Cornwich took care to keep *Nancy Biggins* as far from the shore as possible, and kept slow-matches burning in tin cans for instant use to set off the swivels and grenades, and of course he had his main battery run out and ready, even if it was just three six-pounders on either beam.

Then, when finally we came up alongside Fort Alexander, it was all anti-climax because nothing was going on. The fort was a decent construction of timber palisades and corner bastions. The Russian America Company flag was flying over it, it stood on high ground looking down on a sandy beach, and the gates were swinging open for folk inside to come out to greet us. There was no sign of trouble at all, and the peacefulness cheered up my musketeers something wonderful.

"Hoooo-rah! Hoooo-rah!" says they. They yelled and danced, and waved muskets and grabbed hold of each other, while the Yankee crew sneered, since they despised all the Rusky-Alasky kissing and hugging. I felt the same when Father Nikolai threw arms around me and had to be fended off.

"I'll lower boats and get you ashore, Cap'n Fletcher," says Cornwich. "Then I'll anchor out where it's safe. But I'll be here if'n you need me." He looked at the fort with a distinct uneasiness. "So you keep a good lookout, Cap'n. I can't see no Tlingit right now, but that don't mean they ain't there. So listen hard to this: if'n things do turn nasty, I'll up anchor and be gone. But then I'll give it a day or two and come looking for you. D'you hear that?"

That made me wonder. Baranov was paying him to take me and the rest to Fort Alexander, but that was the extent of his duties so far as I knew. There was no payment for bringing us back.

"Well," says I, "that's more than generous, Captain Cornwich, but why would you take the risk?"

"'Scuse me, Cap'n," says he, and went to the rail to spit. Then he turned and grinned. "I'll take the risk 'cos I like your style, Cap'n," says he. "You got Yankee style about you, even if you was born in the wrong place." He laughed, I laughed, and I made a friend, and I thought even harder about Boston: Boston rather than England. But then we were busy swinging out the boats and getting my Rusky-Alaskies aboard, and it was all neatly done. It was done in Yankee style.

Then, once ashore with Father Nikolai translating, I got my fifty men in best order that could be got out of them. I made sure they had their marching rations, I made sure their muskets were primed and loaded, I made sure they had more cartridges in their pouches. I did all that and I wished ten times over that their cheap Russian trade muskets had bayonets, which they did not. At the same time the commander of the fort and his officers were all around me and gaping at me, and gabbling and pointing. They were a dirty crew, all dressed in furs and skins, with a mixture of Aleut, Russian and who knows what in their faces. There wasn't a uniform among them, nor badges of rank, and they didn't smell too good neither, though there was a decent-sized garrison with lines of men looking down on us from the firing platforms behind the palisades. Also, as with Fort Arkhangelsk, there were guns in the bastions, so the fort looked capable of defending itself.

But, but, but … even if I couldn't understand the fort commander and his men, I could see that something nasty was under way, since they were frowning and they all kept looking back at the forest behind the fort. Worse still, where were Lieutenant Dawson, Mr Midshipman Blacker and the rest? They certainly weren't here on the beach! So I was dismayed, but not surprised, when Father Nikolai said, "Da, da, da," to the fort commander then turned to me. "Your people not here, Captain," says he. "This fort—" he pointed — "is storehouse for furs from up-country fur stations. Your people gone up-country to see fur stations. Gone to see big one: the biggest, and that station very close to the Tlingit." He shrugged. "We can do nothing, Captain. Is only few miles but too dangerous. Too dangerous."

Well my jolly boys, you can probably imagine what your Uncle Jacob did next, in explaining to Father Nikolai that there was *very much* that we could do. I would only point out that you need something like my strength if you are going to take a Russian Orthodox priest by the scruff of his neck, hoist him off his feet and hold him kicking and strangling while you give him his orders at two inches' range, straight into his face in a mighty shout. Then I let him down just before he entirely choked, turned him to face the Rusky-Alaskies and gave him a final order.

"You tell *them* that, you swab!" says I. "Tell them that, or this time I'll wring your bloody neck!" So he uttered some Russian in the voice of a half-throttled mouse.

"Louder!" says I. "Or up you go again!"

"Da, da," says he, "yes, Captain." And he managed to tell them what we were going to do: that's my fifty men and as many others as the fort could spare. We were going up-country this very instant to bring back my people and whoever else might be in danger in the fur station.

So that's what we did, and you might wonder how one man — myself — could make so many others do something that they really didn't want to do, especially if you consider the situation reversed. Thus, if a lone Russian tried to choke an English village parson in front of a congregation of farmers, the Russian would find himself battered senseless and dumped in the village pond in double-quick time.

But Russians are different. They are obsessed with this idea of a *silny lider*, a strong leader. It's what Admiral Adamovich said all those months ago, when I knocked down the ship's bully-boy Veleslav on going aboard *Enable*. It's deep in the bones of Russians that they must have a strong man in command of Russia to hold it together against attack from without and rebellion from within. They want a strong man at the helm, and while they might not have *liked* what I'd done to Father Nikolai, I think they admired it, because when he was done passing on my orders, I looked at the Rusky-Alaskies and saw them gazing at me as if I were the prize bull at a county show.

So there was a deal of yelling and shouting, the fort commander gave us another ten men together with a guide to take us to the fur station, and off we set down a wide-beaten track in the forest, that was rutted with the wheel-marks of wagons, and was wide enough that I didn't get the blue demons for fear of ambush. I had a musket, my sword and pistols; the Rusky-Alaskies were clumped behind in columns of fours, and I felt that with over sixty muskets we had at least a chance of getting to the fur station and back out again with my people, and all of us alive.

Which, my jolly boys, brings me right back to the beginning of this particular tale with the attack by forest monsters — the Tlingit — who fell upon us just before we actually reached the fur station. You will therefore remember that later your Uncle Jacob was in dense forest off Bannerman's Bay with Father Nikolai, watching the Tlingit burn down Fort Alexander having killed every living thing within its walls, while a force of Rusky-Alasky musketeers, plus Lieutenant Dawson, Mr Blacker and the other mids, and a dozen Rusky-Alasky civilians, were in hiding awaiting my orders: them and a huge quantity of sea otter furs in wagons.

156

But we didn't perish because the Tlingit — having just scored the most colossal victory over the Russian invaders — were not entirely burning everything to ashes, because even as the flames roared, they were breaking doors, smashing windows, opening boxes and looting like tars in a treasure ship. Father Nikolai and I saw them running about, in Russian hats and coats, waving things that they prized: copper pots, boots, axes and much else. Then — and probably most valuable of all to them — some of them ran out bearing small copper-banded casks containing gunpowder. They whooped something terrific when they carried those off. Believe me they did, but they didn't whoop as much as they did when they got hold of the fort's store of vodka.

Now it's a sad fact that peoples who can't make alcohol for themselves, have no tradition or drill for the drinking of it. They just sink it down as fast as they can get it. Our tars drink hard, and Russians drink worse, but even they don't tip up a bottle of vodka and take it down in heavy gulps, the whole bottle, in one go. So some of the Tlingit must have killed themselves doing it. They must have, because occasionally some damn-fool seaman, fresh ashore after a cruise, will drink a whole bottle of rum; he usually does it for a bet and he usually ends up dead.

So, what with one thing and another, the Tlingit were too busy enjoying themselves to bother searching for anyone who'd escaped the massacre. But when finally they were done … they vanished! Father Nikolai and I looked at one another in amazement. Without a word of command but by mutual agreement, they looked at each other, and were off through the forest, back the way they had come, thousands of them until none were left. They were gone in minutes and the beach was empty of anything other than dead Russians.

"Come on," says I to Father Nikolai, "let's go back to the others. I think we're safe for a while."

"But what we do?" says he.

"Don't know," says I.

"But you are leader," says he, forlorn as a man who's pissed himself.

"Oh shut up," says I, and set off without bothering to see if he was following. But of course he was. He almost climbed on my back for fear of being left behind. Then, at the hiding place everyone was sat down quiet, but they all stood when we arrived.

"Sir," says Lieutenant Dawson, "what's happened?" And the rest gabbled the same thing in Russian.

So we told them. Between us, Father Nikolai and I told everyone. They all nodded, they were all delighted that the Tlingit were gone, and that was all very nice. But then they looked to me.

"What now, sir?" says Dawson, and I was reminded of the fact that the commander of a fleet lives in royal state aboard ship. He inhabits great and lofty cabins with servants around him. He is lavishly paid, and takes a colossal share of any prize money. But he also takes a colossal share of the responsibility: the desperate forming of a plan, the agonies of indecision, and the nighttime worries that keep him from sleep. So ponder on that, my jolly boys, should ever you seek to rise in your chosen profession.

But this time I was saved from worry by two things: first, my certain conviction as to what the Tlingit warriors would be doing over the next few days; and second, Captain Cornwich's promise. So I got everyone sat down again, and gave a speech to all hands, with Father Nikolai translating.

"Now then," says I, "we're perfectly safe here because the Tlingit will be back among their people celebrating their victory as heroes. They'll be gorging on food, swilling down Russian vodka and rogering their women cross-eyed. That'll likely go on for days."

"Ahhhhh!" says all the Rusky-Alaskies, and they nudged one another in delight.

"Very good, sir!" says Dawson.

"Aye-aye, sir!" says the mids.

"Better still," says I, "Captain Cornwich's ship was gone from the anchorage but I have his promise that in case of trouble, he'll come back after a few days to take us off."

"Hmmmm," says my audience.

"Are you sure, sir?" says Dawson. "Sure that he'll come?"

"Completely sure," says I, "because for one thing he's promised and

I trust him …" I paused and pointed to our wagon-loads of furs. "And for another thing, he knows we've got them, and he'll want his share!"

"Ahhhhh!" says everyone, and they were happy to stay put even if what I'd told them was only half true, because Cornwich couldn't possibly know about the furs. Then, after that, we settled down to wait for Cornwich. There was plenty of food in the Rusky-Alasky knapsacks, and the weather was mild, which was good because I wouldn't allow fires for fear of who might see the smoke. I had Dawson set up a watch-keeping rota among the mids, to watch out for Cornwich coming back with *Nancy Biggins*, and I gave Father Nikolai the job of keeping the camp clean, with latrines dug downwind, and himself to keep order among the people, keeping the men apart from the women. I set Dawson to work because I trusted him. But I gave Father Nikolai his job to show all hands that there was discipline in the camp, and a chain of command. After all, he was a priest, and there was some respect for him among the Rusky-Alaskies. In the event, I was right about the Tlingit — almost right — and both right and wrong about Father Nikolai. I was wrong in giving him responsibility, but the wrong led to a great right, at least for myself.

Thus on the second night — such night as it was — I was awoken by raised voices. It wasn't especially loud but a seaman sleeps light and he knows when there's trouble in the offing, so I was up and looking and saw one of the Rusky-Alasky women bent over talking to Father Nikolai, who was half-asleep and trying to push her away. It was the little blondie who'd kissed me when we first arrived at the fur station.

"Gabble-gabble," says Father Nikolai, all bored and tired, but the blondie shook him, and her voice was near tears. Others were stirring from sleep around the camp and everyone was soon looking at what happened next.

"What's afoot?" says I, going over to Father Nikolai and the woman. He blinked and got up and she looked at me, and poured out a stream of gabble. She was quite lovely but in great distress, with tears on her cheeks, hair pulled out of its plaits, and a bare arm and shoulder where her clothes had been torn. So it took no flights of genius to guess what

159

had gone on. "Well?" says I to Father Nikolai. "What's this? You're in charge of the camp!"

"Pah!" says he, sneering. "This girl is Siupuk. She make trouble. She Aleut half-breed, and all them is easy. They lay with anyone, then argue the price." So I looked at her and wondered. What did I know of Aleut women? Could Father Nikolai be right? But then she surprised me.

"No!" says she, because she had some English. "Not whore! Good woman!" She looked around and pointed to a couple of Rusky-Alaskies who were stood on the edge of the camp, leering at Siupuk. "Those men want rape!" says she.

So I looked at them and the leering stopped. They couldn't meet my eye. "You two," says I. "At the double, come here!"

"No," says Father Nikolai, "she is trouble, like I told you."

"Shut up!" says I. "Mr Dawson! Mr Blacker! Clap hold of those lubbers and bring 'em forward."

"Aye-aye, sir!" says they, already up and awake.

So I held my own little court martial, right there in the Alaskan forest under the Northern Lights, with all present gathered around except the lookouts, and I made judgement on the two villains, I made judgement on sight of them! They were red-faced and stuttering, and looked guilty, so something dirty had gone on, and in any case I didn't like Rusky-Alaskies, while Siupuk was a lovely woman in distress. So what judgement would you have given, my jolly boys? I do hope it's the right one, 'cos otherwise you won't want to read any more of your Uncle Jacob's writings. But blondie — Siupuk — was speaking again.

"They come when I sleep," says she. "Pick me up. Put hand on my mouth. Take me in forest. But I escape."

"Well enough, ma'am," says I, turning to the Rusky-Alaskies. "And what have you two got to say?"

"Gabble-gabble-gabble," says they, very quiet and never looking at me. I turned to Father Nikolai and he shrugged.

"They say she is whore," says he. "Is no surprise. They all whores."

I looked at Siupuk, and she actually sobbed at those words. So that was it. I didn't care then, and I don't care now who was innocent and

160

who was not, for I can't stand to see a woman abused: any woman, even if she ain't so tasty as Siupuk.

"Right," says I. "Mr Dawson?"

"Sir?"

"Stand up these two, apart from one another."

"Aye-aye, sir!"

"And Father Nikolai?"

"Captain?"

"Tell them to put up their fists."

"Gabble-gabble," says he, and the two of them gaped and looked at each other and looked at me, and raised hands in hopeless defences. So I let them off light, or maybe I didn't. *Smack! Smack!* Each one got a full, swing-of-the-arm clout round the face with my open hand, and down they went. Now, a blow from a fist is manly, while a clap round the chops is an insult, and is humiliation before all the world. But serve the buggers right. A decent man *asks* a woman, he does not take. Not when I'm about. So I acted instinctive, but two very fine benefits flowed. Siupuk looked at me, her lashes went up and down and she stopped crying.

"Thank you," says she, and I got the likely look as fine as ever I've had it in all my life. But more even than that, Siupuk knew things that others did not, and life-saving things they were too, since — as I have said — I was not entirely right about the Tlingit.

CHAPTER 22

We were all against Captain Cornwich, but he would have his way, and I suppose he was right, since there was five dozen, what we saved from hideous slaughter by the savages.

(Extract of the sea journal of Ephraim Hampshire, First Mate aboard Nancy Biggins.)

Cornwich went to the rail to spit: to spit and to control his temper. He took a breath, got his telescope comfortable under his arm, and went back to the ship's wheel, the binnacle and the helmsman, and his first and second mates. Once there, he stared steadily at the set of the sails as *Nancy Biggins* crept up the safe channel, under reefed tops'ls with the lead going, and the leadsman chanting.

"By the mark four ... and a half four ... a quarter less three ... "

Then, still staring at the sails, he spoke. He spoke first to the two mates.

"You two fine gentlemen will get to your goddam duties," he said, "you'll do it goddam now!" Then he spoke to the helmsman. "And you look to your goddam steering, and don't run the whole goddam ship of us into the mud, with the bottom coming up as it is!"

"Aye-aye!" they said. They all said it. Even the hands looking on said it too, since Cornwich was a good captain who always paid a man's wages and only booted those up the breech that deserved it.

"Good enough," said Cornwich, "so we'll not hear another word about Cap'n Fletcher and his men, and my promise — my faithful promise — to bring him off safe, if the goddam Tlingit turn bad." But silence followed.

"Did you not hear me?" said Cornwich. "Are you all struck goddam deaf?"

"Aye-aye!" said some.

"No, Cap'n!" said others, searching for an apt reply.

Cornwich filled his lungs and bellowed, "And you aloft!" he cried. "Sharp lookout!"

"Aye-aye!" cried the men in the tops.

"First sight you get of the goddam Tlingit, I goddam want to know!" cried Cornwich, and then he glared at the two mates. "And will you two go to your duties now, or will you not?" he said.

"Aye-aye," they said, and touched hats and went to their stations.

"Deputation indeed!" said Cornwich to himself, though the helmsman heard him. "Deputation from the goddam ship's people!" Cornwich went to the rail again, but this time to look up the inlet — and he sighed. Six days ago he'd upped anchor and filled sails as soon as the Tlingit struck. He'd had to. There was nothing he could have done, and if there were thousands of them ashore — which there had been — then they might also have turned out whole fleets of their goddam war canoes. And then, who knows? Maybe a ship wasn't so safe after all?

But he'd promised, and that was that. So he was going back, and *Nancy Biggins* was coming round a headland, and Fort Alexander was coming into view, which is to say the remains of Fort Alexander, which was largely a smoking wreckage of half-burned timber, and there was a communal groan from the crew at the sight of it.

"Clap a hitch on that, you swabs!" said Cornwich. "What did you expect? A county fair with music and dancing?" The groaning stopped. "And you there, Mr Hampshire," said Cornwich to the first mate.

"Aye-aye," said Hampshire.

"Swivels primed and loaded? Guns charged with grape? Grenades ready?"

"Aye-aye!"

Cornwich nodded. He knew all that already, but couldn't help checking. Then the maintop lookout yelled.

163

"Men on the shoreline!"

"Where away?" cried Cornwich.

"Fine on the starboard beam, Cap'n!"

Cornwich raised his glass and looked.

"Ah!" said he, with huge relief and huge satisfaction. "Fletcher!" He was easy to spot, hulking and towering over a handful of men on a scrap of high ground: a lookout post most likely, and Fletcher's men watching out for *Nancy Biggins*. Cornwich hailed the maintop. "What sign of the Tlingit?" he cried.

"None, Cap'n!"

"So all hands get up off your butts!" Cornwich cried. "Lower the boats and stand by to bring off every man of them ashore!" He turned to the first mate. "Mr Hampshire, I'll thank you to back topsail, bring us about, and stand by to make sail for the open sea, at my instant command!"

"Aye-aye!" This time from every man of the crew, because themselves and their ship would soon be forging away to safety from the savages, with Fletcher's shore-folk safe aboard; not that anyone cared for them, but they tolerated the eccentricity of their captain in this regard. So Cornwich's men, being Yankee seamen born and bred, and being delighted to be bringing an end to this mad and dangerous venture, set to with a will, hauled longboat and cutter off their skids amidships, got them afloat and under oars, and pulled for the shore, with Mr Hampshire in command.

There were cheers as the boats grounded, and a rushing forward of bearded Russians, until Hampshire saw a huge man — obviously Fletcher — seize a couple of Russians who were elbowing some women aside, to get to the boats. He took one in either hand and threw them head over heels into the water.

"Belay that, you bloody swabs!" he cried. "Wait your turn and act like men!"

"Da! Da!" cried the Russians, and Hampshire gaped as Fletcher physically heaved the Russians aside, and pushed some half-dozen women forward, picking up one who was unsure of boats, and shoving her

164

into the longboat as the oarsmen made way for her. Hampshire was impressed. He too was a big man, accustomed to using his fists in the name of ship's discipline, but he wasn't of Fletcher's class, and he nodded in deep approval of Fletcher's words and deeds.

"Now then, you buggers!" said Fletcher to the Russians, "you can get aboard now, but God help him as oversets a boat and don't take proper time!"

"Da! Da! Da!" said the Russians, and Hampshire shook his head in amazement at the control Fletcher had over them, and the fact that one — who looked like a priest — kept turning Fletcher's words into Russian. Then Fletcher was standing aside, with some Russian girl at his elbow, making sure the Russians got into the boats, then turning to Hampshire.

"Who are you, then, mister?" he said. Hampshire touched his hat and stood straight.

"I'm Hampshire, Cap'n. First mate."

"Good day to you, Mr Hampshire!" said the huge man. "I'm more than pleased to see you. But where's Mr Cornwich?"

"Aboard ship, Cap'n. He was fierce determined to take you off."

"God bless him for that," said Fletcher, "and can I leave you in charge of the embarkation, Mr Hampshire?" He looked at the crowd of Russian men — over fifty of them — who were pressing forward and beginning to look over their shoulders in fear of what might be lurking in the woods. "Can I leave you to get these no-seamen swabs aboard? For it'll take more than one trip with the boats you've got." He turned to two men who didn't look Russian. "These here are Lieutenant Dawson and Mr Midshipman Blacker, they'll lend a hand."

"Aye-aye, Cap'n," said Hampshire. "You can leave that to me." He nodded to Dawson and Blacker. "Me and them," he said. But then he frowned. "But ain't you coming aboard, Cap'n?"

"Not yet," said Fletcher, "there's something to fetch. I'll be back directly." Then Fletcher was off, running back towards the woods, with the Russian girl chasing after him. Hampshire was puzzled, but he did as he'd been bid, and got all the Russians off the beach, and aboard

Nancy Biggins in good time, and the longboat hoist aboard, while the cutter-crew pulled back to the beach with Hampshire aboard, waiting for Fletcher to appear on the beach.

But Fletcher did not appear. Fletcher didn't, but the Tlingit did. They came swarming out of the forest in their battle gear, and some with muskets. They came with speed that shocked Hampshire.

"Pull for the ship!" he yelled. "Pull your blasted hearts out! Pull! Pull! Pull!"

He needn't have bothered yelling. The men pulled like madmen, and the cutter was soon bumping against *Nancy Biggins*'s planking, with lifting tackles waiting to heave the cutter aboard, with her men still in her.

"Hampshire," cried Captain Cornwich, even with the cutter still in the air, "where's Fletcher? I saw him run into the woods!"

"He's …" said Hampshire, but he never finished the sentence because a rattle of musketry came from the shoreline, where Tlingit warriors were crouched down to take careful aim, with puffs of smoke on the beach, and musket balls whistling — which almost entirely missed, except one that killed the cutter's coxswain stone dead with a ball in the back of his head that blew his teeth and lower jaw out of his face and into Hampshire's lap.

"Get that boat secured," cried Cornwich, "and give them goddam whoresons a taste of grape! Do it slow an' careful and don't miss!"

"Aye-aye!" cried the men at *Nancy Biggins*'s guns, and they gave their broadside such as it was: one nine-pounder and three sixes. But the range was long for grape, and only three Tlingit were knocked over while the rest capered and jeered, except those that re-loaded muskets for another volley.

"Give 'em round shot!" cried Cornwich, but the Englishman Dawson stepped forward, the one that was a lieutenant.

"Sir," he said, "Captain Fletcher is still ashore, he might be hit by your fire."

"Goddam!" said Cornwich, and stared hard at the beach, now full of Tlingit in their bizarre wooden helmets, as another spattering of muskets came from the beach — and this time, musket balls smacked hard into *Nancy Biggins*'s sides. "Well, I ain't leaving Fletcher," said Cornwich, "but I ain't taking fire from no savages and not giving back." He turned to the gunners. "Round shot, lads!" he cried, which brought a cheer, a busy use of sponges and rammers, and the guns run out and fired. Another cheer came from *Nancy Biggins*'s people and the Russians cramming the ship, as a whole line of Tlingit was mangled by a shot shrieking and smashing among them. But then the Tlingit — not being fools — just disappeared. They ran into the woods. They ran into the woods and somewhere else.

"Where the goddam helluv they gone?" said Cornwich, while all those with telescopes scanned the beach.

"Look there, Cap'n," said Hampshire. "There's some of them going into the corner of the fort."

"The bastion," said Lieutenant Dawson. "It's nearly intact. And there's guns mounted. Cap'n Fletcher said they're twelve-pounders."

"But they're savages," said Cornwich. "They can't do nothing. We're safe aboard ship and I'm damned if I'm gonna leave Fletcher behind."

"Indeed, sir," said Dawson, "they're only savages. They can't possibly know the workings of heavy guns." Dawson said that, but he wondered. He wondered hard. Captain Fletcher had laid great stress on the ingenuity of the Tlingit.

So there was uneasy silence for some minutes, as *Nancy Biggins* wallowed and rolled, creaked and groaned, and all aboard her looked to the half-burned but still-standing southern bastion of Fort Alexander. They looked until there was a sudden gout of smoke, a bright orange flash, the bellow of a gun and the fearful howling of a twelve-pound shot hurtling over the fore topmast of their ship. This brought cries and yells from the Russians, and a great tumult of voices yelling in their language, and one of them — the one in black clothes who wore a cross round his neck — coming up to Captain Cornwich and yelling at him in English.

"We go!" he said. "We go or we be killed. Or ship be sunk!"

But Cornwich sneered and shoved him off. Cornwich recognised a Russian priest when he saw one and he didn't like them, not one bit. He thought they smelt of drink and sweat.

"Don't you goddam tell me what to do," he said, "not a goddam heathen like you." But the priest wasn't the only man who wanted *Nancy Biggins* to be gone.

"Cap'n," said Hampshire, pointing to the bastion, "they've got powder and shot and they *do* know the workings of a gun. So if they—"

"Shut your trap," said Cornwich. "I made a promise!" Then he yelled at his gunners. "Fire on the bastion! Fire on it!" The gunners looked at one another in dismay. Ships didn't fight shore batteries. They couldn't win. Everyone knew that. Cornwich saw the hesitation and stamped his foot in anger then tried to shout.

But *flash-boom-smoke* from the bastion, and a shot came aboard that smashed through the ship's rail, and three men were killed outright. They were Cornwich and the Russian priest, who were blown into meat and rags, and another man who was killed without a mark on him, by the wind of the shot. Five others were wounded by splinters, and every man aboard was shocked.

That was enough. Not even Dawson and Blacker could argue that it was wise to remain, or indeed that there was any point in remaining, so first mate Hampshire made sail, got *Nancy Biggins* under way and up the safe channel to the sea.

"God help Cap'n Fletcher," said Dawson.

"And God forgive us for leaving him," said Blacker.

"He'll be dead by now, anyways," said Hampshire. "How could he not be? Them savages is everywhere."

CHAPTER 23

I did have my doubts about Siupuk the blondie, because I thought of Father Nikolai's words in the matter, and also because she followed me around constantly during our long wait in the woods, and smiled with lovely white teeth in a neat little heart-shaped face. So I don't doubt that if I'd suggested we take a walk in the forest, then she'd not only have come with me, but she'd have led the way. Perhaps it was only gratitude? Also, the ladies have always liked me, but Siupuk was just a mite forward. Perhaps it was the Aleut way. How should I know?

So I was sorely tempted. For one thing, she didn't smell of dirt like all the rest out of that fur station. She smelt good. But aside from Dawson, Blacker and the mids, I didn't trust anyone around me — Rusky-Alaskies as they were — and I wanted them kept together, not scattering, lighting fires, getting drunk, fighting, or otherwise attracting whatever might be hiding in the woods. I was very worried about that. I was worried all the time. I worried at every twig that cracked, and every bird that took off with flapping wings. Therefore, I judged that I must not be seen to be taking a carnal interest in little Siupuk while everyone else was under discipline. And that, my jolly boys, is one of the burdens of command that they don't teach in the Royal Naval College at Dartmouth.

I say it was a long wait, but in truth it was only six days, and I was sat eating, with Dawson, Father Nikolai and the mids, and of course Siupuk, who sat just outside the circle of men, smiling at me, when one of the mids came running into camp. I could see it was good news, but he didn't shout. He was a good lad and I'd forbidden any noise-making. He just ran up to me, stamped foot like a tar and touched his hat.

"Permission to report, sir?" says he.

"Carry on," says I.

"Sail coming up the estuary, sir," says he. "Could be *Nancy Biggins*, sir. Could be Mr Cornwich, come to the rescue." That caused a stir, believe me. Everyone jumped up with radiant smiles and hope of salvation. But I wanted no fuss, not now when it seemed that we were coming away safe.

"Stand fast!" says I to the lot of them. "Mr Dawson, you have command here. Keep order among the men."

"Aye-aye, sir!" says he.

"Father Nikolai and Mr Blacker," says I, "you come with me." Then I made a point of *not* running, to set the example, and was off with those two — plus Siupuk, who followed behind and I hadn't the heart to send her back. We walked to the lookout post, on high ground, just outside the treeline, with a fine view over the estuary and bay and a dismal view over the remains of Fort Alexander. At least we'd buried the dead. I'd insisted on that, and all hands took a share of the work. We did have a priest to do the honours, after all.

"There, sir!" says the mid on watch as we approached, and he handed me his telescope.

"Ah," says I, focussing the round image on a two-masted ship, bearing down under reefed topsails, as she felt her way down the safe channel. She was still a way off, but any seaman recognises a ship by its rig. It's like a man's face. "Yes," says I, "that's *Nancy Biggins*." Then: "Mr Blacker?"

"Sir?"

"Get back to the camp, present my compliments to Lieutenant Dawson, and ask him to bring up all hands for embarking aboard ship." I was being carefully formal, to maintain discipline at a moment when it might be swamped with emotion. So we very nearly did it. We very nearly stayed hidden and got everyone safe aboard, together with the wagon-loads of furs. But very nearly means not quite, because Cornwich brought *Nancy Biggins* as close in as he dared, then came about ready to make sail for the open sea as fast as fortune might require. Then he backed his fore topsail, hove-to, and lowered his boats, and by Jove we were pleased to see that. As the boats pulled for shore with oars clanking, I couldn't hold back the Rusky-Alaskies from cheering.

"Hoooo-rah! Hoooo-rah! Hoooo-rah!" But when the boats grounded I had to knock a few heads together to keep the Rusky-Alaskies from swamping the boats as they fought one another to get aboard. Fortunately, there was a large, bruiser-looking man in charge of the boats: Hampshire by name and first mate aboard ship. So I got him, Dawson and Blacker to keep order and get the Rusky-Alaskies aboard, taking care to favour the women, since under my command the order of rescue from any peril shall forever be women and children *first*!

Then once I could see that Hampshire and my lads were in good charge, I excused myself, to attend certain matters demanding attention in the forest camp. Off I ran, never noticing Siupuk astern of me, and was soon in the woods, seeking anyone paralysed drunk or fallen into the latrines — which was much the same thing with Rusky-Alaskies. I was there for those slovenly lubbers, but also — perhaps mainly — for a particularly large handcart of furs which I was sure I could move on my own, rather than face the tragedy of lost profits. Sadly we had to leave most of the carts behind, and the furs with them, but I was jolly well minded to take the big one, and it saved my life.

I was just getting a hold of the shafts, with Siupuk getting in the way trying to help, and I was just telling her to stand clear, when — silent as ghosts — the Tlingit appeared: four of them, charging out of the forest with their helmets and battle gear, and some wicked-looking spears and knives. They didn't whoop or howl, they just came on at a trot, all neat and silent. So I never saw them until they were nearly on me, I certainly never heard them, and I'm alive only because some lazy swab of a Rusky-Alasky carpenter had used a ship's copper bolt to mend one of the shafts of the handcart rather than shaping a new one: a ship's bolt being a powerful fastening used to clamp together the great timbers of a ship's keel. But this bolt was stuck into a hole drilled in the sawn-off stump of the right-hand shaft, such that it extended the shaft to a length easily grasped, and it was a loose-enough fit that I could pull it out in an instant, because I didn't have time to draw pistols or sword.

And then, my jolly boys, the bolt was six feet long, two inches wide and ponderous heavy. But for a man of my strength it makes the finest war club that the heart could desire, such that a wooden helmet — even awesomely carved and painted — is no defence. Mind you, I must warn you youngsters that when it comes to fighting for your life, there's nothing for it but to go in hard and loud, roaring in anger and swinging left and right with every atom of your strength, while bearing in mind that any attempt at fencing — or being clever in any way — is the surest way to get yourself killed. Forgive me if I have said this before — which indeed I have — but it is in your own best interest to take note of my words.

Smash-bang-crunch! Three of the rascals went down faster than you took to read this. One was very likely a dead 'un, from the way the bones of his head crunched. But although they went down, I can't speak for the rest, because the fourth Tlingit did indeed try to be clever, and drew all of my attention. Thus he took hold of Siupuk, threatened her neck with his knife, gabbled at me, and tried to back off, using her as a shield. But she wasn't having it, and she wriggled and beat at him with elbows, then most neatly hooked her leg around his till the pair of them stumbled and went over. After that, it was one kick to get her out of the way, followed by a two-handed swing of the bolt to split the helmet, and a second to end the battle with Tlingit brains all over my boots. So that one really was dead, believe me. He was the deadest Tlingit in Alaska.

I stood gasping, sweating and shaking, as you do after a fight, and wondering what to do because I didn't know where to go. "Come," says I to Siupuk. "We hide. No noise." Then there came a whole volley of musket fire from the direction of the beach, then the *boom* of a ship's guns, and while we stood wondering, a still heavier gun spoke, with a thud that shook the leaves of the trees.

"Come! Come! Hide!" says Siupuk. "Hide! Then later we go."

"Go where?" says I.

172

"Hide, hide, hide!"

So that's what we did, with her leading. I had no better idea, something bad was afoot on the beach, and the Tlingit were out in force again, while Siupuk seemed adept at woodcraft. Thus she pushed into the deep of the forest, found a hollow in the ground, and pulled me down to lie with her, and the pair of us enclosed in leaves, twigs and branches, neat as a coverlet. At first we lay there with myself exhausted from the fight, and no use to anyone, in any sense whatsoever. But after a while, what with being snug and close, and her so fresh and warm, we *did* take that "walk in the forest" after all, because it's amazing how you can wriggle out of your clothes without even getting up. Mind you, once we came to close action with nothing between us, I was surprised by the tough muscles in her arms and legs. Not that it stopped either of us, and we went at it hammer and tongs.

So here I must make apology for the bad example which I set you youngsters after all my advice on how to preserve your precious lives, because with the Tlingit wandering the woods, the pair of us should have kept still and quiet, and not bumped about so much, with some squeals and groans besides. But sometimes, my jolly boys, you just can't help yourself.

Then later, having wriggled back into our clothes, Siupuk began to amaze me in several of ways. To begin with she really was adept at woodcraft: and she was so good at giving silent commands by sign language, that you'd have thought her a sergeant of light infantry. But there was even more. She led me through the trees, going I knew not where, and she found the handcart full of furs! There it was, with the copper bolt lying on the ground among the four dead Tlingit ... except that one wasn't quite dead. He was twitching and trying to call out, which he couldn't do because of the damage I'd done him, and which I'll spare you the description of. The best he could do was gasp, but he soon stopped doing that, because — having first raised a hand so I should stand fast — Siupuk crept forward, knelt on the Tlingit's chest, lifted his chin, drew a knife and slit him from ear-to-ear. I'd never seen a woman do that before — never before and never since — and it made me gasp louder than the Tlingit! Then, even before he'd stopped spouting blood, she was hauling some sort of pack off his shoulders, and rummaging in the other two Tlingits' packs and stuffing things in the first one. All that in seconds, then she was beckoning me to follow her again.

So I followed her. I followed her for a considerable while in complete silence, stopping only once at a small stream where we could drink, and top up a leather water-flask from one of the Tlingit packs. Then off she went again, with myself in tow, and her steering by signposts I couldn't even see: types of tree? Bushes? Rocks? I didn't know then and I don't know now, but she knew. Much later, and with never a word said, she stopped and we made camp without a fire. She wouldn't have that and I agreed the sense of it. We camped under the half-light with the aurora above.

"Eat!" says she in a soft voice: the first word for hours. She said that, reached into her Tlingit pack, and took some dried meat and beans which I took to be Tlingit marching rations. Clever girl for knowing what to look for, or we'd have been very hungry indeed. But we weren't, because dried meat and beans, washed down with leather-flavoured water, goes down very well on some occasions.

Later we got together again — just to keep warm, you understand — and when we'd completed our manoeuvres, and I had a close hold of her and she of me, I whispered in her ear.

"Are we going somewhere or just running?" says I.

"We go to my father," says she.

"What?" says I, unsure I'd heard right.

"To my father," says she, "he is voyageur. We go to him."

"What's voyageur?"

"Talk tomorrow. Not now. Tlingit! Danger!" She wouldn't say more. She just put a finger to lips when I tried to speak. So I gave up and went to sleep.

Next morning, we carried on as before. She led, I followed, we didn't speak. I couldn't judge where we were, except that we were going somewhat downhill, until just after noon, we found what she was looking for, or rather *it* found *us*, when two men appeared out of nowhere in front of us. They were small fellows, with woollen caps on their head, checked shirts all greasy and worn, buckskin breeches, moccasin shoes and bearded faces. They weren't natives, but they had feathers in their caps, and each one had a native bow with an arrow drawn to full length, and aimed at me. A nasty moment indeed. But then it got worse as one of them said something in French, which language I abominate but can easily recognise. It was a challenge, most likely "*kee vallah*".

"Qui va la?" Who goes there? Fletcher's prejudice! In fact he could understand very much of French but would never admit it, nor would he ever have it written down except phonetically, and he would never, ever speak a word of it. S.P.

Fortunately, Siupuk surprised me again; she leaped forward, gabbling French, and the two men dropped their bows, and laughed and threw arms around her and danced up and down. One of them — the cheeky swab — even hugged her tight and kissed her on the lips and she kissed him right back, which I supposed was the way these folk behaved.

"Siupuk! Siupuk!" says they. They cried it aloud, as did the two men who'd crept up behind us with their bows, and that I never saw. So it's just as well that I hadn't attempted to fight. Then Siupuk broke free, took my hand, led me forward and gabbled out my name, gabbled a lot more while pointing at me, until the four blighters behaved just like the damn Russians: they grabbed me and kissed me on the cheeks. God shrivel and blast me if ever in all my life I should understand foreigners! Why do they have to do such things? Can't they behave like us?

Note well that the above is a very much shortened version of Fletcher's original rant, and with all the oaths and curses removed. In fact, and at great length, he expounded upon his oft-repeated conviction that the British and Americans were put on Earth by Almighty God, as an example of righteous conduct to all the lesser folk. S.P.

Nonetheless, and despite all, being kissed by a clutch of garlic-breathing Frenchies was a damn sight better than being shot full of arrows.

Then, once I'd shoved them off me, Siupuk laughed, led me forward into a considerable and carefully hidden camp. It was right next to a wide, slow-flowing river which I'd never have guessed was there, since it was surrounded by dense forest, and it was a landing place as well as a camp since there were five great big native canoes, hauled up on a little beach and laid on their sides. They were made of birch-bark stretched over cedarwood frames, sewn with spruce roots and caulked with a gum made of pine sap mixed with fat. Very neat and lovely they were too, and most excellent fine for their purpose, but hugely bigger than those of the native peoples.

The canoes I saw were near forty feet long, six feet wide in the waist, narrowing sharply to up-curving bow and stern. They were propelled by at least a dozen men paddling — six on each side — while one steersman stood at the stern with a long paddle and another at the bow. They were built for cargo, the cargo was fur, and each canoe would carry at least three tons of it. They were voyageur canoes, and the voyageurs were all around me, standing up from their camp fires, and pressing forward grinning, and what a swaggering company they were too because voyageurs, my jolly boys, were the men who used the extensive rivers of North America as trade routes linking the city of Montreal to the vast interior of the continent. They were tough, active fellows who could paddle all day and half the night, singing songs to keep the stroke time. They feared nothing: not rocks nor shoals nor hostile natives, and certainly not the British or Americans, since they were proudly French, which is to say Royalist, Bourbon French from the days before the revolution and the days before the British grabbed Canada in the war of 1759.

You youngsters must surely know my views on anything French, and if you've read earlier volumes of these memoirs (Editor's note: see *Fletcher and the Blue Star*) you will recall that I was in Frenchified Canada in 1801 — in Quebec, to be precise — and I didn't like it one bit, for its festering hatred of the English. But I took to the voyageurs something strong, since they were as close to seamen as can be found inland. They were resourceful and ingenious, intelligent and bold, and they knew all the tricks of the native peoples in living off the land right down to using bows, not guns, when there was a need to keep quiet for fear the Tlingit were about.

Of course, I didn't know any of this when first I saw them, but during the weeks I was in their company I had time to learn, and one of the first things I learned was how very lucky I'd been in taking care of Siupuk. I learned that because of one very tall fellow, a man in his fifties, most handsome and confident, who came forward among the voyageurs with the manner of being a leader, which indeed he was. He had blond hair just like Siupuk, and he swept her up in his arms and spun her round while the rest clapped and cheered and whistled.

"Papa! Papa!" says she, so I didn't have to guess who he was, and why we'd come to his camp. Then, when he'd done greeting her, he came to me and God bless him for holding out his hand like a man and not trying to bloody well kiss me. His name was Jean-Paul Blanchard, known to everyone simply as Jean-Paul, and I took to him at once and he to me. Thus he had us sit down by a fire where a meat stew was bubbling in a pot, and we were given a dinner on tinned plates, and even rum in tinned mugs. All the company — some sixty of them — sat round us other than their sentries, and Siupuk talked and talked with her father. He too had a bit of English — more than her, in fact — and the pair of them spoke it for my benefit, which was most mannerly of them. So I listened with great interest.

"First, Capitaine Fletcher," says Jean-Paul, "I thank you for what you did for my girl."

"Any decent man would've done the same, sir," says I.

"Perhaps," says he, "but you were there, and you did it! So I don't forget." He didn't, either. But then he was straight to business with Siupuk.

"What of the Russians?" says he. "Will there be more furs?"

"No, Papa, they are at war with the Tlingit. A big war."

"Ah," says he, "we heard sounds of battle. We heard cannon fire."

"Furs?" says I. "Do you trade with the Russians?"

Jean-Paul smiled. "Yes," says he, "they are forbidden to trade furs with us, but they do. They need the food we bring. So my daughter makes the trade. That's why she was sent among the Russians."

"So they trade with you as well as the Americans?" says I.

"Yes," says he, "otherwise they would starve." He looked at Siupuk. "So no more furs?"

"No, Papa. No more until their war is ended."

"No more furs? None at all? Not one?"

"Well, Papa," says she, "there are some."

"Where?" says he.

"In the woods. Two days' march. One day if we move fast. A wagon-load."

"Can you find it?" says he. "You who was born in the woods?"

"Of course," says she, and he leaned forward, took her hand and kissed it.

"This girl was raised as a tracker," says he to me. "She is tough. She ran with the boys as a child. She ran with them, fought with them, and was raised with them." He nodded. "She was raised by the Algonquin people."

"Algonquin?" says I. "I thought she was Aleut."

He laughed. "No, no, no," says he, "her mother is my Algonquin wife. It's good to have such wives."

"Oh," says I. "How many wives have you got?"

"Huh!" says he, and turned to his men and gabbled French. He was asking a question. They roared with laughter and shouted.

"Seece!" says they, which is the French word for six. Then he laughed too, and was instantly serious again. "You take four men," says he to Siupuk, "take them right now. Take good men that I choose. You find the furs, bring them back, fast. And then we go. We break camp and go back. We don't stay here if there is a war."

"Yes, Papa," says she, "but what about Capitaine Fletcher?"

"No, no," says Jean-Paul, "too big for the woods. He don't go with you!"

"But after that?" says she.

"Ah," says he, and looked at me, and shrugged. "What do you want, Capitaine? What can I do for you?"

178

"That depends on where you're going, sir," says I. "You said you're *going back*. What does that mean?"

"Back to Montreal, Capitaine. If my girl brings in more furs — a wagon-load — that will be plenty enough with what we already have. So we go to Montreal to sell the furs, and you are most welcome to come with us. You should come — you must come — because it is too dangerous here."

That's what he said, and once again I thought of my future in England, facing a hostile Admiralty, as opposed to a future in Boston. I thought hard but not long, because Jean-Paul was right. I'm too big for creeping through the woods alone, I'd never get back to Russian Alaska by myself, because if I even tried, then the Tlingit would have my tripes for tow ropes. So the decision was easy.

"Thank you kindly, sir," says I, "I'll come with you to Montreal, if I may, and then I'll make my way down to Boston." I smiled, thinking of past times in Boston, the people I knew there, and the money sleeping in my bank. "Best I should go there," says I, "where I can busy myself in trade, which I dearly love, and since America's at peace I'll be busy and safe."

That's what I thought, bless my innocence.

CHAPTER 24

The three scholars were most proper gentlemen. But the Count had the smell of politician about him. He reeked of it.

(Extract of a letter from Mr David Nash to his wife.)

I was content on leaving the library, but we must be very careful with Nash.

(Extract of a letter from Count Pavel to his mistress.)

Mr Nash welcomed these particular visitors at the foot of the stairs leading into the library. He did so, following direct orders from the state governor himself. So Nash received the visitors with his staff behind him, and a considerable luncheon prepared within, rather than the light refreshments usually given to visitors.

"It's this damned count," said Nash to his chief librarian, Mr Evans, who was noted for diligence and for being chairman of the Fifth Street Pistol-Shooting Club.

"Quite so, Mr Nash," said Evans. "The man's been everywhere in the town."

"Yes," said Nash. "State House, City Hall, Governor's residence."

"And all the rest," said Evans, "and now us! Last on his list, d'you think?"

"Not quite," said Nash, "he's at the penitentiary tomorrow."

Both men smiled at this small blessing, since — as in all cities — the institutions of Philadelphia were locked in eternal rivalry.

180

"Ah," said Evans, "here they come. Look! Three carriage-loads."

There were indeed three carriage-loads, since Count Pavel was now the foremost celebrity of Philadelphia, and a train of dignitaries was constantly in attendance on his tours of the city: these dignitaries and their ladies.

"What a shame it is, that we haven't got grenadiers to present arms," said Nash as the carriages rolled forward, raising dust.

"And a band of music," said Evans.

Then the carriages stopped, brakes were clapped on, horses tossed their heads, steps were let down, and a privileged selection of females — all in their finest — was alighting, assisted by a man in the most swaggering and magnificent of cavalry uniforms, complete with a huge fur hat and plume. The ladies gazed upon him in rapture, even as their husbands alighted from the second and third carriages. So Mr Nash had not the slightest difficulty in naming the man.

"Welcome to our library, Mr Count," said Nash, extending his hand. "We're entirely at your disposal." Nash smiled, expecting some hesitant reply from a foreigner awkward in English, but Count Pavel's reply was so perfect that Nash was taken aback.

"My dear Mr Nash," said Count Pavel, "I am delighted to meet you. For myself I am a simple soldier, but I come with scholars of the University of St Petersburg, who are most eager to discuss library matters with you." It was a clever speech, cleverly delivered, because Count Pavel managed — all in the same instant — to be charmingly polite, yet convey that he personally had not the slightest interest in *library matters*.

"I see," said Nash.

"Ah," said Evans.

Then Count Pavel turned his charm upon his accompanying squadron of over-dressed, middle-aged plumpfulness. "These ladies are surely known to you," said Count Pavel. "These lovely ladies." He bowed to them and they simpered most tremendously in reply.

"Indeed, ma'am, indeed, ma'am, indeed ma'am," said Nash nodding towards familiar faces. Of course he knew them: they were the dominant matrons of Philadelphian society. After that there was a considerable amount of introducing, and words and smiles, as the husbands of the matrons came forward in their dignity, every one a holder of some city rank or other and every one as fully dressed-up as his wife, and equally out for a jolly jaunt. But among them were three gentlemen who impressed Mr Nash very differently.

"May I introduce," said Count Pavel, "Professor Fitzhummer, Dr Barkovskiy and Dr Menchikov. They are among the finest intellects of St Petersburg University, and they are most anxious to meet the Principal Officer of the Library Company of Philadelphia." Once again, Nash was taken aback with his excellent English, as three men in their fifties came forward: intelligent faces, greying beards, and dressed in the unselfconscious untidiness of the true academic.

"My dear Mr Nash," said Fitzhummer, "we have heard much of your library."

"Even in St Petersburg," said Barkovskiy.

"Even so," said Menchikov.

Nash looked at them carefully. He looked for flattery or insincerity. But there was none. The three gentlemen meant what they said, and later, when Nash conducted the usual tour of the building, Nash noted with approval that while some of the Philadelphian visitors displayed wavering interest, Fitzhummer, Barkovskiy and Menchikov were clearly fascinated, clearly enjoying themselves and displayed the most remarkable knowledge of the history of the American Constitution.

"Of course this noble document represents the second attempt at a constitution," said Fitzhummer, gazing at the sacred vellum.

"Yes," said Nash, smiling.

"The first was the Articles of Confederation of 1777," said Barkovskiy.

"Yes," said Nash, impressed.

"Which failed," said Menchikov, "for a variety of reasons ..." Which he went on to list as Nash gaped in amazement. "So this final and perfect version—" Menchikov bowed towards the vellum — "was not signed until 1788." Very much more discussion followed: discussion between Nash and the three Russians, and so deep into scholarship it went, that all those not involved became bored and wandered off into clumps of more agreeable discussion concerning Philadelphia's news and scandals. Only Mr Evans and Count Pavel stayed right to the end, when servants reminded Mr Nash that luncheon was served. Thus Evans and Pavel stayed to the end and kept careful watch.

Later, when Count Pavel and his entourage had gone, Nash and Evans sat down to a well-deserved brandy, in Nash's office on the first floor. Evans spoke first, looking at a carriage clock mounted on a shelf.

'My apologies if I leave early tonight, Mr Nash," he said.

"Ah, it's Wednesday," said Nash.

"Club night!" said Evans.

"You and your pistols," said Nash, smiling. "Blowing holes in paper targets."

"It's a *discipline*, sir," said Evans, "of *self-control*. But what did you make of our guests today, Mr Nash?"

"I'm not sure," said Nash. "Not sure at all. The professor and the other two seemed straight-forward men, and I believe that they really wanted to come here."

"Yes, yes, yes!" said Evans. "Who'd have thought Russians would show such interest?" He took a sip from his glass. "What about the count?"

"Wouldn't trust him an inch," said Nash. "He'll have some reason for coming here, and it'll be something political. He's too smooth for his own good, that one. Cunning too, I shouldn't wonder. I'd be wary of him."

At the very same time, in Count Pavel's lodgings on Chestnut Street, a conversation was under way which was identical in tone except that it included someone who had not been at the library: Mr Ducaine of South Carolina, who — with other leading men of that colony — wanted to take that colony out of the Union.

"My dear Fitzhummer," said Count Pavel, "what did you think of Mr Nash?"

Fitzhummer looked at Barkovskiy and Menchikov, who nodded. "He's the one, Your Excellency," said Fitzhummer. "He's our man. He is ideally placed in American society."

Count Pavel turned to Ducaine. "Do you agree?"

"Of course," said Ducaine. "Everyone respects him. His opinion would be vital. It would be definitive."

"Good," said Count Pavel. "So we have found the man, and now we must secure him." He looked at Ducaine. "Have you any suggestions?"

"Yes, Mr Count," said Ducaine. "There are several possibilities."

"Good," said Count Pavel. "Meanwhile, we have done well so far. We went to the library late in our tour of this city, so that the library and its documents should seem unimportant to us, and we have achieved this objective. See how those who were with us today — these Philadelphians — were actually bored! They paid little attention to Nash, and that is good. But we must be careful of Nash himself. He is extremely clever. We must be wary of him."

CHAPTER 25

It would be a good idea now for you youngsters to find an atlas and look at a map of North America. You'll have to do that if you are to understand the vast journey that my voyageurs had to take, in order to get from Rusky-Alasky territory, across Canada, to come safe to Lachine, the traditional home port and destination of the east-bound voyageurs, which was located to the south-west of the city of Montreal.

First of all, to get out of Rusky-land, they had to find rivers navigable for their big canoes and with currents not so strong that the paddlers couldn't master them. Then it was a long and complex passage through the numberless lakes and rivers of the north-west, navigating without chart or sextant, entirely by tradition and memory. So the man who knew the way — Jean-Paul — was valued beyond gold and beyond diamonds. In rough summary, the route was from Lake Athabasca, down to Lake Winnipeg, finally skirting the northern shores of the colossal Lake Superior, then the colossal Lake Huron — each of them inland seas rather than lakes, such that the far shores are beyond the horizon. After that came a relatively easy home run down the Ottawa River to Lachine and Montreal.

But now, take a pause. Take a pause and consider the list of lakes and rivers that you have just read. Consider that, and the 3,000-mile journey involved. Consider that, and forget your modern overland journeys by railroad with restaurant-cars, sleeping-cars and a thundering steam locomotive hauling you along at a mile a minute. Forget all that, and think of a birch-bark canoe laden down with furs, while the voyageurs strained fourteen hours a day, at fifty strokes per minute, while singing their repertoire of songs to keep time, to keep morale, and keep going.

More important, sometimes the journey wasn't just hard and demanding: it was outright dangerous — so I'll give you just one picture of what was called "shooting the rapids", which we did times without number, on too many rivers to recall. But I'll describe just the first time for me, because although I was a seasoned mariner who'd rounded the Horn, it scared the willies out of me.

It was our second day on the river and I was no use as a paddler since it was a skill, like deep-sea rowing, which took time to learn. Besides that, Jean-Paul had looked at me the first time I went aboard. He'd looked at me and laughed.

"You are an elephant, Capitaine," says he, "too big, too heavy! We put you with the furs in the centre. You are good for ballast. Nothing more!" I suppose he was right. He was the expert after all, and with my weight I might have overbalanced the canoe if I'd sat at one side, to paddle. But I wasn't used to being useless in a boat, and it was embarrassing to see that Siupuk took a paddle right next to me, and dipped and heaved with the men. She was used to it. She'd done it before. But I had to accept that I took no part in navigation nor paddling, which was bad enough, but when we came to white water, it was terrifying. The trouble was that I had nothing to do than look on, while praying to a God who'd doubtless lost interest in me. But I prayed nonetheless, because it's what a man does when he's helpless.

The day's paddling began at dawn, always at dawn. There'd be a breakfast of thick pea soup with bacon strips, and ship's biscuit boiled in it to become soft, and a mug of sweet coffee to go with it. Then camp was struck, fires doused, all tackles and kit cleared away quick-sharp, then the canoes were launched which overnight had been hauled clear of the river, and turned on their sides as shelters. Then all aboard, with myself and the furs in the middle of the flagship — that's Jean-Paul's lead canoe — then all hands to the paddles, on a nice broad river, flowing through the most lovely pine forest, with hawks overhead, the sun rising and hardly a current worth mentioning.

It was all so smooth and calm that the paddlers of the five canoes, being easily able to hear each other, took to singing the same song. They sang it as a round, just as you may have heard "London's Burning" sung, with each crew starting a phrase *after* the one in front, so as to generate harmonies and melodies. It's hard to do, but these fellows — and Siupuk — did it without breaking stroke. They were fine singers, and a joy to hear. So weren't we all merry and bright, my jolly lads? Yes we were, until the nice broad river narrowed down to something nasty. So instead of lovely pine trees on either hand, there were greeny-black cliffs draped in weed, and the water roared in anger as it crashed into a dreadful hazard of rocks that seemed totally impassable, since our speed was now tremendous. Thus one touch of those rocks on our canoe would split it from end to end, and throw all hands into half-frozen, seething water, with the choice of either miserable drowning, or being battered brainless on the rocks.

I couldn't help looking back at Jean-Paul, who was stood in the stern as helmsman, heaving this way and that with his paddle. He saw my face and laughed, and he shouted something that nobody could hear over the dreadful noise of the river. And that wasn't the worst of it. It wasn't because — at first — while the river was maniac fast, and while Jean-Paul darted us round the rocks like a master, at least the river was level. But soon it wasn't! I heard what was coming before I saw it, because the noise of the river arose from being merely deafening, to absolutely painful. It was like those storms at sea, when you have to shout direct into another man's ear so he'll hear you. I heard the noise, and looked ahead and wished I hadn't.

What I saw was a white steam that utterly filled the canyon ahead, though it wasn't steam, but water smashed into such a dense spray as to rise up like a cloud. It rose up and the noise grew even louder and I knew for sure that I was going to die, because we were tearing lightning-fast towards a great waterfall, that must overset us, and break us and pulverise us into fish food.

Well, my jolly boys, I've faced the broadsides of three-deckers, the typhoons of the West Indies, and the tsunamis of Japan. But never in all my life was I so afraid as I was in that moment. Perhaps it was because I was helpless — I don't know. All I do know is that I felt a stab of terror, that couldn't possibly be worse … until it did become worse, because the canoe went at the waterfall like a charge of the devil's dragoons, and over we went, and down we went and my stomach leaped sickening up into my mouth at the ghastly drop, and I knew that I was done for.

But I wasn't. Perhaps Jean-Paul and his men were the finest in their trade — and I think that they were. Or perhaps the canoes were works of genius — and I think that they were. But for whatever reason, the canoes — all five of them — dipped their rounded noses, dived twenty feet at least, then hit with a splash that threw the waters out to either side and not back into the craft. I was strongly reminded of the way that a Newcastle collier like good old *Enable* would do the same and stay a dry ship. So it was a fine thing to see once I'd got used to it; not that I ever did, not entirely, because we faced these white-water perils time and time again. To the voyageurs it was the routine of their craft: to them, but not to me.

But, my jolly boys, by extreme contrast to the white waters, there were times when our adventures were dry-footed, shore-bound and precious slow. That was when we had to pass from one river to another, to make our way east. That meant a "portage", as the voyageurs called it, which was going ashore, unpacking everything from the canoes, then carrying everything from one river to the next, and of course that included the canoes themselves. If that wasn't hard enough, I would add that every damn single time we seemed to be going uphill, over rocky ground that tried to throw a man over or snap his ankle.

Fortunately — or perhaps not — I was very far from useless at the portages. I even got cheers.

"Up! Up! Up!" says Jean-Paul, at the first portage. He pointed to bundles of furs laid in neat rows by the beached canoes. They were crammed tight into so-called pieces, each one ninety pounds in weight which had to be carried to the next river a quarter-mile off. Jean-Paul grinned at me. "How many, Capitaine?" says he to me, and all the voyageurs and Siupuk were whistling and stamping and clapping hands.

"Oh, that's your game, is it?" says I, and I started by picking up a piece in each hand and I set off nice and steady.

"Oooooooof!" says all the voyageurs, and those that fancied their chances heaved up some bundles and followed on behind myself and Jean-Paul, who was also loaded with two. After that we grew foolish, as men will on such occasions, lifting more, and more, and staggering under stupid loads. But it was a pleasant day, with bright sun and a bit of wind to cool us, and if they were mad enough to compete with me for brute strength, then more fool them, and more fool me for giving the challenge. Thus we were at it for hours: trudging, burdened, uphill over a crest then sliding down through the bushes and trees to the next river, and each man piling his pieces into a heap to see which of us was the greatest ape.

I'll let you youngsters guess who won, and won by a considerable margin. They might as well have attempted fisticuffs against me. It is so easy for me that I never boast of it.

This is true. I have mentioned previously in these volumes that when quite old, and pressed by ladies of his party, Fletcher faced a professional pugilist at a county fair. He later praised the pugilist for lasting nearly half a minute before going down, and gave him a golden guinea for pluck. He took no pride in such matters. S.P.

Then we had a canoe-carrying competition with an identical result. But after that, Jean-Paul brought out the rum, which was traditional after a portage, and we were singing round the campfire late into the night. Since I was now champion gorilla, they pressed me for a song.

"*Chantez!* Chantez!" says they, with faces gleaming in the firelight and the rum well at work.

"Give us a song, Capitaine!" says Jean-Paul, and Siupuk snuggled up against me and whispered in my ear.

"Sing!" says she. "Sing an English song. Do you not have a song in England?" Well, my lads, I have a deep, loud voice, and I have been told that I keep melody fairly well. Also the rum was working in me as well as them. So I got up, stood forward, took a deep breath, and gave them one of my favourites, "Spanish Ladies", which tells of the sea life, and this is the first verse:

Farewell and adieu, to you fair Spanish ladies,
Farewell and adieu, to you ladies of Spain,
For we've received orders to sail for old England
And sail with the fear we shan't see you again.

They liked that, did the voyageeurs, and they joined in with the melody if not the words. So I was singing as if accompanied by an orchestra, and it was a fine moment. Siupuk gazed up at me as if I was something special, which I suppose in that moment I was, since I was very happy. Then when I was done, they gave a great shout, while beating the ground with their hands.

"Encore! Encore!" says they.

"Go on!" says Siupuk.

"Another!" says Jean-Paul. "Give another!"

So I did. I gave them my favourite song of any that I know, and which always makes me smile for its quick beat, its merry tune and its humour. I gave them "The Lincolnshire Poacher". This is the first verse:

When I was bound apprentice,
In famous Lincolnshire,
I served my master faithfully,
For nigh on seven year,
Till I took up with poaching,
Of which you soon shall hear,
For 'tis my delight of a shiny night,
In season of the year!

They loved that one right up to the stars. They loved it and they were so marvellous quick as to learn the chorus. They even got up and danced round and stamped feet and cheered. More than that, they adopted it and used it — with their own words — as a paddling song. It's a fine tune, after all, and well done him that made it, whoever he might have been, long ago.

So everyone slept sound and snoring that night. But we were up at dawn, next day. The voyageurs were like that.

Beyond that, as with my account of rounding the Horn and sailing up the coast of South America, while every day with the voyageurs was an adventure, it becomes tedious to repeat what sounds like the same thing over and over again. So I'll give just one more account of what happened on that long journey eastward. I'll give it for the fact that it was so different from everything else, and for the astonishing surprise that it gave me. It had to do with hot springs and the Makishwah people of Lake Makishwah, some miles south of Lake Athabaska.

Thus about a week after we set out, Jean-Paul came to me just before we embarked at dawn. He came up to me and Siupuk, and smiled.

"Today we take a bath!" he said, and she laughed.

"A bath?" says I.

"Yes," says he, and the voyageurs all looked on and grinned.

"Hot water!" says he. "Oceans of it!" That brought whistles and cheers, and many winks and nudges between the men.

"What's this, then?" says I to Siupuk.

"Wait and see," says she. So I did, since she wouldn't say more. Then later I noticed that the paddlers laid on even harder than usual, and their singing was most merry and loud. Then we came down a stretch of river, that became shallow, and clear, with the bottom looking up at us, while the trees and foliage around the river looked odd, and different, and there was a distinct smell coming up from the water. Then there was a shout from the man in the bow of our canoe, and he pointed down at the water and everyone cheered.

"Look!" says Siupuk, paddling hard and never breaking stroke. "Look at the river!" I looked and saw that the river was bubbling. It was the oddest thing I ever saw. There were big bubbles coming up from under the stones of the river bed, and as they burst, that strange smell came out. More than that, the river was warm and not cold. "Look ahead," says Siupuk, "it's the Makishwah. They make camp here. They trade with the voyageurs." I looked and saw a settlement of native people in a bend of the river. It was a village, almost a small town with two or three kinds of houses — Siupuk called them *maysons*. There were long houses built of heavy planks split from cedar wood, and roofed with wooden tiles. Then there were light-weight domes of deer-skin sewn over latticework wooden frames, and there were dugouts, half buried in the ground, built of tree trunks covered with turf. There was all that, and there were dozens and dozens of people: young, old, men, women and children and dogs yapping and barking. They were standing at the water's edge, waving and calling, and beating on drums, while the voyageurs yelled out greetings in return.

"Who are these people?" says I.

"I told you," says she. "Makishwah."

"What do they want?" says I.

"You'll see," says she.

So I had to be patient as the canoes beached and were hauled up, and secured, close to the biggest of the long houses, and Jean-Paul was embraced by a native — obviously a chieftain — with a fine robe and a headdress of bird feathers, accompanied by an elite group of elders, who wore lesser versions of the feathered headdress, and all of them were friendly. They couldn't have been more friendly.

Thus there was a parlay, where everyone sat down in a circle, and gifts were exchanged on either side. Or rather, gifts passed from Jean-Paul to the chieftain: axes, knives and a bundle of furs, though nothing came back the other way, while Jean-Paul chattered away to the chieftain, in whatever the Makishwah language was. Then food was brought out from the longhouse, and just enough was eaten for politeness, then the chieftain stood, waved his hands, and all the voyageurs cheered, and leaped and started clapping hands and singing, as the chieftain led them off through the village, and Jean-Paul laughed and threw an arm around my shoulder.

"Now for the bath!" says he. By then I was fed up with being kept in the dark, so I said nothing. But Siupuk came close and smiled. So I did ask a question.

192

"You said these people trade with the voyageurs," says I.

"Yes," says she.

"Well," says I, "I saw your father hand over some goods, but what do the Makishwah give in return?"

I was quite annoyed when she just laughed, so I plodded on as the voyageurs sang and clapped hands until we came to a series of small pools with steam rising out of them, and that odd smell stronger than ever. There was a great number of these pools: all about four or five feet deep, with smooth round stones at the bottom, and the waters bubbling up from below. Various scientific gentlemen have since explained to me that it was subterranean heat and gases that were the cause of this, such as those that send hot water rising out of the ground in our own city of Bath. But the customs of Makishwah-land weren't those of Bath.

Not one bit they weren't, since many of the rock pools were already occupied. They were occupied by Makishwah women: young women stark naked, waving and smiling. And after that, my jolly boys, I've never seen a company of men throw off their hats, boots and clothes with such joyful abandon, and some falling over with britches round their knees and laughing all the while. Nor had I ever seen such a collection of galloping tackles, all bouncing and jogging, and such a regiment of lily-white arses behind them, and believe me that Jean-Paul was in the lead, taking a header straight into the nearest pool. But this time, his men didn't cheer. They were too busy for that.

I think I actually blushed, and turned to Siupuk, wondering if I should cover her eyes. But she ran off, beckoning me to follow.

"This way," she said, "the best one is over there!" She pointed, I nodded and didn't need encouragement to run after her, through a natural screen of bushes to a pond that was positively seething with bubbles. Then she too threw off her clothes. It was the first time I'd seen her in entirety, and a very neat and tidy little creature she was too: built like an athlete, smooth and brown, and every part of her standing up firm. So I wasn't slow myself in getting ready for my bath. But I did stack my clothes in a neat pile: them and my pair of pistols. I wouldn't have wanted them to get wet, now would I?

Then I was in with a great splash, and the water amazingly warm, and I was grabbing hold of Siupuk, all slippery and lovely as she was, and wriggling most wonderfully. And so to work, though first I nearly drowned the pair of us. You see, once in water up to your chest, the entire business must be transacted standing up. Indeed this is obvious. But fortunately there is an established drill for this. It was a drill I learned at the Theatre Royal Dublin in September of 1803, where I entertained a lady in a box next to the dress circle, and which had curtains at the back for privacy. All this is in an earlier volume of these memoirs (Editor's note: see *Fletcher and the Flying Machine*) so you might like to read it for the instruction it will give your young selves.

Because, my jolly boys, this is how you must carry on. First your partner takes a double-arm grip around the back of your neck. Then you grasp cheeks and hoist, making sure that close contact is maintained, and the gun deck is stood to attention, and all parties merry and bright, which latter is most important, since it ain't just yourself that's in action, but the two of you. Then, finally, lower away! But take care, since aim must be by *feel* not *sight*, and this at a moment when urgency fills the mind rather than precision.

Consequently, what with the pair of us laughing fit to bust, we entirely ruined the dignity of the moment, slipped over and went bottoms up, gulping and swallowing and breathing water. But we recovered, and after a pause we managed to get things right a number of times and for a very pleasant while. But later came the great shock of surprise, while we were dozing in each other's arms, and relishing the warm water.

We heard voices and some voyageurs and Makishwah girls came through the bushes and past our pool. They were done bathing, out and dressed, and I recognised one of the men. He was the cheeky swab who'd kissed Siupuk on the lips. But now he was walking past, swigging a flask of something — doubtless rum — then passing it to the girl he had his arm around. He saw me and Siupuk, smiled, blew a kiss in our direction all casual and easy, and off he went with the rest.

194

"Who was that?" says I.

"That was Alphonse," says she.

"Do you know him?"

"Of course."

"Why"

"Because he's my husband."

"Your bloody what?"

"My husband."

"But, but ..." says I, half-strangled.

She just shrugged. "We are voyageurs," says she, "we have our own laws."

She was an odd little creature. One of the oddest that I ever met, and when we reached Lachine, she kissed me goodbye with a smile, and went off with Alphonse. But I was involved with too much else to worry about that. I was involved with the great love of my life.

CHAPTER 26

He paid in Russian gold, dear heart. He told a Russian fairy tale that nobody believes, and he was so drunk that he could do nothing with my girls, who laughed behind his back. But here's the tale …

(Extract of a letter from Mrs Louisa Yarwood, Madame of The Coffee-Pot Cat-House, Philadelphia, to her sister, Mrs Dora Banford, Madame of Banford's Bagnio, Boston.)

Precisely on time for his appointment, Ducaine rapped on the door-knocker of 25 Chestnut Street. It was dark and cold and he was wrapped in an overcoat. An obsequious butler answered, took Ducaine's hat and coat, and led him down a corridor full of young Russians in uniform. They were most polite and bowed heads in deference, but Ducaine received less respect when taken into the parlour, where several more Russians were sat around a table, likewise in uniform. They wore more elaborate uniforms and the wearers stared at Ducaine and said nothing. But Ducaine wasn't a little lamb that follows its mother. He was confident and full of himself. So he spoke.

"Evening, gentlemen! I'm here to meet the count, so what might you be doing here?" But there was no reply. Not in English at least, though one of the Russians said something in Russian. He pointed at Ducaine, chattered at the rest, and they all nodded heads in understanding.

"Ahhhhh!" they said, looking at Ducaine as if he were an exotic beast in a menagerie. But the butler was soon back, and he did have a few words of English.

"If the gentleman would follow me?" he said, and Ducaine was taken upstairs to find Count Pavel, sitting around another table with more Russians in extremely more elaborate uniforms all hung with gold lace and orders of chivalry. But Count Pavel stood to receive Ducaine, so the rest did the same.

"Good evening, Mr Ducaine," said Count Pavel, and waved a hand at his colleagues. "We have been to a reception at Carpenter's Hall, thus I took the opportunity to bring you here, in the presence of my most senior officers, to show you something, and to give you some final details."

Ducaine considered those words and his heart began to thump with anticipation. He stood looking at Count Pavel and his officers as they sat, and noted the chair kept vacant for himself.

"Do sit down, Mr Ducaine," said Count Pavel. "Will you take wine or brandy?"

Ducaine hesitated, but the emotion of the moment overcame reserve. "Brandy, sir; it's a cold night."

"Really?" said Count Pavel. "You should see Moscow in winter!" Count Pavel laughed. So his officers laughed, too. Ducaine looked at them.

"Do they speak English?" he said.

"Enough for my purpose," said Count Pavel.

"And what is your purpose, sir?" said Ducaine. "Why am I here, this night? You know what we want: myself and my party in South Carolina. We want out of this damned Union! So what will you do to help us, and what's in it for you?"

"More brandy, Mr Ducaine?" said Count Pavel. "I see that your glass is empty."

Ducaine held out his glass. "And what is it that you're going to show me?" he said.

Count Pavel nodded, stretched out a hand, and one of his officers drew a scroll from a velvet bag, then stood and bowed and handed it to Count Pavel.

"Look at this," said Count Pavel, "and be extraordinarily careful with it. You may unroll it on the table here, but do be careful with it."

Ducaine took the scroll, which was made of vellum, and looked to the light of a pair of candelabra on the table. He unrolled the document, laid it on the table, pressing it with his palms against its tendency to roll up. He stared at the document. He stared at it closely and Count Pavel and the rest stared at him. They stared at him, as he gasped, stood up out of his chair, gazed in amazement at the document, then turned to Count Pavel.

"So this is it," said Ducaine. "You told me about it, but I can't believe it! This ain't possible! Is it genuine? Is it real? Is it … ?"

"May I take it?" said Count Pavel. "It is very precious and I shouldn't want you to damage it in your passion." He took the document from Ducaine and passed it on, so that it went safely back into the velvet bag.

"But do you know what this is?" said Ducaine. "Do you know what it means?"

"Of course I do," said Count Pavel. "Did I not tell you about it?"

"Yes, but …"

"Oh do sit down and take another brandy."

"But do you know …" said Ducaine.

"Of course I know!" said Count Pavel. "This document breaks and shatters the Connecticut Compromise and the Union."

Ducaine blinked, gulped and fell silent. For the moment he had no words. But then he found some. He frowned and spoke.

"Where did you get it?" he said. "How in the name of Jesus did you get hold of it?"

"Does that matter?" said Count Pavel.

"Yes!" said Ducaine, and Count Pavel shrugged.

"It was given to me in England, by the celebrated Lady Sarah Coignwood, who got it from her late husband."

"That one?" said Ducaine. "I've heard of her. She's famous. But what I want to know is … is this document genuine?"

"My dear sir," said Count Pavel, "if Mr Nash proclaims the document to be genuine, then nothing else matters."

"Hmmm," said Ducaine. "I suppose that's true."

"It is emphatically true," said Count Pavel. "So this is the way forward. Mr Ducaine, you have been most helpful in identifying Mr Nash as the greatest expert on Constitutional documents in all the thirteen colonies, so thank you for that." Count Pavel bowed and Ducaine nodded and gulped brandy. "And now, Mr Ducaine," said Count Pavel, "it shall be yourself who leads Nash towards the document, because any such approach by anyone Russian would stimulate Nash into distrust and alarm. So you, Mr Ducaine, will act exactly as I shall tell you, and I shall then convey Mr Nash to Washington where the original will be presented to the Continental Congress, while several thousand printed copies will be distributed through the streets so that the document cannot be denied or hidden."

"But why take Nash to Washington?" said Ducaine.

"So that he shall convince the Continental Congress that the document is genuine!"

"Of course, of course," said Ducaine, holding out an empty glass which Count Pavel filled.

"The entire Union will then be thrown into chaos," said Count Pavel, "while you — Mr Ducaine — you and your party in South Carolina will take your opportunity to leave the Union. You will leave the Union protected and safeguarded by Russian troops and Russian guns."

"What troops? What guns?" said Ducaine.

"Be patient, sir," said Count Pavel, "let me explain. We shall not present the document to the Congress until I have been reinforced by a Russian fleet that has been sent after me, and which will rendezvous with my ship at …" He turned to one of his officers.

"In latitude thirty-seven degrees north, Excellency," said the officer, "the fleet will join us at the mouth of Chesapeake Bay."

"And the fleet will consist of?" said Count Pavel.

The officer spoke again. "Three line-of-battle ships, Excellency, plus transports bearing over two thousand foot, two hundred dragoons, plus a dozen field-batteries. Also engineers, a medical corps and transport wagons."

Count Pavel nodded and turned back to Ducaine. "While the Union government is in confusion, that force will take initiative."

"What initiative?" said Ducaine. "And what about the British, the Spanish and the French? Won't they react to what you're doing? The damn British fought a war to keep hold of America. So if they see you Russians ..."

Count Pavel raised a hand to stop Ducaine's flood of words. "Please believe me, sir," he said. "The supposed great powers will do nothing because everything will have been achieved in a swift coup de main." Count Pavel smiled and waved a graceful hand. "Indeed the entire world will stand back amazed at Russian efficiency in achieving our objectives."

Ducaine frowned. He wasn't quite following. "Efficiency?" he said. "Efficiency in doing *what*?"

Count Pavel paused.

"Now listen to me," he said with his most charming diplomatic smile. "Our first objective is to reward you — and South Carolina — by preventing any interference with your leaving the Union. Do you understand?"

"Ah!" said Ducaine, and he smiled too.

"Good," said Count Pavel, "but that cannot happen until you have dealt with Mr Nash. Do you understand? You must deal with him in a manner that I will explain later, with the result that he — who loves the Union so dearly — will be the man who blesses the document as genuine." Count Pavel pointed to the velvet bag. "The document that breaks the Union."

But Ducaine was struggling to get a grasp on all this enormity. He blinked. He shook his head. He puffed out his cheeks. Then finally he sighed and spoke. "I see," he said, "and what will you do after that? What will you do when we've broken the Union?"

"After that," said Count Pavel, "we shall take, capture and claim some territory *far* from South Carolina, as the basis for expansion of the Russian empire." He smiled again. "Though of course we shall make entirely sure that the chaotic remains of the Congress do not interfere with our plans. We shall do that by occupying Washington."

Ducaine was dazzled. He hated Washington. He hated that sweltering, mosquito-ridden town and everything that it represented. So he was amazed. He was stunned. He left the meeting shortly afterwards with his head spinning. It was spinning with ideas, spinning with hope and spinning with brandy. It was spinning with brandy because although Mr John Howard Ducaine was an exceedingly talented man — ruthless master, tenacious organiser and swift opportunist — despite all that, Ducaine had two faults.

The first fault was weakness for drink: especially ardent spirits. Once he'd taken one, he had to take more. Usually, he could stop himself taking the first. But if he took the first, he was lost.

The second fault was weakness for women: especially those who were young and fresh, like those to be found in Mrs Louisa Yarwood's Coffee-Pot Cat-House, which was no more than ten minutes' walk from 25 Chestnut Street.

CHAPTER 27

The love of my life is trade. Thus you youngsters should know that I never did choose the sea life, since I was press-ganged as an apprentice clerk and have ever since tried every means to get out of King George's Sea Service, only to be dragged back into it.

Indeed Fletcher loved trade, but note this further and tedious repetition of his supposed detestation of the sea life, while many times admitting his profound love of it, and of the Royal Navy in particular. S.P.

Thus I was happy to come to Montreal, which city was bound up with trade. It was bound up with the fur trade of the great interior, and with sea-bound trade, since Montreal lies on a great island within the Prairies river and the Ottawa river to the north-west, and St Lawrence to the south-east, and the St Lawrence is a sea-highroad leading to the Atlantic and all the coastal cities of America: Boston, New York, Philadelphia, Baltimore and Washington. Thus all those cities were now beckoning, and most especially Boston, where I was known, and knew people and had money in the bank!

But first I had to make my farewells to Siupuk and her father Jean-Paul, and the voyageurs who had become shipmates to me. This I did at Lachine, a combination of home port for the voyageurs and a major trading post for the furs they brought in. It was some way west of the city walls of Montreal, on a small river. It was alive with business, since many other voyageur canoes had arrived, and you should now forget all images of timber-built log houses of the wild frontier. Indeed you must, since the depot at Lachine was all stone buildings, with glass in the windows, counters, clerks, weights and scales and wagons and horses ready to carry off the furs. It was strange to see the fierce bargaining under way between weather-beaten voyageurs in their beards and buckskins, and fresh-shaven office clerks with white collars and clean fingernails.

But it was all very efficient, and Jean-Paul did our bargaining, being well known and respected, and of course it was all in French. But I went with him into the counting house, for the love of it and to see the action. I was further impressed to note that very much of the final payment for our sixteen tons of fur was by note of credit to Jean-Paul's bank, and believe me, my jolly boys, I was surprised that he even had one! But he certainly did. Apart from that, we came away with spending money in Spanish dollars, which as I've said were the world's currency. That went into a leather satchel along with the bill of payment.

"How do you pay your men?" says I, on the way out of the counting house. "They'll want coin, not paper."

"They see me later in Montreal," says he. "I pay them there. It's not good to carry too much money."

"Indeed," says I, "and what about my share?"

He gaped at me as if amazed. "Share?" says he. "Are you saying that you want money? I thought you came along just for my daughter!"

"What?" says I. "When I saved her life a dozen times? No, no, m'sieur, I'm due at least half of your profits." So he laughed in my face, and I laughed back in his, and we were off! We both enjoyed it. When we were done, he pulled out a paper from his satchel.

"This for you, Capitaine Englishman," says he, handing me a bill of payment made out to me, signed by him and by the senior clerk of the counting house clerks, but with a space left clear for the sum. He grinned at me. "I write in the sum later," says he, and he did too. What a man! We were almost brothers. More than that, he gave me a purse of dollars on top of what we'd agreed, and I would point out that the agreed sum was a very considerable one indeed, and my first personal taste of the vast profits to be made in the fur trade.

Later on, we enjoyed a farewell dinner in a big tavern built close by the depot. This *was* a frontier-style timber-and-shingle construction, with long benches, and serving girls who chuckled and giggled and sold a lot more than food and drink. So it was a good evening, with many embraces, and kisses on the cheek and tearful partings. I was used to such behaviour by then, but I didn't do much kissing. Neither did I kiss Siupuk, who smiled at me when we went into the tavern, then went and sat with Alphonse, her husband. But later on she did bring him to where I was sat with Jean-Paul, and she and Alphonse displayed the utmost goodwill. Then she said goodbye, and he gabbled at me in French with a big smile, and both of them waved and were gone.

I never did understand that woman. She was special to herself. She was unique. I never met one like her in all my years.

After that, we all slept in the tavern that night. We slept on the earth floor, but that was no hardship, since it's what we'd done for weeks. Then next morning I began the shift from being a frontiersman to being a gentleman, which had to be by stages. Thus first I got myself a thorough scrubbing with soap and hot water, in a tub that served as a bath. Then found a barber to trim my hair and shave me. Then I got into whatever clothes I could buy at the Lachine trading post. It was very hard finding anything big enough, but I did my best. Then I got a bag for my pistols and other traps, and hired a cart to take me into Montreal.

Montreal, of course, was within King George's realm, having been took off the French in 1759. So there was no more French nonsense after that, except that the city fortifications had been built by the French, who'd done the job with French thoroughness. So coming from the west, as I did, with the horse trotting and the driver whistling, we came to massive walls, and three huge bastions bristling with cannon, and red coats with muskets up on the walls, and at the gates. But there was a busy traffic going in and out and we were waved through without challenge.

It was a fine, lively town, with traffic and bustle on all the main streets. So I got the driver to take me to a good lodging house on the wharf side of Montreal facing the St Lawrence, then I paid him off and hired a room. Later I walked the wharf, and fortune favoured me, since I found a fine three-masted trader — the *Hingham Bay*, out of Massachusetts — loaded and bound for New York, and ready to sail in three days' time. This was indeed a piece of luck, since otherwise I might have waited weeks for a ship. So I went aboard, and made a deal with the captain then and there, to give me passage and put in at Boston, since Boston is the northernmost of America's principal cities, with New York and the rest to the south, below. This was a huge relief, and we sealed the deal in rum.

"Cap'n Fletcher," says he, raising a glass in his stern cabin, "pleasure to have you aboard." He'd recognised me, you see. Groves was his name, Captain Arthur Groves of Colesharbor, Massachusetts, who was master and part-owner of *Hingham Bay*. He'd spotted me even as I came up the gangplank, which is the penalty of being as big as I am, and having that white streak in my hair, and the press reporting my career as they do, complete with descriptions of my person. So it was common for me to be recognised, and commonest of all to be recognised by seamen, who necessarily take interest in seamanly adventures.

Of course, not everyone knows me all the time, but it happens a lot and it's troublesome when I want to be discreet. But there it is, I had to put up with it, and at least I went down Groves's gangplank content with having got a swift passage to Boston.

After that, I found a good tailor to kit me out properly with fitted clothes together with linen, a hat, boots and even a pocket handkerchief, which were to be ready next day following an advance payment, which was a heavy payment but necessary, since a matter of business was involved: business involving money.

For here's a great truth. When most men get hold of money they think they've done well, and either spend it or hide it away in a bank. But when a man of business gets money he thinks, how can I increase it? I was therefore determined to do this, to give myself a proper launch into the life I was seeking in Boston.

So, next afternoon, I presented myself to Jean-Paul's bank: the Commerce Generale of St Jacques Street, facing the Place d'Armes. It was a fine, ponderous building, in white stone with a dome on top of a triangular pediment, supported by Grecian columns, and a broad row of steps to the fore, with all the gentry of the town passing by in admiration.

In addition there was a pair of heavy minions on the big double doors — minions in livery with shiny buttons and laced hats — ready to swing the doors open. So I nodded sternly and pressed a Spanish dollar into each man's hand. That was vastly excessive for a tip. But it was policy, because if you're trying to get money out of a bank, then first you have to prove that you don't need it, and the doormen would certainly gossip.

Once inside I sighed with pleasure, since it was vast and high with great windows, marble floor, the soft hush of finance under way, and long counters with thin brass railings on top, to separate the staff from the clients. Then, as I entered, every eye was on myself since I am so big. I was immaculately dressed, and I've always had the manner of a man who takes no nonsense. So it was very easy for me to dominate the little grubs who sat on tall stools behind their brass railings, peering out at the world. So I picked a likely lad, and slid Jean-Paul Blanchard's bill of payment under the railing and into his hands.

"I'm Fletcher," says I. "Late commodore of His Majesty's Sea Service. I shall need payment on this bill, and I shall need to speak to the manager in person." Now, here I was taking a risk. I was taking the risk that word might have reached Montreal of my dismasting that revenue cutter, and if so the bank might call in the colonial government to look me over. But as I've said, it's hard for me to pass unnoticed, so it's best to come straight out with who I am.

Meanwhile, the clerk took a look at the bill of payment, and another look at me.

"Yes, sir!" says he. "Yes, Commodore Fletcher! At once, Commodore Fletcher!" Then he beckoned at a messenger boy, whispered into his ear, sent him running and within minutes I was in the manager's office — all mahogany furniture and velvet curtains — sat facing the manager and his chief clerk behind a big desk. So I gave them my prepared story, and you youngsters must take careful note that a story must be delivered with utter confidence and boldness if it is to be believed, when in reality it is a steaming pile of codswallop. And so:

"I am here in the King's service," says I, sitting straight and glaring them in the eye.

"Oh?" says they, and looked at me closely. Then they looked at one another. Then they frowned for a long, and tense, and nasty moment, since they were mature and serious men with mature and serious responsibilities. But I stared back as if never a doubt existed, I knew that my bill of credit from Jean-Paul made me worthy of respect, and finally — God bless their innocent souls — they believed me! I saw it in their eyes. So I nodded and pressed on.

"I may not give details of my responsibilities," says I, "but I must ask, in the King's name, for absolute confidentiality."

"Yes, yes!" says they, nodding to each other.

"Now gentlemen," says I. "You have seen Monsieur Blanchard's bill of hand?"

"Yes, yes!"

"Good," says I, "since I shall need payment of three times that sum ... and in *gold*." I waved a hand in depreciation. "Silver is useful for tips and small expenses," says I, "but my purposes are political, and I can at least tell you that there is an *indispensable* need to demonstrate the capacity of Montreal's institutions to pay in gold!"

"In gold, sir?" says they.

"In gold, gentlemen!" says I. "And the monies must be delivered to my ship with an armed escort."

"Armed escort, sir?" says the manager. "That means soldiers from the garrison."

"Which is usual in such cases," says the chief clerk.

"Well and good," says I, "providing they know nothing of my mission."

"All this can be arranged, sir," says the manager, "but there remains the question of ..." He paused. "Of how might the bank be recompensed for sums beyond that covered by Monsieur Blanchard's bill of payment?"

"Easily, sir," says I. "I shall sign any document that you may prepare, declaring that you acted properly, and thereby enabling you to obtain recompense from the colonial government."

"Excellent," says they, smiling in relief.

"But gentlemen," says I, "I must charge you in the King's name not to seek recompense until at least a week after my ship has sailed. This is vital to my mission."

After that things went smoothly, and soon my money — in golden guineas — was sent aboard *Hingham Bay* under guard of a dozen men of the 14th Foot, with bayonets fixed, a beating drum and a pinky-faced ensign in front with his chest puffed out and his young voice yelling at the people to make way. I was already aboard, and the little pip-squeak got me to sign a receipt, which was one of several documents that the bank had drawn up, all of which I signed with a flourish and a solemn frown. I signed such that the bank might recover the extra two-thirds of its money, though for all the good these documents would do in that respect, they'd have been better employed as bog-house bum-fodder.

So things went smoothly, and I was comfortably aboard ship, where I had a little cabin to myself and the crew were prime seamen. But I worried non-stop until we upped anchor and Groves was working his ship down the St Lawrence, heading for the open sea. I worried, even with the ship heeling hard and the river thrashed into foam under the bow, for she was a fast ship, and Groves worked her hard. I was worried because there'd been a couple of armed brigs flying King George's colours anchored at Montreal and all the while I feared that the bank might come to its senses, go to the Governor and have a chase sent after me.

So as *Hingham Bay* tore down the St Lawrence at a fine rate of knots, I was togged out in my nice new seafaring rig, bought from a wharf-side warehouse — pea jacket, fur cap and sea-boots — as I stood at the stern just aft of the mizzenmast, ship's wheel and binnacle, while Captain Groves conned his ship. I was braced against the heel of the deck, but couldn't help going to the rail to look back towards Montreal. I kept doing that and Groves was a sharp 'un and he noticed. So he nudged his first mate and called out.

"Have you left something behind, Cap'n Fletcher?" says he. "Or is someone in Montreal coming after you?" He, the mate and the helmsman all grinned. But I chose not to discuss the matter. I looked ahead, down-river, where we were just coming through the shoals and dangers of the Grodeau Islands into the broad expanse of Lake Saint-Pierre — ten miles wide and fifteen long — which I would have found a considerable relief in the ease of navigation. But Groves had taken his ship through the islands with never a pause, and that was either risky or fine seamanship if a man didn't know the passage well.

"I see you don't use a pilot, Mr Groves," says I.

"No, sir," says he. "I know the St Lawrence and I ain't payin' for what I don't need."

"Won't pay?" says I. "Even in a river full of islands? And never a reef in your t'gallants and the ship running so hard?"

"Ah-ha!" says Groves. "*T'gallants*, says you? *No reefs*, says you? So what sail would you set, if'n you was master?"

I'll spare you the discussion that followed, for it would sound like a cannibal's gobbledegook to a landman, but Groves and I enjoyed it and I was reminded of my bargaining with Jean-Paul. Then, later, the discussion turned to the ship herself, *Hingham Bay*. She was a true Yankee beauty, and an early ancestor of the famous clipper ships that came later. She was near 300 tons burden, flush-decked, heavily sparred to wear a great spread of canvas, and while she bore mainsail, topsail and t'gallant on the fore and main, the mizzenmast bore only a huge spanker with gaff and boom, balanced by a spread of staysails to the foremast. She was built for speed, and if that meant a sharp prow and a wet ship, with spray coming aft from the bow, then that was the price you pay for speed, since no ship can have it all, not in this world, my jolly boys, not in this life!

So those were her sailing qualities, and in addition I saw at once — in fact I'd seen it even as I first went aboard her in harbour — I saw that she was pierced for a line of guns. I counted ten ports each side, even though they were mostly secured with lids lashed shut and just four guns mounted — twelve-pounders they were — two on either beam, which was not unusual in those days when most merchant ships went armed. But if need arose, then *Hingham Bay* could turn herself into a lightning-fast frigate, so I easily guessed that she had another purpose entirely than trade, and Captain Groves was most happy to admit it.

"She's been a privateer, Cap'n Fletcher, since you ask," says he, with his head on one side. "Though who's askin'? Are you an Englishman or an American?" I just smiled, since I never could answer that question. He smiled back and waved a hand at his ship. "Damn fine privateer she was too," says he. "Last time we was at war with the British, was that little war in 1794: the one that everyone's forgot!" He shook his head wistfully. "We was licensed by Congress to 'take and capture'." He shook his head again and sighed. "And never in all my years did we get so rich."

I nodded. It was the way of any country without a strong navy, that in time of war it would issue letters of marque to private-built warships to go out and chase the enemy's merchant fleets, keeping a good share of the ships and cargoes taken. The privateers usually avoided real warships, but they were a serious threat to the enemy's seaborne trade and both the French and the Americans were famous for their privateers.

"But what of the US Navy?" says I. "Hasn't the Congress built ships of war? I remember some frigates, but no ships of the line."

"Hah!" says Groves, and looked to his first mate in a disgust that was deeply shared, before turning to me. "Congress, says you? Congress? Them whoreson, sonovabitches? Them pollywog bastards as won't see the need for a real, seafarin' navy? They *talk* about building ships of the line, but they damn sure never find the money."

"So what ships has the US Navy got?" says I.

"Well," says he, "there's brigs and launches and there's gondolas with oars for inland work. But there's just three big ships, which is frigates all three. There's *Declaration of Independence*, which is laid up in Charleston, Carolina, not fit for sea, and there's *Constitution* away in the Mediterranean fighting the Barbary pirates, and *Founding Fathers*, which is manned and ready in Boston."

"Yes," says I, "I've heard of them." Indeed I had. I'd actually served aboard *Declaration* as told in an earlier volume of these memoirs — the one concerning the Glorious First of June — while *Constitution* and *Founding Fathers* were famous as a new breed of super-heavy frigate mounting a prodigious battery. They were also fast and densely built of thick timbers. So thank you Captain Arthur Groves for sending my mind in that particular direction, and thank you for a good passage past Quebec, Anticosti Island, Nova Scotia, then westward and southward past Maine and New Hampshire, to Massachusetts. We were just three weeks at sea, and when finally we approached Boston, even Captain Groves wanted a pilot to con his ship through the vast sandbanks of Noddle's Island, which lay to the north of Boston, and the Dorchester Flats to the south, both of them the graveyard of unwary skippers.

And so to my favourite city of America: Boston, which in those days was on a peninsula that looked very similar in shape to the North American continent, with the vast outflow of the Charles river to the west — leading into the interior — and which on the eastern side had more piers and quays reaching out towards the Atlantic than an octopus regiment has arms. Better still, Boston threw up a skyline of steeples, domes and grand buildings to rival any town in the Americas, Boston's population was dense, the smoke rose from a thousand chimneys and the people were eager for business. I'd been there many times before and I had friends there, and I felt as if I was coming home. But this time I was coming home rich! So I was very happy, because I'd mapped out my future and I was going to be one of the great trading businessmen of the Americas.

Which all goes to prove the old saying, that if you want to make God laugh, then tell Him your plans.

CHAPTER 28

Mr Nash was in such a passion of anxiety as to be not his normal self. I feared for his safety and did my best to prepare him against harm.

(Extract of the 1805 diary of Mr J. C. Evans, Chief Librarian of the Library Company of Philadelphia.)

Ducaine was useful, but proven to have a loose mouth. My agents have therefore acted as follows:

(Extract of a single, handwritten page hidden among Count Pavel's correspondence and written in a Cyrillic-based code.)

Mr and Mrs Evans were at breakfast in the charming little room that was entirely the work of Mrs Evans, who had planned it and decorated it. The room looked out on their small garden through glazed French windows that had cost a fortune, and Mrs Evans had likewise planned the garden, which was her great pleasure, though perhaps not as great a pleasure as a good breakfast, since Mrs Evans loved her food — although slim and shapely, she was a connoisseur of cuisine.

Then everything went wrong. They heard the thundering on the front door, even where they sat at the back of the house. They heard the maid answer the door, the bellow of a familiar voice, the heavy footsteps over planked floors, then the breakfast-room door burst open and there was Mr David Nash, unshaved, distraught, unkempt and the buttons of his coat and vest unfastened.

"Evans!" said Nash. "We must talk, and talk alone! Just you and I!" He stood over the table, with its cutlery, china and silver, and stared straight at Evans, not even acknowledging Mrs Evans, even though Nash was the most polite and charming man where ladies were concerned, and even though he knew Mrs Evans well. Then Nash stepped forward, beat the table with the flat of his hand so that everything jumped, and the milk jug went over with a splash. "We must talk," he said, staring hard at Evans, and totally ignoring his wife. "We must talk, just you and I! Now! Now! Now!"

Evans looked round, hoping for inspiration. He saw the maid, in her mob-cap and apron, stood gaping in the doorway. He saw the look of outrage on the face of his wife, and the heavy frown she directed at himself. But most of all, he saw his good friend David Nash in such a condition of stress and anguish as had never been seen in him before. This was Nash who always smiled, Nash who told stories of pretend, Nash who was the most deep and formidable of scholars. It was beyond belief.

Then Nash sat in a vacant chair, and did something else beyond belief. He leaned forward, threw his face into his hands and wept. His shoulders heaved. The tears flowed. Evans was enormously embarrassed, and knew not what to do. But Mrs Evans did. She got up, went to Nash and threw her arms around him.

"There, there," she said, just as she'd said to her children when young. "My poor fellow. There, there, it's never so bad as we fear."

"But it is, ma'am," said Nash, mumbling between his fingers. "It is most dreadfully bad."

"Is it your wife, sir?" said Mrs Evans. "Or your children?"

"No," said Nash, "they are in New York. They are well."

"Then is it yourself? Are you afflicted with illness?"

"No, ma'am."

"I see," said Mrs Evans, and she stood up straight, suspecting some crisis of money, trust or even morality, for who knew what a man did in his private moments? "In that case," she said, "I shall withdraw and leave you to speak to my husband."

"Bless you, ma'am," said Nash. "Bless you."

So Mrs Evans left, closing the door firmly behind her, and Nash and Evans had a conversation that Evans never forgot.

"Sir," said Nash, "a man has come to me. A man called Ducaine. He is a planter of South Carolina, and deep in politics. I did not like him. Not at all, even before he showed me the document." Nash groaned and raised hands to his face again.

"What document?" said Evans.

"I couldn't believe it," said Nash, in real agony, and stared at the floral wallpaper as if Evans were not even present.

"But *what* document?" said Evans again.

"It was not the original version," said Nash.

"Can you not tell more?"

"It was a printed copy. But everything else rang true."

"Sir, you have not told me what was in this document."

"The consequences are appalling."

"Sir?"

"If the original version is indeed true …"

"My dear Nash, you've not told me what this document is!"

"If true — and I am promised sight of the original — if true …"

Now Evans frowned. He was annoyed.

"Sir," he said. "In heaven's name! What are we talking about?"

"Appalling! Appalling!" said Nash, and at last turned to face Evans. "Listen, old friend. I am to be taken this night, taken by Ducaine to see the original document — the supposed original — so that I can see that it reflects the will of the Founding Fathers."

"Founding Fathers?" said Evans.

"Yes!" said Nash. "The men who framed the Constitution."

"My dear Nash," said Evans, "what the damnation are we talking about?"

"I cannot say," said Nash, "but I am to be taken by Ducaine — whom I do not trust — taken by him to see the original …" He paused. "So that I can pronounce that it is genuine and valid and true!" He shook his head in disbelief. "*Me?* That *I* should do this? *Me!*"

214

After that, Nash was in such a state that Evans could get no more from him. Nothing about the document, nor where Nash was to be taken, nor anything other than horror and despair. Finally, since Evans believed that a little help is worth a deal of pity, he told Nash to stay seated, went into his study and came back with a pistol case that he opened on the table. He took out two small pistols from their green-baize nest among the instruments of priming and loading. Each pistol was less than the length of a man's hand, and was neat and snug and smooth.

"From my collection," said Evans. "These are by Manton of London. Finest maker in the world. They are box-lock pocket pistols. They have folding triggers that spring out when they are cocked, and being screw-barrel breech loaders they shoot very hard. They are deadly at close range, and I shall load them now, and you must take them with you tonight." He looked hard at Nash. "I don't even know why you've come to me, and if you won't say what's afoot then I can do no more, but for God's sake take these pistols with you!"

Later, after dark, a carriage stopped outside the library on Fifth Street. Nash always lived there when his wife and children were away, so as to be close to his work. He loved his work and he loved the library. He was always happy to be in the library, but tonight he was profoundly unhappy and his insides twisted in spasms of pain as he stood in front of the library steps in hat and topcoat. He stood back as the coachman reined in, and clapped on the brake. Then the coachman leaned back, and beat his hand on the side of the coach in signal of arrival. But he needn't have bothered. The door was already opening, and Ducaine leaning out and beckoning.

"Come up, sir!" says he, but Nash was unsure. He looked up and down the dark street. Nobody was about. He looked into the carriage. It was an English-style Hackney coach: enclosed, seats for six, a single horse and the driver on a box at the front. Nash looked into the dark interior. He thought he could see more than one figure in the dark.

"Who's with you?" he said. "Who's there?"

"Mr Nash," said Ducaine, "you have seen what the document contains, haven't you?"

215

"Yes," said Nash.

"So here's your choice," said Ducaine. "You come with me right now, or the original of the document goes aboard a ship destined for Washington to be presented to Congress, to let them decide if it's real."

Nash gasped. "No! No!" he said, snatching at the chance that he might be able to prove the document false.

"Then get up in this carriage right now!" said Ducaine.

Nash groaned, but put his foot on the step and got into the carriage. There were two big men in dark clothes as well as Ducaine. They looked at Nash and said nothing. They just sat with arms folded.

"Who are they?" said Nash.

"Friends," said Ducaine, and sneered.

"What *friends*?" asked Nash.

"Just friends," said Ducaine, as the carriage lurched forward and the horse got into a trot.

"Where are we going?" said Nash.

"To see the document," said Ducaine.

"But where?"

"You'll see."

Nash was afraid. He was very afraid. But what could he do? He had to see the document. He had to find that it was a forgery, a mistake, a piece of malice: anything! He was deep in his own thoughts as the carriage went through the neat, square-grid streets of Philadelphia and headed for the Delaware River, and finally stopped at the entrance to a wharf looking out over the night-gleaming water, with the moon high above, and Petty's Island in the mile-wide span of the river. The night was cold and there was a strong wind.

"We get out here," said Ducaine.

"Where are we?" said Nash.

"Cutler's Wharf," said Ducaine.

"What's that?" said Nash.

"Just get out," said Ducaine.

Nash got out and looked around. They were next to a pair of gates that led into the wharf. The gates were open, and lights shone from

216

windows of a small building within the gates. Nash supposed that to be the offices of the wharf, and a small warehouse lay beyond it. But mainly he noticed that there were more large men in dark clothes standing by the gates, and they stamped to attention in military style, as five more men came out of the office building and walked towards the carriage.

Nash recognised the leading man. He was the Russian count who'd come to the library; the count who was the toast of Philadelphia.

"Good evening, Mr Nash," said Count Pavel, "how very kind of you to come."

Nash knew at once that he'd been deceived: very seriously deceived.

"What's this?" he said to Ducaine. "You never mentioned any Russians!"

"Just get out," said Ducaine.

"Please do," said Count Pavel, stretching out a hand to help Nash, who hesitated long enough for one of the big men in the carriage to push him out into Count Pavel's arms.

"Dear me," said Count Pavel, "I do hope you are not hurt, Mr Nash?"

"What's going on?" said Nash. "Why are you here?"

Count Pavel smiled. "I am here, Mr Nash," he said, "because I need to see your face when, finally, you are presented with the original document."

"And who are these men with you?" said Nash, looking at the four who stood behind Count Pavel.

"My leading officers," said Count Pavel, "who also need to see your reactions."

Nash did his best to break away and run. He tried hard, but he was seized and held and could do nothing other than try not to stumble as he was dragged into the office building and into the light, and forced into a chair.

"What are you doing?" said Nash to Count Pavel. "This is America! You can't do this!"

"Can I not?" said Count Pavel. "My dear Mr Nash, we could discuss that point *ad nauseam*, but it would prevent your looking at the document. If you look in front of you, you will see that it is already laid

217

out before you for your inspection. I believe you to be this nation's greatest expert in such matters: expert in the examination of vellum, calligraphy, guide marks and even the colour of ink, not to mention ..." Count Pavel stopped. He stopped and smiled because Nash was already studying the document, and the expression on his face was everything that Count Pavel desired.

Later and outside, Count Pavel spoke to Ducaine.

"And are you pleased? And satisfied?" said Ducaine.

"Indeed, sir," said Count Pavel.

"It's real, then?"

"It is real."

"What will you do with Nash?"

"He will go aboard my ship en route to Washington."

"What will you do with him there?"

"He will stay aboard ship, and I shall bring people to see him."

"What people?"

"Everyone of importance."

"But will he say the document is real?"

"He cannot help himself. If it was false he'd say so with joy, but it is not false, and he knows it, and his despair will prove it to others. The more miserable he gets, the more proof he gives."

"And at the same time, you'll flood Washington with the printed copies?"

"Oh yes."

"So," said Ducaine, "what about me? What about South Carolina?"

Count Pavel smiled, waved a hand and the large men in dark clothes came forward and seized Ducaine. They seized him rather harder than they had seized Nash.

"What? What?" said Ducaine. "We have an agreement, a bargain, we have—"

"Be silent!" said Count Pavel. "Mr Ducaine, it is easy to admire — or even *like* — an honourable enemy. Thus I admire Mr Nash, because he is loyal to the cause he believes in. But, my dear Mr Ducaine, nobody admires a traitor — and you are a traitor to the nation that bred you."

218

"Traitor be damned!" said Ducaine. "I'm loyal to South Carolina, not the damned Union!"

"Rubbish!" said Count Pavel, and spoke to the men holding Ducaine. He spoke in Russian.

"What was that?" said Ducaine, "What were you saying?"

"I told them to fetch the sack."

"What sack?"

"The sack for your body once they have strangled you. When that's done, they will weight the sack with stones, tie it up tight, row you out into the river and drop you in." He smiled. "They will do this because you talk too much when drunk, and you know things that must be kept secret. Thus you must be eliminated as a risk to my plans. Of course, this is a purely practical matter." Count Pavel smiled. "But as a *personal* matter, you will be killed because I despise you. So goodbye, Mr Ducaine."

With that, Count Pavel walked off, leaving Ducaine still spouting outraged protest even as the cord went over his head and under his chin.

CHAPTER 29

I was three days aboard *Hingham Bay* making my arrangements, and squaring myself with Boston's bureaucracy. Captain Groves dealt with the harbour officials and customs, since he had his own business with merchants ashore. But I needed to prove my American citizenship, having left all my papers aboard *Enable,* and there was a tussle for authority in the matter, between Boston's town government at Faneuil Hall and the Massachusetts government at State Hall. Fortunately, matters were untangled after an exchange of letters between myself and one Ezekiah Cooper, a vastly rich merchant-prince of Boston, whom I'd known following adventures of mine in the war of 1794. Thus he was the man who got me my American citizenship in the first place, and who then made me gunnery lieutenant aboard the heavy frigate *Declaration of Independence.* (Editor's note: see *Fletcher's Glorious First of June.*)

I aimed to hook Cooper's interest, by seeking — or pretending to seek — his advice on where best I might place a very considerable sum of money, in actual gold coin. That alone would have set his mouth watering; but I furthermore stated that I was looking for partners to exploit the North American fur trade, of which trade I had direct and recent knowledge, and which could not fail to bring a tremendous return on investment. That at least was God's own truth, because it was what I really wanted to do.

In the event, my letters brought Ezekiah Cooper in person, coming to meet me aboard *Hingham Bay.* He came with an entourage of like-minded men at the very top of Boston's business community. There was himself and five others, including another beauty that I already knew from the past: Mr Jos Benson, who was not only vastly rich in trade but was deep in Boston politics, being chairman of the Board of Selectmen that ran the city.

Cooper, Benson and the rest were out of the same mould. They were stout men and serious: well fed and rounded, wearing hats and bob-wigs, plain dark clothes, knee britches and buckled shoes. I was on deck when they came aboard, and a little black lad came running before, yelling out their names.

"Mizzah Cooper, Mizzah Benson and gennelmen!" says he. "Mizzah Cooper, Mizzah Benson and gennelmen! Mizzah Cooper for Mizzah Jacob Fletcher!"

Captain Groves and his first mate were standing beside me, and we smiled to see these ponderous nabobs wobbling up the gangplank, hanging on to the hand ropes, with their walking sticks clutched under one arm. The dockside folk outright jeered, but Cooper and the rest had come in carriages, with drivers and footmen and expensive horses. So they were precisely the men I needed to see. Better still, Cooper at least was delighted to see me. Either that, or he was the only one whose greed was more powerful than his fear of falling off the gangplank and into the muck-swilling waters of the harbour below.

"Fletcher!" says Cooper with a sunshine smile. "My dear boy! Do I find you well, sir? You do look well!"

"My dear sir!" says I, with my own best smile. "A pleasure, sir! A pleasure indeed!" So there we stood beside the mainmast, with the nabobs trying not to trip over hatches, tackles and gear, and there was a great shaking of hands, even if the newcomers were uneasy with the ship's rolling in consequence of their weight coming aboard. Then Cooper beamed again.

"Mr Benson, my dear fellow," says he.

"My dear Mr Cooper?" says Benson, with a knowing grin.

"Give him the papers!" says Cooper.

"The papers!" says the rest, and Benson — despite his belly — managed a bow and handed me an oilskin package.

221

"Your citizenship's inside, Mr Fletcher!" says he. "Duly attested before the amanuenses of the Committee of Selectmen, and formally entered into the records of the state of Massachusetts!"

I must confess that this was a great relief, since it's one thing to know you're a citizen, but quite another to prove it with written text. So I took the package and I've kept it ever since, and my certificate of US citizenship hangs on the wall, framed and looking down at me, even as I dictate these words.

After that everything went wonderfully — for an hour or so at least — since I begged use of Captain Groves's great cabin, which had stern windows for light, and chairs and a table, and down we all went: myself, Cooper and his party, while Groves sent some decent wine after us, and some salt pork and pickles on fresh bread from the shore. Once seated and refreshed, Cooper pitched right in.

"My dear Fletcher," says he, "you must not think of taking lodgings ashore, since my lady wife will not hear of you staying anywhere except in our house, and as for safe keeping and investment of your gold—" he turned to those of his companions I'd not previously met — "here is Robert Sanders, principal partner of the Consolidated Bank of Boston."

"Your servant, sir," says Sanders, eyes gleaming at the thought of gold coin.

"And here," says Cooper, "is Charles Dillis, high constable of the Boston Corn and Finance Exchange."

"Call when you need me, sir," says Dillis, merry as a dog in a sausage shop. The final two were similarly eminent in Boston's affairs, and I was both delighted and surprised at the reception I was receiving on my return after so long away. But Cooper soon blew the gaff on the reason for that.

"Now, my dear Fletcher," says he, "you mentioned the North American fur trade in one of your letters."

"Ahhhh!" says all the rest, leaning forward in their chairs. So I saw the hunger for profit on their fine fat faces, and I guessed — and guessed correctly — that the blighters had long since been dreaming of the fur trade, and were lacking only someone with the necessary expertise to help them get their hands on it.

"And you *said*, my dear Fletcher ..." says Cooper, but he paused as his instinct for bargaining came into action, "or rather you claim — you *claim*, sir — to have some knowledge in the matter?" He stopped there, smiled again, and waited for me to fill the silence while all his chums looked at me with big round eyes.

So I filled the silence: indeed I did. I told them everything that you have just been reading concerning my adventures with Rusky-Alaskies and the voyageurs, leaving out only those matters appertaining to Siupuk because that was none of their damned business. Then I finished with a rousing speech on my plans.

"The United Fur Company of Boston," says I, "founded by a fleet of American ships and American adventurers!" I looked round and saw them nodding. "Fine ships, armed ships and strong, with armed men aboard, to sail to Alaska — or just south of Alaska, where no man's flag is flying — and the whole enterprise financed by ourselves as shareholders, gentlemen, and led by myself as admiral, general and advisor!"

"Yes, yes!" says they.

"A substantial expedition," says I, "to found a colony, seize the fur trade, and damn the Russians!"

"Huzzah!" says they, pounding the table and raising their glasses.

Which was the high point of my return to Boston.

The high point before the ghastly drop.

The drop which led to despair.

"Damn the Russians, Mr Fletcher!" says Cooper, laughing. "Damn fine plan, sir! Since these same Russians are about to—" he smirked and looked at his friends — "they are about to smash the Union and occupy Washington!"

All the rest laughed loudly. They laughed as if at some shared joke that had gone the rounds, yet never failed to amuse for its irresistible nonsensicality.

"Your pardon, sir," says I. "Why are we laughing about the Russians? Did you not say 'smash the Union and occupy Washington'?"

"Yes, yes, yes," says Cooper, wiping his face with a handkerchief, "haven't you heard?"

"He cannot have heard!" says one of the others. "He's been at sea."

"Ahh," says Cooper, turning to me. "Well, my young sir, as the seaman you are, you will know that even in Boston there are ... well ... certain ... certain ... *houses of ill-repute*."

"Buttocking shops?" says I. "Pushing schools?" They all laughed at that.

"Quite, sir," says Cooper, "and it so happens that there is a house, run by a Mrs Dora Banford, who is madame of the so-called Banford's Bagnio."

"Mr Cooper," says Benson, straight-faced, "how can you know of such a house? Are you a patron, sir?" Again, everyone laughed.

"Indeed not, sir!" says Cooper. "No more than any other man here!" And still more laughter followed. "Nonetheless," says Cooper, "it seems that in Philadelphia there is a similar house, run by a sister of Dora Banford, and that house was recently attended by a man — a Mr Ducaine of South Carolina — who was so drunk as to be incapable of carnal intercourse, yet who babbled nonsense to all the girls concerning a Russian plot to disprove the Constitution of the United States, and to invade and occupy the city of Washington." Cooper looked at me. "Can you imagine such nonsense? Disprove the Constitution of our Founding Fathers? And a fleet of line-of-battle ships to assemble in latitude thirty-eight degrees north, at the mouth of Chesapeake Bay? It's nonsense, sir. It is the sad ramblings of an old fool from the South. An old fool ... who can't ... who can't ... who can't *get it up* any more!"

"Ooooh!" says the others, pretending shock at the vulgarity. So they laughed, but I did not. I did not, because I was worried. I was worried because my imagination could already hear drums beating to quarters, and guns running out. I was particularly worried because Cooper had said "in latitude thirty-eight degrees north" and landmen don't talk like that. A landman wouldn't know the latitude of his own arse, and even if he did he'd never say "*in* latitude thirty-eight degrees", because that's sea-talk. A landman would say "at the latitude of thirty-eight degrees". He'd say that or something like it. Also, someone knew the latitude of Chesapeake Bay, and that couldn't be a landman either. Beyond that — thanks to Captain Groves of *Hingham Bay* — I knew that *Founding Fathers*, the only heavy ship in the US Navy on this side of the Atlantic, was fit for sail and anchored in Boston. Oh dear. Oh dear. Oh dear me indeed.

So, a long and tedious argument followed. It began with me begging their attention.

"Gentlemen," says I, "I must ask that you listen to me most carefully."

Cooper grinned. "Dear me," says he, "are we about to discuss the sharing out of our profits?"

"No, sir," says I. "We are about to discuss the future of the United States of America, and I ask you to pay close attention, because I know the Russians and you do not! And it is their constantly stated belief that they have a manifest destiny, to spread their empire around the world and take hold of as much of the west coast of America as they can grab, and then the east coast, too."

"Never!" says someone. "Preposterous!"

And another joined in. "How can the damned Russians beat us," says he, "if the damned British could not?"

"The British couldn't beat you," says I, "because the thirteen colonies were united when you fought the British. But you might not do so well if you're fragmented! So what's this about smashing the Constitution? Because that's what binds you together." I looked at Cooper. "What have you heard, sir, in that respect? What do the rumours say?"

Cooper wasn't sure. He looked round and it came out in dribs and drabs, with one man speaking after another.

"There's supposed to be a document."

"That breaks the Connecticut Compromise."

"An old document, but proven genuine."

"Owned by the wife of some Englishman."

"Yes, he's dead but his wife found it. Lady Sarah Coignwood."

"*Sarah Coignwood?*" says I, nearly jumping out of my chair. "That bloody damn bitch? *Her*? Then this is bloody serious, gentlemen, because

I know her and I knew her husband. He was Sir Henry Coignwood and I must tell you — I must insist that you take note of the fact — that he was my natural father by another woman than his blasted wife! It's a long tale, but just believe me that he was my father, who had to abandon me at birth, for fear of *her* — Sarah Coignwood — who'd have killed me if she could. But that was years ago, and I've since read all about Sir Henry, and I can tell you that he was tremendous in business and politics *and* I can tell you that he was in Philadelphia before the revolution! *And* he'd have known every damned one of the men who drafted the Constitution. So this is serious, gentlemen, for God's own sake, believe me!"

It took a lot more arguing than that, but I was making my case to the right people. Cooper and Benson alone wielded huge influence, while together the six of them — in Boston, Massachusetts — could move mountains and make water flow uphill. So, cutting out the hours of talk, here is the miserable course of action that we agreed, and which snatched from my hands all my dreams of trade, because I was now committed to America, and couldn't have America falling to pieces all around me. But it was still precious hard to be dragged back to sea. So here it all comes, as summarised by Ezekiah Cooper.

"I shall speak to the captain of *Founding Fathers*," says Cooper, "to beg, pray and implore that he takes his ship to Chesapeake Bay to oppose this appalling plan of the Russians. And Fletcher must be aboard! So I ask you, Mr Benson, to get Fletcher some sort of commission as a sea officer: a commission properly signed by the state governor! A commission such that Fletcher cannot be hanged as a pirate if the worst happens." He turned to the others. "And I'm sure that you gentlemen can have Fletcher outfitted with a uniform, and all necessary navigational instruments — whatever a sea officer should take aboard — and that the ship herself is fully provisioned for a cruise, and this done with lightning speed." They nodded.

See as follows, that once again the dichotomy of Fletcher's mind is revealed. Thus he truly regretted the passing of his dreams for the fur trade, yet the enthusiasm which he displayed in all matters of naval gunnery is pointedly obvious. S.P.

"And don't forget the extra powder and shot," says I, "that I'll need for live-firing drill. And most important of all, would you gentlemen pull whatever strings may be pulled, that I should be gunnery officer? I don't care if I'm called admiral, midshipman or swabber of the heads, just so long as I'm responsible for the guns."

"If that's what you want, sir," says Cooper.

"It is indeed, sir," says I. "It is indispensably what I want, because I have no doubt that the captain of *Constitution* — whoever he may be — can get his ship off the mouth of Chesapeake Bay, and bring her into action against whatever enemy we may find. But I most seriously doubt that any single frigate — however heavily timbered and armed — can beat a squadron of ships of the line, if that's what is bearing down upon us! Or at least one frigate can't do that unless she is most exceptionally well trained in speed of fire when close alongside, since that's what wins a battle."

The next few days were busy. My gold went ashore into Sanders' bank under armed guard. I moved into the Coopers' house on Tontine Crescent — a fine new building in a terrace fit for any square in West London — and all the town's tailors, cutlers and quadrant-mongers fitted me out, and Mr Benson had me commissioned a lieutenant of the US Department of the Navy. He even got me the right buttons and bullions for the tailor to sew onto my navy blue coats, which coats were damn near identical to their British equivalents. Meanwhile, there was a busy traffic of shore boats going out from the Boston Navy Yard, which was located in Charleston, north of the Charles and the Mystic Rivers. The boats were busy, because Americans move fast when gripped by a plan, and Cooper's chums made sure that USS *Constitution* got everything I'd asked for, and which wasn't too hard a task anyway, since she was anchored close off the wharves and warehouses of the yard.

But I saw none of this myself, nor even a glimpse of *Constitution*, because Cooper said I must "await developments till the time is right", as serious politicking was under way to get what we wanted, and all of it by unofficial — probably illegal — channels. Meanwhile, Cooper's wife saw me as a social prize to be shown off to Boston society. So there were dinners, with silver and candles and French food, and ladies just like the over-dressed, over-powdered, middle-aged Mrs Cooper herself, all giving me the ogle-eye, and myself sadly convinced that all ladies under fifty had been forbidden the invitation list.

Also, there was one social occasion that I absolutely had to attend. That was a full-dress formal dinner at the mansion of Captain Ulysses Alexander Van der Merwe, commanding officer of USS *Founding Fathers*, who was a very great person indeed. Supposedly America has no aristocracy, and indeed there are no dukes and earls. But there most certainly are men — and ladies, too — of the wealthy, trading, land-owning classes, who act just exactly like our own dukes and earls. Van der Merwe was one of these, since his Dutch ancestors had seized lands in America when New York was New Amsterdam, in the early 1600s. Thus wealth had flown down the generations ever since.

So we rode out to his mansion — myself, Cooper and Mrs Cooper — in Cooper's carriage, and Cooper giving a warning.

"Fletcher, you must allow Van der Merwe to direct the conversation," says he. "My influence has limits, and Van der Merwe has the final word on our plans for you aboard his ship. So I ask you to raise no topic that he has not already raised."

"I see," says I, "then I'll clap a hitch on my jawing tackle."

Mrs Cooper laughed. "Oh my dear Mr Fletcher," says she, lightly slapping my hand in chastisement, "you say such amusing things." She smiled and smiled, bless her heart. She smiled and I knew that I could have had the drawers off her in five minutes, given the chance; not that I wanted to.

The mansion was a few miles out of Boston and was just like those of England: raked gravel drive, fine brickwork, pillars, pediment, dome and tall, glazed windows. Van der Merwe greeted us in a huge entry hall, hung with portraits and decorated with marble statues, while liveried, white-wigged servants were everywhere. So you'd have thought that you were in England, except that all the servants were black, and had been Van der Merwe's slaves until Boston abolished slavery in the 1790s.

"Mr Cooper," says Van der Merwe as we entered, "and my dear Mrs Cooper."

"How kind of you to come," says Mrs Van der Merwe, who was definitely not of the middle-aged, over-dressed kind. She was a stunner, in a Frenchified gown that looked like just half a yard of fine muslin, and showed off most of what was beneath. She was in her twenties and quite lovely, which shows what money can buy. Though to be fair, Van der Merwe was a tall, handsome fellow of about forty, immaculately dressed, shaved and trimmed, and he moved as if he had an iron rod for a spine. He had more pride than a real duke, and he greeted me last of all, with barest politeness on top of a stony-faced look that told me I was under inspection.

"Mr Fletcher," says he, "I shall present you to my wife." That was me being reminded of my low status, you see.

"Mr Fletcher," says the lady, matching her husband with equal absence of warmth. She was plain cold, unsmiling, which surprised me because I don't often get *that* from the ladies! I most solemnly assure you of it, my jolly boys.

And so to small talk, and never a mention of ships, commissions or what the hell I was doing in Boston. Then later we moved to the dining room, where at least I was sat next to the muslin gown and its lovely contents but with Van der Merwe constantly looking my way.

Of course, the point of it all was that Van der Merwe was looking me over to see if I was a fit creature to hold rank aboard his ship. I don't blame him in the least for doing that because I've done it myself many times, since a sea officer must be a seaman, a navigator and brave, of course he must! But also he must fit in with the family that you build aboard ship, and especially among the gentlemen of the wardroom. In short, Van der Merwe was checking that I didn't get drunk, put a hand up the maids' skirts, or break wind at the dinner table.

It was only after the meal, when the ladies withdrew and we gentlemen started the port, that Ven der Merwe got to cases, and surprised me entirely, since I'd thought he was against me.

"Mr Fletcher," says he, without a smile on his face, "I know your reputation! Indeed, all Boston knows it." And the blighter raised his glass to me. I could hardly believe it.

"Indeed, indeed," says Cooper, joining in the toast.

"And Mr Cooper has informed me," says Van der Merwe, "of the miraculous work you did, in training up the gun crews of *Declaration of Independence* to give fire with astonishing rapidity."

"Right kindly of you, sir," says I.

"And therefore," says Van der Merwe, "I shall take you into my ship as fifth lieutenant. You shall be junior to the rest in the general life of the ship, but shall have exclusive power over all matters of gunnery."

He was a cold-blooded fish, entirely without passion or emotion, but he was completely persuaded of my arguments concerning the danger facing the United States. "Our nation is indebted to you, sir!" says he. "We are greatly indebted for this warning you have given us, and I shall therefore welcome you aboard ship tomorrow morning, prompt for the turn of the tide at five thirty ante meridian, when I shall make sail and set course for Chesapeake Bay."

Well spoken, that man, even as odd as he was! So I'd got what I wanted apart from certain problems that other men would never have faced, because sometimes it's hard to have a reputation: it's very hard, my jolly boys.

CHAPTER 30

By God's will I was not this time afflicted with the seasickness,
and was able to instil fire into the bellies of my subordinates
of His Imperial Majesty's Sea Service.

(Extract of a letter from Count Pavel to his mistress.)

The frigate *Svatoy Eudoxia* rolled on the heavy swell of the seas off the
American coast where Virginia meets North Carolina. The ship rolled
because she was hove-to with her fore topsail backed, such that boats
could come alongside from the powerful squadron that had found *Svatoy
Eudoxia* so very efficiently. Thus the squadron had met the frigate barely
a day's sail from the mouth of Chesapeake Bay: the bay which was to
be found in latitude thirty-eight degrees north.

Three big line-of-battleships were similarly hove-to: the flagship *Pietr
Velikiy* (seventy-four guns), in company with *Mikhailovich Chernavin*
(seventy-four) and *Oskar Gorshkov* (seventy-four), each of these great
ships being named — most auspiciously — for victorious Russian admirals of past times. It was a most happy sea-meeting because the thousands
of men aboard the big ships, and their accompanying troopships and
supply vessels, had made one of the longest passages in Russian history,
far out from the Baltic, into the North Sea and the distant Atlantic.
Thus the Imperial seamen of the fleet manned the yards, banners were
hoist in profusion, and the soldiers and merchant seamen lined the
rails and cheered.

Meanwhile, launches from the principal ships of the squadron were bumping alongside the lee quarter of *Svatoy Eudoxia*, with coxswains yelling the names of their officers such that due precedence could be observed, in the difficult task of leaping out of their heaving, rolling boats, to make their way up to the frigate's quarterdeck, as marines stamped to attention, boatswains' calls sounded, and the frigate's officers came forward in greeting. They came forward with smiles, but every one of them deferred to a noble landman among them, who was the Tsar's man, and therefore outranked every living breathing creature on the ocean — just so long as that living, breathing creature was Russian.

Thus Count Pavel, in his splendid uniform, took the salutes of the fleet admiral, and the captains, and the first officers and the rest, of the three seventy-fours and of the biggest of the troopships. He took the salutes, made the introductions, and praised Fleet Admiral Chirkov for the skills of his men in coming so far.

"Well done, Feliks Grigoreyvich Chirkov!" he said. "His Imperial Majesty shall hear your name for this triumph of navigation!"

"You are too kind, Most Honoured Count Pavel Pavelovich Stroganov," said the admiral, and gave a court bow. "But perhaps I might present my fleet captain and his navigating officers, who had some hand in the matter?"

Count Pavel willingly accepted, and a considerable number of presentations and introductions followed. Nonetheless, with so many men coming aboard — even such senior men as this — then much of the frigate below the quarterdeck, and from the great cabin forward, had to be struck of partitions as if for action stations, to create a space large enough for all these illustrious men to sit down together. But the people of *Svatoy Eudoxia* did this as smoothly and efficiently as ever could be imagined.

Finally, and to the relief of all those who were uneasy with the ship's motion, Count Pavel spoke to *Svatoy Eudoxia*'s captain.

"I should be infinitely obliged, if now the entire fleet could make sail," he said, and turned to all those who knew his own weakness, "to bring an end to this rolling, which will surely upset my weak stomach."

"Aye-aye, Honoured Sir!" said the captain, and knowing Count Pavel's history of seasickness, all his crew laughed at the gracious condescension of his self-mocking joke, and all those *not* of his crew laughed because they were Russian and they knew what was good for them.

So a lavish dinner followed, with lavish serving of wine and toasts in vodka to the Imperial Family, the Holy Church, Mother Russia, the Imperial Army, the Imperial Sea Service and much else. But the ship was under sail, the rolling had stopped, and Russians have strong heads and well-trained livers. Then afterwards, with servants and all juniors sent away, the serious discussions began. Count Pavel stood and addressed Admiral Chirkov.

"Honoured Admiral," he said, "will you now please report on the state and condition of your fleet and its men?" There was a silence, and everyone looked at Chirkov, who stood, bowed and spoke.

"The voyage was outstandingly difficult, Count," he said. "We lost all but fifteen of the horses, and had to heave most of the field guns overside, to save the ships and men. We have only five guns left."

"No matter," said Count Pavel, "I do not anticipate a need for cavalry or guns. What of the men?"

"There was some scurvy," said Admiral Chirkov. "We lost some men. But we have nearly two thousand left, with supplies, arms and field kit."

"And what of the ships? First the troopships and supply ships?"

"Mostly good," said Chirkov. "We had to abandon three ships, but we still have twelve troopships and ten supply ships."

"Good!" said Count Pavel. "I shall ask later for the most seaworthy of your lesser ships to be sent back to St Petersburg, with my report to His Imperial Majesty, together with my family letters and those of my officers."

"Of course, Most Honoured Sir."

"And now, most important of all," said Count Pavel, "in what condition are your line-of-battle ships?"

"All are strained by the voyage," said Chirkov, "rigging damaged and repaired at sea, and some men lost. Also seams are opened, and the ships are leaking. But we keep ahead by constant manning of the pumps."

"Good!" said Count Pavel. "So can your ships fight?"

Chirkov smiled. "Like the Devil himself," he said.

"Hoooo-rah!" said Count Pavel and raised a glass to Admiral Chirkov.

"Hoooo-rah!" said Admiral Chirkov and raised his own glass.

"Thank you, Admiral," said Count Pavel, "you may sit in comfort of a great task well done!" There was drumming on the tables and more cheering as the admiral sat. "Now," said Count Pavel, "listen to what we shall do for the glory of our Tsar, our Faith and our Nation." There was more cheering and table-drumming. Count Pavel smiled and waited for the noise to subside. Then he spoke. "I have, aboard this ship," he said, "a document that proves the Constitution of the United States to be a fraud. I also have aboard the foremost American expert in Constitutional matters — Mr David Nash of Philadelphia — who will prove this document to be genuine. We shall take him and the document to Washington, and use him, the document and thousands of copies, to smash the United States into fragments, such that those states — especially the southern states — that wish to break from the Union, will do so ... and in the confusion, we shall land troops, arrest the American Congress and declare martial law, before seizing territory to become the first Russian colony on the east coast, with many more to follow!"

The cheers rocked the very timbers of the ship, save only that they were young men's cheers. Admiral Chirkov and others of his generation did not cheer. Instead they looked at one another, until Chirkov found courage to speak.

"Most Honoured and Noble Count Pavel Pavelovich Stroganov," he said. "It seems that your excellent plan depends utterly on the document that disproves the American Constitution. It depends upon that, and upon the testimony of the man Nash. Am I correct?"

"You are correct, Feliks Grigoreyvich Chirkov," said Count Pavel.

"So what if the document or the man were to be lost?" said Chirkov.

"That will never happen," said Count Pavel.

"But if it did," said Chirkov, "then the whole plan would fail, and we might as well go home."

Count Pavel was not pleased. His smile was strained. But he gave a proper answer.

"That will never happen," said Count Pavel, "because Nash and the document are safe aboard my ship, and my ship will never be brought to action, since the three warships under your command, Admiral, are now absolutely the most powerful fleet off the coast of America. The British and French are busy with the European war, while the American Navy has no line-of-battle ships at all, and only the frigate *Founding Fathers* is in America and seaworthy."

"May I ask," said Chirkov, "may I ask — with *utmost* respect — if Your Honour is entirely sure of that? That the Americans have no ships of the line?"

"Absolutely sure," said Count Pavel. "I know this from certain and recent information. Thus your ships, Admiral, will brush aside any attempt at interference with our plans, and I most directly order and command, that given *any* attempt by *any* American ship to stand in your way ..." He paused, then concluded in a powerful voice, "Then you should instantly fire into that ship, without warning, and with deadly effect!"

All present cheered at that, and even Admiral Chirkov smiled.

"Hoooo-rah! Hoooh-rah! Hoooo-rah!"

It was a great and important moment for Russia and for Count Pavel, but a moment came later which was even more important, since Count Pavel was obliged to make an unforeseen decision. Thus, with the officers of the fleet returned to their ships, and the whole squadron under way, Count Pavel was on *Svatoy Eudoxia*'s quarterdeck with his usual suite of advisers and followers, when he was approached by Lieutenant Aleksandr Mauritz Vasilovich, who raised his hat in respect and bowed. Vasilovich was a pinky-faced young man, whose rich merchant father had sought to lift Aleksandr Mauritz above commercial vulgarity by means of a sea service commission obtained by bribery. Young Vasilovich was now the ship's most junior lieutenant, but had the useful skill of being fluent in English, having grown up in London, where his father had business interests.

"Excellency," said Vasilovich, "may I have the honour of your attention?"

235

Count Pavel nodded. "Of course, Lieutenant," he said, "since you are the officer in charge of Mr Nash." He turned to his followers with a smile. "Mr Nash, the ship's guest!" Good courtiers that they were, everyone laughed at this. "So, how is Mr Nash?" asked Count Pavel. "I am pleased to have seen him going about the ship with you."

"Yes, Excellency!" said Vasilovich. "He seems more cheerful, and has asked me to show him the ship and explain its workings. So — as he cannot possibly escape — I have taken him to see everything."

"Good!" said Count Pavel. "I approve of this. Mr Nash should be on deck, in the sunshine and fresh air. We cannot have him falling into misery and despair, since he has a vital duty to perform." He waved a hand expressively to encompass all the ship. "I have given orders that he may go wherever he pleases and be welcomed."

"He is grateful for that, Excellency," said Vasilovich, "but he now begs a favour of you, and which I would ask on his behalf."

"Then ask!"

"He has learned that mail from our ship will be passed to one of our merchantmen, to be taken to St Petersburg."

"Of course. This is by my command."

"Then Mr Nash asks if he might send, with our mail, a letter which he has written to his wife, to explain himself and reassure her. He begs that she should at least know that he is alive. So, may he send the letter?"

Vasilovich bowed again, and Count Pavel considered the request. Any such letter would be a year or so in transit, since it would have to get to St Petersburg, and then back to America. That was if anybody bothered to send it back to America!

"Have you read the letter, Vasilovich?" said Count Pavel.

"Yes, Excellency," said Vasilovich.

"So what did it say?"

"Endearments to his wife and children, Excellency, and protestation that he was forced aboard our ship and into our service."

"Nothing more?"

"There are two lines in Greek, Excellency, which I cannot read, but Nash says that they are poetry: ancient love poetry."

"Hmmm," said Count Pavel, who most certainly could read Greek, having studied Greek, Latin and French as a student at St Petersburg University. So Count Pavel wondered if he should read the letter himself. But …

He knew that the letter would take years to reach Nash's wife.

He respected Nash as a patriot loyal to his own people.

He wished to offer Nash some little grain of comfort.

He therefore made a small decision of colossal consequence.

"Send the letter," he said. "I shall not bother to read it."

CHAPTER 31

I once met John Quillam — he was then Captain John Quillam — who was first lieutenant aboard Nelson's *Victory* at Trafalgar. He was a beaky-nosed creature who didn't like me, as many did not in the sea service. But he told me that there were some dozens of foreigners aboard *Victory* among the hundreds on the lower deck, including even four Frenchmen. More to the point there were over twenty Americans aboard. Which is not surprising, since trained, able seamen were an international commodity, immensely valued for their skills, and easily able to pass from one service to another.

So why should anybody be surprised that when I finally went aboard *Founding Fathers*, there were men leaning out of the gunports and yelling out my sea-name, even as the boatmen pulled me alongside? They were either Britons who'd heard of me, or they were Americans who'd listened to such as did know me.

"Jacky Flash! Jacky Flash! Jacky Flash!" says they, and I wasn't pleased since they had merry, cheeky faces and seemed to regard me as a figure of fun. But as I went aboard with my traps, saluting the quarterdeck and being greeted by the officer of the watch, I had no time to do anything else than keep out of the way, and settle myself into the little cabin they'd given me off the wardroom. I stress that I kept out of the way since I had no duties, as had been made clear to me by Captain Van der Merwe.

But I was up on deck to see *Founding Fathers* make sail, and set course, out through the hazards of Boston Harbour, the sandbanks and islands beyond — then steering eastward into the Atlantic to clear the hooked peninsula of Cape Cod, south of Boston, which juts out fifty miles to trap the unwary, then finally, steering south with the states of Rhode Island, Connecticut, New York, New Jersey and Delaware on the starboard beam, heading for the mouth of Chesapeake Bay.

I note here my amazement that Fletcher sought my opinion on the spelling of Connecticut, admittedly a difficult word. But this was the only time in all my years in his service that ever he asked such a question, since usually he insisted that foreign words should be spelled phonetically. He explained that American words were different, since he believed that nothing American could be foreign, and he even thanked me for my advice. He was irrational in this, since he never inquired as to the spelling of Van der Merwe. S.P.

This was a voyage of some 650 miles, which lasted fifteen days with foul winds, when so fast a ship as *Founding Fathers* might have run those sea miles in less than four days. But this was a great blessing, as I shall explain later. Meanwhile, what of *Founding Fathers* and her people? Although rated as a frigate, she was close on the size of a ship of the line, being 2,500 tons burden, over 300 feet from bowsprit to spanker book, and with twenty-four-inch thickness of timbers.

She had some 450 men aboard, with five sea service lieutenants including myself, plus a marine lieutenant, fifty marines, twelve middies, and every trade on the lower deck from barber to butcher, which was no more than usual in those days. She wasn't so lovely a ship as *Constitution* but easy on the helm, and a dry and weatherly ship. But what mattered to me was her thirty twenty-four-pounders on the gun deck, backed up with twenty-two thirty-two-pounder carronades on her spar deck. Such a battery was never meant to equal that of a ship of the line, but it was something awesome powerful for a frigate.

As for the people, those closest to me were the gentlemen of the wardroom, the lieutenants, surgeon, chaplain and sailing master. It was one of the most spacious wardrooms I ever encountered aboard a frigate. It had the usual long table down the middle with chairs and benches, and with cabins on either side, which ran out to the full extent of the ship's beam. This wardroom, and those who lived in it, were most remarkable similar to their Royal Navy equivalents. They were the same in attitudes, strengths and weaknesses, and they were a cheery bunch who instantly treated me as a shipmate. The reason for this was made clear when Captain Van der Merwe gave a dinner in the great cabin for his officers on this first night at sea, which again was remarkable similar to Royal Navy practice, except that we toasted President Jefferson instead of King George.

Other than the lieutenant on watch, all the wardroom gentlemen were there, a white cloth was spread, Van der Merwe's wife was represented in no less than three portraits on the bulkheads, and seamen in white jackets and white gloves stood behind each chair, as servants. The ship was under easy sail, the motion steady, lamps swung overhead, and the dinner was excellent, with vegetables and bread still fresh from the shore. Also being a mess dinner — as in our service — there was no talking shop. So our mission was not discussed. Thus everything was familiar, except that I was not captain and at the head of the table. Instead, I was a prize oddity of a guest.

Van der Merwe tapped a fork against a glass, and the company fell silent.

"Gentlemen," says he, "we have a most strange man aboard." He turned to me. "Because here sits Mr Fletcher, who sank *Calipheme* in Boston Harbour with an infernal device." There he paused, leaving me with no idea what course he was steering, since never a twitch of emotion was on his po-faced chops. But then he continued, "Mr Fletcher," says he, "we are agog with wonder for your prodigious feat. So would you give us an account of your adventure in undersea navigation?" And then he smiled. The blighter actually smiled, and the rest cheered and beat their hands on the table with the very greatest enthusiasm.

It was all very, very strange, my boys, because I had grown used to keeping silent about *Calipheme,* since so many people in England — and not just in the sea service — thought me a tremendous villain for showing our French enemies how to attack our ships from below. Indeed, until that moment I had not realised how reticent I had become in the matter. But now these Yankees wanted to know everything in every detail, and so I told them. I told them how I'd navigated a wooden submarine boat named *Plunger*, which was driven by myself cranking a screw propellor, and how I'd towed an explosive mine beneath *Calipheme* and blown her to splinters. I'll not give full details here, since it's all in earlier volumes of these memoirs, but the telling of it was all exceedingly pleasant ... except that aboard *Founding Fathers*, just as the lower deck had taken me as Jolly Jack the Joker, these officers were slapping me on the back in the most familiar manner. The first lieutenant, Mr Seeker, was a considerable leader in this respect. He even patted me on the head. But he was the oldest man at the table, in his seventies with white hair in an old-fashioned queue. So perhaps he was acting as a fond grandpa? But all the rest laughed, and I felt more like a trained ape than a seafaring hero.

And so to the next day at dawn, just after five bells of the morning watch, when the trained ape — myself — was let loose on the gun deck, and on the spar deck too. Thus Van der Merwe was good as his word, as given to Ezekiah Cooper, and he nodded to Mr Seeker, who yelled out a command.

"Beat to quarters!" says he, and the marine drummer boys flourished sticks and beat out the signal that sent the ship to action stations, and I watched every movement and every piece of tackle and kit, just as hard as Van de Merwe and his officers were watching me, to see what Jacky Flash could really do with a ship's guns. So I watched and I saw that the crew men were smart by normal standards, which they damn well should have been since every one of them was a free volunteer, since the American Navy was so small, and conditions aboard so good, that there was no need for the press gang.

Thus lashings were cast off, port lids opened, charges brought up from the magazine, and guns loaded and shotted, since I'd already explained to Van der Merwe that every gun practice, once at sea, would be a live-firing practice. So they cleared decks, did the all-volunteer crew, some hundreds of them, battering the decks with their bare feet, working in teams, and they manned the magazine, loaded guns and ran out and did everything neatly and entirely without fault or getting any man in any other's way. Then they stood panting by the guns, and grinning at me, well pleased with themselves. They grinned and the lieutenants grinned, and the midshipmen grinned.

But I'd been timing the performance. One piece of tackle I'd brought aboard was a stopwatch, courtesy of Simon Willard, clockmaker of Roxbury Street, Boston, and paid for by Ezekiah Cooper.

So my moment had come. I stepped forward in my Yankee uniform, with my Yankee buttons and my cocked hat, and I made a performance of looking at the watch. Then I took a deep breath, and shivered the ship's timbers with the utmost bellow within my strength.

"Four minutes and twenty-five seconds to clear for action!" says I. "Even the French can do better than that, even the Spanish, and God help every man of us aboard if the Russians can do better still, and God help every man of you aboard should ever you be alongside a British ship that gives three broadsides in five minutes!" I looked up and down the gun deck, at the row of black guns, and the row of faces, and the faces didn't like what I'd said. The faces looked to their officers for sanction and support, and the officers looked to Van der Merwe. But he stayed po-faced, and merely nodded at me.

"Right!" says I, in another bellow. "Fire in sequence from bow to stern, then secure guns, rig ship for seafaring duties … and then do it all over again and this time, bloody well faster!"

They really, truly didn't like that and I saw surly looks and muttering such as I'd never have tolerated an instant on any ship of mine. Then once again they looked to their officers, and the officers looked to Van der Merwe, and once again Van der Merwe nodded at me.

So they did it all over again, and this time they did it in three minutes and fifty-one seconds, which I told them was still a disgrace to their navy, and proof that they'd been slacking the first time. On the other hand they'd fired off two broadsides, powder smoke was in the air and the guns were hot, and I've seen it too many times ever to doubt that seamen love the thunder of the guns and the bounding of the carriages, and it makes them grin. It's exactly the same with landmen and fireworks. Everyone says "Ooooh" and "Ahhhh" when the rockets whoosh or the cannons roar.

So the hands secured guns and went to their duties, displeased as they were but without actually hanging me at the yardarm, and I knew that it was time for a certain demonstration. I therefore went to Mr Seeker, first lieutenant. He was aft at the taffrail, talking to the signals lieutenant, so I went up, and raised my hat in salute.

"Mr Seeker, sir," says I, "might I have a word? A word about ship's discipline?"

"Oh?" says he, and looked to the signals lieutenant and both of them smiled.

"Oh!" says the signals lieutenant, and I frowned because I was puzzled. I was puzzled, but they were not.

"Mr Fletcher," says Seeker, "your reputation has gone before you."

"Has it?" says I.

"It has Mr Fletcher, it has," says Seeker. "Indeed the whole ship is aware of the manner in which you usually come aboard ship, and the whole ship is waiting for you to have—" he smiled again — "a *quiet word* with the ship's bully-boys."

This time, I smiled. "That is my very intention, sir," says I, "and as soon as it may be arranged. So who is he?"

"*They*, Mr Fletcher," says Seeker. "The Porter brothers, who are twins: Nathan and Shadrack, who do all things together. But please note that Captain Van der Merwe must know nothing of this, since he will permit no physical punishment aboard his ship — neither flogging nor the rope's end — and therefore your meeting with the Porter twins may not be on the quarterdeck, where our captain could not fail to observe it."

I smiled again, because that summoned memories of the first fight I ever fought, and which was aboard *Phiandra* frigate, under Captain Sir Harry Bollington, who had similar sensitivities, such that fights were always on the fo'csle where he could pretend not to know.

"Mr Fletcher," says the signals lieutenant, "regarding the Porters — shall you face both of them at once, or one at a time? Bets are being laid throughout the ship. And likewise on the outcome."

Very nice of that lieutenant I'm sure, to take such an interest.

After that it was all very seamanly and Yankee. They fixed the bout for six bells of the afternoon watch, which is three p.m. landman's time, so that all hands had got their dinners down them and digested. Every man not on essential duties was crammed into the fore rigging, on the carronade slides, or into any spare corner where the spectacle could be observed. That was all hands except the captain: him and the purser and his clerk. These two latter beauties were Quakers — peace-lovers who disapproved of violence. So what they were doing aboard a ship of war is any man's guess. But the marines were turned out with their blue coats, forage caps and Charleville muskets, a ring had been rigged with stanchions and ropes, the second lieutenant was officiating, the noise was tremendous, and bets were flying in flocks. So I came up from my cabin cleared for action, wearing just britches, bare-chested with bare feet, and a couple of middies were sent to escort me with a bucket of water, a sponge and some towels.

I got an almighty cheer as I climbed into the ring. I am a very big man with heavy muscles, and sculptors have pestered me for years to pose my physique for them, which I damn well won't, since standing bollock naked except for a loincloth might attract the wrong kind of interest. But I acknowledged the cheers and took first look at the Porter twins, who were ready in their corner, stripped down for action like myself. And by Jove they were a pair of dog-ugly swabs. They were squat and heavy, with arms down to their knees, broken noses, pugilists' ears, and Nathan could easily be told from Shadrack, since one of Nathan's ears had been bitten off to a stump. They stared at me steadily, and the funny thing was that with all their manner of shaved-gorilla thuggery, I saw intelligence in their faces, especially as they whispered to one another, in quick, active speech, which said that neither of them had been the village idiot in the place that bred them.

Then the second lieutenant called us in to the middle of the ring, asking the same question as the signals lieutenant.

"Mr Fletcher," says he, "shall it be one at a time—" he looked at the Porters — "or both together?"

"Any way they please," says I. That got another deafening roar of applause, so I hope the two Quakers were reading the Bible to take their minds off things which are unpeaceful. After that, the second lieutenant delivered some words about rules of the ring, but he was overexcited and gabbled, and nobody took notice anyway. Then he was out of the ring, and we set to, and the Porters surprised me because they were indeed intelligent, and they worked as a team, running round me in opposite directions so I couldn't fix on either. Then Nathan dived at me, fastened arms around my legs and had me over on the deck with a *thump*! But that wasn't near as hard a *thump* as I got from Shadrack, who stamped at my head as I lay face down and helpless.

So, your Uncle Jacob was staring defeat in the eye, within the first seconds. The deck was smeared with blood from my nose and my head was swimming with nausea. All I could do was give every atom of strength to roll over on my back, and get my fists into action, pounding Nathan's head, till his grip weakened and I could kick my legs free and get up. Even so, the swab bit me fiercely on one leg as I shook him off. But I got up with Shadrack hanging on my back, fixing a stranglehold on my neck. Again, sheer brute strength saved me, I broke his grip, took hold of one of his arms and swung him away by it. That left me free, and Shadrack with a shoulder popped out of joint.

That got the pair of them angry and they tried to settle things with their fists, even if Shadrack was one-handed. That was their mistake. They should have stuck with cunning tricks. They should have done that even though Nathan was a formidable box-fighter who landed some good 'uns, and left me bruised, while as for Shadrack you couldn't fault him for pluck, fighting on as he did with one arm useless. But they shouldn't have switched to fisticuffs, since there was no man born who can beat me in face-to-face boxing, not under Queensberry Rules, nor even the punching-kicking-biting style of the Porter brothers. So in the end it was the usual result, with them on the deck, and myself standing looking down at them, while running with sweat and gasping for breath. The cheers were so loud in that moment, that when I hauled the Porters to their feet and called on Mr Seeker to award them double grog, I doubt that anyone heard me. But they got it anyway, since Seeker really did know my reputation very well.

After that, Shadrack Porter had his arm put back by the surgeon, and there was no more trouble on the gun deck, nor were there any more patronising slaps on the back in the wardroom. So my method worked as it always has. But as I have said to you youngsters many times, you should not attempt this — my own style of keeping discipline — unless you are some serious fragment of my size and strength. Also, there wasn't any more *fifth* lieutenant nonsense either, since everyone except First Lieutenant Seeker and the captain now addressed me as "sir". After all, I had ten times the experience of anyone else in a ship where only a tiny fraction of the people had ever faced shot of any kind, let alone a three-decker's broadside, because the US Navy was too young for that in those days.

So I took the gun crews of *Founding Fathers* through such a training as they'd never dreamed of, and once more I give my thanks and gratitude to Van der Merwe, who backed me every inch of the way. So here's some of the drills I put them through. I had the drums beat to quarters at any time, day or night, without warning. I had the drums beat to quarters when the weather was especially foul, because it's a fine thing being able to run out, load, fire and load again, when there's flat calm and the ship behaves herself. But what if she's pitching and rolling? What if the sea's coming in through the gun ports, such that you can't even use the guns on the lee side? And what if the hands are seasick as even veteran mariners can be if the motion changes? And what if a gun captain is killed by the enemy's shot? What if your gun is dismounted and smashed, and half the crew with it?

So I had the carpenter make me a staff, painted red, and I'd go round the gun deck during firing drill, so I could tap men on the shoulder to tell them they were out of the drill and their mates must contrive to keep the gun in action. And I made the gun crews practise each other's roles, so any of a gun crew might be gun captain, swabber, rammer or loader as need shall arise. I furthermore made the gun crews swap guns as well, so they could all fight from any angle at any gun.

246

Then when the weather permitted, because it has to be calm for long-distance fire, then — as ever is my practice — I had them fire careful and slow at a flag on a floating cask, with double grog for the crew that hits it or gets closest. The men love that, and I commend it to you, since distance fire has its uses although it was never a battle winner, not in the days of smooth-bore muzzle-loaders. So, better still, I made them practise quick firing, to deliver the prize of three broadsides in five minutes, because that really is the battle winner. They worked hard, they practised and practised, and they worked with a will.

Thus I still remember the colossal cheers that the whole ship gave itself on the day when I raised my Willard stopwatch and cried out, "Two minutes and fifty-one seconds!" Then, when the cheers died down, I gave my usual reminder. "But it'll have to be faster next time!" And what a changed crew they'd become, because they greeted that with still greater cheers, and a great chant.

"Jacky Flash! Jacky Flash! Jacky Flash!"

All this, my jolly boys, is why I thanked the weather for delaying our passage down to Chesapeake Bay, because if *Founding Fathers* had been on a favourable wind, and had she flown south at the twelve knots that was within her powers, then I'd never have had enough time to get the gun crews fit for what was coming. Thus there came a day, just after eight bells of the morning watch, with the hands at breakfast and myself and my messmates too in the wardroom, when a hail came down from the foretop lookouts.

"Saaaaaail *ho*! Saaaaaail *ho*!"

This caused intense excitement aboard ship, since we were running down the eastern shore of Virginia off the Delmarva Peninsula, with Hog Island in sight, which meant that the mouth of Chesapeake Bay was just under the horizon, some twenty miles to our south. So, if there really was a Russian squadron at sea with evil intent, then it too could be just under the horizon, and likely — at any moment — to come in sight of our lookouts.

Thus there was a general rush of those below, to see what was afoot. I went to the helm and binnacle, doffed hat to Van der Merwe — who was already there with the sailing master and others — just as Van der Merwe raised a speaking trumpet and hailed the masthead.

"What sail?" says Van der Merwe.

"Men-o'-war!" cries the lookout. "Two sail! Ships of the line! No, there's three!"

"What flag?" says Van der Merwe, and the whole ship waited without breathing, as the lookout 100 feet over our heads took a long and careful look through his glass.

"St Andrew's flag!" cries the lookout. "Blue cross on white! Russian Imperial Navy!" At this there was a huge sigh from the people of *Founding Fathers*, something between a groan and a growl, and I looked for Van der Merwe to do what I would have done in that moment, had I been in command. I looked for what any decent captain would have done. I looked for a call to arms! I looked for a rousing speech! I looked for all the guff and nonsense about the enemy who's coming to rape your mother and your sweetheart; the enemy who's coming to steal your goods and burn your house; the enemy who's coming to plant a foreign flag over your beloved homeland. I looked for all that ancient nonsense which has been said before 1,000 times because it ain't nonsense at all, my jolly boys, believe me it ain't. It ain't because it sets the heart pounding and kicks fear so hard up the arse that fear runs away and doesn't come back, and it makes men fight like lions. So that's what I'd have done, followed instantly by beating to quarters!

Instead of that, Van der Merwe — being the man he was — merely spoke to his first lieutenant.

"Mr Seeker," says he.

"Sir?" says Seeker.

"I shall close with the Russian squadron and bespeak its commander to establish his intentions," says Van der Merwe. "You will therefore make ready to heave-to and lower my barge, at the opportune moment. I shall go myself and take Mr Fletcher with me."

Well, it was nice of him to think of me, I'm sure, and what he proposed might have been very wonderfully diplomatic as regards *not* starting a war, should the Russians have no intention of doing so, bless

248

their Russian hearts. But I saw the ship's people looking at one another, muttering and shaking their heads, because three ships of the line were bearing down on us with more men and guns than we had any right to conquer, and everyone aboard — with the possible exception of the cold-blooded Van der Merwe — was wondering what might happen next! More that that, I personally was wondering about what sort of reception we might get aboard the Russian flagship.

It wasn't a good start.

CHAPTER 32

In that moment, it seemed that all my doubts were proven wrong, since that Count Pavel's plan must undoubtedly succeed.

(Extract of a letter from Admiral Chirkov to his wife in Moscow.)

Admiral Chirkov raised his telescope for a good long look at the ship that was coming on under all plain sail, now fully visible over a hazy sea some ten miles off. He could see every feature of her, from main-trucks to waterline. So could the fleet captain, the ship's captain, the first lieutenant and others. They could all see the ship as they stood with their admiral, telescopes raised, on the quarterdeck of the flagship of the Russian squadron, *Pietr Velikiy,* which ship bore thirty-six-pounders on the lower gun deck, twenty-four-pounders on the upper gun deck, rows of swivels on the gunwales and a pair of eighteen-pounder bow chasers which — aboard *Pietr Velikiy* — were exceptionally long guns, and special from the St Petersburg Arsenal.

"So," said Chirkov, "here are the Americans at last. What took them so long to find us?"

"And it's just a frigate," said the fleet captain.

"Count Pavel was right," said the ship's captain.

"Just one frigate," said Chirkov. "But we'll still take care, because anything can happen in a sea fight, and only God knows who might lose a spar, or be holed below." The rest nodded. They were veteran seamen of the wars against the Turks. They understood.

"Shall I clear for action and run out the guns?" said the ship's captain.

"Yes," said Chirkov, "but first make signal to the fleet, that the fleet should heave-to while we engage the enemy."

"Aye-aye, sir!" said the ship's captain.

"At once, now!" said Chirkov. "Make the signal. After that, we shall easily deal with one frigate, but it cannot be ignored in case they have some devil's plan to slip into the fleet and attack Count Pavel's ship, which we absolutely cannot allow!"

"Aye-aye, sir!" said the ship's captain.

"Then make sure your men aim well," said Chirkov, "since we have business in Washington, and cannot waste time on one frigate. We'll give a broadside to settle it and then press on."

"Aye-aye, sir!" said the ship's captain.

"And run out the bow chasers," said Chirkov, "and open fire so soon as the enemy is within range."

This puzzled the ship's captain. "Do you mean warning shots from the bow chasers, Admiral?"

"Good God, no!" said Chirkov. "Not by God and the Virgin! We have Count Pavel's express orders in the matter. Fire into the hull. Fire into the hull with every gun we bear."

Soon *Pietr Velikiy*'s men cheered as the drums rolled and they ran to their stations to make ready. They cheered, because like all seamen, they loved to hear the thunder of their own guns, and gun practice aboard *Pietr Velikiy* was only an occasional event, and usually without powder being burned and shot fired.

Then there was a long wait of nearly an hour, as *Pietr Velikiy* sailed onward while the fleet backed topsails and every man aboard every ship who had a telescope studied events in eager anticipation of watching their powerful flagship pulverise, wreck and destroy the American intruder. While on the fore-gundeck of the flagship itself, the gunnery lieutenant was measuring time and distance. He was peering out through a gun port of the larboard side bow chaser, under the shadow of the head timbers, with the massive bowsprit jutting out above all. He peered out, with the gun crew clustered behind him, eagerly waiting their time, and he

251

took a constant sighting down the barrel of the larboard gun as his ship rolled and pitched, and the long black barrel made slow circles in the air, coming on-target and off-target of the American ship bearing down with the white water under her bows and the gulls wheeling above.

In that moment, if any of the gulls had wished to take note, they would have observed how Admiral Chirkov had deployed his squadron to give utmost protection to the most important ship under his care: Count Pavel's ship *Svatoy Eudoxia*. Thus a total of twenty-five ships were hove-to in rectangular formation, over two square miles in extent, while *Pietr Velikiy* was under all plain sail, forging ahead of the rest, leaving *Oskar Gorshkov* and *Mikhailovich Chernavin* poised to defend the fleet if need be. Then, astern of the two seventy-fours, were ten troop-transports and twelve supply ships wallowing in parallel rows, with *Svatoy Eudoxia* in the utmost centre, supposedly immune to any possibility of coming into action.

The seagulls would have seen all this and they would have seen the white puffs of smoke that erupted, one after another, from the bows of *Pietr Velikiy*. Then, in their high and distant stations, the gulls would have heard the deep and resounding voices of the guns.

THUD!

THUD!

Van der Merwe was what — in later days — the Yankees called "a cool hand". Too cool by half in my opinion, because he hadn't beat to quarters even when a bloody enormous Russian fleet came out of the haze, with banners flying, and dozens of them rolling along towards us as if they owned the bloody ocean. The lookouts yelled themselves hoarse, the hands filled the shrouds and lined the rails goggling, and everyone looked to Van der Merwe for orders, which I suppose he was about to give, when Mr Seeker cried out.

"God damn the bastards," says he, "they're firing on us!" So they were, the swabs, 'cos there was a great, fat line-of-battle ship out in front of all the rest, and with a gold-leaf figurehead and sails bleached by seafaring, and this ship threw out two great balls of powder smoke from her bow chasers, followed by the detonations, and then the hideous shriek of a shot in flight that went over our ship, with a *whoooooosh*, and a howl which made every man duck. But that shot missed us while its partner hit the sea off our starboard beam, with an almighty *chop*! And up went a water-spout high over our t'gallants, and some of it even came down aboard of us.

"Beat to quarters!" cries Van der Merwe, awake at last, and never was I so pleased at the drill I'd hammered into the lower deck hands of *Founding Fathers*. I didn't have my stopwatch, but by Jove, they must have broken all records for speed in getting the ship into fighting condition. But they weren't as fast as the gunners aboard the Russian seventy-four, who already had their guns run out, because more smoke gouted from the Russian's bows, another shot went smashing into the water, and this time the second shot took us clear in the bow, and smashed halfway down the ship before its strength wore out.

Well, my jolly boys, that was battle joined, and no mistake. So was no more nonsense of Van der Merwe's "bespeaking, bespoking, be-buggering" or whatsoever he meant. And at least your Uncle Jacob didn't have to worry about what welcome he might get aboard the Russian flagship. Furthermore, Van der Merwe was honest and grateful.

"Mr Fletcher," says he, yelling over the noise of hundreds of men, running, shifting, loading and hauling out the guns. That, and some grim cries from the gun deck, from those too wounded to keep silent, which ain't a nice sound, my lads, believe me it ain't. "Mr Fletcher," says Van der Merwe, "no man can now doubt the truth of the warning that you laid before us. So God bless you, sir, and I furthermore state that while I shall lay my ship alongside of the enemy, I look to you to achieve best fire from her guns."

"Aye-aye, sir!" says I, and saluted him. Then I was down on the main gun deck.

The men had cleared and ran out with utmost effort and utmost will. But then there was a silence, with marines looking over the rails, gun crews through their ports, topmen looking from above. We were looking and waiting for such time as our broadside would bear on the Russians, but with little wind and slow sailing, we had to endure — and I counted them — three more rounds from each of the enemy's bow chasers, without the chance to hit back. By good luck and providence, only two shots hit us, but once again, they ploughed down our gun deck, killing and breaking and throwing up great oaken splinters. One of these took the hat right off my head, but that was nothing because it might have taken my head off.

And then, and then … Glory be to God in the Highest! Van der Merwe took *Founding Fathers* across the bows of the big Russian, in the most perfect manoeuvre that even Nelson himself couldn't have bettered. He took us across the bows of the Russian ship with utmost opportunity to fire right down the Russian throat.

> I was astounded at their boldness in bearing down upon superior ships, but astounded still more by what followed.
>
> (Extract of a letter from Admiral Chirkov to his wife in Moscow.)

Like any admiral of any sea service, once the ship which he served was in action, Admiral Chirkov had nothing to do. Nothing whatsoever. Nothing at all. A ship's captain might be pressed for decisions on everything regarding any aspect of the action. Lieutenants and midshipmen would direct the fire of the guns, and deal with ship damage, rigging and casualties, while the rest of the crew sweated with the effort of the constant, unremitting demands of their duties. So these lesser beings had no time for fear. But an idle admiral, bereft of duties, merely paced the aftermost poop deck with his bowels churning in agonies of apprehension and his mind wide open to any fear that his imagination could create. Beyond that, some of the things that he saw — in all reality — were both terrifying and horrible.

At least Admiral Chirkov had the company of his fleet captain, who — unlike the *ship's* captain — had as little to do as his admiral.

"Just look at him!" cried the fleet captain, pointing to the oncoming frigate. "He's not steering away! He's coming straight on, and no damn frigate should do that. We're a seventy-four, in the name of God!"

"No," said Chirkov, "he's—"

But conversation was interrupted by a press of men, urged on by a lieutenant, to man the gunwale swivels, and stand ready to fire should the American come alongside.

"Beg pardon, Your Honours!" cried the lieutenant. "Beg pardon! Beg pardon!" But in the heat of the moment the admiral and fleet captain were jostled and bumped by lowly persons, who at least touched forelock as they did so.

"Over here, sir," said the fleet captain, seeking to get Chirkov away and beyond the swivels. But Chirkov ignored him. He was staring in utter amazement at the American frigate.

"Look, damn him!" he said. "He's crossing our bows!"

"By God, he is!" cried the fleet captain as Chirkov pushed through all others on the poop deck, ran down the companionway to the quarterdeck, and yelled at the officers and men at the ship's wheel.

"Come about!" he cried. "Bring her round! He's trying to rake us by the bow!"

But if these men even heard their admiral, in the intensity of their concentration, it made no difference, as they were already trying to do exactly what he was saying, because Admiral Chirkov was far from being the only man aboard *Pietr Velikiy* who could see the danger. Then Chirkov gasped, as it was too late, and the seventy-four could not turn as fast as the frigate, which backed topsails in beautiful coordination, slowed and delivered the most perfect ripple-broadside, guns thundering, one after another down the length of the ship, billowing out massive smoke clouds and sending shot down the length of her big opponent. Chirkov heard — and even felt through the soles of his shoes — the impact of shot that had come so far through *Pietr Velikiy's* bows as to strike even the timbers and fittings of the decks beneath his feet.

But then it got even worse … or perhaps better? Chirkov could not decide, because the American came round and alongside *Pietr Velikiy* such that, looking down from the height of the big ship's poop, Chirkov could see every detail of the American's decks: men, guns, capstan, pin-rails, even the ship's boys running cartridges to the guns. It was a piece of theatre: fascinating and fearful, because the American gave two more broadsides even as she slid past! Her rate of fire was incredible! It was beyond belief! Her shot ripped and crashed and killed. Guns on their carriages were thrown over, and men smashed into hideous meat. But, but, but ... *Pietr Velikiy*'s gunners — ready with guns loaded, shotted and run out — would get their chance, and Chirkov cheered as his ship trembled to the power of her own guns: the thirty-six-pounder lower-deck battery, the twenty-four-pounder upper-deck battery, every swivel that would bear, and the close-range musket fire of the marines in the fighting tops.

Pietr Velikiy was hitting back, and hitting hard.

"Damn you, you damn frigate!" cried Chirkov. "Damn you by all the rules of war. Serves you damn well right!"

They did me proud, did the gun crews of *Founding Fathers*. Not having my stopwatch, I don't know what it took them for the first three broadsides, but it was something amazing quick. All credit, too, to Van der Merwe for the neatness of his ship's manoeuvring, and then he tried to do even better, by getting *Founding Fathers* under the Russian's stern, so our gunners could fire straight in through the weakest part of any ship: the stern galleries and windows, which were matchwood and glass compared with the dense timbers of the rest of a ship of war.

But the Russian wasn't having that! Whoever was in command wasn't a complete fool, and he swiftly put down his helm and changed the rig of his sails: I could see his topmen busy as monkeys aloft. Thus he brought her round to face us broadside-to-broadside for a battering match, which by all the experience of the ages, his ship must win, being so much thicker in timbers and heavy in guns than any frigate, even one such as *Founding Fathers*.

Except that we had on our side such an advantage in rate fire as I never saw before or since in all my years. I can only think that the Russians had neglected their gun drill, whereas we on board of *Founding Fathers* had lived and breathed and sweated and dreamed of gun drill. We'd done it morning, noon and night, and day after day after day. By my count — even though I had much else to do than count — we fired more than three times faster than they did, and even with the damage their bow chasers had inflicted, we'd got in the first few broadsides before they gave it back to us. So heaven knows what damage we'd done to her people and her insides.

But then we did get it back. We got it back at pistol-shot range, and at such range there's no use for ears and little use for eyes. This, because the fire of heavy guns is deafening even if you stand behind the guns. But when you're in front of them, my jolly boys, it's beyond anything you can ever imagine. You have to be there to believe it. Likewise the smoke that pours out from the guns blots out the light on the gun deck, it rolls up above the topmasts, it smothers the ship, and all you can see is what you can touch, and the whole business of serving the guns is done by feel, and by the instinct that constant drill puts in a man's head, and the only things you can clearly see are the luring orange flashes of the enemy's guns, which give you your point of aim. So that's what it's like in a hot action when your captain has laid you so close alongside the enemy that you can't miss, and all that matters is your speed at gunnery.

On top of all that, the business has to be done when the enemy's shot is coming in through your ship's sides. It's coming in and showering deadly splinters in all directions. It's coming in and blowing the limbs off your comrades. It's coming in and smashing massive black gun barrels clear out of their carriages, to come crashing down on the people and tackles of the gun deck. So I do most cordially advise you youngsters to think of that, if ever you dream of a life in the sea service.

As for me, since I wasn't in command, and since I'd done my bit in training up the gun crews, I was mostly concerned with putting right what the enemy had put wrong. That meant heaving broken guns off poor trapped seamen, giving a hand to serve guns with half the crews knocked flat, and even slapping a poor, little, hysterical powder boy to knock him out of the screaming fits of pure terror. Mind you, I was careful not to slap him too hard, and the little bugger ran off and back to his duties. You have to do these things: cruel to be kind.

257

How long this went on, I do not know, but then three things happened in succession. First, the wind got up and blew clear most of the powder smoke, so we could actually see the big Russian through the gun ports. Next, by pure luck — since as I have explained there's no real aiming in a close action —one of our broadsides sent the enemy's foremast into ruin. It went over, cascading and showering his decks with acres of canvas, miles of tangled and matted rigging, and tons of heavy spars, and all this great jam of gear hung over the sides, trailing in the sea and making the ship unsteerable. This caused a cessation of action, since the Russian was in fear of igniting the wreckage into fire, while we could not fire — not properly — for the damage done to our ship. Therefore, as a result of harm we'd done to each other and by order of our commanders — Van der Merwe on our side and some Russian on the other — each ship fell off from the other so that repairs could be done, with the firm intention of renewing the action so fast as might be possible.

I've seen such mutual pauses or truces — call them what you like — many times in my service, where single-ship actions are concerned, and in this case, with the two other Russian ships some way off it might as well have been a ship-to-ship fight. Which meant that a race was on to see which ship's crew could make and mend, heave overside the wreckage and the dead, jury rig sail if need be, then come back into action, with whatever guns might still be serviceable and able to fire into a helpless enemy.

That was the usual way of it, my jolly boys, but what happened next was unique to my entire career at sea.

> I cannot cause the Constitution to fail. I shall act as follows,
> using the weapons given me by Evans …
> (Translation of half of the lines in Classical Greek, written
> by David Nash in the letter to his wife, and sent from the
> frigate Svatoy Eudoxia, by permission of Count Pavel.)

Nash knew that his moment had come, or at least he could not imagine a better time. "I must go below," he said to Lieutenant Vasilovich, who had been so kind and attentive. "The motion upsets me and I feel sick."

"Of course, Mr Nash," said Vasilovich. "Do as you think best. We're rolling heavily. You go below, Mr Nash." Vasilovich said these words, but he was hardly paying attention to Nash. Vasilovich was on the fo'csle with all the mids, and anyone else whose duties allowed. He was there with his telescope, and like all the rest, he was more interested in the coming battle between the American and the flagship than anything else in the entire world.

"Hooooo-rah!" they cried, as the flagship's bow chasers opened fire. They cheered and they grinned at each other, and nobody paid the least attention to Mr Nash, who passed among them and down the companionway to the waist, and then past the larboard, main-deck battery, and the hands all climbed on the gun carriages or up in the shrouds for a good view, and all of them cheering.

"Hooooo-rah!" they cried as the flagship's bow chasers fired again.

Nobody paid attention to Nash, because Count Pavel himself had said that Nash had the freedom of the ship. So Nash found the hatchway that led down from the main deck to the berthing deck, as he had every right to do, since a cabin had been provided for him just forward of the gun room where the ship's officers lived and socialised. But then he took a risk, because he found another hatchway, leading down to the orlop deck, and the hold, then onward into a world of darkness below the waterline, which was lit only by candle-lanterns that swung on their hooks with the ship's sickening, rolling motion. Normally, even these dark, wooden tunnels would have had some life, some men about their duties. But not now, not with all of them fascinated by what the flagship was doing.

So this was the ideal moment, and even the heavy, rolling motion could not stop Nash. He was not seasick, because his mind was consumed by other matters entirely than mere physical anguish; because Nash was under torment of the soul. It had been impossible not to write the letter. It was impossible because — having made his decision — he could not rest if nobody should ever know, and most especially if his wife should never know. But the risk had been enormous. What if somebody on this Russian ship could read Classical Greek? Nash groaned. What if young Vasilovich had been able to read Greek? Him or his superiors?

But in any case, in the event the letter had gone. It had not been stopped. Neither had he been stopped, and now Nash was in agonies of dread, of anticipation, of fear, of uncertainly and of self-doubt. He imagined that every creature on the ship must hear his heartbeats; as he came to the outer door, he thanked God that the Russians had never thought to search him, and he reached into his britches' pockets.

We won the race. We won and I take some credit for that too, because I went up and down the gun deck, as the men were at work, doing some of the dreadful things that must be done. They were picking up the bits and pieces of their late shipmates, that had been smashed and mangled by the enemy's fire. They picked them up dripping and slimy, and shoved them out through the gun ports, and some of the fragments still recognisable by the pale, dead faces. They did all that while the powder boys and surgeon's mates got the wounded down below for the treatment of their wounds, and some of the wounds were most ugly to look upon. No, my lads, it ain't nice. It ain't nice at all. It ain't nice when it comes with the heavy, physical labour of righting overturned guns, hacking away at fallen spars, tangled rigging and broken gear.

So I did what Van der Merwe had neglected.

"Come on you *Founding Fathers*!" says I in a bellow. "Do it for your fathers! Do it for your mothers! Do it for your sweethearts! Do it for your country and your flag!" That was the substance of it, and it was all the tomfool nonsense that every leader ever spouts, because it ain't tomfool nonsense at all. So we won the race, and Van der Merwe brought the ship about, spread main and topsails and bore down on the wounded seventy-four with guns run out — such guns as we had left — to achieve the historic impossible of warfare at sea. Our frigate was about to batter a ship of the line into wreckage or surrender! We were going into the history books for ever and ever amen.

Except that we weren't. With a decent wind at last, the battle smoke had blown away, the sea haze had blown away and there was blue sky above and a clear sight to the coast of Delaware on our beam, to the horizon all around, and to the Russian squadron, down to the south of us. So the lookouts spotted what was coming. They spotted it first and yelled down to Van der Merwe, though I heard it loud and clear on the gun deck.

"Enemy coming up astern! Line-o'-battle ships! Two of 'em!"

I groaned. I looked up and down the gun deck. We'd been bad hit, and at least a third of our guns were knocked over, a third of the guns and maybe a quarter of the gun crews. We still had plenty enough to defeat the seventy-four we'd fought, if only Van der Merwe could get us under her stern where she couldn't return fire. But we could never face another seventy-four, let alone two of them. So it wasn't only me that groaned, believe me it wasn't.

So it looked precisely and inevitably as if, for all our efforts, we were going to be defeated, the Russians would succeed in their plan, and the United States of America was about to be broken in to fragments.

He was a nosy little swab. Always asking questions. So I told him yes, there was always a marine there, and the outer door locked, but the outer door was thin, being only for show, and myself with the key.

(Extract of memoir, published 1852, of Ivan Zhelgov, yeoman of the powder room aboard Svatoy Eudoxia.)

Nash trembled in all his limbs, and most especially in his knees. He trembled but he was now firm in resolve. He looked at the marine who was standing with his musket grounded, and a puzzled expression. The marine said something in Russian, which Nash did not understand. The marine was not unfriendly, he was quite young, and Nash was struck with irrational regret for what he must do next. It was irrational because his overall intentions were very much worse.

So Nash produced, in his right hand, one of Mr Evans' pocket pistols — those made by Manton of London — and fumbled with the lock. But then the trigger folded down with a click and Nash pointed square at the centre of the young marine's chest.

"I'm so sorry," said Nash, "so sorry." Then he pulled the trigger, the pistol flashed, barked and jumped, and the marine gaped in utmost amazement. He dropped his musket, clutched at his chest, tore open his tunic and looked down. But then the light went out of his eyes and he slumped and fell in front of the outer door of *Svatoy Eudoxia*'s powder magazine.

"I'm sorry, I'm sorry," said Nash, "and may God forgive me." But then he took up the fallen musket, cocked the heavy lock and pointed it at the door. The yeoman of the powder room had been most voluble and Vasilovich had translated. It seemed that even with utmost care, there were always a few grains of powder spilt in the outer compartment. Even though everything was lined with copper, and no iron of any kind allowed inside, and even though the powder casks themselves had copper bands, and even though the filled cartridges were carefully examined at frequent intervals ... all these precautions were taken because there were always a few grains on the floor.

"So," the yeoman of the powder room had said, "first duty every day is to mop out, with a damp mop, for the powder grains. But you still find a few of them about, which is why we must wear felt slippers."

So Nash raised the musket. He pointed it at the door. Then he hesitated.

God bless my dear wife, he thought, *God bless my children. God bless the Union!* Then, finally, he thought, *Right against the door so the flash goes inside*, and he stepped back, put the muzzle to the door and pulled the trigger. The musket roared, and kicked back, and blew a scorched hole in the outer door. But Nash blinked, and realised that he was still alive. He looked at the door, looked at the lock, and the lock seemed flimsy, so he beat it with the brass-bound butt of the musket. He was still battering hard when there was shouting and the sound of running feet, and even a hand on his shoulder, and he swung round and struck the musket butt hard into a barely seen face, and hit the door again, and men were shouting and shouting, and he was pushed forward by a press of bodies, and the door gave way.

Nash fell inside, dropping the musket, and he hardly felt the blow as someone ran him through from behind with a blade: a knife, a dirk, a bayonet? He hardly felt it as he got up and stumbled across the copper-lined floor, towards the inner door, and hauled it open, and there were the lines of powder casks, and the shelves of cartridges, all seen in the light from the lamp room. Then Nash was falling again as men grabbed him, but his left hand was free and he drew the second pistol, kicked and wriggled with all his might, and the slippery blood of his wound ran down the hands of the man holding his right arm, and the arm was free, and Nash cocked the pistol.

And in that instant, at terrific speed, all the great things of Nash's life came to mind: his parents, his beloved lady, their marriage, the birth of their children, happy summers and frozen winters ... but also the dreadful document came to mind. Nash saw it in a sharp clarity of horror: the vellum, the penmanship, the colour of ink, all undeniably correct. He saw the powerful names of powerful men, and the deceit that had been practised — the deceit which saved the Union — and most of all, he saw the phrase kept secret these last twenty years, the phrase that explained everything, the phrase which gave the document both its enormous power, and its malignant ability to smash the Union:

We therefore agree upon the substitution of ...

But further memory was unbearable and Nash discharged his pistol into the heart of the magazine.

Fortunately, none of the things I feared came to pass, as surely you must have guessed, because the United States of America stands firm.

What happened instead was the most enormous explosion in the heart of the Russian squadron. I saw it with my own eyes. Most of us saw it aboard *Founding Fathers*, since we were all staring at the Russian warships coming up from the direction of their fleet. So first there was the enormous flash and the huge cloud of smoke, and visible fragments of the ship thrown into the air: masts, shrouds, capstan, guns. All went tumbling up to cascade down on the empty ocean and the other Russian ships in company. All that came first, and then the huge, rumbling, roaring of many tons of gunpowder going up in a blinding instant. That sound came seconds after, and even at such distance it was heavy and dreadful.

To this very day I have not the slightest idea what caused that explosion, but it was the salvation of us aboard *Founding Fathers*, because the Russian squadron made no attempt to attack our ship. Not even the two seventy-fours came after us. Instead, they hove-to alongside the ship we'd battered, and stayed with her to assist in repairs, but made no attempt on *Founding Fathers*. This gave us time to spread sails and run downwind until we were well clear, when Van der Merwe brought us about so that we could observe what the Russians might do next.

I say that I have no idea what caused the explosion or why the Russians gave up on their intention to topple America. But there may be some significance in what the Russians did immediately after the explosion. Thus the wounded seventy-four ran up several hoists of signal flags — incomprehensible to me or Van der Merwe's people, because we didn't know Russian signals. But it was the wounded seventy-four which signalled first, with others responding, so that sounds like the actions of an admiral aboard his flagship. So it wasn't by chance or mistake that the Russians gave up. Also, Van der Merwe said something that made sense. I was with him on his quarterdeck among his officers, and all of us anxiously looking at the Russians for what they might do, with signals going between flagship and fleet.

"All this must be consequent upon the explosion," says Van der Merwe. "It must be some ship of great significance which has been lost."

"And it has to be a ship of war," says I. "Because no merchantman has that much powder aboard."

"Indeed," says Van der Merwe, "and I speculate that something vital was aboard that ship. Perhaps it was this celebrated document — the one which would shatter the Constitution — and which Mr Ducaine mentioned in his speech to the whores of Philadelphia?" There was laughter at that, but I wasn't so sure he was wrong, and even if the document *was* aboard, why should that cause a ship to explode? Who knows? But the sea has its mysteries, my jolly boys. Just think of this business of the *Marie Celeste*, only a few years ago. Look it up in your history books if you don't know about that one.

Meanwhile, we kept watch over the Russians for two days until at last they got their flagship under way, and the whole fleet sailed eastward, out into the Atlantic where we lost sight of them, having given up the pursuit after a day's sailing. We did not attempt to follow them further because *Founding Fathers* had taken some heavy shot between wind and water, and Van der Merwe — wisely, in my opinion — wouldn't risk her on the deep ocean without a dockyard re-fit. After all, *Founding Fathers* was still the only heavy ship that the US Navy had afloat on the seaboard of the blessedly still united United States.

I would add that by some miracle we picked up three survivors from the exploded Russian ship. We found them clinging to the stump of a spar when we followed the Russian squadron. Two of them were bad wounded and died despite the surgeon's best efforts, but one was fit and well, and even became an American in his later years, and sailed aboard American ships. Last I heard of him was that he'd been yeoman of the powder room aboard his ship, but even he didn't know why it exploded, since he was sitting in the warrant officers' privy at the time, far up in the bows, and that is why he survived.

After that we sailed northward for Boston where we were received in considerable glory, since — after all — we'd saved the Union, and much of the glory fell upon myself too, but not without some considerable regret.

CHAPTER 33

The entire enterprise was Count Pavel's. It was none of my doing, and therefore I gave the entirety of my efforts toward salvaging from his disaster, as many as possible of His Imperial Majesty's ships and men.

(Extract of a letter from Admiral Chirkov to his wife in Moscow.)

For Admiral Chirkov it was a most serious and dreadful time, for fear that he might be remembered as the admiral whose flagship was bested by a mere frigate. Indeed, Chirkov would have preferred to have fallen in action to such a disgrace as that. But by God's grace, the man responsible for all these ills could be clearly identified as the object of all blame, and that man was not Admiral Chirkov! Not at all.

Meanwhile there was a squadron to save, and hard decisions to be made. Thus even as *Mikhailovich Chernavin* and *Oskar Gorshkov* approached, and the American frigate hauled off, Chirkov gave orders to the ship's captain, calling him away even from the vital work of supervising repairs.

"Admiral?" said the captain, saluting.

"I shall need your best attention in making signals to the squadron," said Chirkov.

"Aye-aye, sir!"

"Make to *Mikhailovich Chernavin*: I shall come aboard and hoist my flag."

"Aye-aye, sir!"

"Make to the squadron: the squadron will come about and follow my flag."

"Aye-aye, sir!"

"Make to *Oskar Gorshkov* and to all the troop carriers, the signal for their commanding officers to come aboard *Mikhailovich Chernavin*, in conference,"

"Aye-aye, sir!"

Later, in the great cabin of *Mikhailovich Chernavin*, Chirkov made his hard decisions, as advised by his captains and as obliged by the quantities of food, drink and other essential supplies in the squadron. Thus he made a great speech to them all.

"With *Svatoy Eudoxia* lost, with all that she contained," he said, "this mad and foolish enterprise of North America fails before it even begins." He looked round at them all. "Does any man disagree with that?" he said, and there was profound silence, dense packed and anxious as they were, and thinking only of how they might be received in St Petersburg.

"So," said Chirkov, "this shall be our plan."

"Aye-aye," said all present, in a dismal murmur.

"The merchantmen shall be released to make what ports they may on the American coast or in the English Caribbean." This brought mutterings from some who thought themselves out of the admiral's sight. But they were certainly not out of his hearing.

"I know," said Chirkov, "they will not like that! But I am not concerned with merchant captains who have no influence at court. So they will make what shift they can, having transferred all possible stores to the warships and troopships."

"Ah!" said all present, and they nodded.

"We shall then steer north," said Chirkov, "for the prevailing winds to carry us across the Atlantic, towards Europe, the Baltic and St Petersburg."

"Hmmmm," said all present.

"Upon arriving at St Petersburg," said Chirkov, "we shall make clear that my flagship had suffered severe storm damage before the engagement with the American frigate."

"Oh?" they said.

"Indeed," said Chirkov, "how else could a frigate inflict … ah … some small damage … some *small* damage … to a seventy-four, before running away?"

"Ahhhhh!" they said.

"Most important of all," said Chirkov, "the entire responsibility for what has happened here is the fault of Count Pavel, whose deeply flawed plan this was, and by whose ineptitude *Svatoy Eudoxia* was lost." Chirkov looked around the cabin, fixing each officer with his eye. "Does any man disagree?" said Chirkov, "or would any man prefer that we share the blame — and the Tsar's punishment — among ourselves?"

"No," they said, and the matter was closed.

CHAPTER 34

After that, I achieved very much of my heart's desire. I returned to Boston, I was greeted with delight by Ezekiah Cooper and the elite of the city, and I greatly prospered in trade: indeed I did! Better still, I bought a fine house with servants, and my own carriage and horses, the first time in my life I ever owned my own home and horses.

However, I mentioned regret, since I was deep depressed at the thought of a parting between myself, my dear sister, her fine husband and my nephews and nieces. But I was forced into this sadness for reasons made blindingly clear in newspapers arrived from England. You youngsters must remember, that even in those days ships frequently crossed between the American and British ports, invariably bringing newspapers taken aboard as reading matter by the ship's people. All such newspapers were carefully preserved, since folk were eager to read them at the port of destination as the latest information of events on the other side of the Atlantic, even if weeks out of date. In fact there was a busy trade in them, since libraries, coffee houses and gentlemen's clubs would compete to buy them — and at good prices, too — for the benefit of their patrons.

So I represent here, two clippings from such newspapers. The dates are lost, but this is what they said. The first was in *The Times* of London, the second in the *Regent's Chronicle*

JACOB FLETCHER A PROVEN TRAITOR.

We are reliably and credibly informed by no less than His

Grace the Earl Wilshaw, First Lord of the Admiralty, that in command of the armed ship Enable, Jacob Fletcher, once an officer of His Majesty's Sea Service, did traitorously and wilfully cause Enable to fire into the revenue cutter Firefly with intent to break, destroy and sink the said Firefly with outrageous unconcern for the lives of the loyal hands aboard.

THE GALLOWS OR THE FIRING SQUAD?

The heroic Lieutenant Charles Trentham, lately in command of HM's ship Firefly, brought by him safe into Plymouth in near-sinking condition, testifies as follows: viz that THE NOTORIOUS FLETCHER, aboard of the Russian-chartered vessel Enable, when lawfully and properly challenged by Firefly, and Firefly wearing British colours, then FLETCHER directed a full broadside into Firefly's hull such as was intended to kill and maim. Thus who shall doubt that the full weight of HIS MAJESTY KING GEORGE'S LAW must fall upon FLETCHER, leaving undecided only the manner of execution which shall be inflicted upon THE NOTORIOUS FLETCHER whensoever he may be apprehended by His Majesty's forces?

I trust that having read these atrocious lies you will agree, my jolly boys, that my point is made, and that I was left in the full and certain belief that I must now make my life exclusively in America, and never see England again.

EPILOGUE

Letter, undated, from William Cavendish-Bentinck, Duke of Portland, Prime Minister of Great Britain, to Earl Wilshaw, First Lord of the Admiralty.

My dear Wilshaw,

I address you thus fondly, for fear of adding fuel to the fire of my anger.

My sources report that you are stamping and roaring around London among the printed press, dragging behind you Lieutenant Trentham, and the pair of you cursing the name of Jacob Fletcher, whom your own sources report to have "dropped anchor" in Boston with firm resolve to remain there as an American. You are further despoiling Fletcher with accusations of treachery.

I must therefore ask you to desist and abstain from further such behaviour for the following reasons.

Firstly, when you castigate Fletcher's firing on the revenue cutter Firefly you fail to appreciate that Fletcher's vessel, Enable, was crewed almost exclusively by Russians, who may have constrained Fletcher to fire on the British flag in order to prevent interference with their enterprise of furs.

Secondly, I note that while Firefly was dis-masted, none of her crew were killed, and her captain effected repairs and brought ship and crew home to England. This happy outcome, despite the fact that Fletcher's ship was perfectly capable of battering Firefly into sinking condition. I therefore take the survival unharmed of Firefly's people as a demonstration of restraint on Fletcher's part rather than treason.

Thirdly, even if it was the Russian crewmen who caused Enable to fire on Firefly, then given the vital importance of preserving the Russians in alliance with ourselves against Bonaparte, it is fixedly important that no further trouble be made with the Russians in this regard.

Finally — and of supreme importance — a considerable body of papers passed to me by Mr Pitt's administration which preceded my own, proves beyond doubt that Fletcher has in the past proved to be a most tremendous asset in dealing with perilous — but secret — threats to our nation.

In short, Fletcher is as valuable to Britannia as a squadron of ships of the line, and first-rate, 100-gun ships at that!

Therefore, please note that my government seeks Fletcher's earliest return to England and will allow no man to place a barrier in his way, which prohibition applies most directly, personally, and specifically to yourself.

Yours,
Portland.

THE END

THE LUME & JOFFE BOOKS STORY

Lume Books was founded by Matthew Lynn, one of the true pioneers of independent publishing. In 2023 Lume Books was acquired by Joffe Books and now its story continues as part of the Joffe Books family of companies.

Joffe Books began in 2014 when Jasper agreed to publish his mum's much-rejected romance novel and it became a bestseller.

Since then we've grown into the largest independent publisher in the UK. We're extremely proud to publish some of the very best writers in the world, including Joy Ellis, Faith Martin, Caro Ramsay, Helen Forrester, Simon Brett and Robert Goddard. Everyone at Joffe Books loves reading and we never forget that it all begins with the magic of an author telling a story.

We are proud to publish talented first-time authors, as well as established writers whose books we love introducing to a new generation of readers.

We won Trade Publisher of the Year at the Independent Publishing Awards in 2023. We have been shortlisted for Independent Publisher of the Year at the British Book Awards for the last four years, and were shortlisted for the Diversity and Inclusivity Award at the 2022 Independent Publishing Awards. In 2023 we were shortlisted for Publisher of the Year at the RNA Industry Awards.

We built this company with your help, and we love to hear from you, so please email us about absolutely anything bookish at feedback@joffe-books.com

If you want to receive free books every Friday and hear about all our new releases, join our mailing list here.

And when you tell your friends about us, just remember: it's pronounced Joffe as in coffee or toffee!